BRAIN 2000

Also by Ernest K. Gann

SONG OF THE SIRENS
IN THE COMPANY OF EAGLES
OF GOOD AND EVIL
FATE IS THE HUNTER
THE TROUBLE WITH LAZY ETHEL
TWILIGHT FOR THE GODS
SOLDIER OF FORTUNE
THE HIGH AND THE MIGHTY
FIDDLERS GREEN
BENJAMIN LAWLESS
BLAZE OF NOON
ISLAND IN THE SKY
THE ANTAGONISTS
BAND OF BROTHERS
ERNEST K. GANN'S FLYING CIRCUS
A HOSTAGE TO FORTUNE

BRAIN

2000

by Ernest K. Gann

DOUBLEDAY & COMPANY, INC.
GARDEN CITY, NEW YORK 1980

All of the characters in this book are fictitious, and any resemblance to actual persons, living or dead, is purely coincidental.

ISBN: 0-385-14393-1
Library of Congress Catalog Card Number 79–7048
Copyright © 1980 by Ernest K. Gann

To the real Miss Kellogg
With love

And to all the fools who still believe we, and all else, will last forever.

Readers' Warning

If you stop to think . . . don't

E.K.G.

BRAIN 2000

THE FIRST DAY

On this particular night in January the leaning tower of Pisa fell down. Almost simultaneously Natasha Egocina and Vladimir Rabinov, two brilliant stars of Moscow's Bolshoi, thumped to the stage floor while executing an ordinary *pas de deux*. As a consequence of these awkward events there was much more remorse in Moscow than in Italy. Egocina and Rabinov were said to be contemplating a dual suicide on the east and west sides of Lenin's tomb to mitigate their shame, but the fallen tower in Pisa evoked only a Latin shrugging of shoulders. Every Italian knew it was destined to fall down eventually, and the when was now.

Nanoseconds later Michael Piper, in St. Paul, Minnesota, where of course it was morning, experienced a situation which gave him pause for even more thought than usual, and despite his having achieved only age sixteen,

Michael was known as a dedicated thinker. So utterly was young Piper given to this unique habit that among his peers he was known as "Brain 2000"; the first appellation in salute to his unquestionable brilliance in mathematics class and the second to his residence at 2000 Maple Avenue. Michael was known to his parents as "Michael"; to his twelve-year-old sister, Sandra, as "The Brain," and in direct communication with his contemporaries as plain "Mike."

Michael's mental capabilities were sumptuous in some departments and strangely sparse in others, a combination reflected in his physique. His stork legs enabled him to look down on most of his classmates at Central High School and his rusty hair made him conspicuous in any congregation of his hirsute friends. His perfect eyesight enabled him to become an omnivorous reader without resort to glasses and his complexion was extraordinarily free of the various pustules and rashes plaguing nearly all his ilk. The minor galaxy of freckles swirling across his nose from cheek to cheek contributed rather than detracted from his craggy beauty and his smile, in the opinion of all who knew it, was enchanting.

The girls at Central High were more inclined to label Mike's smile as "neat" and found reason to linger in his vicinity as long as possible. Yet even Michael Piper's smile was subject to economic pressures, for he was a businessman, and to support his magnificent example of "early iron" (a 1941 Pontiac, yellow-and-red-flamed across the hood, roll bars, frenched lights, bolt-on stang discs, and the whole tilted front to look sneaky) he was constantly obliged to undertake new enterprises. These included renting his wire teeth retainers at fifty cents an hour (cost of antiseptic solution on exchange of tenancy to be borne by the lessee), and his thrice-weekly "Operation Chicle." This endeavor was conceived as part of Mike's personal conglomerate and involved him in the removal of chewing gum from the seats at the local theater at twenty cents per row.

On an hourly basis Michael Piper found his most lucrative business was the preparation of his father's income tax report, a labor which had engaged him for the last two Januarys. Compiling the first estimate of his father's tax was on his agenda for this day. It was a Saturday, he thought happily, and therefore there was no school to interfere with more important matters, such as the care and feeding of "early iron." He had bought a retread tire for the Pontiac's left front wheel, and now he had fitted it to the rim and inflated it. The glistening stang disc was ready for bolting. He hoisted the wheel preparatory to slipping it on the axle when it happened.

Afterward Mike reviewed the details of exactly what had happened and found himself wondering if he had been hallucinating, or perhaps something he had eaten for breakfast had given him vertigo, or . . . Whatever *had* happened was precisely what he had deduced would happen, but unless his calculations were radically inaccurate such things should not happen for at least another five years.

Yet there it was. Now would the monarch butterflies who migrated every winter to that mountain refuge just north of Mexico City return this spring, or become confused and, instead of dying en route, perish right there?

He had lifted the wheel from the bench alongside the back of the garage. And it had felt astonishingly light. Then, while bearing the wheel to the Pontiac, he had stumbled over a seat cushion and accidentally dropped it.

Even minutes later he could not remember why he had been so clumsy. Was it just carelessness, or inattention? If so, what had been so distracting?

At the age of twelve Mike had decided there was a reason for everything, but now he wondered. Of course the wheel bounced when it hit the garage floor, but not as he had expected. It had bounced so high he was able to reach straight out and catch it almost level with his face. Perhaps instinct could account for this reaction, a natural result of playing on the basketball team. (Score 87 baskets for "Brain 2000" so far this season.) Was he suddenly losing his marbles? A man had to think things out, and when confronted with such a sudden phenomenon he supposed the normal tendency was to fantasize. But here was a fantasy he had seen with his own eyes—right here, for cripes' sake—in the family garage at 2000 Maple Avenue. Far out? Just how super ding-a-ling could things be? Of course like Mr. Trumbull in Social Studies said, "Ask three different people why two cars collided, and one of them will fault a third car that was not really involved." Besides, anyone knew the human memory bank rested on quicksand.

Well then, he thought, which of the ten thousand million nerve cells in my brain has blown a fuse? Have the neurons in the cortex of my brain suddenly stopped exchanging their brief bursts of electrified energy, thereby losing communication and defying Lord Adrian's law?

When he had caught the wheel he had not continued carrying it toward the Pontiac in the normal way, but as if in a dream, he had decided to dribble it. And there he was playing basketball with a fifty-pound tire and wheel, like Gargantua, no less.

Then suddenly it was over. He did not quite make the Pontiac before the tire stopped trying to pretend it was a basketball and assumed an ordinary behavior. How many times had he actually dribbled it? Ten . . . twenty times? It was nine paces from the workbench to the left front wheel of the Pontiac. Say two dribbles per pace would bring the total to eighteen, less approximately three because he had not quite made the target. So he had indeed made at least fifteen dribbles with a heavy tire and wheel. The time space required for such action when simulated several minutes later had been approximately ten seconds . . . maybe twelve.

The whole affair, he decided, was not at all in line with the calculations he had made just after Christmas and then laid aside as perhaps untrustworthy. The computer his parents had given him for his sixteenth birthday was reasonably sophisticated although it went only to the ninth power. Still, with some juggling of numerics he had been able to surmount its limitations and go on to some quite interesting hypotheses. For example, he had been able to challenge Mr. Dodd, the physics teacher, on the matter of the earth's surface gravity as compared with the moon's. If the intensity weakened as the square of the distance by a factor of 3.666 times 3.666, should we not divide earth's innate gravitational intensity of 81.3 by 13.44 and get an answer of 6.05?

Mr. Dodd had not liked that kind of "convoluted thinking," as he called it, and Mike's favor factor with that rather dull man sank to a new nadir. Mr. Dodd felt his students were not yet qualified to postulate and they were not supposed to ask for computers to celebrate birthdays. He had stated openly that God himself must be awed by the present-day inconsistency of teen-agers and he saw no reason to applaud same.

Even without these strange goings-on Mike knew this Saturday was going to be a difficult day to schedule. Now that the Pontiac was "operational," he must make the rounds of the twenty-two clients who were always relieved to see him. These were neighborhood families who saved all the junk mail they received during the week and handed it to Mike on Saturdays. The accumulation never totaled less than fifty pounds, which Mike cached until he had several hundred, whereupon he sold it to a recycling station for two cents a pound. This translated into six gallons of gas for the Pontiac, a gain of three gallons over the amount required for the collection. And then of course there was the neat sensation of tooling about the neighborhood in such a magnificent piece of early iron. There were times when Mike decided he knew how Roman emperors felt in their chariots.

After the junk mail collection he must attend to other matters. Kevin McCoy received his allowance on Saturday mornings and would therefore be in a position to pay the previous two-day rental of Mike's teeth retainers. It was time they were back in his own head anyway, Mike reasoned. The family was beginning to inquire of their whereabouts, and damn all little sisters who noticed and remarked on such details.

"Where are your braces, snaggletooth? Seems to me you don't wear them very much."

Fortunately, Dad had been preoccupied and had not heard the inquiry (he was vague, like all older men), but Mother had picked it up and reminded, gently of course, how very expensive the retainers had been and that in view of the family tribute to the very high life-style of a certain orthodontist Mike should wear them as long as he could bear them. "You'll thank us for it someday, dear."

Cripes. The retainers were doing their bit for humanity by improving more than just one person's teeth, weren't they? They were paying for themselves, so to speak, and their earnings were reflected in the magnificence of the

Pontiac, which everyone agreed was "super-super-neat." There were plenty of long exhaled "wows" every time Mike lit off the mill and let people listen to that 4-71 GMC super charger. No need for speeding tickets with a thing like that under the hood. You *knew* what it could do.

Furthermore, there were other potentials for teeth retainers to which little sisters were not privy. Even now Mike was experimenting with diodes and transistors temporarily fixed to the retainers, and had achieved a mild degree of success. Once the assembly had been connected to the retainer wires, he had driven the Pontiac to the transmitting station of KSTP and, while still three tenths of a mile shy of the antenna towers, had picked up music more or less distinctly and an announcer's voice which had not been so distinct.

Performance improved somewhat very close to the station, but an unforeseen difficulty soon became evident. The vibrations transmitted through the teeth to the nerves and thence to the brain which "heard" the music diminished or increased as Mike turned his head. The unit was directional, and by swiveling his head owl-like Mike found there were two positions where he heard nothing. This had been disappointing, but perhaps there were other uses. Like how about navigating a tiny spacecraft with the astronaut just homing in on a signal?

Then there was Susie, for example, wonderful super-super Susanna York, who made all the girls at Central High look and act like ding-a-lings. Perhaps with expert modification the teeth-retainer radio could make a positive out of the negative of Susie's handicap—the misfortune that kept her in a special school instead of within easy reach. Now to fix that with just tooth retainers would be something to write home about, as the older generation was always saying! People got Nobel prizes for that kind of contribution to humanity.

Some strict programming for this busy day was needed. Susie at ten o'clock, as promised. A little discussion about going to the movies or doing a wax job on the Pontiac tonight. Then it was going to be an all-afternoon session on Dad's tax forms—not that he was rich by any standard, but that break level between what the government called the "poverty class" and the income of a middle-class man who just worked for the power company required a tax form that was so complicated most people had to hire an accountant to do the calculations for them. It was nice to know your dad would come right out and say you could do a better job than most experts and why shouldn't the cost be kept in the family. There were times when Dad was a very clear-minded man.

And now to louse up the Saturday schedule there was this other thing which certainly required further dinking around with the computer. The results would be entirely theoretical, and well, cripes, it really couldn't be. Or could it? And just where it was all going to fit into this jam-packed day was the real question. Right now, with everything so super normal, it was hard to believe it had happened at all . . . and had it really? Mom's breakfast waffles had tasted perfectly normal and so was last night's macaroni casserole, so it couldn't have been some kind of food poisoning. Hepatitis? No, they say that comes on slowly. A normal countdown for the past twenty-four hours no matter where a man looked. This happening was going to be difficult to describe to Susie without using words, but then again that task in itself would be a challenge. But how were you going to come right out and say in sign language or any other form of dialogue that maybe the world was coming to an end? Maybe? . . . no, for sure, it would *re-*

ally go boom if everything added up. The numbers were already there, right? How could a guy convince anyone at all, let alone adults, who seemed to stop thinking after they were twenty or thirty, that right here in the little old Piper garage instead of in some fancy place like the United Nations Building, something had happened that was like the first whiff of smoke in a forest fire? This was a very heavy situation, and something had better be done about it right away. That is, if it wasn't already too late.

* * *

As far as many St. Paul residents are concerned, the biggest event of the year in Minnesota is the Winter Carnival, which is anticipated from the fall of the first snowflake in October to the crowning of the ice queen herself. The Palace Ice Rink becomes a sort of training arena for skaters who intend to participate in the carnival, and on Saturday mornings the professionals are augmented by students of variable skill and talent. This year one of the aspirants was Susanna York, who at age fourteen had been runner-up in the statewide figure skating championship and had been often mentioned as a good possibility for the nationals. At sixteen and one half years of age she was considered "expert," and the graceful rhythm of her routine had caused even rival experts to applaud. Their enthusiasm was based solely on performance, and sympathy had nothing to do with it. Inversely, Susie's total deafness caused knowledgeable spectators to look for mistakes, and then, finding them so rare, they began to question what sweet and secret magic must reside in the silence behind her lovely eyes. Everyone who knew of Susanna's affliction wondered how she managed to coordinate her movements so gracefully with "Scheherazade," the standard background music of figure skaters. A waltz . . . a polka? It seemed to make little difference. Yet Susie York had not heard a note of any known tune since she was five, when calamity struck in the form of scarlet fever and left her in eternal silence.

Susie's own explanation when queried by a newswoman with more gall than delicacy was: "You do not miss what you never had." This retort was reinforced by one of Susie's particularly saucy smiles while the sign-language interpreter, on that occasion her mother, relayed it to the reporter.

Susanna York was much more than a superb skater. Her double axles, splits, butterflies, and double loops were merely a release for the energies of the artist within her. Thanks to her remarkable powers of visual observation, facilitated by a pair of sparkling blue eyes, she was capable of learning nearly anything she could see. She sketched well and created charming little watercolors. Her few pieces of wood sculpture had shown great promise. There was no feeling sorry for Susie because it had never occurred to her to feel sorry for herself.

As if to compensate for an accidental cruelty, nature had endowed Susie with many attributes rarely found among her age group. Every feature of her face was in perfect proportion to its neighbor, and yet somehow the total combination avoided the merely beautiful. Assessed separately (a near impossibility once confronted with the whole portrait), the mouth was somewhat overlarge, but then so were the eyes. The resulting balance became a visual harmony accented by her perky nose and a jaw which suggested great determination. Her complexion, like Mike Piper's, was free of the usual teen-age graffiti, and after ten minutes on the ice her skin glowed with the soft gold and cerise of young blood. Finally her figure, kept free of lean or fat by her daily exertions, was a delight to all eyes. Mike

Piper, who only lately had developed an eye for such matters, had often declared her "real holy," a Central High School localism applied to extraordinary beauty.

Because Mike had been so smitten with Susie on first sight and learned of her handicap immediately, he had applied himself to the art of sign language. He had taken two months' instruction in Ameslan when, still stumbling yet obviously so sincere Susie nearly cried, he ventured their first "conversation." Inspired by Susie's very special presence plus his own desire, his skill soon flourished and he discovered what few others knew. Susie's mind matched her physical beauty, and exploring, he found glittering deposits of brilliance everywhere. Even her humor was relatively mature. When, with their fingers flashing, he discovered she was two months older than himself, he had signaled "Wow! I'm falling in love with an older woman!" And Susie had laughed until her sides hurt.

On this chill Saturday morning Mike entered the Palace Rink and stood at the rail, admiring his Susie from a distance. She was wearing dark blue tights, and as she dipped and twirled and executed what looked like a perfect double axle he saw a smudge of white along her left leg and knew she must have fallen down.

As she split away from the center for one of her breathtaking speed sweeps along the length of the rink, he caught her eye, and holding up his right hand with thumb, second, and fifth fingers extended, he made the simple one-gesture sign, "I love you."

Susie immediately split toward him and came to a hissing stop precisely at the rail. When he had first begun learning to communicate with the deaf, Mike had discerned they were inclined to be great pantomimists—a smile, a twinkle of the eye, a toss of the head could express endless emotions, and he was puzzled now because Susie's usual warmth of greeting was absent. He signed, "Why are you so gloomy?"

She was unusually slow to respond, her fingers moving hesitantly. "I'm all right. But I fell down a little while ago."

"You've fallen lots of times before. Did you hurt yourself?"

"No . . . Well, yes. My pride was badly damaged."

He made the sign for not understanding.

Her fingers started to fly. "I was doing a perfectly simple butterfly, like I've done a thousand times. Then I went into a final stem and accelerated through about five turns. Then all of a sudden I don't know what happened . . . my speed went way up. I couldn't keep track of anything. I kept trying to slow down and couldn't. Then I spun out and slid clear across the ice until I hit the rail. It was very embarrassing. I tried to laugh it off, but I still can't think why it happened."

"Did this just happen?"

"No. It must have been about an hour ago. I had really just started. It was funny . . . the feeling was so strange. I was totally out of control. It was like someone put me in the washing machine at home and turned it on. I couldn't hang onto the spinning."

"Did you feel dizzy? You're not coming down with something? Sam Moseley has the flu, and so do several other people at school."

"No. I feel fine. But when it happened I felt very light on my skates, like I weighed about ten pounds. And I said to myself, 'I'm really with it today,' and then wow!"

Mike checked his watch. He was thoughtful, and wished he had looked at the time when he was in the garage. If it was the same time, then . . . ? But there was no use worrying Susie about it now.

"You want to go to the movies tonight?"

Susie displayed what Mike often thought of as her hundred-million-dollar smile and opened the fingers of her right hand wide to sign "Fine, excellent, super."

"I'll pick you up at six-thirty, but I won't be able to take you for a Coke afterward because I have to do some homework."

"You? Of all people! On Saturday night? The world must be coming to an end."

Mike smiled wryly and made the signs for "It just could be." Then he kissed her very quickly, left her feeling loved if slightly bewildered, and went to his various enterprises.

* * *

As Manager of Projects and Planning at the power company Ben Piper, after twenty years with the organization, was well enough compensated to have achieved what he considered a comfortable life. The Piper home at 2000 Maple Avenue was of middle thirties' vintage, but was well preserved and only 40 percent owned by the bank. It was pseudo-Tudor in style, and the stucco had held up better than the heating system, which Ben Piper often vowed he would replace as soon as he felt just a little bit ahead of current financial needs. Whether that day would ever come was now problematical since his chances for advancement within the company were not encouraging. He seemed to have reached a horizonless corporate plateau, and he knew there would soon be college for Michael to worry about. Thus far in his relatively comfortable life Ben Piper had not found the federal tax gatherers at all sympathetic to those Americans who might be considered in the "executive" or "managerial" class, and even though his decision-making authority was nearly nil his gross salary identified him with the real bosses. He often thought, in rueful company with several hundred thousand other American "bosses," that if his *net* salary were subject to the same social gauging as his gross then he might rank somewhere between a journeyman plumber and a licensed electrician, who were considered "workers" by the Internal Revenue people because they were not required to wear a nondeductible pressed suit and tie while on the job.

Now, since it was Saturday night and the Pipers were not scheduled for any of the usual social events, indeed even the Robert Bucks had declined an invitation to go "dutch" at a restaurant, Ben decided to have a second old-fashioned before dinner. Son Michael was already off to take his Susie to the movies, and daughter Sandy, an unquenchable chatterbox, was spending a "jammie" night with three other twelve-year-olds. Nancy, the good wife and mother who kept tab on such matters, said the mini-convention would be held at the Logans', who had banned television from their home, and consequently the four girls might catch at least a few hours' sleep.

Thus, Ben Piper knew an unusual sense of privacy on this evening, and he found his appreciation of Nancy to be especially keen. Tonight, he thought, she looked much younger than the other wives of their circle, and even (hello there, old chap) quite sexy. Who knew what the evening would bring if Nancy herself could be persuaded into a second old-fashioned?

"How about a wee nip more for you, my dear?"

Nancy Piper removed her glasses, which were designed for close vision only, and she surveyed the individual she had been married to for sixteen years and ten months. She saw a tall man with a once striking face now somewhat spongy as a result of too much precious lifetime in an office. Once, she remembered, he had looked like a young Lincoln; now he suggested an amiable well-fed Ichabod

Crane. But he was a lovable Ichabod, she thought, a man with a multitude of friends and no known enemies. He was patient and kind and tolerant, and did not pinch the fannies of other women—at least any she knew. He was also rather lazy physically (it was almost impossible to get him to do anything whatsoever about the house, even if it was only summoning a repairman by telephone). The roof could fall right in before Ben would become interested enough to do something about it. Perhaps his indifference to seeing clear sky through the rafters and all like domestic developments accounted for his less than spectacular corporate career. A fine choice, Nancy Piper had often thought secretly, for head of the Projects and Planning department.

"Very well. I will join you. It's not every night this house is haunted."

"Haunted?" He asked the question while he was making the two extra drinks—heavy on the ice this time. He asked because he had not really heard, and it was not just because they both often had trouble hearing each other these days. Only the other day Nancy had been momentarily piqued when he had not heard whatever it was she had said. "Good grief!" she had cried out when he failed to respond, "I'm going to send you to an ear doctor. There you are, sitting right across the dining room table, and you didn't hear a word I said. If you were standing before a firing squad and given a last chance to save your life if you could quote what your wife said ten seconds ago, you might just as well ask for the blindfold."

Later Nancy had laughed and admitted there were times when she didn't exactly hang on his every word either. But right now as he handed her a glass he was preoccupied in a different way. He was thinking about his son, Mike, a not unusual preoccupation since he was certainly an unusual boy, and he was thinking thoughts that were a little scary. Maybe the kid was just working too hard in school, a thought definitely not verified by his grades in either English or Social Studies. And he seemed to be in perpetual trouble with his physics teacher. Yet Ben Piper knew it was really not his son's schoolwork that troubled him; hell, he himself had flunked Spanish seven straight semesters. And he still couldn't say anything but *Adios* and *Vaya con Dios*.

"Do you know what our son said to me tonight . . . just before he left?"

"I'd believe anything. He's at that age."

"You may have some trouble believing this. How does this strike you for an opener? He announced it was probably going to be very necessary for him to have a meeting with the President."

"Hmmmm. And what did you say?"

"I told him running a power company was not an easy job and that I had met Mr. Chatsworth only three or four times since he became President and that I was hardly in a position to run personal affairs through his busy day. Does that sound obtuse or unreasonable? I did tell Mike it was customary for the President to attend the company picnic in July and that perhaps he could shake hands with him then."

"Did that satisfy him?"

There was something in Nancy's voice, a recognizable tone that signaled he did not have as much of her full attention as he would like. Joined with her complaints about his not hearing her every declaration was one he did remember, and now the reflection caused him to smile mischievously. She had said, "I worry about the time I may say the house is burning down and you will turn to me and ask if I smell smoke. Doggone it, someday I may

have to get your attention by standing up and taking all
my clothes off and screaming rape."

He had told her that would be a pretty picture. Now he
thought he had something equally demanding of her attention.

"No, Mike was definitely not satisfied. He said talking
with Mr. Chatsworth would not accomplish anything. He
really needed to see the President of the United States."

Ben was pleased to see he now had some 80 percent of
his wife's attention. He watched her limp through her
reply with a strange sense of triumph.

"He must not have been serious. Remember Mike has a
very special sense of humor."

"He was damned serious. He said he thought the time
was not quite right to tell me the exact details as to *why*
he had to see the President . . . something about
confirming certain facts, but he used two words I didn't
even know he knew."

"Four-letter words?"

"No. One was *imperative* and the other was *grave*. He
said it was imperative for him to see the President about a
very grave matter."

"He was translating for you. In his language the word is
heavy."

"I do not particularly enjoy being patronized by my
son."

"Well, I suppose he has a perfect right to see the President. After all, we voted for him."

"You did . . . I didn't. And stop being a mother who
thinks the President of the United States has nothing to
do but see her darling boy—"

"Oh, knock it off, darling. You know I'm not one of
those."

And she wasn't, thank God, he thought. She was a good

mother without the doting. "I'm trying to impress on you the kid was serious. He said if I couldn't help him he'd have to try some other means."

"Can you?"

"Of course not. I don't know the President or anyone within miles of him. I don't even know the names of our state senators. I just can't call up the White House and say, 'Hey there, how about an appointment for my son, who is a bright kid even if his father didn't vote for you?'"

"What are you going to do?"

"I was hoping you might have a few suggestions."

Ben took a sip of his old-fashioned, which was not as tasty as he had hoped. If a person was going to have more than one drink before dinner he should be in a carefree mood—not troubled by family or financial woes—or worse, some petty worry that defied solution.

He looked at his wife and saw she was making a sincere attempt to understand the fix he was in, but the usual animation about her honest eyes and mouth when she was inspired was still not evident. "You are thinking, I see," he said.

She nodded solemnly, and for a moment he was reminded how beauty really was in the eyes of the beholder. Nancy lamented frequently about her self-accused overweight, naming fifteen pounds as a mandatory reduction. It was nonsense, of course. Nancy was on the plump side, perhaps, but certainly not fat, and who wanted some middle-aged sticks and bones like the women on television pitching commercials for menopause pills? Nancy had fine legs, her breasts were still firm and upstanding, and there was hardly a visible wrinkle on her face.

He was surprised that his thoughts should have taken such an analytical twist when what he originally had in mind was a mutual celebration of their aloneness. Right after dinner? He had even envisioned a hand-in-hand parade up to their bedroom, but if they didn't linger too long over the meal, hell, they might even try it on the couch, like in the love-and-glory times, before the kids were so much underfoot.

"I don't hear much from you, Mrs. Solomon," he said, smiling.

"I'm still pondering. The President of the United States? And he meant it?"

"Let me give you something else to ponder. Did you hear the news tonight?"

"No. I was too involved in the chicken fricassee I'm about to serve up. It's a new recipe for the gravy, and I'm a little worried about it."

"You are not aware then that the leaning tower of Pisa has fallen down."

"It did?"

"It did indeed. And our Mike says he thinks he knows why. How do you like *that* for something to worry about?"

Now Nancy took a long sip of her drink and shook her head. He noticed she almost drained her glass, and also that her heavy black hair had only the slightest traces of gray as yet, and he decided it was the damnedest thing how it was possible for the human eye to record such trivialities when the brain was occupied with other matters. Grave matters, as Mike had volunteered.

"Well, golly . . ." Nancy said. "I don't know what to think."

"Thank you for your wisdom and parental guidance. I would very much like to be an understanding father, the kind I've read about but so seldom meet. Long ago I psyched myself in preparation for the day when Mike might come to me and say I'm a fathead, or a capitalistic stooge, or a racist, or a miser, or whatever. I am prepared to smile knowingly and agree with him while he decides what sort of an ogre or fool I am next. But our son does not play such games. While I admit he sometimes appears to see right through me, and let me tell you being transparent is a strange experience, he does come to me occasionally and ask what I think about this or that. And we have a reasonably mature conversational exchange. I have even learned to avoid the subject of his finances versus his Pontiac—"

"I hope you have never made the mistake of referring to it as a 'heap' again."

"No, I have not. *Shalom*, as the Jews say." Ben could feel bourbon getting to him now, and decided he had better space his sipping until he broached what had really been worrying him. One should be wary when dealing with the American flag and/or a mother.

"I sometimes wonder . . . and particularly after my conversation tonight with Mike . . . if maybe he hasn't suffered some . . . how do they say . . . mental fibrillation? Nothing serious, mind you, and don't get excited, but I was just wondering if—"

"Ben Piper, are you trying to insinuate that Mike is mentally ill?"

There was a cutting edge to Nancy's voice that seemed to congeal the ice in his glass. Well, he thought, what must be said must not be postponed.

"I'm only suggesting—no, wondering if maybe we shouldn't ask Doc Jenkins to recommend a reliable psychiatrist. I'm just not at all sure you and I, loving parents though we may be, are equipped to cope with this sort of behavior . . ."

He saw that all semblance of a come-hither look had now left Nancy's eyes, and he stood back for the expected guided missiles.

She launched one immediately. "I suppose you base your assumption on the fact he doesn't smoke pot or drink beer or wreck his Pontiac or write 'Screw you' on the blackboard when the teacher isn't looking?"

Dead on target, he thought. He moved a step backward to throw off her next trajectory. "After listening to a few other fathers I would consider that quite normal."

"Then you are a jaded, cynical, lost-generation red-neck. Why don't you join the Ku Klux Klan?"

"Oh, now come on, Nancy. I was just trying to tell you we have a mutual problem—or seem to have—and I'm beginning to think something should be done about it."

He saw her eyes suddenly lose their anger and become wet and confused. He went to her at once and took her in his arms. He felt her sobbing against his shoulder and he knew it was not the old-fashioneds, and somehow the realization made him feel better. Nancy knew as well as he did something was abnormal about Mike, but she was a mother and until the chips were right down she could not admit he was imperfect.

"I know, Ben, I know." She whimpered so softly against the lapel of his jacket he could barely hear her. "What are we going to do? Who is going to tell him . . . you or me?"

"I'll call Doc Jenkins on Monday and see what he suggests. I'm afraid if we go at this thing too directly we may cause more damage than good."

She sighed, still in his arms. It was an exhalation of infinite trust. "What are we going to do about the President of the United States?" she whispered finally.

"We might put a message in with our tax forms. We could say these were prepared by a sixteen-year-old who is so bright he can understand them and maybe the President should appoint him to his Cabinet."

* * *

They stood talking in the shaft of light from Susie's front doorway. In the beginning of their relationship Mike had found the necessity for light awkward during a conversation. Everyone else talked about serious things in the dark—in the back of movies, or in cars parked in the darkest place you could find, or in someone's house whose parents were out for the evening. If you were in mixed company and you wanted to rap about such things as afterlife, the existence of God, the qualities a girl should have and the faults she should not, the intolerance of parents and their possible senility, the plans for this summer, or next summer, or the year 2020, or how you would prefer to spend the rest of your life, and who was making out with whom—those things were all best discussed in the dark. You talked about grades, money, cars in general, "early iron," sports, and the eccentricities of teachers in daylight. With Susie of course it was different. She had to see facial expressions and hands and fingers or a conversation didn't get very far.

Now, facing the light so she could see his fingers clearly and how very sincere his eyes were, he concluded his lecture, "It's what I call my spinning-top theory. I certainly can't claim it is fully developed, and there's a great many basics I have to recalculate, but judging from recent events, two of which we know about, I can only conclude my premise is probably correct."

"How long will it take you to be sure?" she signed.

"If I go right home and get to work, I should be close to the primary solution in a couple of hours. The secondary resolve will take longer even if I don't run into any glitchs."

Susie signed she did not understand the sign for his last word, and laughing, he apologized. "I just made up the sign. It's a word the astronauts use to indicate something has gone wrong."

She smiled her relief and signed how much she had enjoyed the movie and being with him, as always. He responded instantly.

"That's my first glitch right there. I don't want to go yet. I want to stay right here because I love you. I consider you absolutely the neatest person in the world, and how can I think about this terrible problem when all I want is to think about you?"

He reached for her and brought her to him. Their lips met in silent rapture. Finally Susie eased far enough away to display her hands and signed, "I just can't relax when I think how much depends on you. You better go now. If it works like you think could happen, if all the people in the world could be brought together in a common cause, then wow! Maybe there wouldn't be any more wars; maybe if every single person on earth knew they were needed even a little bit . . . well, the whole idea of such a thing is fantastic. You've just got to see the President."

"That's one glitch. My dad just sat there and smiled and said there wasn't much he could do. I didn't tell him very much because he wouldn't understand. Maybe I should go see Miss Kellogg. She understands a lot more than just teaching English."

"Even I understand about spinning tops, and that's just exactly the way I felt at the time."

"I love you, Susie."

"I love you, Mike. Go home now. Do your work, and I'll see you tomorrow."

They kissed once more, he saw her to the door, and then in one easy leap he cleared the porch rail and landed gracefully on the lawn. He turned to make sure she had observed his unique departure, and then seeing her still in the half-open doorway, he was content.

He trotted down to the Pontiac and let the big mill rumble for twenty-three seconds by count. Then with the comfortable knowledge the cylinder head temperatures were proper for efficient combustion, he eased into old number one gear and let her slide. When he had shifted smoothly to high gear he sat back and cocked his head, the better to hear the sweet and sonorous music from his chromium pipes.

He had only one regret in his whole life. If he had everything pinned down mathematically, say two hours from now, he would be unable to just pick up the phone and tell Susie this was unquestionably . . . *it*.

THE SECOND DAY

As the earth rotated and day gradually embraced the western hemisphere, most Americans began a normal resurrection. The night had passed uneventfully except for the frogs in Louisiana, who experienced trouble croaking in the lower octaves.

Sunday's dawn brought a further inexplicable situation, which led to a coolness between Sergeant Randolph Sutter of the United States Marines and Private Philip ("Hunky") Dory of the same organization. Their duty was to raise the stars and stripes precisely with the sun, and for this purpose Private Dory held the flag in his arms, folded in the proper triangle. Sergeant Sutter lived by the sweep second hand of his trustworthy Japanese watch, bought when he had stood embassy guard in Tokyo, and he checked it every night with WWV, the national time station. He was clipping the flag halyards to the grommets when he heard his inferior mouth words he could not believe.

Dory was looking past his sergeant's rhinoceros-skin neck when he said, "Sarge, I got bad news for you. The sun is already up."

Sergeant Sutter became momentarily paralyzed and even incapable of speech, for of all things Marine he prided himself on punctuality, and raising the flag at Quantico was the symbol of all he held inviolate.

"Goddamnit, the sun can't be up. I checked the almanac, and my watch is never wrong. We got one minute to go."

"You just turn your head and take a look and you'll see I ain't exaggeratin'!"

Sutter pressed his lips together hard. The quality of enlistments the Marines were getting these days was not encouraging. Some could barely see. "Be advised, Dory, you gotta be lookin' at a streetlight."

"That streetlight's got a cloud across it."

Sergeant Sutter rotated his head, and what he saw shook him profoundly. He blinked at the offending sun and whispered hoarsely, "Well, I'll be a son of a bitch. Haul away!"

Neither the bayou frogs nor Sergeant Sutter knew that on this same dawning the tide in New York Harbor began flooding one hour earlier than the tables predicted. The few harbor pilots who noticed the difference put it down to a typographical error.

* * *

In St. Paul, Minnesota, Alice Kellogg yawned and stretched her arms above her head and wiggled her fingers at the pair of pink-cheeked, bare-bottomed cupids who adorned the backboard of her oversized bed. The bed was an unholy extravagance for a high school teacher, she knew, but she would rather skimp on other furniture and indulge herself in the only one of man's creations where it was convenient to escape, exult, recuperate spent energy, and die. She had bought the cupids in an antique shop, fixed them to the headboard with wonder glue, and almost named them Abe and Rose before she caught herself and decided she was being just a bit too coy.

Now, yawning again, she saw the sun strike the cupids, and she hoped it was going to be a nice day because Buck Delaney was coming by to pick her up and they would have an afternoon skating on Lake Como.

She kicked off the covers and stretched her long and lovely legs preparatory to her morning calisthenics. What a bore. Twenty minutes every morning, twisting and turning and jumping up and down and bending for what? To fight thirty-five years on this earth, that's what. Never mind if you still had only one chin and all of your other departments might pass for twenty-five years of use. You should not judge a used car by the sheen on its fenders. And *Mother* had predicted just this: "Alice you are going to become a spinster if you don't watch out. And *spinster* is a nice word for *old maid*. You have just got to find your Mr. Right Man soon or it will be too late. All this liberation stuff is nonsense. You can't argue with nature. Happiness is a woman with a rich man of her very own."

Raising her feet to the ceiling and then lowering them, she counted ". . . eighteen, nineteen, twenty. . . . Whew!" She thought. Well, I *tried*, Mother. But two things got in the way and I don't see much hope of bypassing them. First. I have yet to meet a man with whom I want to spend more than a strenuous weekend, and second, I like variety. No, Mother dear, I do *not* hop into bed with every man I meet, despite your nasty little secret thoughts, but I do very much enjoy a more than occasional roll in the hay, which, if I have my statistics right, is a good deal more often than the average wife enjoys. And I don't have to launder his shirts or spend so many precious hours each year with *his* mother or remember her birthday or her recipe for goulash. Smiling all the while of course. The very few men I do sleep with (you would call it fornicating and tell me how hot it is in hell) do not sleep . . . at least not for very long if they are in this bed. They either have to go home to their wife (you would call it adultery and you'd be right) or they want to move in for a long spell, toothbrush and all, and I'm not interested in providing free shelter, heat, and light to some macho type with a bristle mustache and glistening teeth. And I am strangely not driven to motherhood, Mother. Maybe because I'm den mother to almost one hundred teen-agers, which is enough to turn almost anyone off further procreation of the race, and I'd just as soon face the future listening to other old women talk about *their* children. When eventually they cart me off to a rest home, I don't want obligatory visits from individuals who are wondering if I'm going to outlive my income and theirs.

Alice Kellogg rolled out of bed and stood before the mirror. She reviewed her body long enough to assure herself no serious structural deterioration had occurred during the night. She preferred to sleep in the nude, and this inspection of her parts was a regular morning ceremony. No belly . . . very good. Breasts full but not Holstein and still pointing in the same direction she might be going. A tootsie roll of blubber about the hips. Grief! The first budding of middle-aged spread?

She turned for a profile view and reminded herself to stand up straight. And chin up. Pretend you are Marie Antoinette telling the common folk they can eat cake. And you need a trip to the hairdresser this week. Enough of narcissism. To arms, Joan! The Cardinal's troops are even now pounding on the gates.

She raised her sword arm in salute, and almost simultaneously one eyebrow. What was this? Is your imagination overactivated? No. Someone was actually knocking on the front door. A Cardinal's trooper at this hour on Sunday morning? Unreal.

The knocking ceased and the doorbell rang as she swept back a few errant brushes of hair and reached for her bathrobe. She went to the window which offered a view of the sidewalk leading to her cottage. She recognized Mike Piper's Pontiac parked at the curb.

Through the peephole a previous tenant had installed in the front door she confirmed it was her favorite pupil waiting outside. Mike was a very special boy of course, but wasn't a Sunday visit just a bit odd even for him? She opened the door and bade him good morning.

"Good morning, Miss Kellogg. I hope I'm not disturbing you."

"Oh, not at all. I always get up at seven o'clock on Sunday mornings," she lied. "Not for me a day of rest. Come in, come in."

Mike shuffled his frame through the door and she closed it behind him. He halted in the center of the small living room and stood thumbing the earflaps of his cap. Weaving slightly in position, he reminded Alice Kellogg of a young fir tree in the wind. "Is it cold outside?" she asked.

"Not too bad. The streets are icy."

"Won't you sit down?" She nodded at the couch, where the previous night Buck Delaney, a loquacious lawyer from Minneapolis, had employed his finest forensics to convince her that three dates should be enough to qualify for a total physical communion. She had declined. (I don't succumb to *every* invitation, Mother.)

Mike moved toward the couch, then seemed to change his mind. "The thing is," he said, "I'm in kind of a hurry. I have an awful lot to do for the next several days, and I came to you because I don't know where else to go."

His lanky spare parts, she decided, only rarely appeared to be working in coordination. "I'm not following you, Mike. Is there something wrong at school?"

"Nothing heavier than usual. I guess I'll never learn to tell a dangling participle from a split infinitive even if you are the best English teacher in the world."

"Thank you," she said with what she hoped was proper modesty, and she thought, I haven't brushed my teeth or really started my day. Of all the days in the week this is the one I take at slow bell. Now where, she wondered, did my out-of-concept brain dig up that old nautical phrase? Am I the reincarnation of a southern belle on a Mississippi paddle-wheeler bound for Natchez? Hattie, pack my crinolines.

"Well, Miss Kellogg, I guess you know all your students think you're neat."

Pity, she thought, the faculty, the principal, and the school board are not of the same opinion. If it were not for tenure, you would be lucky to get a job teaching kindergarten in Afghanistan. The teaching body as a whole and the dear stalwarts of the PTA were not enthusiastic about a teacher who was regarded as a "swinger," and a confirmed bachelor girl at that. Well, *semi*confirmed.

"Mike, did you drop by on this lovely Sunday morning just to boost my morale? Has something terrible happened I don't know about?"

"Not yet, Miss Kellogg. But it will."

She sat on the arm of the couch and adjusted her robe to avoid any possibility of displaying her cleavage. Besmirch my name as you will, fellow faculty members, but you will never have reason to accuse me of messing with pupils. She thought for a moment of little Sheila Danforth, the saucy fifteen-year-old who made no attempt to hide her total infatuation with Mike. She was all over the boy whenever opportunity offered, and that usually seemed to be in his English class. Bad little girl, Sheila, a talebearer, or "nark" in the student vernacular. She had a sharp tongue and scheming little eyes. Mike's obvious patience with her antics was nothing short of noble.

"The reason I came to you, Miss Kellogg," she heard him saying, "is that I have to see the President of the United States. And our meeting must be very soon."

She looked at his eyes and saw only sincerity, and she was almost immediately compelled to look at the floor. She knew at once he meant what he had just said, and when a teen-ager tells you something from his heart, that heart could be shattered if you failed to take him seriously. Careful now, she thought. Don't scare him away. Even if his English grades were barely passing, those teachers on the faculty who had been exposed to the Piper boy were uncomfortably aware they probably had a genius in their midst. Via his challenges he drove Dr. Dodd, the physics teacher, to advanced nail-biting and Lucy Bellows, who was probably as qualified a teacher of higher mathematics as any high school rating in the state, was frankly astounded at his grasp of calculus. Even the teaching staff was sometimes tempted to refer to him as "Brain Two Thousand," and now, like so many potential geniuses, had he suffered a sudden collapse?

"Mike, perhaps it's too early in the morning for me to follow you. Why do you think you should see the President of the United States?"

"Because of my spinning-top theory."

Alice swallowed and murmured, "Uh-huh."

"You see, Miss Kellogg, this planet has been in a relatively fixed orbit for billions of years. Now, all of a sudden, that is relatively sudden in terms of years, we have created an imbalance, and according to my calculations, things are going to get very heavy on or about the sixteenth of February. Then our exit from normal orbit will be initiated and, while the consequences will be acceptable for a time—say six months—the situation will soon become terminal. The worst part of it is, once it really starts it will be too late to reverse the trend."

"Michael Piper, are you suggesting the world is coming to an end? Are you all right?" Good heavens! she thought. Some of the students were pot smokers, a few were real "burnouts," and some were into hashish, but Mike Piper? Wow!, as the students were so fond of commenting.

"As we know it, the end will come. The earth itself is just another planet, and will possibly keep on spinning out of orbit for a few thousand years, until it gets too close to a celestial body with a stronger gravitational pull and gets captured. I haven't figured out which one it might be yet, but we will probably crash into it. Of course it won't make any difference because there won't be anyone left to watch the show."

Alice swallowed again. Maybe it wasn't Mike, but she herself. She had taken one Martini before dinner last night and had a glass of sherry with Buck Delaney before he had started his oration on the universal need for voluntary and therefore happy copulation as opposed to performance of duty. Did birth-control pills make a person hear kookie things?

"You mentioned something about a spinning top, Mike. Was that what we call in composition a 'plant' or did I somehow mishear you? Remember you almost flunked composition, my friend."

"That's why I came to you, Miss Kellogg, because like you just said, you are my friend and I need help very badly."

Go along with him, Alice. Humor the lad until he either comes out of it or you can get to the telephone. Help!

She looked through the half-open doorway to the bedroom and wondered if she was still asleep. That was it— had to be. Okay, play along with the dream. "Have you discussed this with your parents?"

"I talked to my dad. He wasn't very receptive, and I'm afraid I confused the issue by starting right out with my need to see the President. My dad said he didn't know how to arrange an appointment."

"Frankly, I don't either."

"But you would try . . . wouldn't you, Miss Kellogg?"

"Maybe you'd better tell me why all this is going to happen. Or is that something I don't need to know?"

"It's pretty complex when reduced to numbers, but I can sort of explain it if you visualize a spinning top."

"All right. I'm trying." She closed her eyes. It was better not to look at the demented, young or old.

"Say you have a wooden top and you spin it in the normal fashion. It will take up a normal rotation about its axis just like the planet earth. And usually it will spin in an orbit which is a smooth elipse or circle, depending on how you originally throw it. But if you take the same top and cut a chip out of one side and then throw it, the rotation will be much more erratic and the orbit will vary according to a predictable equation. Removal of a tiny chip won't make much difference, but if you keep cutting off more and more there is a point where both the rate of spinning and the orbit will reflect the absence of perfect balance. Of course the larger the top the less effect a small missing chip will affect it, but eventually even if the top was as big as this room the effect of gyroscopic imbalance will become apparent. Allowing for some variation in the true weight of the chip, the time of departure from orbit is predictable. Unfortunately, the shape of the new orbit is not."

There followed a long silence. Mike *looks* all right, she thought. And he obviously isn't violent. Was this some kind of student prank, with Mike chosen as the protagonist? No, that didn't make sense, any more than top-spinning on Sunday morning. "Mike, if you're trying to convince me the earth and spinning tops have something in common, I suppose it's true and not a bad simile, but do you really believe it possible for someone to go around carving chips off the earth . . . like peeling a potato?" Page Paul Bunyan, she thought.

"We already have. It's being done every day. And unless it's stopped, I am ninety-five percent sure the terminal data or orbit departure is February sixteenth."

She would have to respond, she thought desperately. Humor . . . humor.

"Why are you only ninety-five percent sure? What about the other five percent?"

"My computer only goes to the ninth power. But by interpolating some of my figures I can eliminate the five percent gray area. It's a time-consuming process, and I've been so short of time. I took Susie to the movies last night when I should have been calculating, and yesterday the Pontiac needed—"

"Mike dear, you must get hold of yourself. You are trying to tell me the end of the world is coming and you haven't got time to find out exactly when or why?"

"I do know why. And the when is February sixteenth. I just don't know the hour . . . yet."

All right, den mother, what do you do now? Athena, Goddess of Wisdom! Reach down and tell Cleopatra what

I should say? He's sticking by his story. Should I get on the telephone and tell his parents to come and get him? But if I do that he'll run like a deer and maybe hurt himself. And I'll certainly destroy his confidence in me. When in doubt, procrastinate—which is precisely why the telephone was still in the living room when more than three months ago you had resolved to have it reinstalled in the bedroom. Procrastination is the art of keeping up with yesterday. Archie and Mehitabel. Just because a classic cockroach was unable to utilize capital letters is no excuse for so many students—including the one now standing before you and scratching at his rusty locks. "Who is doing all this carving away at Mother Earth?"

"OPEC," Mike said flatly.

"Say again?"

"OPEC. The Organization of Petroleum Exporting Countries and ourselves. Since the introduction of oil as an energy source we have been removing weight from our planet and expending it as gas into the atmosphere. That weight is gone forever. If the removal was taking place only at mathematically selective locations on earth the balance could be maintained, perhaps indefinitely. But the removal of trillions of tons occurs in small areas, mostly located comparatively near the equator, which is the worst place it could be done from a rotation and orbital aspect."

"Supposing it was stopped, then what about your precious Pontiac?"

He laughed, and she was relieved to see that utterly disarming smile again.

He said, "I'm sure glad about your sense of humor, Miss Kellogg. Most teachers could use a little more."

"Well, it's a rather difficult thing to maintain when I face instant destruction on the sixteenth of February. That's not very long from now. Let's see, this is—"

"Oh, it won't be instant, Miss Kellogg. We have to remember this planet with its atmosphere and mountains and oceans is just one big living organism and if we louse up even one cell then the whole system gets poisoned . . . and like any disease, it takes time. Cripes, I guess you know all about the ozone layer which protects us from the sun . . . the sort of greenhouse effect? Well, if we increase our rotational speed or slip out of orbit just a smidget, we will change the altitude of the ozone layer and its shape—"

"And there everyone is with instant skin cancer?"

"You catch on real quick, Miss Kellogg. Everything else being equal and ignoring the oil weight-loss factor, there will be a great change in our environment anyway. By the year three thousand temperatures around the world may increase by as much as nine degrees centigrade."

"I read somewhere we are headed for an ice age." I have to say something, she thought. Stall . . . stall.

"You probably have been exposed to the Milankovitch theory. I don't buy it . . . that is, in its entirety."

"Why not?" God, who besides Mike Piper had ever heard of Milankovitch? Help!

"It ignores the acceleration of all Earth physical events caused by the removal of a heavy viscous liquid from a globular body which is subject to powerful gyroscopic and magnetic influences. Milankovitch maintains the summer sunshine varies according to changes in Earth's axis and the shape of its orbit, which of course is elementary, and no one who has his marbles can disagree with him on that, but whether the variations govern the aggrandizement or reduction of glacial episodes is another matter."

"Mike, where did you get that word *aggrandizement?*"

"Milankovitch uses it, and I like it because it does suggest a mighty development. And if we lived for forty thousand or so years, maybe we'd see the whole cycle . . . like for instance the pyramid of Cheops, which has a shaft constructed to admit the light of the star Thuban. Cripes, now the shaft opens to an entirely different part of the sky and Thuban won't be back on target for another nineteen thousand years. Theorizing is fun and Newton was full of it, but we've got to think about right now. At present the tilt of our axis is twenty-three point five degrees, and if all remained as is we would diminish to a minimum of twenty-one point eight. But all isn't remaining as is. Recent phenomena have proved it."

"I'll admit it's been an unusually cold winter. I've never seen so much snow. I hope it's not too much for the Carnival."

Get him on the Winter Carnival, she thought. Distract him with fun ideas. Did teen-agers *have* to be so serious all the time?

"Isn't your friend Susie going to skate in the Carnival?"

"You bet. She's out to win the gold trophy."

"She's such a lovely girl." Indeed she was, Alice remembered. How pleasant it was to think of Susie's extraordinary serenity and just momentarily postpone the end of the world.

"Are you going to help me see the President, Miss Kellogg?"

Bang! Right back in the soup. Where was the exit?

"Of course I'll help in any way I can, but I'm still confused—"

"I don't want to go into plate tectonics now, Miss Kellogg, but even if the weight of the oil removed was not so important it has been pressing on the earth's mantle for eons and as a result the mantle has sunk. Now suppose that in a relatively few years the pressure is released. The result can be like a kernel of popcorn. Poof! Somewhere there will be a pop-up in the earth's crust, the balance of the globe will be further disturbed, and we're on our way."

"Oh-lay-oh-lay-ee-ooo," she yodeled softly.

"I sure like your sense of humor, Miss Kellogg. I always have."

"Have you any kind of *proof* this is going to happen, Mike?" That ought to hold him, she decided.

"Sure. I've been wondering about this whole thing for a long time and I've prepared a pretty good list. Certainly the gravitational eccentricity should be apparent to any thinking person. The night before last the leaning tower of Pisa fell down."

"According to Jules What's-his-name, that TV commentator, it was in bad repair and about to collapse anyway."

"Yesterday morning Susie fell down, which she just doesn't do, at least not in the manner it happened. But these things and something that happened to me at the same time only triggered the thinking I've been doing."

Suddenly she saw Mike lose interest in her and all around him. It was as if he had physically removed himself from her living room and stood somewhere in space, contemplating infinity. She shivered slightly and pulled the bathrobe tighter about her. For the first time, she thought, I am just a little frightened.

She heard him saying, "I guess I really dug it last summer when I built my spectroscope and recorded the changes in the speed of light I received from the sun. Instead of blue being a hundred and twenty-one thousand miles per second and red a hundred and twenty-two thousand, I got a hundred and twenty and a hundred and twenty-five. At the time I thought it was because of my crude workmanship, and also I was over budget on the Pontiac, so I couldn't afford the best prisms. And then maybe my calculations were wrong, but the differences between what I recorded and what is supposed to be was discouraging. It's not very interesting trying to observe the Doppler effect with an inadequate tool, and so I got into other things."

For a long moment he seemed uncertain of himself, then she saw him regain confidence.

He said, "There are a lot of unrelated factors which distracted me last summer, but now with some more work I'm sure I can pull them all together. Last night I did some more calculations and found we have discharged at least ten and possibly twenty million tons of trash into the atmosphere just since the industrial revolution. Maybe that junk bent the light and threw my spectroscope figures off, so I failed to recognize a slight orbital change. I do remember theorizing that, if my readings were correct, by the time I'm forty we could be approaching a little ice age, and I didn't much like the idea of being cold when old."

"Forty is not so awfully old, Mike." Especially, she thought, when thine hour is nigh. "And I thought you just said when we first started this . . . May I call it a conversation? I thought you said the world was going to get warmer."

"Only if we maintain our present orbit. That's the glitch."

"All of us, Mike, are very concerned about what's happening to our atmosphere. I've thought we're very lucky living in Minnesota, where we have so relatively little pollution." If I can't divert him, then I'll join him, she thought. Clean air was a crusade anyone could encourage. Yet either he had not heard her or did not care, for his speech quickened.

"I did some more checking and found how failure of the monsoons south of the Sahara occurred for six years starting in 1968. The result was a terrible drought, and almost everything died. We've had very erratic changes in our North American climate . . . Look at 1976, when the winter drought killed so much of the wheat crop here in Minnesota and in all the big producing states. The same year Western Europe had the longest hot and dry weather since records have been kept. Water was rationed, a lot of animals were slaughtered for lack of feed, and there were forest fires in England and France. And look at our winters in 'seventy-seven and 'seventy-eight. But all that sort of thing is really small potatoes."

"Unless you're a potato trying to survive under such conditions."

"Most people don't believe that every day our atmosphere is bombarded by more than a million billion meteoroids, most of which are no bigger than a potato and most are much smaller, but the number seems to be increasing, and so more and more tons of meteor dust— that's after they burn up, Miss Kellogg—fall down to earth every day. I can't equate the weight of that dust to the immediate problem, but it certainly must have some effect on our weight distribution. The thing is, in August and October we just missed passing through a meteor shower by a few million miles. Just a little change in the earth's orbit and we would have gone right through it, and the earth's surface would look like the moon's and I wouldn't be standing here talking to you. Did you know Hermes missed us by only four hundred thousand miles in 1937 and if it collides with us, which can happen with even a little orbital change, it can release the energy of ten million hydrogen bombs? Think about it."

"Oh, I am. Indeed I am."

But probably, she thought, not just as you would have me think. I am really listening to my addled mind, which is monitoring my troubled heart while it asks how I am going to get this poor boy to go home and lie down with a cold compress on his head. And there we have a quartet of adjectives in the same sentence for which I would flunk any student in my class. Oh, dear God, why have you brought me such a Sunday?

"Mike, what has the President of the United States to do with all this? Even the Republicans could hardly blame him for your special brand of gloom and doom."

"The President must gather all the world's heads of state immediately. Oil production in certain areas must be stopped and various compensating procedures followed. It must be a common effort by all the people on this earth . . . to save themselves. I haven't got all my numbers straight yet, but it can be done. Best of all, Miss Kellogg, maybe people working together for survival instead of fighting all the time might start people putting more value on each other. Just think what that might do for the human race."

She forced herself to contemplate the human race for five seconds, which she decided was enough for a Sunday morning. Then she was infinitely relieved to hear the telephone ringing, and went to it with an eagerness she had rarely known. Whoever interrupted this educational seminar was welcome. She hoped it was Mike's parents saying they were on the way.

It was Buck Delaney, who responded to her "Hello" with one of his lesser greetings: "Good morning, light of my life! Did you sleep well?"

Buck could be an ass, she thought, and maybe the time had come to start phasing out their relationship while it was still platonic. Some night he might bring a bottle of champagne and you might feel like tearing down the Bastille. "I slept like the angel I am," she said, wondering if an afternoon of skating with Buck was not just a little more than she could bear after such an uneasy start for the day. Maybe a solo trip to the movies was the answer, or even meditation in some handy church. Funny she had never thought how really convenient they might be. If she could find a veil and a dark outfit she could pretend she was a widow, and everyone would leave her alone.

"Have you heard the news this morning?" Buck was asking.

"No. I just got up . . . Well, not exactly . . ."

"It's wild. It just came on the radio and it's on TV. It seems that sometime last night the level of Lake Superior fell six feet. No one can explain it. They say the sound of the ice cracking is just like cannon fire." He chuckled happily. "I'm sure glad we're not going skating on Superior."

I am going to hang up this phone, go back to bed, and wake up normally, she resolved. All will be well. Mike will not be here, and Buck will call about noon and confirm our skating date on Lake Como, and maybe afterward we will take in an early movie. And then tomorrow morning I will go to school, and at eleven o'clock, along with the rest of his class, Mike will be trying to conjugate verbs and thereby prove he is far from the brain he is supposed to be. And little Sheila will be making goo-goo eyes at him and I will know this is all some kind of a nightmare caused by eating overcooked fettucine.

"Buck, I'm not feeling very well. I shall have to cancel our afternoon. I hope you'll forgive me. Have a nice day." She hung up the phone without waiting for a reply. Then for a long moment she stood staring at the instrument. Finally she turned to Mike and watched his eyes as she asked, "Have you heard any news broadcasts this morning?"

"No. The folks weren't up yet, so I made my own breakfast. I like to read the funnies on Sunday morning at breakfast before my kid sister gets to them."

Again she allowed a silence to fall between them, and she thought it was almost so heavy she could hear it thump as it hit the carpet. The answer was simple. Someone trained in treating people gone hopelessly bananas should be called in and assigned the task of deprogramming Alice Kellogg. They should eliminate even a lingering suspicion that maybe—just maybe—the world really could come to an end. And don't make your usual Sunday call to Mother. She would be full of what the Bible had to say on the subject. The telephone wires should be cut and manacles applied as needed.

"Mike," she said solemnly, "are you *absolutely* sure of what you've told me? Can you back it up with your figures?"

"I sure can, Miss Kellogg."

"Then we have a lot of work to do in three weeks."

THE THIRD DAY

Ben Piper brooded the Monday morning through at his desk, then at precisely twelve past twelve (must not seem too hasty) he went to the company cafeteria. There he decorated a plastic tray with the usual white-collar luncheon, a sawdusty chicken croquette he knew would be cold in the middle, string beans boiled to glandular limpness, rusted lettuce salad, and a bowl of Jello. He joined his peers at a table for six. They were the department managers and submanagers who were not yet and possibly never would be eligible for lunch in the executive dining room.

His fellow diners were a good bunch, Piper thought, if inclined to be overloud and jolly, considering that all they were really doing was sustaining life. Sometimes their laughter at the usual run of barbs and company jokes became so loud Piper wondered if he were not somehow part of an audience witnessing a hilarious play which was invisible only to him.

His colleagues, Burr in Substations, Truax in Accounting, Maxwell in Legal, and Hardesty in Personnel, were given to another habit which he found particularly annoying on this noontide. They bragged about their offspring, and particularly their sons. If he were to believe half what they claimed in public, all their sons were models of enterprise and guaranteed a brilliant future. A few of the more honest sometimes expressed doubts in private about their sons' common sense, and very occasionally they might confess their beloved image was a pain in the ass. But never, ever, had he heard any of his fellow fathers suggest there might be something mentally wrong with their boys.

Thus, on this day while he listened to the clink-dinking of tableware and the guffaws about him, and a series of speculations about the strange behavior of the ice in Lake Superior, Ben Piper felt very alone. When his sense of isolation persisted, he finished his Jello and, claiming he was behind in his work, left the table. His dining companions knew his excuse was nonsense since no one in the power company offices ever had a full day's work at hand. Leaving a trail of bad puns and innuendos suggesting he was off to rendezvous with a blonde, Piper left the table and proceeded to his small office, where he sat looking at the wall until one o'clock. At that hour John Jenkins, the family doctor, should have completed his hospital and other calls and would be in his office.

He dialed the number and, after giving his full name, confirming he was a U.S. citizen, a resident of St. Paul, an employee of the power company, not a subscriber to Blue Cross or other hospital insurance organizations, and that indeed he was known as a former patient to Dr. Jenkins and there were records in his office to verify that fact, and finally that he was not calling in an emergency, the female voice at the other end of the line informed him she would put him on hold. He waited for exactly three minutes and twenty-seven seconds by the wall clock before Dr. John Jenkins, a man he had known since their high school days together, came on the phone.

"Hi."

"Hello, John. How's it going?"

"The situation is unchanged. I am overpaid and undersexed."

Piper thought of Saturday night, when a parental exchange with Nancy had completely shot down a possible erotic interval. John Jenkins had four teen-agers. His frustration was understandable.

"John, can you recommend a good psychiatrist?"

"I didn't realize the energy problem in this country was so bad people like you would need a couch."

"The problem is son Mike. I'm worried. So is Nancy."

"That's not so funny. Are you sure a psychiatrist is the answer? Maybe it's something else. Kids get strange diseases . . . allergies we never heard of. What are his symptoms?"

"He insists it is imperative for him to have a meeting with the President of the United States."

"You're kidding."

"I wish I was. And don't get the idea he's on any drugs or anything like that, because he's not. I know the boy means it."

"Did he give you any inkling why he wants to see the President?"

"I think he tried, but the generation gap got in the way. Probably my fault, but how would you handle a discussion of gravity acting on swirls of matter, the Doppler effect, something called nutation, which I gather has to do with the way the earth nods on its axis, and something else called 'Roche limit'? And in case you were not aware, the earth is not really round."

"Don't tell me he has joined the Flat Earth Society."

"You're not far enough out, man. He says the shape of the earth is—I wrote it down so I won't forget—*oblate*."

He spelled the word, and there followed an ominous silence until Jenkins recovered his professional tone. "I realize you do have a special problem with Mike. Has he been under any great stress lately?"

"Cut out the bedside manner, John. The boy is in real trouble and we're the ones under stress. Besides the weirdos I've just told you about, Mike's only stress in life is how he is going to keep his Pontiac running. I'm just about totally convinced he is sick and needs help."

"I don't like amateurs like you making diagnoses, but if you insist maybe you can persuade Mike to talk with Dr. Dennis Patcheck—"

"Hatcheck?" Piper was writing.

"Patcheck. He's new in town, eager, and has lots of moxie. And he's young enough so that maybe Mike will open up with him."

Piper scribbled the number, thanked his friend, and hung up. Then he turned back to his wall staring again. Life on earth, he thought, was difficult enough without worrying about earth itself.

* * *

Alice Kellogg drove a fourth-hand Porsche, which usually gave her a sense of release from her secret fear of becoming stodgy. She considered it a one-thing-after-another car, and its various malfunctions had taught her the average male pupil in Central High School was a far more competent mechanic than most of the professionals who had tinkered with it. The boys kept her mobile, and she employed them as often as necessary. They cared, she decided; in fact, it was a pity they cared so very much about all four-wheeled vehicles powered with reciprocating engines they could scarcely care about anything else. She had heard, with mixed feelings, that it was considered an honor to work on Miss Kellogg's Porsche.

Now in the raw steel light of a far northern afternoon she steered the Porsche toward the State Capitol Building, where she had an appointment with Lieutenant Governor Rudy Distancia. Arranging it had been much easier than she had dared hope. Sunday evening before she had made a phone call to the Chairperson of the Republican District Committee and reminded her that next year was critical to the party's future if it had any at all, and also how as Spokesperson for the Teachers Coalition against Racial Bias in Tenure Vulnerability (TCRBTV), she had persuaded more than two hundred votes toward Republicans in the last election and would be willing to try for more in the next. Provided the Chairperson might do a little favor. That was the way things were done, was it not? All she wanted was an appointment with the Governor as soon as possible. Certainly he would know some way Mike could meet with the President.

Even on the telephone Alice sensed the Chairperson was squirming uncomfortably, but she had finally come through with a promise to see what she could do. Surprisingly, she had called back within an hour and, gushing with officiousness, declared Rudy Distancia had agreed to see her at four on Monday afternoon. The Governor himself, it seemed, was in the Himalayas, trying to sell off surplus Minnesota wheat, and would not return until the middle of the week, at which time his schedule was understandably jammed tight. His detractors said the Governor had gone to Tibet to learn more about ringing prayer bells, a hobby he was as enthusiastic about as he had ever been about anything.

Alice was committed now. She had told Mike about the appointment after class, and they had discussed strategy. They had agreed that for this initial step it would be a mistake to fire all their ammunition through the rigging of an underling. Alice would test the waters, explaining the importance of Mike's message, but the main show should be held back for the President. To penetrate his isolation they must proceed one step at a time while still not forgetting that time was of the essence.

And how do you like those clichés for getting in a political mood? Alice thought as she jogged up the Capitol steps. Will I find myself viewing with alarm and visualizing the broad concept just by entering these hallowed halls? Yoiks! Suppose we do actually get to see the President? Will I feel an irresistible urge to drape Old Glory across my bosom and sing "America the Beautiful"? No way. They had agreed it would be more impressive if Mike saw the President alone.

Rudy Distancia, eighth son of a hard-working Italian immigrant to the steppes of Minnesota, often announced he knew quality when he saw it, and on first sight of Alice Kellogg he considered canceling the rest of his day. He was a middle-aged chubby man, a gregarious and professional political balance to his aloof and sometimes rather vague young Governor. In something less than one tenth of a second he appraised Alice Kellogg from toe to hairline and graciously moved a heavy leather chair as close to his own as the cumbersome neo-Edwardian furniture in his office would permit. "Now," he said, exhaling in the manner of a man whose patience would survive under unbearable pressure, "what can I do for you, young lady?"

Alice told him briefly of her remarkable student and his background. Then, once more daring the impossible, she wondered if Distancia might help them to meet the President. "I have enough money. I will pay our own transportation and expenses."

Distancia brushed a fat paw several times across his right ear, a habitual gesture he employed when stalling for time. Was this some kind of a gag? Maybe the press boys, goddamned their spoiled brats' hearts, were out to embarrass him with some cockamamie about a local boy who wanted to see the President. But if this broad was a setup she sure didn't look it. Could the bastards be trying to involve him with her? A little gentle blackmail was not entirely unknown about the Capitol. Since the Governor managed to convey the image that his morals matched any Benedictine monk's, maybe someone was trying to get something on his Lieutenant.

"Let me understand you, Miss Kellogg. Your friend Michael wants to see the President of the United States, right? And this is because he thinks the end of the world is coming, right? Why do you come to us? Aside from my questioning the validity of your friend's forecast, may I remind you that I am only the Lieutenant Governor and even if our President were a Republican, which he certainly is not, I do not have ready access to the White House."

"We have to start somewhere. The Governor is not available . . . and I just couldn't think where else to begin."

"Don't misunderstand me. Our supporters, and yes, even our enemies, are always welcome here. The Governor's entire philosophy is based on citizen input."

"Mr. Distancia—or do I call you 'your honor'?—we are talking about the end of the world."

"Just plain 'Rudy' will do," he purred. How could such

a good-looking broad be so nuts? It was a goddamned shame, a crime against nature. For a moment he visualized a quiet little motel near White Bear Lake. If she were told enough about the terrible burdens daily fallen upon the office of the Lieutenant Governor, would she be sympathetic enough to go for a late matinee? Let the voice of reason now echo between the marble pillars of this structure. Shake up and divert, then get on to the really important rewards of power.

"May I ask why Michael's parents are not here? You recognize that since he is a juvenile many problems arise. Have his parents authorized you to speak in behalf of their son?"

"No, I . . . Frankly, I hadn't thought of that. Perhaps I should have. . . . It's all been so sudden, perhaps my priorities—"

"Do his parents know we are all about to go skittering off into space?"

"Yes, they do—that is, I think they do. Mike said he explained things to his father. How can I tell you, your honor—"

"It's just Rudy . . . remember?"

"How can I tell you what an extraordinary boy Mike is? I believe him with all my heart or I would not be here, sir. We must stop this terrible thing from happening."

"You have omitted telling me how that miracle can be accomplished."

"Mike says the solution must be for the President's eyes only. In the wrong hands it could become the most powerful blackmail weapon the world has ever known."

Distancia duly noted the new tone of desperation in her voice. It was a good sign, he thought, a signal emitted innumerable times in his office every day when some citizen

52

with a cockamamie beef suddenly realized his or her pitch was not as meaningful as they had thought.

"Did my secretary get your number?" he asked, being careful to remove any hint of the personal from his face.

"I can be reached at the school."

"That might be inconvenient in case the Governor would like to talk further with you. As you may have heard, he keeps rather untraditional hours."

She gave him her home number, which he inscribed on a note pad as carefully as an accountant reaching a six-figure sum. Then he led her to the massive door, gently, ever gently, the great statesman bending to succor the troubled. "I promise you I will speak about this matter with the Governor as soon as he returns. Perhaps he will agree to funding a study. Whatever the outcome, I will report to you within forty-eight hours. Meanwhile you may be sure my lips are sealed."

When she went through the doorway and passed his secretary's desk, Rudy Distancia stood for a moment admiring her retreating figure. He was once again the shrewd appraiser. Blackmail? A little of what that bird had to offer might be worth the risk. Still, a man must protect his flanks as well as his back, so before proceeding further maybe it might be worthwhile contacting the Superintendent of Schools. Could be one of his employees needed investigating. What the hell kind of people were teaching our kids these days?

*   *   *

In Seoul's most elaborate brothel the decorative pond just inside the entrance suddenly vomited thirty-seven carp beyond its rock-strewn shores. The carp went into hysterics, as did the eleven resident girls. Chasing the frantic carp, one of the girls fell off the rainbow bridge and broke her right ankle, and the whole interlude was very bad for business. Later inquiries revealed no indications of a local disturbance on the Richter scale.

* * *

The Pipers were having Monday night supper, which, according to tradition in Nancy's family, relieved the refrigerator of various leftovers from Sunday's dinner. Everyone in the Piper family viewed the Monday night suppers with disdain, and even little sister Sandy, who Mike said would eat gorilla entrails, frowned at the fare. But Nancy thought tradition was the anchor of family and hers were going to sit up and eat their bubble and squeak, come what may. "Waste not, want not," she admonished.

"Mother, you've said that fifty million times," Sandy commented dryly. "Have you ever thought of putting it on a record?"

"You may spend a month in solitary for smart remarks like that," her father growled. "Think of the poor starving little girls in Africa."

"Oh, come off it, Daddy. If there really are a lot of starving girls in Africa, why don't we take some of the food we have too much of and send it to them?"

"Frankly, I've often wondered."

"Well, Daddy, if you don't know, then who in the world ever would?"

"I thank you for your confidence, but in this matter I fear it is misplaced."

Mike was swabbing at a puddle of yesterday's turkey gravy with a slice of day-before-yesterday's bread. He did not look up from his task when he said, "If all the people in the world can be brought together in a common cause, then we can really communicate and get things distributed around."

"Okay, Brain," Sandy interrupted. "Just how do you think that could be done? If you'd watch the box like I do, you'd know people are shooting at each other just about everywhere. And something else. I have never seen a girl starving on the box. Not one. The girls I see are all eating their heads off . . . cereal, chocolate bars, potato chips, and their mothers are slurping mayonnaise right out of the jar. Why don't you wear an apron in the kitchen, Mother?"

"I don't like aprons, dear."

"Mothers on the box always wear aprons. All the time except when they're dressed for church. Sometimes you don't even look like a mother to me."

"May I ask what I do look like to you?"

Sandy hesitated as if giving the matter her profound consideration. "I would say you look like . . ." She turned to her brother. "Mike, what do you think she looks like?"

"My mother."

"Is that all? Well, I think she looks like sort of half Queen Elizabeth and a little bit of the Avon lady crossed with Mrs. Yates."

"And who is Mrs. Yates?"

"Holly Beckly's Sunday school teacher. She says we are all going to heaven or hell depending on how we behave down here."

"Which do you think you qualify for?" Nancy asked, using her best mother-is-listening tone.

"Heaven. God says He means to even things up for my having such a brain for a brother."

"All right, that's enough of that kind of talk," Ben Piper said with surprising sternness. What Sandy had said was really not that offensive, he knew, but he was edgy tonight. In the few minutes of privacy he had with Nancy before dinner he had told her he had arranged an appointment for Mike with a Dr. Dennis Patcheck right after school on Tuesday. Nancy had bristled even more than he had expected, and a decided coolness between them had prevailed ever since. She had insisted an interview with a psychiatrist would only confuse Mike. "But he's my son too," he had agonized. "For God's sake, all I want to do is what is best for the kid. We can't just let him run around loose like he is. Among other things, I happen to know he's reading *Playboy* in the bathroom."

"Didn't you?"

"*Playboy* was not in existence when I was a boy. And that's not the point. I want to detour him before he becomes a menace to society."

"If you were a boy right now, I'd tell you to go wash out your mouth with soap and water. Mike a menace? You ought to be ashamed of yourself! He's a fine upstanding young man in every way. He's just going through a stage . . . growing pains."

"Nancy, when I came home tonight I said, 'Hi, Mike, how are things going?' And at first he looked right through me, like I was someone he'd never seen before. Then to be more specific I asked him how things were going in school, and he said he didn't know and didn't have time to care because he'd been up in his room all afternoon . . . thinking and figuring. It was a sorry day when we bought him that computer."

"He's just sharpening his skill."

"Darling, we have *got* to get him squared away so he can lead a normal life . . . not to mention the rest of the family."

"Supposing he's right."

"Oh, come on. Let's be sensible. *Please*. The boy has this fixation which is just close enough to sounding real that he could cause a lot of trouble. We can't challenge him scientifically—he'll drown us in numbers. We have to direct him on to other things, and that's where Dennis Hatcheck comes in. Everyone likes to talk about themselves."

"I thought the name was Patcheck."

"It is . . . was. I'm so worried and confused I only know half what I'm saying."

"You better get hold of yourself. In all the years of our marriage I've never seen you like this."

"I've never felt like this. The boy I love is in trouble I can't seem to handle. If he wrecked his car or got in a fight or the police called and said he was selling pot, I would know how to handle it. But this? I even thought of going to his girl friend, Susie, and asking her to suggest something, but of course I can't talk to her."

It had been then, as if on cue, that the phone had rung and terminated their discussion. Nancy reached for the phone at the second ring and heard her son on the upstairs extension. She heard a woman's voice—a grown woman's, she thought. She heard her say, "I saw the Lieutenant Governor today and I think we should try something else—"

That was all, for Ben Piper's hand pressing firmly upon her own returned the receiver to its proper place. "Shame on *you*," he said, unsmiling. "What do you mean listening in on another person's phone conversations?"

"But he's my son!"

"All the more so. He is a person and deserves the same privacy we do."

"He was talking with an older woman."

"How do you know? Have we installed Phonovision around here?"

"I could tell by her voice."

"What did she say?"

"I'm not going to tell you. Mike has a right to his privacy."

The Monday evening meal did not improve the overall mood of the Piper family.

* * *

Later, in his room, Mike Piper continued with what he called his "verifications." As a challenge to himself and his theory he tried working backward, beginning with the primary fact that earthlings had discharged 1.7 billion pounds of flurocarbon into the atmosphere during the year 1973. It was reasonable to assume the amount had increased rather than decreased since that time. Therefore two billion pounds per year, an increase of only three tenths of the earlier total, was a conservative starting point.

Even that approach was pure theory since the weight of oil removed versus gaseous release was not paramount to the real-life effect. He had decided to ignore the factor of coal removal for the present. It was near the surface, it was nearly all in the northern hemisphere, and the rate of removal was relatively slow. Coal also left some residual weight.

He warned himself that to recognize the complete concept was far more than a series of equations in nicely arranged juxtaposition. Lord Adrian's law, destined, he thought, someday to become as important as Newton's laws of motions, was even now taking over. He could almost feel the voltage as the neurons of his brain communicated with a rapidity he had never sensed before.

"You are not tired," he repeated softly to himself. "You will think at full amperage for one hour. But who was it said, 'To think without imagination is like trying to fly without wings'?"

It was no use just playing around with a lot of figures.

Newton's *Principia* and Johannes Kepler's discovery that the orbits of planets are ellipses were not conceived by brains fixed to a catalogue of mere numbers. Based on current knowledge of why planet earth was where it was, there should be clues to show where it was going once the anchors started dragging. And do not neglect history, Mike old boy. Consider the separation of continents . . . Atlantis disappearing . . . the creation of mountain ranges. . . .

And now back to basics. Put away the vision of that dual carburetor plus twenty dollars' extra charge for chromium and remember the earth's bulge at the equator is now fourteen miles. Okay, back to Susie. The bulge is there because of the twirling ice-skater effect. Now, if the speed of rotation is increased, if we start having twenty-three-hour days then twenty-two, and so on, so will the bulge increase and the speed of rotation even further accelerate. Or the other way . . . if we slow down and start having twenty-five-hour days? Will the resulting lack of centrifugal force replace the present bulge with a vast depression and suck the oceans toward it? Will New York or San Francisco be a hundred miles from the sea and all the equatorial lands under water? Wow.

Cut out the science fiction stuff, Mike. This is for real and you know it. Mind the neighbors for a minute . . . Venus, which is about the same size and mass as earth. Someone ought to think of a prettier name for this beautiful place. *Earth* sounds like a grunt. Whoa, Mike, now concentrate! Venus circles the sun in 225 earth days. It doesn't have as far to travel as we do. It has retrograde rotation because it is closer to the sun and the sun's gravity slows down the rate of rotation.

So? To speed our rate of rotation we would have to move farther from the sun and to slow it move in closer.

Okay, once again, Finnegan. We are a moon and the sun is our parent. Every planet and star has its so-called "Roche limit." The Roche limit for the sun is half a million miles above its surface. Any planet that tries to form within that limit will be destroyed before it can really begin. If we slip inside that limit, will our destruction be instant, a slow crumbling, or take a few thousand years?

Mike rose from his desk and went to the window. Organized thinking was the most difficult of all the arts, he decided. A person should have something working nights for him, like right now his braces were in his own mouth instead of Kevin McCoy's and were therefore not picking up any rent. If you can find something to work for you while you sleep, then it won't be long before the Pontiac can flash those dual carburetors. Cripes, were they expensive!

He stared down at the moonlight on the snow and found the sight tended to calm his thoughts. Newton. The gravitational force between two objects varies as one over the square of their distance. So if the distance is doubled, the strength of gravity *decreases* to a quarter of its original power. You bounced a tire, Susie spun out, the leaning tower of Pisa fell down. Any relation? Certainly. The moon, the moon! There it was in essence—right there! Newton also said gravity falls off as one over the square of the distance to the *center of the earth*. Then there *had* been a variation in the distance between the normal location of those areas where the strange events occurred and the earth's center. It would be like the present equatorial bulge, but perhaps much less. A mile? Two miles, probably depending on the amount of wobble. And the new wobble pattern was caused by a relatively new change in the balance of the whole sphere.

As if it were written in the snow, Mike saw the equation, Force$=\dfrac{m_1\,m_2}{d^2}$. The moon was held in orbit according to that formula, and also the earth. And if there is the slightest change in the object itself, then according to the inverse square law of attraction, there must be a corresponding change in orbit. No question about it, we were on our way . . . somewhere.

Mike returned to his desk, his mind clicking off figures even before his fingers began touching the buttons on his computer. He revived the same calculations he had developed the preceding summer when he had been toying with hypothetical plate tectonic situations and had first conceived his spinning-top theory. He remembered how it had been fantasy then . . . the unbelievable was fun as long as it remained unbelievable. But now he was no longer playing games.

He must be very careful and precise. No one should be able to disprove his calculations. No one in the world. And no one must know his exact predictions, much less the ultimate solution—if (cripes, what a project) he could really pin it down. No one should be trusted with such vital data except the President of the United States.

THE FOURTH DAY

On the fourth day after Mike Piper dribbled the wheel and tire of his early iron across the family garage, nothing extraordinary happened on planet earth and the morning news commentators were obliged to vamp through their pontifications just hoping for the best. They reported a study was to be made of the Lake Superior ice phenomenon at a cost of one million dollars. They were not aware that Michael Piper had chosen this day to plead illness and thus persuade his mother he should not attend Central High School. Nor would they have thought it newsworthy that a sixteen-year-old boy spent the entire day in his room working furiously with computer, pencil, an ordinary school writing book, and the stack of reference books he had accumulated since he was twelve.

Timing, as all resourceful politicians know, is the key to

the launching of any project. Rudy Distancia had devoted a whole hour to the various requirements he considered might guarantee a satisfying matinee with his caller of the previous day—a Ms. Alice Kellogg, according to his inexhaustible mental name file. She was crazy, he had decided, but then one might tolerate an addled little Red Riding Hood if she would be led safely through the forest and eventually warm Papa Bear's bed. If she were under the illusion that the world was in real trouble unless the President intervened in some yet undefined manner, then who indeed might come to the rescue? Rudy Distancia, sometimes known as Rudy the Nimble. Kooky? No, he decided, titillating.

With his plan still in the preliminary stages, and finding it quite as stimulating as a hot political campaign, Distancia telephoned the Superintendent of Schools, a man who had once worked for him in the House Committee on State Employee Pensions.

Distancia's keynote speech was intended to inspire his audience, and in that respect did succeed admirably. ". . . Charlie, I am aware you have now been running the city school system for two years, and I wish to congratulate you on a difficult task well done. These are difficult times, Charlie." Was there ever a nondifficult time? "Now I trust you have not forgotten the circumstances leading to your present highly rewarding position?"

The Superintendent ahemmed three times while he forced himself to recall the circumstances and identified himself with a troubled soul named Faust.

"Very well then, Charlie old boy. One of your teachers has come to the attention of this office, and since the matter is confidential I cannot now share it with you. However, I would like a full report on Alice Kellogg, who I assume is a Miss, or is it a Mrs.? It's not easy to be sure these days, ho-ho. Now, Charlie, I would like that report in my hand no later than this afternoon."

The Superintendent promised a messenger would be dispatched with such data as he had at *his* hand within the hour. He added that if his memory served him correctly, an Alice Kellogg was one of their better teachers, and he wondered if she was being considered for a possible position with the state itself.

"That is not impossible," Distancia replied with just the right amount of solemnity; then both parties hung up their phones with a sense of accomplishment.

Afterward Distancia spent some time buffing his fingernails against his pants leg while he marveled at the strong impression Alice Kellogg had made on him. Very strange, he thought. Rudy the Nimble had a covey of birds who were available for various reasons. Yet his name was not given for naught; he would never countenance his high office being sullied with females in cushy jobs. Never would any investigator be able to point a finger at Distancia and accuse him of exchanging posts in his immediate bailiwick for political favor. He hired on merit and qualifications, a policy so unique in state government that everyone mistrusted him. But ah, the dividends. With a staff such as he had assembled, his time could be devoted to the pleasures of life.

One of those pleasures was baiting his young Governor.

Governor Preston Granger, scion of a wealthy Minnesota family (lumber, iron, railroads, beer), was said to be honest to a penny, which was more money than he customarily bothered to carry. He was also straightforward, a complete idealist, and passionately interested in leaving both his office and the state in better condition than when he had been elected. As a consequence of these curious beliefs few people believed what he said and a number of powerful figures had dedicated themselves to thwarting his every attempt at improving the environment both within the Capitol itself and the vast geography surrounding it.

In the most powerful circles Governor Granger was referred to openly as "that goddamned do-gooder," amid prophecies that he would wreck the state if given the chance. Since he betrayed his heritage by daring to cross swords with the establishment, it was obvious to most of the electorate that he would not be given a next chance.

When dealing with his Governor, Distancia kept an unerring eye on the future of his own backside, and in the process had acquired a marvelous expertise in shifting from counselor to confidant and from court clown to faithful chamberlain. It was in the latter role that he attended upon his political superior on the morning after his return from India.

He found Granger by the large window which graced the Governor's office. A shaft of sunlight spotlighted Granger's handsome head and revealed him on the window seat sitting in the lotus position. Distancia knew he was in meditation, but as long as Preston did not come out of it with one of his commonsense ideas like legalizing both marijuana *and* abortion, allowing fags and dykes to live as they pleased, to say nothing of insisting young and able-bodied people on welfare show proof they were trying to get work before largesse was distributed, he could meditate twenty-four hours a day for all Distancia cared. There was no harm thinking about things as long as the Governor did not act upon what he thought.

"Welcome home, Preston," Distancia said with his finest blend of one part sincerity, one part respect, one part contempt (what the hell did you come back for— everything was going along fine), and one part just plain folk greetings from a good old boy. He capped his salutation with a touching falsehood: "We sure did miss you around here," and he thought how marvelous it was that so much could be transmitted in so few words. Someday he would take out a patent on the formula and bottle it.

Now Distancia sniffed unhappily. "What's that funny smell in here?"

"Incense. It's called, 'Message from Kandu.' I find it helps me solve problems."

Maybe, Distancia questioned secretly, I am thinking of bottling the wrong stuff? He stood patiently, waiting for the Governor to break his trance. At last Granger uncoiled his long legs, sighed regretfully, as if he had left something exceedingly pleasurable, and extended a limp hand toward his Lieutenant. "How are things in the great state of Minnesota?" he inquired with a vague smile.

Distancia was about to recite his usual report, which was *always* highly positive (remember what happened to the guy who brought bad news to that old king), when some new and mischievous genie possessed him. Later he could not for the life of him analyze why he had responded, "Well, Preston, not so good. I assume you heard about Lake Superior getting shallower?"

"Yes. I can't understand it. Imagine a lake as big as an ocean springing a leak. I'm afraid getting things fixed up is going to cost the state a lot of money. What about the fish? Did any survive?"

"Nope. All three died."

"Maybe it was sabotage by some anti-environmental group. Anyway, I'll have to declare it a disaster area. The President will send money and we can get some more fish."

It was just then that the genie took charge and Distancia found himself saying, "Speaking of the President, I had a caller yesterday who hoped we could help her get a

White House appointment. She says the end of the world is coming . . . or have you heard that before?"

While he was waiting for a laugh or at least a chuckle, Distancia was astonished to see Granger lower his head and peer at him from beneath his bushy eyebrows. "Oh, I've known that for some time. It's only a question of when."

Distancia grasped desperately for a lifeline from the real world. What the hell had he just done? New rule. Never bring two kooks together or you might start a convention.

Seeking to stuff his own thinking back into perspective as well as his Governor's, he said, "I hardly think we need pay much attention to the lady involved. She is an English teacher who has some sixteen-year-old kid she thinks is some kind of a genius and he has it all figured out."

"Maybe he has."

"Aw, now really, Preston . . . this is idiotic stuff. You take my advice and stay clear of it or the news media will have a field day. I can see it now—'Governor Declares End of World in Sight'—based on secret information the Governor has received from an adolescent guru. We just can't let that sort of material go around these days, Preston. The Senate is already suspicious of your trip to India and they don't understand things like incense."

"I paid for the India trip out of my own pocket."

"Of course. The problem is always to get anyone to print five consecutive words in favor of any public official."

"I'd like to see this schoolteacher, and of course the boy."

"And I should keep my big mouth shut," Distancia groaned. In no way could he allow his Governor to become mixed up with any more gnomes and elves and witches than he already was. The teacher should be transferred immediately to a school north of the Mesabi iron range and the boy sent off to a distant military academy. Maybe the parents were reasonable people.

"Try to get them to drop by this afternoon," Granger said. "I haven't anything to do anyway."

Distancia concluded he would remedy that situation forthwith. A Governor with a loaded calendar was a good Governor. It kept him out of mischief.

Preston my boy, he thought, you'll never believe how busy you're going to be. By this afternoon you'll be lucky to find time to go to the bathroom.

Within fifteen minutes Distancia had his entire staff at work lining up appointments for the Governor. Most were with people who could not remember what their original beef had been, and others thought it might be fun to just pass the time of day with such an eccentric and rich young man.

* * *

Since she normally ate a light breakfast Alice Kellogg was always ravenous by noon, and she noticed that her patience shortened with her degree of hunger. Thus she often dismissed her class a few minutes before noon and, once by herself, propped her feet on the lower drawer of her desk, opened a book placed handily for the occasion, and enjoyed an hour of solitude. During this time she consumed two sandwiches, an apple, four cookies, half a thermos of tea, and enough of Lawrence Durrell to leave her feeling so like a seductive Alexandrian that she sometimes fanned her brow to relieve the intense North African heat.

She was rarely disturbed during these very private interludes and had come to rely on nearly a full hour until students for the 1 P.M. class started filing in. Hence she was surprised when she heard the door open and, turning away from the searing blaze of the Egyptian sun and the soft humming of flies, she observed none other than William Wordsworth Bunker enter the room. He was a small man, often given to sniveling, and some of his ways, Alice had thought, suggested a not so bright Uriah Heep. He had other problems, which she suspected might be deeply psychological. His frequent sniveling was probably in reaction to an asthmatic condition, but the snowdrifts of dandruff which always accumulated on his shoulders in spite of their steep slope were the result of either perpetual tension or extreme myopia. Yet in many ways Alice felt compassion for William Bunker, who as principal of the large Central High School held a position far beyond his capabilities. She knew he must suffer untold agonies of indecision and consequent fretfulness. She saw the permanent wistfulness about his eyes as a signal regretting his very being, an open apology for his presence on any scene. The student body, unaware of Bunker's notable scholastic achievements, used their principal as a butt of their jokes and a convenient target for their defiance of the establishment. Certain members of the faculty who should have known better were not above snide comments upon his various bouts with indecision.

Now Bunker came to her, thumbs protectively in his vest pockets, and said, "May I disturb you at your repast, Miss Kellogg?"

"Welcome," she said, kicking the desk drawer shut and rising. "We of the English Department are honored that you could find your way to our humble surroundings."

Bunker endeavored to smile and failed, in keeping with almost all his other endeavors.

He looked about the room as if he had never seen a school before. Then he took off his glasses and massaged them with the overused handkerchief he pulled from the side pocket of his jacket. He asked if he might sit down, and when Alice brought him a chair he squinted at the window glare and cleared his throat several times. Resuming her luncheon, Alice asked if he would like a cookie, and when he declined she became vaguely unhappy. She thought it would be rewarding to give Mr. Bunker even a few moments of sensual pleasure—even munching on a store-bought cookie might provide more enjoyment than he had known in a long time.

"Miss Kellogg," he finally sighed, "I don't know how to begin, but there is something I must discuss with you. I . . . find it most embarrassing, one might say even distressing—"

Not knowing what else to say, Alice inquired if his wife was unwell.

"Oh, dear me, no. Sadie is in splendid spirits, thank you."

And I'll bet she is indeed, Alice thought. The apparently indestructible Sadie, in strong contrast to her melancholy spouse, was given to spirits of any kind at the slightest excuse. Her boisterous conduct when "in good spirits" had resulted in no less than eight probables and five confirmed crashes while at the helm of their car. Fortunately, all the encounters were with solid objects such as garage doors, curbs, trees, and an illegally parked cement mixer. With no other cars involved, the police were spared a contest with her rambunctious personality.

"There are times in one's life when one must face up to one's duty," Bunker droned on, "and while I have been aware of this matter for some time, I had discounted it as idle gossip. Now, I fear, the time has come when I am forced to discuss it with the individual involved."

She watched him cross and recross his legs, smoothing

out what was left of the press in his pants after the exchange of limbs had been made. "You will forgive me for being blunt, Miss Kellogg?"

"By all means, try it." What in the world was on his convoluted little mind?

"I refer to the matter of your personal conduct. We prefer our teaching staff to be above reproach." He held up a frail hand defensively. "Lest you take offense, please remember that I am on your side. That is why I did not ask you to come to my office, but instead came to you. In my office the atmosphere might be that of an official inquiry . . . even censure, and I should prefer to avoid such an aura . . . at least for the present. Unfortunately, the impetus for this matter seems to have been initiated in a much higher office than my own."

Alice finished the last cookie and washed it down with what remained of her tea. She waited for Bunker to say something more and found it easy to imagine she was one of the Czarina's ladies-in-waiting being interrogated by a Tartar commissar. ("Which way did the droshky go, you miserable aristocrat?")

("I will not tell you though I may die here in the snows of Siberia. Mujik! Mujik! Bring my sable lest I take chill.")

"Miss Kellogg . . . I hope you realize this is very very difficult for me?"

"I would realize a lot more, Mr. Bunker, if I knew what the hell you were talking about."

"Perhaps it is a question of attitude, as in the statement you just made, or should one say the way you phrased it."

"I asked you to come out of the bushes and you keep ducking back in."

"Obviously you feel no remorse."

"I feel considerable remorse for my lunch, which is not

resting well in my esophagus." Alice Kellogg's eyes were beginning to take on the look of highly polished granite.
"Now don't get upset. Remember I am only doing my duty. You must understand that when the State Superintendent of Schools makes inquiry about one of my staff, asking for such information as is available to me, I must respond in some way. I certainly cannot ignore his request, but before I send along the information I must reassure myself that what appears to be common knowledge is not based upon fact."

"Mr. Bunker, are you trying to suggest that I am not a virgin?"

He blushed to an alizarine crimson, which Alice decided with some satisfaction was quite a feat for a man whose normal coloring resembled the interior of an eggplant.

"Good heavens! I would not presume to suggest *any*thing of a personal nature. However, it is well known that you do occasionally exhibit, shall we say, a certain instability of conduct."

"Shall who say?"

"It is difficult to correlate your splendid teaching record with what is sometimes, shall we say, considered your eccentric behavior. It draws attention to yourself."

"Und dot is verboten, Herr Bunker?"

"*Please.* This is a very serious matter. I am trying to make it easy for both of us."

"Well, you aren't. If you don't come to the point, I'm going to ask you to leave so I can finish my lunch in peace."

William Wordsworth Bunker sighed, and with his exhalation her anger subsided. Poor man. When, if ever, had he known of either real passion or compassion? Since he was human, there must be buried somewhere within him a poet, or even a rake capable of wild emotion. Mike Piper had once explained how all humans were simply the end result of hydrogen gas and amino acids, yet after several billion years there was some question if this invertebrate had graduated to real creature status.

"Are you by any chance referring to the car I drive, Mr. Bunker? If so I must agree it is not only an eccentric pose, but also unwise. Never have I had such a perpetual drain on my finances."

"Ah! Yes, the car you drive is, shall we say, a symbol of the other things. Away from school your personal life is rightfully your own . . . with certain moral limitations of course. You are a young and attractive lady, and it is perhaps only natural that a number of eligible men would seek you out."

"Some of them are not so eligible. Alas."

"Please, Miss Kellogg. I am trying to avoid a confrontation on a nonschool basis. What worries me is the rumors of your conduct with your own male students. I am embarrassed to tell you—"

Alice held up her hand to interrupt him. For suddenly she knew why her superior had come. Baring her teeth, she spoke slowly, enunciating each word as if she relished it. "Don't be. I cannot wait to hear how an evil high school teacher lusts for the bodies of the young gods who must submit to her will."

"Well . . . that is why I am here. One mother called me last week and said something must be done about your apparent infatuation with her boy."

Suddenly Alice Kellogg thought she was going to be sick right on the podium which supported her desk. And right in front of Mr. Bunker. No angel I, she thought, but this was too much like daytime television. The notes of a once popular song flickered across her thoughts. Woe to me,

Mrs. Robinson. My God, it wouldn't be Mike's mother, would it? Or would it?

"Who brought this ridiculous accusation?"

"Mrs. Trilling. I believe her boy is named Roger."

"And what were Roger and I supposed to be doing?"

"That was not specified, but the suggestion was made that Roger was kept after class three times in the last week, during which you laid a hand on his shoulder in a way that distracted his concentration."

"Mr. Bunker, let me assure you that Roger is nearly incapable of concentrating on anything. I put my hand on his shoulder in an attempt to encourage him beyond the mental threshold of a baboon. The attempt was unsuccessful, and now I know where he got his mental genes."

"There is also the matter of Michael Piper."

"What about him?"

"I do not know the original source, but the word is—even among certain members of the faculty, I fear—that you are prone to hold his hand."

Alice Kellogg rose slowly and stood in silence before her principal. At first she wanted to reach down and seize his wisps of mousy hair and pull him up and shake him until the roots gave way. Here she was in real life, sort of a poor woman's Medea. Bring the hemlock! Let the blood flow lest the venom of my lascivious desires destroy the lovely romance between Michael Piper and Susanna York. But first let us kill Mr. William Wordsworth Bunker.

"Go," she said hoarsely. "Get out of this room, and don't you ever come back. Yes, I love my students, every last one of them . . . even Roger Trilling. And because this is my life I like to think some of them love me. And if you're thinking of making a case out of what you seem to believe, be forewarned you'd better have proof. I have tenure and a lawyer, and I'll fight you down to the last rumor. Now beat it before I throw up in your lap."

* * *

Since Ben Piper pleaded he could not possibly leave the heavy pressure of a Tuesday in his office, it was Nancy who escorted her son to the leather couch of Dr. Dennis Patcheck. They drove in separate cars at Mike's insistence. Nancy understood. No young man wanted to be taken to a doctor by his mother unless he was paralyzed beyond hope or had come down with advanced leprosy. "And besides," Mike had said, "I have things to do afterward."

It had not been comfortable at the breakfast table when Mike was informed the later part of his afternoon had been scheduled with a doctor.

"There's nothing wrong with me. Today I feel super neat."

Both father Ben and mother Nancy had then tried to explain why he must see Dr. Patcheck. "Just an exploratory visit which it is really your duty to humanity to take in good grace. The doctor will try to find out why you are so good in mathematics, thereby helping students who have great difficulty. . . ."

"Is he a Doctor of Education or a headshrinker?"

They were obliged to confess that Dr. Patcheck was indeed a psychiatrist, but Mike's immediate protests were finally worn away with the call to duty for humanity. Aware of the pleading in his mother's eyes, Mike agreed to give the interview one hour of his valuable time and no more.

Due to his relatively recent arrival in the city, not to include the professional handicap of being clean-shaven, Dr. Patcheck still had a practice so thin he had no trouble whatsoever in reserving the four-to-five appointment slot for Mike Piper. Nancy was somewhat taken aback at his youth when he emerged from his inner office and advanced to greet his only patient of the afternoon. She decided he did not look at all like a headshrinker, and found she was even a little disappointed in his lack of mysterioso as he discussed the cold weather and how early in the day darkness fell.

Mike resisted an attempt to tell him why the sun was going down three minutes ahead of schedule this day. There was no use inserting disturbing thoughts into the head of a man like Dr. Patcheck. A jolly doctor was better than an old gloom-and-doom, and if it would make him feel any better believing Mike Piper was crazy, why not? Older people should be treated with respect and care, and the doctor was probably thirty (as anyone could tell by observing the craters on his carrot nose and his half-eye spectacles). He also reeked of tobacco, and therefore, in Mike's opinion, he could not be very smart.

After the amenities and assurance that if Dr. Patcheck would mail the bill to 2000 Maple Avenue payment would be prompt, Nancy wiggled her fingers in uncertain farewell and left the scene. In anxiety for her son she had great trouble concentrating on her homeward journey, barely avoiding two accidents, and she took a wrong turn down a dead-end street she knew perfectly well led to the back-wire fence of an industrial park. When she finally arrived at 2000 Maple Avenue she committed an act hitherto unthinkable to her. Striding resolutely from the garage to the kitchen, she took down the bottle of sherry Aunt Lucille had sent the family for Christmas and poured herself half a tumblerful. Then, still clad in hat, gloves, and coat, she stood watching the sink as if it might suddenly rise from its mooring and fly away. And, swallowing, she thought, Eeny, meeny, miney, mo. The question is who should really be hitting the leather in Dr. Patcheck's office? Maybe it should be Ben . . . ? Or, come on now . . . maybe it should be me?

* * *

The interview had not been going at all as Dr. Patcheck had anticipated. He had been prepared, as always, to share the grief and joy en route to his patient's unconscious. Steeped as he was in Binswanger, Boss, Kierkegaard, and Ferenczi, he knew he was a Freudian at heart and that the "royal road to the unconscious" was via the interpretation of dreams. Yet now he was finding young Michael Piper anything but fertile ground.

Patcheck paused in his questioning to review a few shorthand notes he had made which normally would provide cues for his later analysis.

"Tell me about your dreams, Mike."

"I almost never dream. Of course if I come home on Saturday night from a basketball game or a dance and I raid the icebox, then sometimes I dream."

"Is your icebox raiding against your parent's wishes? When we come right down to it, isn't that symbolic of your defying authority?"

"No. I'm just hungry."

"Were you deprived of food during your childhood?"

"Cripes no. What's that got to do with why I'm here?"

It was such responses that persuaded Dr. Patcheck he should forsake his professional mien and get closer to his patient. Friends they would be, pals across the abyss of distortions and self-deceptions which so afflicted this poor young man. "Mike old pal," he had commenced in his most easygoing manner, "deep down you and I know the world is *not* really coming to an end. You and I recognize this is a fixation in your mind . . . an obsession, if you will. We have to find out why this troubles you—"

"It ought to trouble everyone."

"I don't mean it that way, Mike. The *cause* of your problem must be determined before any real therapy can begin. You do not seem to have a thyroid condition, myasthenia gravis, or any of the multitude of chemically induced psychoses. Perhaps the key lies in your past, in some infantile sexual conflict, something in your childhood which was repressed and hence relegated to the unconscious. Tell me, do you ever ask, *Who am I?*"

"I know who I am. Mike Piper."

"Hmmmm. Are you ever lonely?"

"I don't have time to be lonely, what with school, basketball, homework, my car, my business, and trying to see Susie once in a while. I'm pooped when I go to bed. Maybe that's why I don't dream."

"Everybody dreams, Mike. If you must vent the hostility you feel toward authority figures such as your parents, then go right ahead and take it out on me. That's part of my job."

"Was I being hostile? I just said I didn't dream very much. And besides, I love my mother and father. They're neat people even if they are kind of stuffy."

Dr. Patcheck puffed vigorously on his pipe, and created such a cloud of smoke Mike wiped at his eyes. He remained silent while Patcheck looked at the ceiling and remembered how adolescents must be advised of the interdigitating, overwhelming forces created by the impinging and shifting pressures of the familial field.

"I suppose you consider your parents reactionary?"

"What's that?"

"If you were to quote Castro, or Che Guevara or praise Ho Chi Minh in their presence, which is a common signal of youthful rebellion against authority in our country, what would your parents think?"

"They would think I was bananas."

"Exactly. And that would infuriate you, right? In your superior knowledge of the modern world you would then tell them where they were wrong? Would you perhaps link their decadent philosophy with your belief that unless our civilization rectified itself soon the end of the world was inevitable?"

"That's what I've been trying to tell you. It is inevitable, and the Republicans don't have anything to do with it."

"Of course, of course." Humor the patient, Patcheck remembered, while leading him toward the light. He also recalled that intellectually gifted adolescents were not inclined to display any high incidence of social responsibility. Many teachers considered superior adolescents to be more rebellious and aggressive than those of average intelligence. "Mike," he said gently, "we must integrate."

"I have nothing against blacks. We have a whole bunch at school and most of them are nice guys."

"I'm talking about you. Somehow we must integrate your manifest and latent personalities. We must uncover any feelings you may have of personal inadequacy and dissatisfaction with yourself and with our society."

"Okay, you ask Miss Kellogg, our English teacher. She knows I try hard but I can't ever get the past perfect tense straight and I can split an infinitive at a thousand yards. She may have to flunk me, and that really bugs me."

Dr. Patcheck sighed. "Mike, we have to come up with some meaningful conclusions about why you think you should see the President of the United States."

"If you don't mind my saying so, Doctor, *meaningful* is not a word. At least I know that much about the English language."

It was Dr. Patcheck's turn to retreat into silence. Did his reprimand suggest defiance? Rapaport and Schafer hypothesized that intelligence bloomed in childhood when nourished by the ego and involved the postponement or even the concealment of impulse gratification. Was Mike simply kicking shins? Was he bawling, "Look at me, pay attention, I want to be in the spotlight"? And to accomplish his desire he had consciously or perhaps subconsciously set himself up as a juvenile Messiah who knew more than anyone else and would in his cleverness lead his audience to salvation? By God, Dennis old boy, you may be on to something here.

"How do you feel about your sister, Mike?"

"Okay. But she talks too much."

"How about your mother?"

"She's my mother. She's neat. How do you feel about yours?"

"May I remind you that I am conducting this interview, which, I assure you, is very preliminary."

"Miss Kellogg would say you don't need the word *very* there, Doctor. Something is either preliminary or it is not."

"And who is Miss Kellogg?"

"My English teacher."

Dr. Patcheck had difficulty in stifling an involuntary "Ah-hah!" There was indeed more than met the eye here. The lad was obviously under the influence of an older woman. Rebellion again—the substitution of an outside maternal factor for the traditional family member. Or was there something even more insidious? Perhaps for a meaningful exploration of this bizarre situation it would be helpful to call in Miss Kellogg. Feedback in this dimension was vital to recognizing a flagrant disorganization of thinking and disorientation such as Mike was experiencing.

Dr. Patcheck purred solemnly while he heard Mike saying, "Miss Kellogg believes what I say is going to happen really *is* going to happen. Right now she is working on getting me an appointment with the President."

"Is she, really." Patcheck allowed his voice to remain flat. He wanted to make a statement, not a query. "Really? And I suppose there are other matters on which you are in complete agreement."

He watched Mike carefully for any autonomic phenomena such as blanching or a dilation of the pupils. And he reminded himself that the neurotic were often emotionally unstable—a handsome lad like Mike could be persuaded into almost any sort of action if he were told repeatedly that what he must do in the company of his persuader was fine and meaningful.

Dr. Patcheck found this new avenue intriguing. He uttered a second "Ah-hah" as he considered how Miss Kellogg could be included along with the rest of the family in group therapy. Who knew? The total analysis sessions might take as long as a year.

"Mike, there is a very apparent chip on your shoulder. It may take us a long time to knock it off, but if you'll stick with me we'll win eventually. Think of me as your friend . . . call me Dennis if you like. Or pretend I am the President of the United States."

"You don't look like him. And none of us have a long time to solve this problem. In only a couple of weeks it may be too late. Can I go now? My hour is up and I've got a lot to do today."

Dr. Patcheck watched Mike stand up and decided to remain seated. It was not the time to be negative. Adolescent self-determination was still in command. The torments seething within Mike Piper must be allowed to cool slowly. It would be chancy, perhaps even dangerous, to attempt a siphoning off of Mike's defiance syndrome by guiding him into physical aggression. Massage? The specter of such a tall young man relieving his tension by beating a pillow with a tennis racket (which had been so successful in the case of Miss Wilma Nogurt, his patient of the morning, who had recently developed a powerful urge to break all the furniture in her house) was not a pretty picture. No. Whether Mike's family was centripetal, centrifugal, or mixed must be articulated before any meaningful perception of his discrepancies could be achieved. The hierarchy of adaptive ego mechanisms must, as always, determine the mass of the iceberg though merely the tip was visible.

* * *

As he drove from the doctor's office to the Palace Ice Rink, Mike became lost in the glorious music of the Pontiac's exhaust pipes. Their throaty basso enabled him to dream dreams he found most soothing to his earthly troubles. He saw a large ranch somewhere—in the Argentine pampas, probably—and he was descending upon the landing strip in his own Lear jet. He swooped down past the figure of a woman, Susie of course. She waved to him as he executed a spectacular chandelle, then eased down for a perfect landing. He was a wealthy man, this Yankee who had come to dominate such a huge section of Argentina. Through the cockpit window he saw Susie sign "Welcome home!" and he was relieved that the long flight from Zurich, where he had been conferring with the Bank for International Settlements, was done. Now for an evening with Susie in their specially built observatory, where a twenty-inch reflecting telescope would help him discover a new star in the heavens. He would name it Alpha Susanna

78, honoring the year they had met. And probably he would win the Nobel.

For this temporary peace of mind it was doubtless better that Mike could not be aware of two other significant events transpiring in the relatively short time of his drive. The first occurred at Mission Capistrano when the swallows returned in great numbers. Knowledgeable swallow observers were shocked because the arrival of the birds was more than one month ahead of schedule.

Next, in Yellowstone Park the geyser Old Faithful, which had been dormant for two weeks, suddenly spewed stinking water three hundred feet straight up.

Three scientists, part of a USIRCAGV group (Interdepartmental Research and Correlation of Active Geysers and Volcanoes), were on a two-million-dollar government grant and were actually on the site when the eruption occurred. They were enjoying pine needle tea and pemmican, as they had done every afternoon for the past six months of their strenuous study, and were discussing the need for another million funding before they could really scratch the surface of their subject. It was then the surface bubbled beneath them and the ensuing cascade nearly drowned the lot. After PCR (pulmonary cardiac resuscitation) by the stronger members of the team, all survived, although they were pronounced socially unacceptable even after rigorous bathing.

By the time Mike arrived at the Palace Ice Rink, it was dark. He went inside, kicked the snow off his boots, and made his way along the empty rows of seats until he came to the center of the rink. There he waited impatiently until Susie left a trio of figure skaters who were watching her do flick turns. When he finally caught her eye, she came to him breathless and smiling her multimillion-dollar smile. She banked to a hard stop directly in front of him, deliberately shooting a little fountain of ice chips at his face.

Laughing, he thought she had never looked more beautiful. She had obviously been skating hard, for tiny beads of perspiration glistened on her cheeks and forehead and she was still panting when she signed how happy she was to see him.

"Did you fall today?"

"No. No trouble at all."

"No funny feeling . . . like maybe you were suddenly lighter or heavier?"

Susie shook her head negatively, and then much more positively when he asked her if she would like to watch the night ski-jumping practice at Lake Como. "And I invited Miss Kellogg. She said she would like to get her mind off her troubles."

Susie signed her lack of comprehension. Miss Kellogg was too neat to have troubles.

"She hasn't heard anything from the Governor. I don't know what to do next. And maybe—just maybe—I could be wrong."

"Do you really doubt yourself?"

Mike hesitated. After a moment he waved his hand rapidly, flat and outward from his hips, signifying "Not yet." Then he signed, "It's just that no one else seems to realize what is happening. Everybody just seems to be going about their business. Today I had to go see a head doctor, and I'm sure he thinks I'm so far out I'll never come back."

"I don't. And I never will." She reached for his hand impulsively and looked into his eyes. She raised his hand briefly to her lips.

"Wow," Mike said softly to himself. Then he signed, "Get out of your skates, Susie. I'll take you home."

* * *

A fine snow sifted down from the black sky, and the crowd assembled to witness the hopeful ski jumpers was composed almost entirely of family and enthusiasts. Hence, there were not more than a few hundred people clustered in a half circle near the finish area and along both sides of the slope. The jump structure itself was brilliantly illuminated. It rose impressively above the summit of the hill which supported its underpinning, and the highest lights flickered weakly through the snow. Occasionally those in the crowd below could see one of the jumpers or officials moving about the top of the tower. They were tiny dark figurines against the void.

Everyone knew this was not going to be a very exciting night, for the jumpers were all young aspirants, eager to improve their status in the sport and perhaps even qualify for Winter Carnival events. The real pros would be jumping then. They were usually of Scandinavian descent and soared through the air as much as three hundred meters before they touched down. Their technique was nearly flawless, but of the fifty candidates already on top of the jump and those still climbing the hill only a few could hope to compete.

Among the hopefuls was Sven Neilsen, a powerful youth of eighteen. Perhaps because he was a plodder and not overly bright even his physical strength had not been enough to hoist him into the upper class of jumpers. He was a senior at Central High School and therefore was so far exalted above a mere sophomore like Mike Piper that he would normally see right through him. Yet this night Sven was lonely and somewhat frightened at the questionable visibility and he was very glad to see a familiar face. Possibly that need for reassurance obliged him to pause when he saw Mike standing with Alice Kellogg and a girl unknown to him.

"Hi, Miss Kellogg. Hi, Brain. How's it goin'?"

"Super! Good luck!"

"Thanks. Tonight's the night I'm gonna do it."

He resumed his upward march, and Mike signed to Susie that Sven hoped to qualify and he hoped he succeeded because he was a nice jock and was not afraid to talk to people who were not seniors. Susie waved to Sven, and so did Miss Kellogg, and the jumper waved back, thus creating a warm sense of belonging to each other. Mike glanced down at Susie, whose face was mostly concealed behind the fox fur fringing her parka hood, and he decided even her nose alone was beautiful. Turning away, he noticed Alice Kellogg's face outlined crisply against the lighted snow, and he thought she was also beautiful even if she was pretty ancient.

He was still appraising his English teacher when he saw a man come up behind her, hesitate for a moment, then reach out and cover her eyes with his hands. He heard Alice Kellogg gasp, then start to laugh as the man said, "Guess who?"

"How can I? Give me a clue."

Hearing the tone of her voice, Mike decided she was in no need of his protection. The man was obviously a friend. He was tall, clean-shaven, and of course also pretty ancient. He wore a muffler around his neck, and the snow had formed a white cap over his dark hair.

"Think back to the summer you worked for the Pioneer Press," the man said, still covering her eyes. "Think back to your girlhood before you became a teacher and remember, if you can, your first open-cockpit airplane ride."

Mike was relieved to see his teacher smiling. She said, "Marty Martinson. You've got to be."

She spun around, laughing, and somewhat to his amazement, Mike saw them embrace—as older people do, he thought, right out in public. He was not surprised at their performing subsequent rites since he had seen it before: the gentle pounding of hands on arms and shoulders, the cocking of heads as if the participants in reunion could not properly view each other with their heads held straight— then the gushing of phrases interspersed with frequent "whys" and "wheres" and the gradual subsiding of greeting noises as their pleasure at seeing each other became firmly established. Mike suddenly realized with regret that he had never missed seeing a single person for more than a few days because every person he had ever known was always around. And he thought it must be very wonderful to see a friend after a long time of not seeing that friend. He turned to Susie and signed his thoughts to her, and she agreed it must be a very strange experience.

Then Alice Kellogg introduced them, explaining that Marty Martinson's first name was really Digby, which was enough reason for everyone to call him "Marty," and that once upon a time he had a sport airplane and owned part of the Pioneer Press.

Mike liked the way Mr. Martinson took his hand and smiled and then gave Susie a little salute when she turned to him. He heard Alice Kellogg ask him where he lived now and what was he up to, and what brought him home to St. Paul at this time of year. He lost interest in their further chatter when he saw the first jumper rocket past the upper lights and sail gracefully across the night sky. The jumper seemed to hover for a moment, then the swift descent began. Ten seconds later his skis slapped the snow and he rattled on down the slope to the finish area. Mike heard a loud-hailer announce, "Number seventeen, Gary Sundstrom . . . one hundred thirty-seven meters. Very good, Gary."

Another jumper followed, and then another, until five had sailed across the sky. And all the while Mike was conscious of the continuing conversation between Miss Kellogg and the man Marty Martinson who had owned an open-cockpit airplane. There were some questions he would like to ask about that kind of flying, but the time seemed wrong.

Mike was signing to Susie about the apparent versus the true velocity of the jumpers when he heard the loud-hailer announce, "The next jumper will be number eighteen Sven Neilsen, in class three."

They watched the little figure poised at the top of the jump, then saw him descend and shoot off the end of the ramp into the night. He rotated his arms only twice, then held them close to his sides. His feet were together, and he was leaning forward nearly to the horizontal. Mike thought Sven Neilsen had made a nearly perfect entry into his flight envelope, good speed and posture, well laid forward and head down. He should make a good jump—perhaps as long as the others had achieved.

But something was going wrong, and as Sven flashed past he seemed to hold altitude rather than start the usual descent. Obviously Sven knew something was not right, for he began to straighten his posture before the glide was finished and he was all out of position for touchdown.

Mike watched in fascination as Sven descended toward the circle of finish-area spectators and scattered them like birds. His actual touchdown occurred in a snowbank more than a hundred meters beyond the usual area. There was only a little blossoming of snow to mark his actual contact, and he had landed so awkwardly it seemed certain he could not have escaped without serious injury. As several people ran toward him, Mike saw that his body lay very still.

Mike found his voice. "Did you see that?"

He was disappointed. How could Miss Kellogg and Mr. Martinson still be jabbering away while a miracle passed right by them? He turned to Susie, and she signed she could hardly believe her eyes. They heard a crackling from the loud-hailer, then a man who sounded like he was forcing himself to contain his excitement announced, "The last jumper, number seventeen . . . no, sorry, number eighteen . . . What was the name again? Sven Neilsen is disqualified since . . . Wait a minute. Sven Neilsen is shaken up, but he is not seriously injured. I say, who wouldn't be after that jump, which has to be a world's record. . . . We are checking that right now. . . . Wow! I still don't believe it. . . ."

Mike reached for Susie's hand and started down the slope. "I have to talk to Sven," he called to Alice Kellogg. "Meet you at the car." She waved at him and smiled, but he was not at all sure she had understood him. He signed to Susie that Miss Kellogg sure was interested in her old friend.

When Mike finally got through the press of people who felt compelled to talk to Sven Neilsen, he found him even more inarticulate than usual. His reaction to his phenomenal jump seemed to be that of a spectator rather than the originator, and for a time Mike wondered if he had suffered some brain damage. "There I was just, you know, and you know, I felt pretty good, you know, and my goggles, you know, were slipped down my nose until, you know —well, it felt just right, you know, and I let everything hang out, you know, trying to stop, and I just couldn't . . . You know?"

"Did you feel anything special when you were on top of the jump?" Mike asked.

"No. I don't like all the falling snow."

"Did you feel any different during the slide?"

"No. I got to buy a new pair of goggles so they don't slip, you know."

"How about after the launch? You're in the air. Did you feel any different? Or anything strange?"

"Yeah. No. I guess not. I just, you know, kept on a-goin'!"

"How do you feel now?"

"Great. Who wouldn't? Maybe I got some kind of a record. You know?"

"Do you think you could do it again?"

"I don't know why not, you know. They said I could go again so I could, you know, officially qualify for the Carnival."

Mike wished him good luck, but he was not in the least surprised when thirty minutes later Sven Neilsen made his second jump and touched down so far short of the other competitors he barely qualified for class four.

When the jumping was over, Marty Martinson invited all of them for ice cream at the famous downtown Sweet Tooth Saloon. They sat around the marble-top table and washed down their sundaes with hot chocolate while their host spoke of the world. Only the night before he had been in Berlin. Now he held his small audience spellbound as he spoke of the eerie sense of depression he had felt when visiting the huge Soviet war memorial. He seemed to have been everywhere, and spoke so casually of great events and great people that Mike's fingers flew almost continuously while he translated for Susie.

When they had finished and Alice Kellogg had reminded them all that tomorrow was a school day, Mike helped her with her coat. And while Marty Martinson paused to pay the cashier, Mike had his first chance to pose the question that had been burning within him. "Your friend sure is neat. Do you think he could help us?"

"Help us?"

After assessing the puzzled look in her eyes Mike decided Miss Kellogg was obviously on a different wavelength. A far-out wave pattern.

"See the President. Remember? Something has got to be done right away. You saw what happened tonight . . . No, you didn't see it, but I'm sure now it was just another demonstration—"

"Oh, that— Yes, yes . . . I wonder . . ."

"Do you think you could get him to drive you home? If Susie and I weren't hanging around, maybe you could talk about it easier."

"He's already asked. I'll accept."

Mike thought he would have felt much better about Miss Kellogg's resolve if she had not seemed so preoccupied. Ever since Mr. Martinson's appearance she had acted strangely. Driving Susie home, Mike stopped for a traffic light, and there was enough illumination for him to tell her Miss Kellogg seemed to have suddenly left this world. Susie signed, "She had that look about her."

"What look?"

". . . wishing."

"Well, cripes! She even seems to have lost her sense of humor."

After agreeing the behavior of adults was unpredictable they shook their heads in wonder and signed how in later years they would never be that way.

* * *

It seemed so natural for Marty to be sitting on the couch, Alice thought, sitting in the same place where Buck

Delaney had made such an oratorial ass of himself. She remembered that Buck's copulation argument had been declared on three premises—as a sharing of mutuality, whatever that was, as an exaltation of common need, and when that had failed he had tried the copulation-as-a-healthy-form-of-exercise routine.

Listening to Marty's easy banter was refreshing. He addressed her as an equal, as a rediscovered individual of some value, and at least for the moment seemed devoid of the usual macho hang-ups, which, translated into real-time lingo, so often became "Let's-lie-down-and-talk-this-over." Alice concluded she could spend a long time on a desert island with Buck Delaney before his head would start looking better to her than a coconut. But with Marty Martinson? Why wasn't there some lusty pirate around who would threaten a fate worse than death so he could come to the rescue?

Maybe it was his tweed suit, she thought. It hung loosely on his big frame, and looked as if it had been hanging so long enough to make a revealing statement. This man does not feel the need to impress, she thought. He does not drive a Cadillac while he is overdrawn at the bank; in fact, he avoids Cadillacs as well as mispronouncing French words when within sniffing distance of a restaurant, and he does not pretend to enjoy baroque music.

If it isn't the suit, she thought while he flipped through an album of their time together at the University of Minnesota, it might be his bearing, a dignity without any hint of pomposity. All right, so we were *not* together at the university by any stretch of the imagination. He had graduated at least five years before an Alice Kellogg even registered. But the album was something to show him, was it not? Something to keep his attention until you could think of something else to keep him from rushing back to his hotel. It was too bad about those ice-cream sundaes. The man could hardly be blamed for declining a scotch and soda or anything like one. Mother dear, you were always harping on my need for a real man, but you neglected to tell me how to entertain him once I got him in my clutches.

In a voice she hardly recognized as her own (a new and throaty contralto), she heard herself saying, "Of course I could show you the album which covers my girl scout days. I am devastating in my culottes. And then there is a smaller volume on my camp fire girl days. Would you care to bet I can't make fire by friction?"

"If I remember rightly, you were the girl everyone agreed could do anything. It was a disaster when you left the Press. By the time I heard about it, the paper was in serious trouble."

Of course that made a lot of sense. Because a summer hireling in the mail room left the job to complete her Master's, a great newspaper almost fell on its face. "Come on, Marty, you don't even remember where I worked."

"I do. In the mail room. If you had been in charge of the editorial policy or advertising revenues, who knows how much better the paper would have done?"

"I know," she said, confounded. Twitter, twitter, pray tell me, lady, how could he possibly remember poor little you?

She caught herself before her further inspection of Marty Martinson became too obvious. He looked different now in the light; his nose was almost too large, but then it matched his mouth, which was full and generous. His jaw was certainly right there, stubborn and hewn, the kind of a no-nonsense projection that didn't have to hide behind a beard. And at this hour it could have used a bit of a shave. But where did he live now, and how? At the ski jump he had mentioned something about being responsible for more than he wanted to be, but . . . ?

He had slipped on a pair of shell-rimmed glasses when he flipped through the album. Let us see . . . he must be in his mid-forties . . . then whoa! How long would you allow Marty to chase you around the Sahara dunes before you deliberately stumbled and begged him to take you to the Casbah? And good grief, maybe William Wordsworth Bunker had pegged you rightly. A nymphomaniac. Slow down, Alice. The man just happened to run into an old acquaintance, which does not mean, my silly friend, that you automatically wind up in the goose feathers. It does mean you don't even know where his wife is, plus all the children. Remind yourself it may not be many minutes before the orchestra plays variations on a theme; this time with Marty wielding the baton rather than Buck Delaney. Strike the overture: "I am very sorry to say my wife and I are about to be divorced . . . of course the final papers haven't gone through yet." Next cadenza: "Funny thing the way my wife feels about other women. As long as I don't embarrass her . . ." And now the percussion section: "It is now a marriage of convenience. We get along, mind you, mainly on account of the kids. But any relation between us is ended. . . ." And finally the violins: "I can't believe that after searching all my life I've finally found that magic person who seems just made for me. My wife is a nice gal, but—"

"Can I make you anything," she offered again, "like a cup of tea or a triple vodka martini? There isn't any vermouth in the house, but some people just like to pretend their pet martini at least knows there is a bottle around somewhere."

"No, thanks. I'd better be getting along to bed."

What a jolly good idea, she thought before she could

stop herself. I might even be able to dig up a spare tooth-brush. Stop that, Alice Kellogg, or I'll tell Mr. Bunker on you. Oh, the shame of it all!

"I suppose you do have a big day tomorrow?" Why didn't you say *full* day, then he could say "Not quite" and perhaps he would suggest some time in the late afternoon when you might join up for tea and further reminiscences about people neither one of you can remember?

"My problem is I never know when I'm well off. When I was working for the Press here in St. Paul, I had a little money and a little job and I could goof off whenever I felt like it, and I did. Then one day an acquaintance of mine who owns a chain of newspapers said he wanted younger people in the head office. In a weak moment I said yes, and before I knew what struck me they made me sort of top sergeant. Obviously they couldn't find anyone else. Now, if I take off to go sailing, skiing, or even play a game of tennis, I feel like I'm cheating. The syndicate doesn't pay me all the money they do just to enjoy life . . . and people down the line trust me to keep their jobs so they can enjoy life—"

"You run a whole bunch of newspapers? Are you Hearst's unrecognized grandson?"

"And some radio stations. Of course as soon as they catch on to me my head may roll, but for the time being it's a challenge."

To Alice's dismay, she saw him walk to the rack by the front door and take down his overcoat. No vanity. In the center of the rack was a mirror, and he had not even glanced at it. She followed him, and as she reached to help him into his coat she was amazed to hear an involuntary chuckle escape her. What was so funny? And Marty was smiling also, looking down at her as if they had just shared a secret joke. But there had not been any joke or so much as a single word exchanged since he had said he enjoyed challenges.

And there had not been anything so very funny about that. Then for no apparent reason they were holding onto each other, Marty with one arm of his coat still empty and dangling and Alice Kellogg still chuckling. "What's so funny?" he asked.

She shook her head. "I don't know. I can't explain. . . . Somehow I feel wonderful, like . . . like bubbles in a glass of champagne."

"I like that. And I guess being with you is good for me. I feel like I'm back at the Press again . . . twenty-five years old. I was tired a little while ago . . . now I feel light and wonderful, like I could go on forever."

"Then why go?"

A moment's silence passed between them, long enough for him to encircle her in his arms. She laid her head against his tie. And she murmured, "Forget what I just said. All my inhibitions have suddenly come unzipped. I'm giddy . . . I can't explain . . . I've never felt this way in my life . . . as if I were riding in a balloon. . . ."

She tipped up her face, smiling. What should have been a platonic social peck on the cheek became a sudden and passionate joining of their open mouths.

Then as suddenly as the urge struck them, it passed. Alice shook her head and pushed herself back. He made no attempt to hold her. "Wow," she said, bewildered. "*That* was a strange sensation. I don't understand what could make me so bold. You . . . somehow . . . seem to have a very strange influence on me."

"Then it's mutual. That was a great moment. But I guess jet lag has got to me. Now that I know I'm no longer twenty-five I'd better get some sleep. If I stayed over tomorrow, could I see you?"

"I'm in school almost all day." School? *What* school? Return to earth, Alice. The wonderland you just saw and felt is not for you . . . yet.

"How about dinner?"

"Yes. And I promise to behave."

He kissed her again. This time as no more than a salute between friends. Then he was gone before she could remember exactly what it was she had intended to ask him. It was something important. . . . Oh yes, did he know anyone in the White House?

She came to an instant halt, square in the middle of the living room. How *could* she have forgotten?

She stood utterly motionless, staring at the open door to the bedroom, her arms fixed at her sides. Wait a minute! Just pause one damn minute here, Lady Macbeth, while you taste what kind of witches' brew is bubbling in the cauldron. What happened when you were standing together in the hall . . . when you were helping him with his coat? You wanted to tie his arms behind him, and you almost tried. Why did you feel so marvelous . . . like . . . as if you weighed fifty pounds instead of one twenty . . . and light-headed also? Was it Marty's sheer maleness that made you so randy? Or something else? He said he also felt strange; and younger. Just fun talk? Badinage? *Alors, enfants . . . ?* Was something or someone trying to tell you something?

Was that moment—one minute, two minutes—was that little space of time a prewarning of Mike's . . . *it?*

At precisely the same time Mr. Digby Martinson and Miss Alice Kellogg were discovering the magnetism of each other while simultaneously wrestling with an overcoat, an epileptic at the Mayo Clinic in Rochester suddenly recovered from a violent fit. He stopped slathering and insisted on telling the attendants who were doing their best to ease his discomfort that he felt fine.

Also at Rochester during the same moments and in the same clinic six arthritic patients who had been watching a late-late television show from their beds found themselves in such a state of ecstasy the nurses could not keep them out of the hallways. Laughing and cackling at their nearly total relief from excruciating pain, they demanded their street clothes and began planning a chartered tour of Europe with concentration on Parisian hot spots.

Unfortunately, the euphoria at Rochester lasted only a few minutes and the events were not understood or coordinated with other phenomena which occurred almost simultaneously. These also featured an almost total loss of standard inhibitions. In Lima the American Ambassador was concluding a late evening reception for prominent Peruvians. During the gist of his speech his wife, Clarissa, broke wind long and resoundingly. The Ambassador covered immediately with an aside concerning the alarming increase in the number of Japanese motorcycles given to roaring past his residence and the serious effect thereof upon the Peruvian balance of trade. His guests were so impressed with the American's swift diplomacy a new high was reached in relations between the two countries. Later in the privacy of their sleeping quarters the Ambassador's Clarissa, who had never before embarrassed him in public, wept pitiably and said she could not imagine what on earth had tempted her to imitate a Honda.

THE FIFTH DAY

The pallid sun of January did nothing to warm the Minnesota countryside, and in St. Paul a chill mist hung over the streets. It softened the figures of people hurrying to work until they appeared to be moving behind a curtain of gauze. The vapor of their breathing, sprouting from mouths and nostrils like the smoke of miniature dragons, contributed to the aura of unreality.

Ben Piper, having left his car across the street from his office, became a pedestrian for the few minutes required to reach the main building, and as he stamped his feet in the cold gray slush while he waited on traffic he brooded on a matter that troubled him.

Today, he thought as he snorted a cloud of vapor and started across the street, we will hear from Dr. Hatcheck. *Pat*check, damnit. For his fifty-dollar fee he had better

come up with some good answers as to what makes
Michael Benjamin Piper tick.

* * *

Rudy Distancia had never developed the talent for clock
watching which so many civil servants had brought to perfection. All of his life he had been too busy "spreading the
word," a phrase he employed only very privately lest his innumerable memos, messages, admonitions, supplications,
and reports be misinterpreted. Enemies were to be cultivated until they became friends, and if they declined that
role they must die. The substance of his continuous campaign would not bear close scrutiny since the whole of the
many parts was directed toward one target—to prove to the
world first that Rudy Distancia was a man of the people
and therefore a regular guy, second that he was a man of
the utmost discreetness and therefore to be trusted with
the most valuable secrets, and third that he was the person
to call when anyone of influence wanted a certain thing
done. He who knows what others do not carries a priceless
weapon. He who is willing to do what others are not rules
the unwilling.
As a consequence of his diligence Distancia's campaign
had succeeded admirably and he was regarded by all his
contacts almost exactly as he wanted to be regarded. Furthermore, his acquaintances were a multitude and his contacts so widespread there was virtually nothing of importance occurring in the state of Minnesota which sooner or
later did not feel the touch of his fat finger. Rudy the
Nimble worked from predawn to long after dark of every
day reestablishing contacts long in disuse and maintaining
those more often employed. Sometimes, he had found,
just a chat on the telephone rendered a tidbit of valuable

information. Birthdays, anniversaries, and special occasions were not only recorded in Distancia's thick book of contacts, but also engraved in his brain—ever deeper according to the clout of the personage involved.

On this morning he remembered it had been some time since he had spoken with F. Leslie Nash, now Chairman of PCA (Petroleum Council of America), and Distancia scored himself a zero for allowing such a long time to pass without communication with so mighty an individual. Not only was F. Leslie Nash powerful and astute, he was also *very* rich, and who knew when the day might come that Distancia would be trying to shove some fathead into a governorship or even a presidency and need piles of moola to do it?

The problem with calling Nash was finding some excuse, however slight, to make the call seem important—thus causing him, of course, always to remember the name Distancia. The other problem was Nash's preference for his San Francisco office and the consequent two-hour time differential when phoning from Minnesota. Because of it Distancia monitored the clock carefully on this morning. He had further reason. According to information furnished by the Superintendent of Schools, who had, like a good old boy, contacted the Principal of Central High, a certain Miss Kellogg might be free to answer the telephone between noon and one o'clock. Let it never be said that Rudy Distancia failed to carry out the wishes of his Governor, but there was no point in risking too much outside interest in this particular request.

When it was nine o'clock in San Francisco, Rudy Distancia placed his call to F. Leslie Nash. In Distancia's considered opinion, only the very poor of the United States were truly equal. All others were divided into various layers of society and should be treated accordingly. Now in phoning Nash he followed a certain protocol which was dear to him, and one he had found effective. If you wish telephonic communication with someone below your own status (which of course includes most citizens of the United States), have your secretary place the call and get the other party on the line before you deign to pass the time of day. The callee then might be persuaded he had been honored; a space of time had been reserved for him by a man who obviously must count every second and certainly did not have leisure to do the dialing himself. On the other hand, *never* have your secretary initiate a call and then request a party of higher status to come on the line before yourself. Such conduct was unthinkable. It suggested you believed the callee was not busy enough with great affairs and might even have a few seconds to spare. It also eliminated the symbolic fist-to-the-forehead or topknot yank, a social grace expected from the humble by the more powerful. Distancia was convinced their egos must be fed constant diets of juicy delights and any variation toward the bland or unusual was likely to leave them peevish, or even angry. You did not approach the throne of a discontented monarch and expect to come away with a knighthood.

The determination of status could be tricky in a borderline case, but with Distancia versus F. Leslie Nash there was, in Rudy's very own words, no ball game. Therefore Distancia placed his own call to San Francisco, and after identifying himself to Nash's outer-office secretary, who pretended not to remember him (also according to protocol), he was transferred to the executive secretary, a Miss Perkins, according to Distancia's long-ago recorded note, and after some refreshing of her memory she did remember he was presently the Lieutenant Governor of some state . . . somewhere. All of this was expected by Rudy Distancia and did not offend him in the slightest.

Then at last, after a due period of silence, the great man came on deck and sniffed to windward.

"Well, well . . . how are you, Rudy? Good to hear your voice."

Distancia made proper obeisance by expressing his own pleasure at hearing the cultivated diction of F. Leslie Nash, who, as a graduate of Harvard (class of '32), spoke quite a different variety of American. (The same god-damned bored drawl as his Governor, Distancia noted.) He then gave Nash the pleasure of describing the San Francisco weather in comparison with the Minnesota product and reminded him a hunting lodge in northern Minnesota, owned by a mutual friend, was always at the disposal of Nash and his executives. Rudy Distancia would be happy to arrange their trip anytime.

With all bases covered and with a gentle patina of Republican squareness established, Distancia eased into his real message. He knew he must approach it most delicately because Nash was an exceedingly smart man even if he did go to Harvard and the least hint of exaggeration or something misinterpreted as deception, God forbid, would certainly bring disaster. But did Rudy the Nimble know his business or not? Some mark must be made upon Nash's intelligence to assure his thinking further about his caller and, if he was lucky, cause Nash to initiate a further call in the future.

". . . now because of my sensitive position I would not want to be quoted, Leslie, but something has come to my attention which I thought might interest you. Possibly it doesn't mean a damn thing, and I'm aware that by now you and your associates are experts at fighting off all the nuts, kooks, and environmental ignoramuses who would solve this country's energy problem by not having any energy at all. I keep telling such people there are going to be a lot of singed beards around when we're all working by candlelight. Come to think of it, you and I just might have to grow a beard to keep warm. . . ."

Distancia tried a little laugh for size and found it either too big or too small since he could not detect so much as a chuckle in San Francisco. Why was it the very rich never seemed to have much sense of humor?

"Here is the thing, Leslie, and perhaps your people might want to look into the matter so they could cut any problems off at the pass if necessary. Now mark my word, I'm not saying there is anything at all to the idea. It sounds kookie to me and doubtless will to you . . . but the point is we had a caller in here the other day who was very firm about going to the highest Feds with the proposition you people must stop drilling as of now or very serious geographical calamities would result. Of course it's a bunch of cockamamie, but you never know about these things. If left unattended, they sometimes get out of hand."

Distancia waited for the silence he felt confident would follow; then gauging his timing with instinctive skill, he offered his clincher—something to remember Rudy Distancia by. "Now as you are doubtlessly aware through the media, Leslie, we've had a little problem with Lake Superior, although we've been able to keep it much quieter than I would have guessed. I think people just refuse to believe that the lake is getting shallower. But if taken up by the wrong hands, this Superior thing could be dynamite. Everyone would be running around looking for someone to blame, and I suspect you know who that would be? I certainly don't want to be an alarmist, *but* . . ."

Distancia decided to play the fish now that it was so

well hooked. For F. Leslie Nash's willingness to listen
without interrupting was not characteristic of the man. He
simply grunted during the pauses, and that was a good
sign. Therefore Distancia moved to the political scene and
inquired, as if only by accident, what effect even a rumor
that oil drilling and pumping must be halted would have
on the stock market.

The conversation ended very much to his satisfaction.
What could be better than a don't-call-us-we'll-call-you situation when you knew damn well they could hardly wait
to call? But they would wait. The Lieutenant Governor of
Minnesota was going to advise his secretary that when a
Mr. Nash called—tell him to try later. Mr. Distancia was
in conference. Just a little harmless titillation, enough to
engrave the name Distancia just a little deeper than a com-
petitor's. One of these days F. Leslie Nash might need a
manager for one of his oil companies, at say a few hundred
grand per annum?

Distancia watched the clock for another ten minutes,
and then, after admiring his yesterday's manicure, placed a
second call with his very own pudgy fingers.

* * *

Alice Kellogg had just propped up her feet on the desk
drawer and was unwrapping a sandwich when Maxine
Berry, the clerk in the faculty office, appeared in the doorway. She was a scrawny young woman who carried a heavy
pair of glasses low on her nose and an air of perpetual
loneliness about her person. No one knew much about
Maxine. She made herself part of the office furniture and
was so timid that Alice's attempts to bring her into the
real world had always failed.

"There's a telephone call for you, Alice. A gentleman."

The pleasant sense of anticipation which Alice had enjoyed all morning now collapsed. It would be Marty saying he had to leave town . . . suddenly, unexpectedly . . . a board meeting, a financial crisis, war declared somewhere . . . something that might mean good-bye forever. And he would be rushing back to his svelte, beautifully groomed wife and their eight children, arriving just in time to take her to the posh local country club for a candlelight dinner. Damn. How was it so many other girls got all the good cookies in the jar and some were left with the crumbs?

She took her time following Maxine to the phone. Should she be brave and just say jolly good seeing you and do drop in again someday when you have more time? Or shake him up with the basic truth: "Listen, Mr. Martinson, how dare you come to St. Paul and in only a few hours stir up a fire in a gal who is much too vulnerable for her own good? How dare you give me a sleepless night and a distracted morning (unfair to my students—should they picket him?)? How dare you cause your name to roll over and over in my head when I should be thinking about better things?" Better things? Like what was better than Marty? Ugh, she thought, am I about to come down with the world's oldest disease?

"Hello," she said, striving to recapture the soft contralto which she thought had served her so well the night before. Then, listening, she breathed a great sigh of relief.

"Rudy Distanica here, Miss Kellogg. And how are you this fine day?"

Alice submitted she was quite all right, a considerable exaggeration considering her overall gratitude in discovering her fears had been unwarranted. For a moment she even had trouble remembering who Rudy Distancia was.

"I'm calling about your project," he was saying. "I have discussed the matter with the Governor, who would be interested in meeting with you and your pupil as soon as he can arrange an open spot on his calendar. Be assured I will press him for an earlier time, but I must say that in all honesty I doubt if he can get to you until the early part of next week."

"I suppose that's better than nothing, but isn't there some way . . . ?"

"There just might be. First I must become more familiar with the project than I am now so that I can make sense when I brief the Governor. I'm sure you wouldn't want to be cut off in the middle of your pitch, if I may call it that. Now I assume you are really serious about the matter and are willing to go to some rather special lengths to achieve your purpose?"

"I'm not sure I understand—"

"Oh, nothing extraordinary, mind you; it's just that I may be called out of town tomorrow and the one time slot I have available is late this afternoon, between four and six. Could you make that?"

Alice groaned. Marty was going to come by the cottage at six for a drink and then they were supposed to go on to dinner. "I'm not sure I can get Mike for that time," she said lamely.

"As a matter of fact, I would prefer not having the lad present during this exploratory meeting. I would not like to fill so young a mind with extravagant ideas. I would prefer to approach this thing at first in an unofficial manner; that is, not involving the state or its officials until certain guidelines are established. I'm sure you understand our position."

Alice was beginning to think she did understand, and yet . . . ? "Mr. Distancia, Mike is a very mature young man in addition to being brilliant. As for officials, you must bear in mind that he intends to see the President of the United States."

"Exactly. Which is precisely why we must be so discreet at this stage. I recommend we do not even meet in this office, which is always swarming with the press. Perhaps you have not considered the impact on the public if they got hold of this thing and, in their usual fashion, blew it out of all proportion."

"Considering the alternative, I think that would be pretty hard to do. But all right, where would you suggest?" She was tempted to ask, "Your place or mine?" but then decided against it.

"I have a meeting at the Holiday Inn out by White Bear Lake which should be concluded by six at the latest. Would it be too much trouble to ask you to meet me in the coffee shop?"

At last, Alice thought, bless your lecherous little heart, my pirate has appeared. Now for a hero to save me from that fate worse than death. Regaining her contralto, which had somehow become lost since her initial hello, she said, "No trouble at all, Mr. Distancia. I may be a bit late, but see you there about six."

"Wonderful. I'll be waiting."

"And I see you leering through several miles of telephone wire," Alice said aloud as she replaced the receiver. Maxine Berry, whose sterile life had left her nearly a cipher, peered over her glasses at Alice and sighed her envy.

* * *

Mike Piper had great trouble remaining awake in his physics class this day. Much of the previous night had been spent sailing through the night sky with Sven Neilsen, dream after dream lofting him beyond earth's envelope. Long columns of figures and equations had marched through his mind, troubling his subconscious and seriously interfering with the normal ninety-minute cycle of his light sleep.

Why was this? If humans followed a sleeping cycle which could bear only minor alterations and adjustments, as did all other creatures of the earth, including the simplest multicellular animals of the sea, and all of this is based on the same old dependable rate of earth's rotation, what happens to sleep if the rotation speeds up?

The incredible jump he had witnessed last night had been more disturbing than helpful. His original spinning-top theory had been based on a gradual *slowing down* of rotation and a consequent increase in the earth's wobble, which must eventually become so eccentric it would cause a departure from the traditional orbit. But reason insisted Sven Neilsen's jump had been the result of a sudden increase in rotational speed with a corresponding loss of gravitational effect. Or was it just a local bubble in the crust, which, according to Newton's equations, would accomplish the same thing?

Wow. It is said that rabbits can perceive a movement as slow as the sun moving across the sky. And if there really were animals who could detect the presence of a magnetic field, then how did they do it and why couldn't we do it? Was it safe to assume that the force of gravity was the same every place on earth and all the time? Any major variation, Mike now warned himself, could throw his calculations right out of gear. He had a great deal of pure thinking to do. Mr. Martinson had talked about East Berlin and the Russian influence. They would be just as much subject to the spinning-top theory as anyone else on earth. If the President failed to listen, maybe a rap with the Soviets might help. Wow.

When his last class was finished, Mike decided, he was going right home and to bed. He leaned forward and tapped Kevin McCoy gently on the shoulder. "You want to make yourself some easy money?" he whispered.

"Yeah. Always."

"Then do the gum brigade by yourself. I can't hack crawling around theater seats today."

With one responsibility out of the way, Mike decided he would postpone checking on Miss Kellogg's progress toward a meeting with the President. He would catch up on his sleep first, then drop by to see her tonight. There was so little time, but the limping of a weary brain at 2000 Maple Avenue could screw up important decisions to be made at 1600 Pennsylvania Avenue in Washington, D.C.

*　*　*

It seemed to Marty Martinson that he had spent the better part of his life turning in a rental car, then getting on an airplane and losing a few more hours in a sort of pressurized trance while his carcass was being transported to the next rental car in another city. Then there followed the same old routine—drive to the best hotel and if lucky be assigned a room that was made up after the depredations of the previous guest, who, it seemed, was always a heavy smoker of cheap cigars. And the guest's wife, or whoever his bed partner had been, was always devoted to scarlet lipstick, with which she branded every towel and glass in the room.

Marty had developed the greatest sympathy for hotel maids, whose life, he thought, must be made up of overflowing ashtrays, rumpled beds, soggy towels, and discarded newspapers. Sometimes he wondered about his chosen business—well, *half*-chosen, since it was his grandfather's stock which had eased him into the original job with the Pioneer Press. Sometimes he found it discouraging to remember how much effort and devotion went into producing a daily paper and then seeing the useless pile of unread debris it made in hotel rooms. God save our national forests, he thought. If a foreign army of vandals made the same depredations upon our land as the lumbermen, we would remember them as the Jews did the Nazis. So much destroyed forever just to produce a few minutes reading for some character who sat on a hotel room toilet.

And yet, Marty kept reminding himself, the work is invigorating. It made the monthly tour from city to city a daily challenge since he was obliged to remember the names, faults, and qualities of a great many interesting and sometimes very sensitive people. Only the weekends, when there was so little work to do, were dull, and it was then that Myra came to haunt him. As long as he could keep moving he could handle the specter of Myra, the most stunning woman he had ever met . . . once upon a time.

Now, driving to pick up Alice Kellogg, who could hardly be classified as an ugly duckling, he found Myra once more an uninvited guest in his mind. The truth was, he reminded himself for the ten thousandth time lest he somehow begin twisting the truth and start idolizing her, Myra had been a drunken slob. He had paid very little attention to her fondness for a little "tiddly" before they were married—looking at Myra's face and succumbing to her very special charm prohibited logical thought. The little glow she maintained for the first two years of their marriage had been tolerable because she managed to act more sober than most people. But then things suddenly started going downhill and picking up speed on the way. He had tried everything, but Myra just did not want to quit drinking. "What the hell do I care if I die," she had once exulted, "if I'm having a good time doing it?"

She must have been having her idea of a good time when she turned onto the freeway that night and was dead four miles later. By some miracle the people in the car she collided with were not seriously injured. There had not been much left of Myra's lovely face—

Martinson blinked and shook his head to drive away the all too familiar image. He had seen it too many times before, and never wanted to see it again. And he had vowed that he would never again entangle himself with another Myra. It was a self-promise he had found much easier to keep than he had expected. Lately he had noticed how more and more he was becoming disenchanted with the so-called "free" life. Sure he was free to wine and dine Jenny Phipps when he was in Fort Wayne. And Jenny, who was still most pleasant to view, became a bore when she carried on for hours about her children's every accomplishment and her failure to settle the long and bloody war with her ex-husband. In Charleston there was Anne Powers, who looked so young it was almost embarrassing to be seen escorting her anywhere. But Anne was only twenty-four and had already had three husbands, all of whom she still slept with when opportunity offered. Quite some gal, Anne, but not exactly the kind a man wanted to come home to more than very occasionally. As for Patsy Corona in San Francisco, it depended upon how fascinating you found politics, and particularly women's rights as expounded by a nonstop talker. A shame, too, since Patsy was otherwise refreshingly unspoiled.

Sometimes, when stuck for the weekend away from the Manhattan home base of Media National, Martinson would take out his little book and flip through the pages. Surely there must be some name somewhere that he could not resist calling. Helen in Butte, Montana? How badly did you need to know the latest market price of cattle? Shirley in Seattle? She would give you the business about staying in better physical condition—the woman climbed mountains as if they were molehills. Lou-Anne Sessonier in Baton Rouge? Bring on the honeysuckle, honey; there was just so much of Cajun history a man could stand. All bachelors in strange towns, he decided, should be given a discount at the movies.

The more he thought about Alice Kellogg, the more special she seemed. Enjoy yourself, now, Marty thought, before you find out too much about her. She might be a three-time loser, with all husbands still lurking in the background, or maybe her regular boyfriend was a former heavyweight wrestler.

Thus prepared for the worst while still hopeful for the best, Marty kicked the snow off his shoes and entered the cottage two minutes before six o'clock. He had envisioned quite a different sort of greeting. Alice was already dressed for the street. She took his hand, looked him very straight in the eye, and said, "I promised you a drink by the hearth, but that will have to come later. Right now we're due at the Holiday Inn . . . or rather I'm due."

"I thought we had a date for dinner."

"We do. But first things first. Let us go thither. When we have time, I'll try to explain."

As she eased him out the door and half propelled him toward the car, he was saddened. Here was a different Alice Kellogg than he had remembered from last night. The other Alice had somehow given him hope she might be worth phoning from anywhere.

He kept his silence as she directed him toward the Holiday Inn, where, she explained as if she always accepted two dates simultaneously, she was scheduled to meet a man. Fine beginning.

"I'm not going to take you to dinner there," he said. "After so many years on the road my digestion demands something better."

She apologized for the diversion and said it would not be for long. "All I ask you to do is wait outside in the car for twenty minutes, then come into the coffee shop, where you'll see me sitting with someone. Don't come to the table, just wait in the doorway and I'll come to you. Then we can go anywhere you want."

Marty considered he might not want to go anywhere except back to the hotel, where he would lock the door and have dinner for one sent up to the room. He should have known better than to expect an attractive woman of, say, thirty-five to be entirely free of entanglements.

"I don't want to seem too personal, but is the gentleman you're meeting . . . could he have possibly been your date for the evening until I happened to arrive?"

"God forbid."

"I didn't mean that to sound the way it did. I didn't mean to suggest you would cancel a date just for me."

"Oh, come on, Marty. Leave the pebble-kicking to John Wayne. Probably it isn't wise to admit it, but I'd cancel a date with the King of Siam just to share a bowl of chili with you."

"Remember my digestion. I can't eat chili . . . and besides, there is no King of Siam."

More silence. She was preoccupied. He thought he could sense it as surely as he saw the distant neon proclaiming the Holiday Inn. Was she a fruitcake or just whimsical?

"Why are you ringing me in on this expedition?" he asked. "Couldn't we have just met a little later?"

"Because I might need you, and because I don't want to miss one minute of the pleasure of your company if I can avoid it. How's that for a not so subtle answer?"

"Refreshing. If you want to play international spy I'm happy to join in, or are you dealing with the Mafia?"

"Well, someone has to supply pot for the poor little kids at Central High."

"I gather you're not going to tell me who the guy is."

"Maybe later."

* * *

Rudy Distancia waved from a corner booth, and she went to him quickly. He was still trying to rise when she slid into the leather seat and placed her bag on the table. She opened her coat, pushed it back from her shoulders, and apologized for being fifteen minutes late. "I had a slight transportation problem," she said.

"The snow too deep for your Porsche?" he laughed.

"How do you know I drive a Porsche?"

Rudy chortled again, somewhat louder this time. "Lady . . . May I call you Alice? In my job I'm supposed to know everything. What'll you have to drink?"

"Nothing, thank you."

"Good for you. The only drink fit for a gal like you is champagne, and they don't serve it in the coffee shop. But I understand the room service is very good here."

"Really."

Distancia braced his milk-bottle figure against the leather settee and tipped his face upward as if he were looking for something on the ceiling. Then he sighed, the weary man exhausted from his day's labors yet still willing to take up the cudgel for the good of society. With his stare fixed on the ceiling he intoned solemnly, "Would you believe, Alice, that I am a very lonely man?"

"I find that inconceivable."

He closed his eyes as if to reflect upon his martyrdom. "The pressures in my office are terrific. Just keeping the Governor out of trouble is a full-time job, and my nights are rarely my own. When they are, I really want to cut loose, understand?"

"Of course."

"Good. Because my wife doesn't. She thinks I ought to quit work every day at five o'clock. She doesn't understand the burdens of politics."

"Life is a bummer."

"Politics is a strainful business. Just one damn thing after another. I've been thinking about going to the Caribbean for a little sun and relaxation, but I hate to go alone."

"Your wife doesn't understand the Caribbean?"

"She hates travel. Do you?"

Alice Kellogg cocked her head toward him, captured his line of sight, and blinked eleven times. With her free hand she made a sweeping gesture toward the coffee shop. "Born of the sun, they traveled a short while toward the sun, and left the vivid air signed with their honor."

Distancia sighed heavily and happily. "Ah . . . I like that."

"I tell my students a little Stephen Spender never hurt anyone."

"I don't suppose you've been to the Caribbean lately?"

"Never have been there."

"Then maybe . . ." Distancia allowed his eyes to slide away from her and return to the static display on the ceiling. Hoisting his most sincere banner, he said, "Hey! Something just occurred to me! Maybe you might be interested in a little sunshine at this gloomy time of year. Not for long, understand . . . I couldn't be gone for more than a week."

"Neither could I. Strange, isn't it? Kismet?"

"Who?"

"Never mind. Go on."

Now Distancia placed a moist paw on Alice's hand and assumed his most reassuring pose. "Now, now . . . don't get scared, Alice. I know the kind of a girl you are. I was just fantasizing for a moment. It's the loneliness gets to me sometimes. And I say more than I should." His voice took on a boyish quality. "But it sure would be a rare day if I happened to be walking along the beach in the Bahamas someday in February maybe, and whaddya know, there you just happened to be because lo and behold you went to your mailbox one rare day and found a round-trip ticket to Nassau. Now wouldn't that be quite some little surprise?"

"Indeed it would. Especially since I wouldn't have the faintest notion who in the world might have sent it to poor little me."

She pulled her hand out from under his, and placing her fingers daintily upon her throat, she found her contralto. "And I wonder if someone I *did* know would be so kind as to expedite a meeting with the Governor for Mike and me. I wonder if then I might run to my mailbox with greater anticipation. I wonder if I wouldn't be inclined to think a little sun might do me good . . . say over Lincoln's Birthday? It works out we have a four-day holiday then. . . ."

Distancia wiggled in the pleasant realization that his original analysis had been correct. Any broad who was kooky enough to come in with a pitch about the end of the world and ask to be taken seriously was also kooky enough to think Rudy the Nimble was just dying to have his picture taken by some nosy reporter strolling down a gorgeous beach with a package on his arm like this one while the rest of Minnesota, including the Governor, froze their asses off. Some promises were like walnuts. You handed them to the person involved, but sort of forgot to give them a hammer. Meanwhile, if this very good-looking dish was willing to entertain the idea of a rendezvous, there were a lot closer places than the Caribbean.

And since she was obviously willing, there was no cause for rush. "Tell me a little more about your pitch," he said.

Alice told him exactly what she had told him two days previously, and now she included the strange behavior of Lake Superior as proof. He listened with apparent interest.

"Yes, that drop in the water level has been something to think about," he grunted. "We have some people working on it, but of course it will take at least a month or two before their report is completed."

"Mr. Distancia, how can I convince you this thing is very real? Think a minute. Have you felt strange, or any unusual sensation within the last twenty-four hours? Light in weight, for example."

"Oh boy! How I wish I did. But with some sunshine and swimming I should lose—"

"If I put on my track shoes and jogged along a beach, do you suppose someone might chase along after me?"

"Ho-ho!" Distancia laughed so loud and hard several diners turned to look at the corner booth. His laughter deteriorated into a coughing spell, which he finally soothed with a glass of water. "By God, I like that. I like the picture. Let me tell you, ever since women's lib all the gals I know seem to have lost their sense of humor. You are something."

Suddenly, with a growing sense of alarm, he wondered if she was quite as kooky as he believed. Christ! Supposing there was something to what she was raving on about? F. Leslie Nash, remember who told you first.

"Now about that appointment, Mr. Distancia—"

"You gotta call me Rudy if I'm going to chase you along a beach."

"All right, Rudy. When do we see the Governor?"

"This is Wednesday. How about Friday? But before we set up an appointment I'd better brief you on how to handle him. Then you'll get what you want instead of a definite maybe."

Distancia surveyed the coffee shop unhappily. "With all the rattling of dishes and Muzak I find this place very distracting. It so happens there is a room left over from the conference. Why don't we go up there for a little while? I'll give chapter and verse on how to capture and retain the attention of one Preston Granger, who is no ordinary individual—as you may already know. Approaching him just right could mean the success of your project, but if you go at it the wrong way forget it."

Now it was Alice who passed her fingers across his hand ever so gently. "Oh, Rudy, you are being wonderful. But it will have to be another time. That big man standing over there by the door is my brother, who is here visiting. He wouldn't understand. As for a briefing, Mike is the one who will need it because he'll be doing all the talking. What time Friday did you say? You can give us a few minutes of your priceless advice just before we go in. Then I'm sure Mike can handle the situation."

Distancia's eyes took on a glaze as he watched Alice rise very quickly. Belatedly he started to push himself to his feet. Alice pushed him back down.

"No. Don't get up because I must run. Mother is not feeling well and we're late to a family reunion. Just tell me what time Friday."

Distancia was confused. What the hell was wrong with his contacts? No one had mentioned a brother. "Let's try for two o'clock," he said grumpily.

"Two o'clock. Your office. We'll be there."

She was gone and had joined the man at the door before Distancia could cue her (in the roundabout way he had planned) that Wednesday, when his wife played bridge with her club, was the only night in the week he could safely call his own. Reminding himself that patience must eventually triumph, he wondered how he could gracefully get his money back for a room which was not going to be used. The trouble was that his superb catalogue of names had on this occasion proved too much for the master. For the life of him he could not remember the name under which he had registered.

* * *

They were in bed, which under the circumstances Ben Piper thought was the very best place to be. People—even mothers, he hoped—were inclined to become less aggressive if they were in a supine position. And something would have to constrain Nancy when she read Dr. Patcheck's report. She had always been a most even-tempered woman, but there was simply no escaping the fact that Mike's interview with Dr. Patcheck had been his father's idea and his mother was not going to like the results of it one damn bit.

According to her long-established custom, she was reading Anne Lindbergh before she dropped off to sleep. Thinking to start things off in the lightest possible vein, he laughed gently and said that by now she must have memorized every word the woman had ever written. And he added carefully, "But for a little variety I just happen to have something different for you to read."

He withdrew Dr. Patcheck's report from the drawer of the night table on his side of the bed.

"I'll read this to you because we might want to discuss it

as we go along. There could be some points of . . . contention." Oh brother! Points of contention? That was putting it mildly.

He cleared his throat solemnly and began. "'During recent times it has become obvious the social climates in high schools have changed drastically. Adolescents have become more and more isolated from adult society, which has resulted in the establishment of teen-age subcultures wherein the young live by their own social standards and are governed by their own scale of social values—'"

"Baloney," Nancy said. "There's nothing new about that."

"You must take a positive attitude now, damnit, because you're going to need it."

"All right, all right. Go ahead, but I don't need any essays about the state of my country. Mrs. Lindbergh has enough to say about that. I want to know about my son."

"*Our* son," he corrected, and then taking a deep breath, he resumed reading aloud. "'There is no question that Michael is an exceptional youth with a very high IQ, probably on the order of a hundred and forty to a hundred and fifty. As a consequence his reactions may be heightened throughout the entire spectrum of adjustment problems, anuresis, masturbation, stuttering—'"

"*What* did you just say?" Nancy sat straight up in bed, and he thought he could hear the hair on the back of her neck bristling. "*What* was that you just said? What, may I ask, is anuresis?"

"I didn't say it, Dr. Patcheck says it. Anuresis is bed-wetting . . . I *think*."

"Preposterous! Mike hasn't wet his bed since he was a baby!"

"All right, all right, now—"

"And as for masturbating . . . look how tall he is!"

"What's that got to do with it?"

"Masturbation stunts your growth. You know that."

Ben Piper decided not to say anything. At this rate he estimated they should finish reading the report about 4 A.M.

He read on. "'While I did not have the opportunity to administer the Bernreuter Personality Inventory to Michael, I did feel that he would score very highly on the Neurotic Scale and would therefore be subject to emotional instability—'"

"Emotional instability?" Nancy's voice rose to a high soprano. "Why, Michael Piper is the most stable young man in St. Paul. You name me one other boy in this whole city who works at as many jobs as Mike does! Go ahead, I dare you to name just one!"

"Nancy, dear wife of mine, I am simply reading a report by a professional—"

"Professional horse's ass, that's what he is."

"Now don't go judging the man before you've heard him out. May I continue?"

"Proceed," she said coldly. "But I knew he was a horse's ass when I saw him."

"Quote: 'I would have preferred to base some of my diagnosis on Michael's score in a Group Rorschach Test, thereby correlating his measure of intelligence and the measure of his psychological health. Several studies have concluded that the adjustment problems of the intellectually superior child are relatively the same as those of the average young. These may be evidenced in hysteria, various obsessions which I shall pinpoint later, temper tantrums—'"

"Stop! Mike has never had a temper tantrum in his whole life! This whole thing is preposterous!"

Nancy threw a pillow across the room, and Ben Piper

wondered if the gesture was but a preview of things to come. Or go?

"Do you want me to read this report or not? May I remind you it cost a hundred dollars?"

"One hundred dollars' worth of bullshit!"

"*Nancy!*" Ben Piper was shocked almost beyond his comprehension, for never in their eighteen years of married life had he heard his wife use a four-letter word, let alone one of eight letters. "I am astounded," he said.

"Well, I'm astounded at you setting us up with that quack. Read on. I just want to see how crazy he is."

"I might as well tell you right now that he seems to think it is our son who is at least a little crazy." He thumbed through to page seven of the report, which he had read and reread several times and remembered all too vividly. "Here he says, and I quote, 'Lewis, parenthesis, nineteen forty-three, parenthesis, concluded that gifted children exhibited their maladjustment by withdrawing or by egocentricity. They are inclined to daydreaming—'"

Nancy snorted. "Daydreaming is a vital part of growing up. Why, the best time of life was when I was a little girl daydreaming I was the Queen of England."

"I had hoped you would say the best time of your life was when you were married to such a handsome, patient, loving husband, but perhaps the timing is wrong. Meanwhile may I remind you Mike is not a little girl?"

He found his eyes returning to the paragraph on page seven he thought he would now know by heart if it had been in plain English. "Listen to this. I quote: 'A neurotic personality may present himself to the outside world as devoid of the repressed fears and hostilities which torment him within. In defense he may fix upon an obsession with another person or, as I believe in this case, an idea. Locked to this support, he will *ipso facto* endeavor to prove its value in every manner at his command. In Michael's case I believe this has taken form in his obsession with the coming end of the world, a subject with which you are no doubt now very familiar."

There was a long silence. Nancy remained sitting upright, absolutely motionless, her husband noted, and that was a bad sign. Somewhere farther down on Maple Avenue someone honked a horn, and he found himself strangely grateful for it. It was comforting to know they were not entirely alone in a hostile world.

"Nancy? Did you hear what I just read?"

Still silence. Out of the corner of his eye he saw her bow her head, then he heard her whisper, "Yes . . . I did."

"Well? Does what Dr. Patcheck said strike you as being pretty much on target?"

"I just can't believe there is anything wrong with Mike . . . mentally. Oh, I wish I didn't have such terrible visions . . . of maybe it's somehow my doing. I had an uncle who, I remember, was very old, and I remember he was sent away because . . . well, I've never been sure of the because."

He heard her whimper and reached for her hand. She withdrew it and pushed her knuckles against her teeth, and he knew she was trying not to cry. "Now take it easy," he said with such reassurance as he could spare. "This is not the end of the world." He wished he had bitten his tongue. Now why the hell did he have to bring that up? "What I mean is, there are also some bright spots here." He flipped frantically through the report searching for another paragraph he remembered. "Listen. Quote: 'A highly intelligent adolescent like Michael may be expected to display a greater autonomy and dominance in social relationships than his average peers.' Unquote. There, isn't that better?"

"A little."

He heard her sob and saw her shoulders trembling. Aware that maternal panic was near, he kept the tone of his voice as pedantic as he could manage. "I quote: 'In the case of Michael Piper it is tempting to conclude that his open refusal to allocate more than one hour of his self-valued time to his interview with the undersigned is clear indication of his dissatisfaction with self and his latent hostility to personal investigation, which he considers a threat to his secret self-condemnation (a symptom often evidenced in the aggression-rebellion syndrome by more average individuals). Thus his preoccupation with the coming end of the world and his unshakable conviction that it is going to happen may be taken as bold evidence of his repressed fears, i.e., he fantasizes the most terrible catastrophe imaginable and then implants himself not only as its prophet, but also as the only individual who can rescue the world's people from such a tragedy—' "

Ben Piper broke off his reading, for although she made no sound he knew instinctively that his wife was weeping. Enough was enough, he thought as he turned out the light. He took Nancy in his arms and pulled her down into the darkness. She was like a helpless little bird in his arms instead of the tigress he thought she might be. Goddamn Dr. Patcheck, he thought, for breaking the heart of this great little woman and using fancy language to call a spade a spade. As if from a different world he heard her whisper, "Ben . . . what are we going to *do?*"

* * *

Le Bistro offered French décor, a menu in French only, and was manned by an Alsatian maître d' who passed on their order to a Croatian, who took it to the chef, who was an Algerian insisting he was Portuguese.

They began with a brace of champagne cocktails. During this cockle-warming procedure Alice told Marty the man she had met at the Holiday Inn was none other than the state's Lieutenant Governor. While she did touch ever so lightly on why a high school English teacher should be meeting at odd hours with such a personage, she emphasized that she had agreed to the last-minute meeting only in behalf of her student, Mike Piper. And she reminded Marty he was the pleasant youngster he had met the previous evening. Throughout her story Marty was frequently distracted by the maître d', who knew very well the printed menu was sheer pageantry. He kept steering Marty back to what was really available in the kitchen. By the time he had settled on a rack of lamb for two and a bottle of Chardonnay, he had lost track of Michael Piper and his special talent for mathematics.

There was the further and much more heady distraction in the person of Alice Kellogg, whose eyes sparkled with excitement and whose very skin seemed to glow in the candlelight. By the time the vichyssoise arrived, Marty had already concluded she was the most beautiful woman he had seen in the past five years. He informed her of his impression, garnishing his declaration with specific remarks on her pulchritude, and saw she was genuinely pleased; consequently he could not avoid comparing her to a certain Katherine Pringle, to whom he had made a somewhat similar if less enthusiastic address on the occasion of their dining together in Little Rock a week previously. La Pringle, a better than average beauty for a television reporter on one of the stations owned by Marty's conglomerate, and therefore at least a little beholden to him, hurled his bouquets right back in his face. "Don't give me that male chauvinist talk," she had announced fiercely. "I look no better nor worse than any other female, and you should regard me solely as a person and not a sex symbol. I am not a toy to be set up and played with by some immature male as a successor to his electric train. I am fucking well tired of having my identity buried between the sheets."

It had not been a successful dinner for two, and it was not until three days later that he learned Katherine Pringle was inclined to be a switch-hitter. In no sense, he thought, could his experience with her be compared with the rapidly growing ambience of this evening. By the time the Chardonnay arrived ("You don't mind a white with your lamb?"), he was telling Alice that he was not married and that no children had resulted from his unhappy union with Myra.

The rack of lamb was displayed with great ceremony, but as far as Alice was concerned the silver platter might as well have held the head of Samson. She was also aware of a growing rapport with her host, and she thought that if she did not stop tilting her own head so coyly from side to side as he talked on about his views on life, love, and the pursuit of happiness, she would probably have to visit a chiropractor in the morning.

Thanks to several toasts to old times in St. Paul and their chance reunion, they each managed to swallow a glass of the Chardonnay before they fell upon the rack of lamb. Masticating with the enthusiasm of male and female who have just discovered what troubadours have been singing about for several thousand years, they sloshed down the balance of the bottle, and after some determined arm-waving Marty managed to order another. Sniffing the proffered cork, he saw Alice smile and salute him with a twenty-one blink of her eyelids. Never in his life, he decided, had he become so enchanted in such a short time.

Strangely, the application of additional wine to their palates caused no diminuendo in their spirited assault on the lamb, new potatoes, and broccoli. Likewise the salad gave only momentary pause while Alice told him of her amusement with a world which apparently refused to believe she was happy if occasionally quite lonely.

With the cheese they were both exploring the reasons for any loneliness which might be her lot, and they found it astonishingly easy to shift the scenery and discuss those complex reasons why a man of his ability and resources should also know frequent periods of isolation.

Two hours and twenty minutes from the time they entered Le Bistro they finished their coffee and brandy and reached an unspoken agreement on what they were going to do next. All of this time their eyes had been so locked upon each other instead of the food that Alice decided it was wondrous they had not stabbed or cut themselves or knocked over a single glass. Only at long last, when they sighed in mutual contentment and the Croatian brought Marty the check as if he were delivering a manifesto, did his companion's attention drift away. She was considering it might be a convenient time to make for the powder room when for the first time she noticed the huge crystal chandelier hanging from Le Bistro's ceiling. And her mouth—which Marty had described variously as sensual, sensitive, provocative, and tantalizing—fell open. For the handsome chandelier, glittering in the soft candlelight from below, was swaying slowly back and forth in an elliptical pattern.

He had just signed the check when she reached for his hand. "Marty . . . do you see what I see?"

He followed her eyes until his own fixed upon the chandelier. He watched it swing through the ellipse three times before it settled down and behaved as a chandelier should.

"Did you see?" she asked again.

"Yes. I guess I did. Maybe it's got some kind of a motor in it or something. I'll ask."

"Maybe we had too much to drink," Alice said, feeling more sober than she had been at any instant during the entire evening. "But then maybe not. I think we had better go to my place and have a little talk. There is something I have been sort of postponing telling you."

Marty, still in the mellowest of moods, said he certainly thought going to her place was the best suggestion he had heard in several years.

Because he bore the aura of white man's burden and was therefore considered the sort of gentleman who knew the maître d' and the hat check girl would prefer being tipped in cash because of tax matters, Marty was greeted warmly at the street exit. While he waited for Alice to reappear from the powder room, he asked the maître d' if by any chance there might be a motor in the chandelier.

"Oh no, monsieur! It would be a pity to desecrate such a beautiful object."

"Does someone live on the next floor above?"

"Oh no, monsieur. It is only a storehouse for our linens, chairs, tableware, et cetera."

"Would anyone be inclined to go up there and run around at night?"

"You make a joke, monsieur. Of course not, for why should any person do such a silly thing? We go up there . . . perhaps only once a week."

"Then why does the chandelier swing?"

The maître d' arched his considerable eyebrows and smiled knowingly. "Monsieur! You did *indeed* enjoy the Chardonnay."

* * *

In contrast to their previous verbosity, they were very quiet while en route to Alice's cottage. Once inside the door, they removed their hats and overcoats as if they had been years at the identical routine (Alice noticed that he again ignored the mirror), and then while still in the hallway, without word or signal of warning, they fell into each other's arms. Their lips met half open, and they explored each other without haste, caressing and twisting, altogether silent except for an occasional soft humming of their pleasure. "Why are we standing here?" he whispered finally.

"I don't know." She took his hand and led him from the hallway across the lighted living room and into the bedroom. There they embraced in the darkness and she managed to kick off her shoes while still caught in his arms.

She wished she could be more original when she said softly, "I have too many clothes on."

And he replied in kind, "You sure do." Then, almost before he could believe his fortune, she stood naked before him.

"Well?" she said, reaching for his tie. "Are you going to just stand there?"

In his haste to remove his tie he nearly choked himself. He then popped only two buttons removing his shirt and was reaching for his belt buckle when the doorbell rang. "Who the hell is that?" he asked hoarsely.

"God only knows. If my mind hadn't been so busy with delicious sin, I'd never have left the light on." She was up from the bed and into her skirt and blouse almost as quickly as she had removed them. "It couldn't be Mother at this hour."

The doorbell rang again, and was followed by a polite but firm series of knocks. "Stay here," she said. "I'll get rid of whoever it is." Mumbling about her difficulty in believing this could really be happening, she tried to compose herself en route to the door. Once arrived, she listened at the door a moment then raised her voice and asked, "Who is it?"

"It's me, Miss Kellogg. Mike Piper. I have to see you."

"Heavens to Betsy," she said, trying to compensate with a prim phrase of yesterday for a lustful mind that had decided there was no torture quite like coitus interruptus. "Just a minute please, Mike."

She ran to the bedroom. "Are you decent?"

"I can't find my tie. Is it your husband or the police?"

She detected a bitter edge in his voice. "Don't be silly. It's Mike Piper . . . my student."

"That young man seems to have become very much a part of my life. Do you always hold classes at this hour?"

"Forget your tie. Come on out and sit down as though we were just having a nice little after-dinner discussion."

"Weren't we?"

She half shoved him into the living room, kissed him, whispered "I promise" as seductively as she knew how, then went to the front door.

When Mike entered he looked at her and said flatly, "Your hair is all mussed up, Miss Kellogg."

She patted anxiously at her hair and, assuming her teacher's voice, replied, "Well, yes, and no wonder. Mr. Martinson's been massaging the back of my stiff neck . . . you know, the one I get from looking up too much at the blackboard—"

"Oh, is he here? Good. I hope he fixed you up."

The rascal, she thought. Was he smiling? I'll kill him.

They moved into the living room, and Alice was pleased that the exchange of greetings went off quite well . . . all right, fairly well, she thought.

Mike held out a large manila envelope. "I had to see you tonight because it's all done and every hour counts now more than ever. All my calculations check out, and I wish I could say I'm entirely satisfied about everything, but I did make a mistake. The big day will now be February fifteenth, not the sixteenth, as I previously figured. So we've got to hurry. See . . . I've marked the envelope FOR THE PRESIDENT'S EYES ONLY. Do you think that will do? Everything is in here except the solution, and I think it best to keep that to myself until the President has a chance to read this part."

"Mike, I haven't told Mr. Martinson about your . . . project. Would you mind running over it once more . . . lightly?"

"Well . . ." Mike hesitated unhappily. He looked at his shoes, then at the ceiling, and finally directly at Marty. "You're a newspaperman, aren't you, Mr. Martinson?"

"Not in a journalistic capacity, no. I do work for people who own several newspapers."

Mike turned to Alice. "Well, cripes, Miss Kellogg. I just don't think the public should know about what's going to happen . . . at least right now. There could be all kinds of trouble if everything that has happened and I'm sure is going to happen is put together in the wrong way, or even the right way. People might panic. Why, wow, there's no telling what they might do. They might even think I'm crazy and put me away somewhere, and there would be the solution gone and . . . that would be it."

Marty said, "Mike, I don't know what it's all about, but if it will make you happier I'll give you my solemn word that whatever you have to say will not go beyond this room."

Still hesitant, Mike looked at Alice and saw only appeal in her eyes. She said, "Something happened tonight that we saw together, and Mr. Martinson knows as well as I do that earthquakes in Minnesota are unknown. I don't think it would take very much to convince him you are right. He might even be able to help us."

Mike fingered the envelope nervously; then, as if pulling an invisible trigger of decision, he launched into his spinning-top theory.

Almost at once Marty began to wonder if he had, unbeknownst to himself, suffered a blow on the head and the entire evening was part of a recovery program. Sooner or later, he thought, he must wake up in intensive care. Indeed, if anyone had suggested he might be sitting up at ten-thirty listening to a high school boy talk about the end of the world he would have suggested they be sent away to rest. And yet . . . ?

Mike was saying, "Things don't stay the same in our galaxy. They are always changing and there is always a reason. I'm surprised that anyone would be surprised this is happening. Cripes, anyone knows the center of the earth is nothing but a pool of molten iron. If you tip it just a little this way or a little that way, gigantic forces are set up. The imbalance is like frizzing up the stitches on a baseball or a pitcher rubbing it just so. The result is a curve ball, an eccentric orbit, whatever you want to call it."

"Would that make a chandelier sway?"

"Sure. Figure it out for yourself. There is the inner core which is a viscous liquid. Suppose you had a baseball with a liquid center, then you wrap it in a mantle which is a little over two thousand miles thick. Then you enclose the whole ball in a hide that is rock only ten miles thick. Fine. If you throw it straight, it will go straight. But if you start monkeying around with the hide, it's going to assume an eccentric throw path, and on a large scale that's just what's happening—"

"But what about coal? We've been taking that out for a long time."

"The removal of coal certainly contributes to the bruising effect on the earth's hide, but alone it has not been enough to have a significant effect. It is the culmination of all the various factors which is getting us into trouble. The removal of oil weight just happens to finally be tipping the scale. Have you ever played with any Silly Putty?"

"No, I can't say I have." Here he was a grown man, Marty thought, having almost completed one of the most pleasant evenings in his life, perhaps even having fallen more than a little in love, and he was sitting up beyond his bedtime talking about Silly Putty.

"Try it sometime," Mike said enthusiastically. "In many ways it resembles the earth's crust. If you hit it hard and quickly it's like solid rock, but if you just apply steady pressure it behaves like a thick liquid. That's the kind of thing that's happening right now somewhere right below our feet, and we absolutely have to stop it. We have to get all the world's people on this right now, and the only man who can do that is the President. Even now it may be too late."

Mike continued his oration with a brief description of plate tectonics and the apparent changes in the earth's magnetic field resulting from an increase in the planet's speed of rotation, and he concluded with a barrage of quotes from Einstein, Lemaître, De Sitter, Friedmann, and Ernest Rutherford. "Well," he said finally, "do you believe me now, Mr. Martinson?"

There followed such a long silence that Alice felt she could not endure it another moment. "Would you like something to drink, Mike? You must be thirsty. How about a Coke?"

Mike smiled. "That's a no-no in our house. It might rot my braces. They provide me with a fairly good income. And every little bit helps. But I would like a glass of water."

Alice rose at once and went to the little kitchen. They

could hear her rattling ice cubes beyond the door, but Marty said nothing to break the silence and Mike said nothing. Then just as Alice reentered the room holding a tinkling glass, Marty stretched his legs and pushed himself to his feet. He stood thoughtfully for a moment, his eyes studying the youth, who was already somewhat taller.

"Okay . . . Mike," he said slowly. "I'm leaving for New York very early in the morning. As soon as I arrive I'll make a few calls. Where are you going to be about five tomorrow afternoon?"

Mike took a small notebook from his shirt pocket and flipped through two pages. He frowned. "At five I'm scheduled to meet Barney Polsky and talk to him about trading my lamb for his leopard."

"I don't quite follow you. Are you running a zoo?"

"I have lamb's wool on the seat of my Pontiac and he has leopard in his Chevy, see? And I like the leopard better because I like the way Susie looks sitting on it."

"You don't think lamb's wool is becoming to her?"

"Susie would look good sitting on a donkey, but I like to go first class. The trouble is, Barney is trying to squirm out of our deal. I can see it coming."

"Among other things, do you think you could reschedule that conference and be here at this number, at five tomorrow? I am fairly sure someone will want to contact you. Or would you rather take the call at home?"

Mike looked at Alice, and the poise he had held since his arrival suddenly left him. Now his words came hesitantly. "Miss Kellogg, I haven't been able to catch up with you long enough to tell you what happened yesterday . . . and I guess Mr. Martinson might as well know it too, before he starts anything."

Avoiding their eyes, he straightened his posture slightly, as if he were prepared to make a momentous announcement. Then he could not seem to find the words.

"Yes, Mike?" Alice said in her classroom helpful tone.

"Well . . . yesterday my parents asked me to go to a headshrinker, and I did."

"Hmmmm. How did that come out?"

"He is the first psychiatrist I've ever met, and I was surprised because he was really a nice guy, but kind of patronizing. I also thought he might be a little crazy. There . . . I've said it."

"And what did he think of you?"

"I don't know. Not very much, I'm afraid. He just thanked me for coming." Again he hesitated while looking skeptically at Marty. "But I think if I'm going to get any long-distance telephone calls I'd better receive them here. My parents can only take one shock at a time. Also this is much closer to where Barney keeps his Chevy and I could just tell him I'll be late."

Much later, when their libidinal passions had subsided, Alice Kellogg reached across her bed to touch Marty. He was not there, she knew, but her dreaming had left her nearly as satisfied as if he had been. She squirmed against the sheets, touching herself as if by accident, her fingers hesitating, then moving on to another part lest she start something she had little desire to finish.

Too bad about Mike's inconvenient arrival, but then in a way it was good. The whole mood had changed by the time he was ready to leave; Marty was yawning, and she had seen him glance at his watch. He had left with Mike— a handshake which had really been a tender squeeze, and he was gone. Damn.

She rolled to her side and opened one eye. Through the window she saw a gray dripping dawn. And she told herself there would be a night in the future when there would be no interruptions, when Marty could be hers alone until they were exhausted. There had to be such a night. And soon! Why, she asked the cherubs above her bed, why when I am finally in love, when I finally stumble across the man I would like to spend the rest of my life with, why— oh, why—does the world have to come to an end?

The telephone rang and she reached for it quickly. At this hour she knew it could only be one person in the out-of-whack world. "Marty?"

"How did you know?"

"I used ESP. All my other friends always call me at six-thirty in the morning."

"I just wanted to thank you for the pleasure of your company."

"Ho-ho. It is I, monsieur, who must thank you for your favors. That's pretty fancy talk for this hour, but what I'm trying to tell you is please patronize this establishment again soon. Should I even say . . . before it's too late?"

"You really believe the kid."

"How can I help it?"

"So do I, and I'm going to try to do something about it. Can you be there with him when I call at five?"

"You bet your life."

"Okay. Now listen carefully. It's very early in the day for this sort of thing and I know it sounds immature, ill considered, impetuous, and just plain nuts . . . but I'm very much afraid I've fallen in love with you."

She caught her breath. "Incredible. . . ." She was about to say "Keep me in mind" when he said they were closing the gate to his plane and good-bye.

She hung up the phone as gingerly as if it contained a land mine and lowered her head gently to the pillow. Then she stared out the window at the frozen and dismal gloom and decided that without any question it was the most glorious morning she had ever witnessed.

THE SIXTH DAY

Twenty-seven minutes after Alice Kellogg awoke to such a sublime day, Excaliber Lincoln, a maintenance worker in the Bronx holding yards of New York's IRT subway, raised his mop to remove certain graffiti which a local artist had placed on a car window. He made but one wipe from right to left when to his astonishment the entire train, consisting of eight cars, started sliding past his upraised mop and continued for 106 yards before easing to a gentle stop. Excaliber Lincoln was a calm and dignified man, so he was believed when he claimed there was no crew or anyone else within two hundred feet of the train. There was, however, some doubt as to his integrity and that of his fellow workers when an investigation revealed the brakes were locked according to regulations.

Also in Manhattan, but nearly two hours after Alice Kellogg's memorable telephone conversation, August Pierhof, of the Otis Elevator Company's maintenance staff, was making a routine check of the units servicing the Chrysler Building. He noted a somewhat less than normal wear on the main cable sheaves and assumed, because he was a logical man and not inclined to argue with the obvious, that the traffic to the various offices in the great building had been less than normal. Last month's Christmas holidays, he decided, were responsible. As anyone knew, the whole world was going to hell with everybody, and his goddamned brother stopping work for the whole month of December, and how did anyone expect the gross national product to increase if the whole of the national work force was going to be screwing around playing Santa Claus when they ought to be producing? Mr. Pierhof was even more disappointed in the work ethic standard of his fellow Americans when he examined the graphs recording the daily amounts of power required to operate the elevators. He scratched at his groin and his head and nibbled his mustache (all indications that his logical mind was at work) when he discovered a small but definite decrease in electrical usage during the month of December and the first two weeks in January. On this particular morning the recorder showed a remarkably sharp drop in use at ten minutes past ten and then a rise to near normal again at ten-fourteen.

Obviously, August Pierhof decided, the graph proved more accurately than any stock market averages that his belief in the decay of American society was sound. The graph also reaffirmed his belief that it was unnecessary for him to watch the evening television news with all that crap about gloom and doom. No TV schmuck had to tell *him* anything.

Finally in Manhattan a taxi driver, one Morris Liebwitz, suddenly found himself compelled to scrunch out of his driver's seat, walk around his cab, and hold the door open for a passenger. Next, he found himself saluting the passenger with a cheery good morning and a smile. When the shocked passenger inquired of Mr. Liebwitz if he was ill, Morris replied, "Hell no, I feel great. Indecent, sir. Light as a feather." He closed the door gently, then went whistling back to his post. The fact that this incident occurred at precisely the same time August Pierhof's firm beliefs were vindicated and Excaliber Lincoln found his mop wiping nothing but air was never correlated by anyone.

* * *

Rudy Distancia frowned at the wind-bells Governor Granger had brought him as a gift from Tibet, and he decided it was good for a man to have some handy object to hate. After the proper expressions of gratitude for the Governor's thoughtfulness he had hung the wind-bells in the corner of his office, where, quite to his surprise, the circulating air from the heating system played upon them just enough to provide a constant tinkling. Distancia found the unpredictable rhythm of the tinkles nerve-wracking, and when the heating system reached an off cycle the silence was nearly unbearable. Yet it was too early in the game to junk the darn things since Granger himself had called twice to ask how the wind-bells were doing.

"Beautiful!" Distancia had responded while his hatred multiplied with every tinkle.

At three-fifteen this afternoon Distancia was glaring at the wind-bells and still trying to digest the lemon meringue pie which had crowned his overlong luncheon with a party fund raiser. He was belching unhappily and visualizing clots of ulcers scratching at the walls of his abdomen when his secretary announced that a Hymie Markel was on line six. Distancia pressed the button which would connect him with line six immediately, and in spite of his gastronomic distress assumed his jolliest good-old-boy manner. There was good reason: Hymie Markel was his very best contact at the White House, a man personally close to the President and the major factotum in his office of special projects. You did not call Hymie if you wished to sell American machinery to Surinam or hoped for help in establishing a naval base in Morocco. You did call Hymie if your problem was getting the President to back a candidate, speak out for the Cancer Association, or pry a nephew out of jail in Helsinki. You called Hymie only when normal channels had been blocked or declared themselves disinterested, and you never called Hymie until you could prove to him you had tried everything else. Then, like Billy Graham, whom he vaguely resembled, he sometimes felt it his pleasure to reach down and with one hoist of his expressive eyebrows pass a miracle.

Distancia treasured his long relationship with Hymie Markel. Their understanding was nearly complete in all matters political and otherwise, including the necessary frolicking with beautiful and willing women after involvement in heavy thinking on behalf of the American people. Like Distancia, Hymie Markel had come up through the hawsepipe, never forgetting along the way who had been helpful or, even more important, who might *be* helpful.

"Hymie! How are you? Long time no see."

Hymie at once confided that while his general health remained passable he was having "occasional trouble raising my thaliwacker." An occupational hazard, he supposed.

"Not you, old boy," Distancia protested. "When the scroll is drawn up in heaven naming those who have most gratified three generations of women, yours, like Abou ben Adhem, will head the list."

"For which tribute, however magnified, I thank you," Hymie chuckled. And while still chuckling he asked, "How's that Governor of yours doing these days?"

"He's in rut."

"He's in a rut?"

"No. He has forsaken women and is rutting with his new religion."

"I'm afraid I don't understand."

"He's bewitched. We now call his office his tent and are arranging to light his lamps with yak butter. Have you any old goatskins to spare from the White House?"

"We might have a few. God knows we have everything else."

"How about some prayer bells? We're thinking of changing the Capitol Building into a monastery if we can find some prayer flags and tritons."

"I could send you the antlers of a Sikkim stag. Someone presented the President with a pair not long ago, and we've been wondering what to do with them."

"Perfect. And send along a few ravens for atmosphere."

There was a long pause which Distancia enjoyed hugely, for now within a boundary of microseconds lay his opportunity to switch the usual by asking "And what can I do for you, Hymie?"

"As a matter of fact, maybe nothing, but as happens to me no less than twenty times a day, I've been put in a spot and I thought I might as well check with you since my problem originates in your territory."

Distancia offered that he was listening—how very intently he was listening Hymie would never know. If Hymie was going to ask for a complete Minnesota lake to be shipped to Saudi Arabia, thereby appeasing the pique of a sheik, one would be sent this very afternoon. After all, Minnesota had ten thousand lakes, which was too many.

"Rudy, the President has been asked to see a young Minnesota boy named Michael Piper. Ordinarily this would present no great flap and I could set it up sometime a month or six weeks hence . . . you know, combine it with a salute to the Boy Scouts or get a black boy in at the same time and show how well integration was working . . . something along that style. But my problem is the kid wants an hour of the President's time when, Christ, you can't believe how busy the man is. Everyone in the world is on his back night and day about every damn ill wind that blows in the world, and there are times when I think maybe he is the one who should relax with a few prayer wheels, but—"

All of the sensitive electrodes which controlled Distancia's long and successful political life were now glowing white-hot with the reception and transmission of vital messages. A kaleidoscope of possibilities, opportunities, fears, and warnings flashed across his brain. He said cautiously, "Tell me, Hymie, does the President *have* to see the kid?"

"In my opinion, he does because there's a lot of press clout behind the requesting source. As you well know, the President's relations with the media have been a bit sticky lately."

As I well know, Distancia thought. And I am not going to ask who the source is because I also know Hymie is not going to tell me.

"What I wondered," Hymie was saying, "was if you know anything about the kid. Or can find out. His sponsor is not talking. He just asks us to make room for the kid with no briefing, nothing but his name and assurance that a meeting is urgent. Christ, I can't go into the Oval Office and say, 'Hey, sir, look . . . I've got this kid from Minnesota who wants to see you about something, although I don't know what the hell it is, and how about canceling your reception for the President of Ecuador and squeezing the kid in?' The boss doesn't go for vagueness. He wants to be briefed beforehand on every damn little thing, and I can't blame him. Can you understand my situation?"

Ho-ho! Distancia thought, do I ever understand his situation! There Hymie is, sitting in the big house trying to protect a reasonably rational man from making an ass of himself while I am stuck with metaphysical speculations and Zen. Whose Karma is out of joint here?

"Hymie," he said, allowing the tone of a true confidant to enter his voice, "I know about the kid as I know about so many things within the great state of Minnesota. May I say that the kid is supposed to be some kind of a mathematical genius, which is the first so what? May I suggest that it would be unfortunate if the President wasted two seconds of his valuable time on the kid or his sponsors? From what little I know, the whole thing smells of a publicity grab at the very least. Even worse, if the press ever gets wind of what the kid is trying to sell—"

"A fragment of the press is his sponsor, but they are not talking—which I'll admit is unusual. Just tell me all you know so I can protect my backside."

Rudy Distancia settled back into the leather and regarded the wind-bells which he yearned to destroy with a baseball bat. He told Hymie Markel a carefully censored little of what he knew about Michael Piper, including a report on the call at his office, and he told a great deal he did not know. Thus by the time he had finished he fancied he had convinced his White House contact that he knew a great deal more than he did and that his treasure chest of information was always open to qualified parties such as the likes of Hymie Markel.

On his part Markel's supersensitive antennae detected specious signals early on in Distancia's fable, and he silently chastised himself for tossing balls at a minor league player.

"Of course," Distancia concluded, "if you want your man to be stuck with some juvenile mental case raving on about the end of the world because of imbalances caused by the removal of oil, that's your business." He paused significantly, then asked, "Is anyone but you listening on this line, Hymie? Are you tapped, or anything like that?"

"That's a nasty word around here. I'd better not be."

"Okay, my friend. There are mitigating circumstances in all situations. If there is no way out of this thing, may I recommend that you insist the kid's English teacher accompany him? And arrange to meet her yourself. Get acquainted. All I'm suggesting is, for old time's sake, don't miss having a little chat with Alice Kellogg. The rest is up to you, of course, but I think you know what I mean?"

"I know exactly what you mean, and shall attend to the matter. Let joy reign through the land. My Washington flock has all been rustled by visiting cowboys. So long, and thanks."

"*Om mani padme hum . . .*"

"What the hell does that mean?"

"Damned if I know. It's what we say around here to the nearest prayer wheel. So long."

* * *

The suite of offices of F. Leslie Nash occupied a corner of the Bank of America Building's forty-first floor. In keeping with the desired low profile of Nash and his associates there was no name on the polished mahogany door, nor for that matter was there any listing of the Petroleum Council of America on the list of tenants in the lobby. Those invited to visit Nash or one of his several perfectly mannered assistants were either escorted to the offices by one of the staff or expected to know their way. Drop-in visitors, entering by mistake, were politely but firmly directed to wherever they were supposed to be.

The direct route to Nash's private domain passed through an outer office, followed by an inner-outer office, followed by an outer-inner office, then turned left through an inner office occupied by Miss Perkins, his executive secretary of nineteen years, whose facility with Arabic made her even more valuable when the occasional sheik passed through San Francisco.

The view from Nash's indigo-blue-carpeted office commanded the most of San Francisco Bay, the city of Oakland, where Nash would not think of going, and of Berkeley, where Nash would be even less likely to be encountered unless he was kidnapped by the local terrorists. Against that very real possibility (as it existed in the subterranean reaches of Nash's complex mind) there was a secret exit from Nash's office. A magnificent Charles Stanford marine of a Nash tanker laboring in a heavy sea embellished one panel of the mahogany wall opposite the windows. Miss Perkins was instructed to press a red button on her desk barometer at the slightest sign of a suspicious character appearing on the horizon, whereupon various actions occurred almost simultaneously. The button activated a relay which sent an electronic signal to a motor concealed behind the Stanford painting. The motor powered a hydraulic system which opened the entire panel in three seconds. Nash himself, alerted by the humming motor, dropped whatever he was doing at once (which was usually not very much) and vanished into the panel. As he proceeded down a short tunnel to the freight elevator, an electric eye closed the panel behind him.

Regular monthly rehearsals, known to Nash and Miss Perkins as "fire drill," proved the system worked perfectly.

What to do if the alarm went off when Nash was in conference with one or more individuals had been resolved according to the basic law of the jungle, which Nash knew so well. In that unfortunate event he would proceed to the artistic exit at flank speed, leaving his guests to the mercy of whatever coalition had invaded the premises.

At one thirty-three San Francisco time a secretary in the outer office handed off a call to Miss Perkins from a Rudolph Distancia, which was described as urgent. Miss Perkins explained to the caller that Mr. Nash was at lunch and suggested three o'clock as a convenient time to call back. She listened while Distancia vastly inflated her longingrown sense of self-importance by confiding to her that his was no ordinary call. Indeed, the matter he wished to discuss with Mr. Nash was so pressing he thought it would be extremely unwise to wait for three o'clock since her employer might well want to communicate immediately with his representatives in Washington, if not with the White House itself.

At last Miss Perkins weakened and suggested Distancia try Jack's, where the great man would be lunching, as he did every weekday. She did not tell Distancia, nor had she ever told anyone else, that in fair weather F. Leslie Nash would be more likely discovered having lunch with his mistress on the terrace of the Alta Mira Hotel, across the bay in Sausalito. There, tieless and disguised in a Levi jacket, he enjoyed dining with his current favorite.

Miss Perkins recorded the time of Distancia's call with a razor-sharp pencil, then typed it neatly on a slip of blue paper which she later deposited on Nash's immaculate desk. White slips were used to remind him of insignificant calls from such peasantry as his banker, broker, lawyer, and accountant. Red slips were reserved for mandatory and immediate responses required by the royal family: his yacht captain, his daughter, Gwendolyn, who was usually bombed out in the Sequoia National Forest with several of her communal cult and needed money, or his son, Roger, who was normally stoned to incomprehensibility and kept trying to jump off the Golden Gate Bridge. A red slip with the corner turned down indicated Nash's wife, Isabelle, had called and was "in her cups"—Miss Perkins' way of saying she was roaring-drunk and in serious trouble. If the corner of the red slip was not turned down, it meant Isabelle had called in a sober mood. Such slips rarely appeared on Nash's desk.

It was a pity, thought Miss Perkins, who loved her employer very much and therefore qualified as one of the few people in the world who did, that F. Leslie Nash was so very much put upon. Statements from his financial advisers which came to her eye even before he bothered to glance through them indicated his net worth at some seventy million dollars on the hoof, which she thought was quite enough to make even a few sheiks sit up and take notice. A man who had accumulated a fortune of that size deserved a little fun instead of being so perpetually abused. He gave hundreds of thousands to charity, he had endowed a fine art gallery, and was a strong supporter of the San Francisco Opera, even though he had attended but one performance and remained seated for only ten minutes.

Miss Perkins was not surprised when she listened to Nash's well-measured tone some fifteen minutes after her conversation with the man from the hinterlands of Minnesota. "Miss Perkins, I'm still with my salad and do not expect to be back for a bit. Would you be good enough to set up a conference call with Mr. Marcusi in Washington, Jack Eldred in Houston, Lee Brubaker in Los Angeles, and Peter Leonidopolis in Athens—it should be midmorning there now, and not too troublesome for him. If for some reason Mr. Millbank is not available in New York (some little kink in my memory tells me he's off shooting in Scotland), perhaps you could locate Mr. Henshaw in Dubai. Set it up for three if you can, and I shall be back in the office shortly before. Right?"

"Right," Miss Perkins said crisply, and went to work at once. It was three minutes to three when Nash moved silently over the indigo carpeting and slipped behind his desk with the ease of a man who kept himself in splendid physical condition. He had long ago forsaken tobacco and allowed himself only a single and very thin scotch and water on certain social occasions. Even then he nursed it until the time of his departure, which was usually far in advance of other participants. Last to arrive and first to leave had governed his social credo for thirty years, and he saw no more reason to change it than to abandon his morning calisthenics, which occupied a strenuous hour. Evenings, before dressing for dinner, he often enjoyed a few rounds of boxing and karate practice with Woodrow, his chauffeur bodyguard, a two-hundred-pound ex-Marine who had never been known to smile.

A gentleman was a prompt gentleman, Miss Perkins thought as she explained all of the parties he had requested were already on the Watts line with the exception of Peter Leonidopolis, whose secretary had apologized profusely for her employer's unavailability. It seems he was exploring for amphorae off the shore of his island in the Cyclades.

When Nash announced himself as ready on the line, he cut politely through a scattering of greetings from his conferees, all of whom knew each other.

Jerry Millbank was in his yacht tied up alongside a distillery in Inverness and having a jolly good time of it, he laughed.

Brubaker was about to board his yacht and go to Catalina for a little fresh air as soon as this call was finished.

Jack Eldred in Houston laughed as he complained he could not afford a yacht because he had traded in his Grumann G-2 for the new long-range international version and was three million poorer as a result. There was considerable badinage about his plight since all knew Eldred had forgotten where his first fifty million went.

Henshaw in Dubai, an employee rather than a principal amid this court, was an Englishman long skilled in getting along with sundry international potentates, and now displayed his usual aplomb by stating he had been run over by a local taxi driver and had merely suffered a fractured rib. The driver had not paused long enough to apologize.

Leo Marcusi in Washington, a direct employee of the combine and rated as one of the most astute lobbyists in the capital, suggested the wild drivers of Dubai had nothing on the variety in Washington, where, because of traffic, driving was impossibly slow. All laughed at the reminder that wherever they might be, fast or slow, vehicular traffic was keeping certain people in business.

When the conversational dust had cleared, F. Leslie Nash cut straight through to the chase. ". . . terribly sorry to trouble any or all of you, but we have a new problem which may or may not be of some significance. If I had a little more confidence in the judgment of our President, then I should be inclined to forget it, but under the circumstances, and particularly in view of our continued efforts to develop the Atlantic shelf with all its touchy implications, perhaps we should nip this thing in the bud, so to speak."

Nash was particularly fond of verbal clichés; they served

him as a masque of the common man, leading his opposition into laziness and dangerous underestimation of his mind. Now it occurred to him that he had not nipped anything in the bud for a long time, and instead of the genuine alarm he might have felt at the situation he found himself enjoying the challenge. "We must not bury our heads in the sand," he went on, "the boy may be mad as a March hare, but nonetheless we should be on to it. Are you listening, Leo?"

"Hip, hip, hooray," Leo Marcusi quoth from Washington.

"Leslie, just what the hell is it you are talking about?" Jack Eldred boomed from Houston. He was old-style oilman and was not altogether sure he trusted the cultured style of F. Leslie Nash, let alone anyone else in the world except the brewers of Southern Comfort.

Nash then gave them a résumé of his previous conversation with the Lieutenant Governor of Minnesota and of a certain schoolboy who by some miracle was about to have the ear of the President. He explained how, from what he had learned, the petroleum industry, at this point in time, was going to be in very serious trouble if the President believed so much as a word the lad said. "This is really your bag, Leo, but I called in the rest of you so you would be warned. We've taken our lumps before and survived, but we may have to get very rough before we can eliminate this one."

Brubaker grunted ominously from Los Angeles and said, "If it isn't one goddamned specie of kook it's another. There ought to be some kind of a hunting quota for such people. In season, say, five ecologists per oilman."

From Washington, Leo Marcusi said, "I'll get through to my contacts in the White House right away. It might be useful if I knew more about the boy."

"Check with Rudy Distancia in St. Paul, who is best informed. Miss Perkins, are you on the line?"

"Yessir."

"When we have finished, be so good as to give Distancia's number to Mr. Marcusi."

The conversation then drifted to other matters—the newest reports on the very deep drilling for natural gas in the Anadarko basin, where one wildcatter had penetrated below thirty thousand feet, which all agreed was a hell of a long way through the earth's crust; the problems with the Rocky Mountain Overthrust Belt, which were making the Canadians nervous, and what Getty Oil International was up to in their deep-water drilling off the Congo. During all of this Marcusi, who was a master of self-effacement when necessary, remained silent while the oilman talked. Sooner or later they must come back to him, he knew, and the two-hundred-thousand-a-year retainer he received from the Council would seem worthwhile—no matter what he had to do to justify it.

Marcusi was right. At last Nash said, "So much for all that, but let us not forget the primary reason for this conference. It's your ball game now, Leo. Tackle the situation any way you think best . . . and don't hesitate to play rough. This boy and his crazy crusade might become a sort of Joan of Arc situation, and our present public image will not tolerate further erosion."

"You will hear from me within twenty-four hours. May I coin a phrase and say John of Arc will be parboiled at the stake if necessary?"

"I like that." Nash smiled into his telephone. "Let's lock the stable door before the horse bolts."

Miss Perkins' typewritten transcript of the conference call concluded:

MILLBANK   "If you guys want a little relaxation, come on over and watch me fall in the Caledonian Canal."

HENSHAW   "You've got to watch the bloody Scots or they'll steal your foreskin."

(Note: uncertain of last word. Miss P.)

ELDRED   "I just might crank up my little flying machine and join you, but I hear they don't have bourbon over there. A man could die of thirst."

NASH   "So long, gentlemen. Let's keep our ears to the ground."

(Conference call completed 3:47 P.M. PST.)

H/P

* * *

When Nancy Piper brought the macaroni casserole out of the oven, she thought, Well, that's one thing I do right, anyway. Cook. I may be a dingbat intellectually and maybe I'm no glamorous social butterfly, but at least I can say that my contribution to the Piper family cause is not precisely nil, and I do not think that I am considered entirely superfluous . . . at least not yet.

Nancy had promised herself she was not going to be resentful, but here was rancor slobbered all over the kitchen like spilled gravy. Go on, admit it, you refugee from some soap opera. Jealousy mixed with nasty, peevish, miniature delusions of ownership led to resentment. All right Mrs. Oedipus, so Michael *was* going to the White House and he was going to meet the President and Alice Kellogg was invited to chaperone him instead of you, so what was wrong about that? Good grief, you don't own the boy. You're just his mother. Mrs. Stage Mother.

After inspecting the casserole she covered the pot quickly lest one of her tears flavor the contents—over-seasoning would never do. And of course Alice Kellogg, who had come home with Mike and brought the big news, had to be invited to stay for dinner; I mean after *all*, you just couldn't say, "Well, gee, that's very interesting and thanks for being so wonderful about Mike and good-bye, and out into the cold snow you go." It just was not the Piper way. Ben had asked why didn't she stay, and of course you opened your big mouth and said well, there was plenty of macaroni for all if she didn't mind eating macaroni, and Sandy, who was looking forward to having Miss Kellogg as her teacher in the future, jumped up and down and urged her to stay. Mike said nothing. Maybe he knew she was going to stay whether she was invited or not. The casserole smelled delicious. Nicely done by that old indian squaw, Mrs. Nose-out-of-joint.

Well, the whole thing *was* pretty outlandish. A Piper invited to the White House to see the President? Even though their name was Phipps and not Piper, Mother and Father must be spinning in their graves about their grandson. Why, the boy doesn't even have a decent full suit, and no time to get one. Leaving tomorrow, so he would be all ready for a presidential appointment 10 A.M. the next day? Was that all the President had to do . . . see sixteen-year-old kids?

Nancy picked up two hot pads and hefted the casserole onto the dining room table. She was tempted to yell, "Come and get it!", which under normal circumstances she would never think of doing, but she decided Alice Kellogg would not understand why she felt such an insane urge to return to the Wild West range for chow call, thereby proving the Pipers were just plain apple-pie Americans who were not really very much impressed by an invitation to the White House.

During dinner Nancy was proud of the way her husband asked questions she would never have dared to ask.

"Doesn't Mike have to have some kind of permission to be out of school for tomorrow and the next day?" he asked Alice Kellogg.

"First thing in the morning I'll go to see Mr. Bunker. I'm sure there will be no problem."

"How about yourself?"

"Mr. Bunker will have to arrange for a substitute."

"How long will you be gone?" Nancy ventured.

"Mr. Martinson said he didn't know. But all arrangements are made. We'll be staying at the Hay-Adams Hotel, which he says is right across the street from the White House. We will arrive about six tomorrow night. Then at ten the next morning, one might say, will be the big show."

"One might say," Nancy commented dryly. "Is this Mr. Martinson a friend of the President?"

"No. I don't think he even knows him. One might say he knows the right people."

"One might say," Nancy repeated. Did this woman really believe what Michael was predicting? Did Mr. Martinson? Do you, little mother of all the Russias? Good grief, would the President? Things were getting very much out of hand here. The trouble was they couldn't discuss it at the table with Sandy's big ears rotating like radar antennae. There was no use scaring her silly. Scaring her? If it really was true what Mike claimed, then the whole family had a right to be scared, not to mention every other family in the world.

"More macaroni, Miss Kellogg?"

"No, thank you very much. It was delicious. How I envy your talent in the kitchen! Unfortunately, I'm only a can-opener chef."

If she thinks she is going to woo me with women talk, she's got another think coming, Nancy resolved, and then bit her underlip in shame for such pettiness. Damn it all, Miss Kellogg was a wonderful teacher and person, and had certainly done more than her share for Mike, and who knew now what she might do for the world? Nancy Piper, you sit up like a good girl and thank the lady for her blandishments and say you really do hope she'll come again and it was so nice at last to have some real contact with the high school. There's a good girl, and you also ask her to come for dinner when Mike returns so she can give her version of all the goings-on in Washington and what kind of a man the President seemed to be from a woman's point of view.

"I'm afraid I'm not going to meet the President," Alice Kellogg explained. She glanced directly across the table at Mike and added, "That's the way Mike wanted it and that's the way Mr. Martinson fixed it. I go with Mike to the White House, but he goes in to see the President alone."

"Why would you want things that way, Mike?" his father asked.

"Just in case. It's a question of needing to know. If Miss Kellogg knows just the basic principles involved, no one would be interested in taking her hostage, or anything like that. But if she knew the details, and especially the solution, and the wrong people knew she knew, Miss Kellogg could become very valuable."

"From that standpoint, how about you?"

"No one knows how much I know."

"But if the word gets out?"

"Then the President is a blabbermouth and we are all in deep trouble."

There was a long and rather embarrassing silence.

Nancy wished Sandy would stop squirming in her chair, and she saw her husband rolling his paper napkin into a tight little ball—a sure sign he was trying very hard to hold something back. Finally, the very thing he did say was what she was afraid he would say.

"Son . . . have you told Miss Kellogg about your visit to Dr. Patcheck?"

"Yes. And Mr. Martinson knows."

"Then can we assume the President knows?"

"I think that would be assuming a lot, Mr. Piper," Alice said. "But I'm sure Mr. Martinson will brief the President's assistants before the interview. The one thing he asked is that all of us avoid mentioning the real reason for Mike's journey. It's perfectly all right to admit he has an appointment if some newsman calls you, but when it comes to the real why, there should be no comment. Which is a convenient way of not having to lie—"

"All right," Sandy, who had maintained a rare silence throughout the meal cried, "all right . . . why?"

"That you will discover in due course," her father said pompously.

"I know why. I peeked through the keyhole and saw Mike working with his calculator. He's found a way to balance the national budget."

"How did you guess?" her father responded airily while he muttered to himself that he wished it were true.

* * *

Soon after they rose from the table, Alice Kellogg said she hated to eat and run but she had a million things to do if she was going to be ready for tomorrow's flight. And Mike said that since he could not telephone Susie he must go see her and tell her why he would be gone for a few days. Nancy retreated to the kitchen with a sense of genuine relief. She stood betwixt the dishwaster and the stove without moving for several minutes, and she found it astonishing how valuable familiar things had become to her. Whatever was going on was not of her world, she decided. Who brought this boy genius into the world—if that was what he really was? He looked like Ben, but he didn't think like Ben. Could there have been some kind of a hangover gene in her system from one of those very few young men who had caught up with her *before* she married? Nonsense. It was genetically impossible, and looking back, she could not recall one of those "experimenters" who might be remembered as overbright. Then what was happening to her familiar world? (The people of Pompeii must have felt this same way.)

Elsewhere in the world, far removed from Nancy's kitchen, various earthlings were having their own problems with what they came to think of as mighty strange developments. Maximilian Braganza, master of a large tuna seine boat, lost his extremely expensive net just after he had made what promised to be a record set. While he was cursing the porpoises who kept jumping in and out of the net, bent in his estimation on suicide and therefore bound to get him into much trouble with environmentalists, he saw his entire net start for the depths. Were it not for quick action on the part of Tony Sciarso, the winchman, in releasing the main cable the vessel herself might have followed it.

Captain Braganza knew he was fishing in fruitful waters. What he could not know even if he cared, since the information was not on marine charts, was that his set had been made along the Clarion fracture of the North American continent. Crew members, who were all on shares, found their captain's tears pitiful to behold.

As if to challenge Captain Braganza's and Nancy Piper's

encounters with the unexpected, André St. Bharhol, a Parisian painter famous and rich for superb abstract murals depicting his very own private parts (exhibited with especially recorded background music), was at work on a masterpiece he entitled, "Piss and Remorse." Knowing the true value of things, St. Bharhol always signed his paintings before he painted them, thus guaranteeing hysterical reviews by the critics (". . . the ultimate of the absurd, magnificent insignificance, splendid shaping of the spleen and deltoid, ecstatic rendition of the anus," etc.).

It had been St. Bharhol's intention to express his current interest in urination and regret with three bold strokes of his toilet brush dipped in a solution of kerosene, laundry bluing, and a bottle of Dr. Pepper which an admirer had sent all the way from Atlanta, in *les Etats Unis*. Culminating the masterpiece would be a generous blob of his very own semen held in a solution of phenolphthalein. To St. Bharhol's dismay, some maverick optical illusion caused him to stagger when he was cold-sober and he misdirected his three inspired strokes of bluing until they were slanted instead of upright. Worse, he discovered that his sexual excesses of the previous night had exhausted the supply of that element he considered so necessary for a true *coup d'art*. Since neither of these things had ever happened to him before, he sat until closing time in the teensy Café Balthazar, on the Boulevard Montparnasse, without spending a centime. Instead he led his coterie of admirers in a mass lamentation for the fate of the world.

And in Penang it rained up.

THE SEVENTH DAY

Michael Piper and Alice Kellogg arrived at the north portico of the White House at nine forty-seven. Hymie Markel was waiting for them at the entrance door and introduced himself immediately. "Welcome to the White House, Miss Kellogg. And here I assume we have the very special Mr. Michael Piper?"

Smiling warmly, he extended his hand and asked if either of them had ever been to the White House before. "Oh sure," Alice was tempted to say, "many times. I'm always being asked to entertain foreign dignitaries with my imitations of Dracula's anemic sister." Instead she returned Markel's smile and said she hoped they were not too early.

"As a matter of fact, a miracle has happened and the President is slightly ahead of schedule for today, so it should only be a few minutes."

As they left the portico for the marble-floored entrance

hall, Markel assured them of his high regard for Marty Martinson and the wonderful job he was doing with Media International ". . . although I sometimes wish his papers were a bit more tolerant of our occasional mistakes. Oh, we do make them, you know. The trouble is so many people think we who operate out of this establishment are not really people . . . something, I assure you, we are."

Markel remained silent for a few moments while his guests examined themselves in the entrance hall mirrors and glanced up at the great cut-glass chandelier hanging from the ceiling. He saw that Alice's eyes lingered on the chandelier and thought to query her. From the moment she started up the White House steps, he knew he recognized the sort of woman he admired, and now he hoped to establish a closer rapport with her. He needed something to ease these first few minutes. "You approve, Miss Kellogg?" he inquired while momentarily diverting his attention from her to the chandelier.

"It reminds me of a recent very wonderful evening," she said softly.

"Aha! Waltzing at the Senior Prom with a student everyone else despaired of and you inspired to graduate? That's the way the old story goes, isn't it?"

"Not exactly. There was no waltz music. Just roast lamb."

Reluctantly, Markel turned away from her.

How did a schmuck like Distancia ever get near such a lovely creature? he wondered. He studied Mike Piper for a moment. Nice-looking kid, tall for his age, and very inquisitive if his examination of the presidential portraits hanging in the hall were any indication. What was all this flap with Leo Marcusi about? And Distancia, who of course was so far out of the mainstream he would not understand true pressure from all sides? On the other hand, Leo Marcusi *did* understand, and he also had said the kid was addled. Well, he certainly was not going to be alone with the President. You could not be sure what a sixteen-year-old would try these days. The two photographers who would also be in the Oval Office were really bodyguards from Treasury.

As he escorted them toward his office, Markel thought sourly that things had come to a pretty pass when a guy who had practically the whole civilized world on his shoulders had to waste his time with some kid from the sticks whose sanity was suspect. Just to please the press.

This whole affair was out of context, like quotes from some of the old man's policy speeches. While the connection between Rudy Distancia and this doll of an English teacher was barely understandable (thank you, Rudy; you'll be remembered in my will), why should Leo Marcusi be so damned interested? Marcusi had called in the middle of the night and explained, rather lamely, that he had been playing pinochle with the boys at the Press Club and one of them had dropped some kind of a remark about seeing the presidential appointments list. The informant claimed he had recognized a name on the list as being the son of a friend of a friend's father in St. Paul, and the son had long been known to be mentally disturbed. A sad case, and tough on the parents. According to the informant, this particular boy had from time to time even claimed to have seen visions. Sort of a boy Joan of Arc, Marcusi had suggested, and he had wondered what the hell the President was doing with such people. Was there a new story there? Was he going to announce some kind of a new program for the mentally handicapped? And if so, how many millions is it costing?

Markel knew that no self-respecting lobbyist ever called him about anything unless there was a reason; just passing the time of night, Leo? How nice. You get the Yon Cassius award, and never mind about the lean and hungry look.

"And this is my humble digs," Markel said as he ushered them into a pleasant office in the West Wing. He introduced his secretary, a clean-cut antiseptic lady who offered Alice Kellogg coffee "while you are waiting," and said Mike looked very much like her nephew in Virginia, who had also met the President during one of his visits to Camp David. She seemed about to make a further comparison with her nephew when a flasher on her phone twinkled and she picked it up. She smiled enigmatically at Markel and said, "The President is ready for you now."

"Okay, Michael. Let's be on our way." Markel started for the door leading to the corridor, which in turn would lead to the Oval Office. He halted when he saw that Mike was not following hard on his heels. "What's the matter, Mike? Man, this is it. Let's get moving."

"There's been some misunderstanding. I thought I was to see the President alone."

"Oh now, come on, Mike. You must know we can't do that. This is the President of the United States you're about to see."

"I'm very much aware of that, but I have extremely important information in this envelope which is for the President's eyes alone."

"Look, Mike, and I hope you don't mind my calling you that. Since Security X-rayed and passed your envelope, I certainly am not going to advise the President not to accept it. But seeing him alone is out of the question . . . and that goes for almost anyone except the recognized heads of foreign governments."

Markel allowed a patient half smile to play across his mouth. After all, the teacher-doll was listening and watching. "Look. It's this way, Mike. Sometimes in life you have to play by the other fellow's rules . . . in this case ours. Either we go now together or I'll be forced to call the President's secretary and explain as easily as I can that due to a sudden illness or some other little white lie you are unable to make your appointment. The fact that you have already been admitted to the White House and then the situation changed so suddenly will not be easy for the President to understand. I suggest it would be a very long time before a similar opportunity could be rearranged."

Mike hesitated. He glanced hopelessly at Alice Kellogg. "What do you think I should do, Miss Kellogg?"

"There doesn't seem to be much choice. Maybe . . . you could just hand him the envelope and hope for the best."

"But if it falls into the wrong hands?"

Alice Kellogg shrugged her shoulders so eloquently that Markel thought her message was unmistakable. What the hell went on between these two? Was this kid her guru or something? Christ, these days you couldn't trust even Salvation Army girls. Not that the teacher looked the type. Take a vow in your own blood right now, Hymie Markel. Never, *ever* again get talked into one of these deals without at least a week of prior investigation. And cancel any idea of becoming intimate with the teacher-doll, who could just as easily be a witch in disguise. You know fifty guys who have wrecked a brilliant career chasing female rainbows.

He saw Mike turn toward him and heard him mumble, "Okay, Mr. Markel. Let's go."

As Markel started again for the door, he wished with all

his heart that his guest had made the opposite decision. The boss was not going to be delighted with this interview.

* * *

Twenty-seven minutes later Hymie Markel cradled the telephone in the well-worn depression between his shoulder and his left clavicle, the instrument seeming so solidly fixed it was like a permanent growth on his body. He had shrugged that very same shoulder when his invitation to take Alice Kellogg to lunch had been declined. He had thought to make special arrangements for Michael at the Smithsonian, and that offer had been declined. "Right now I'm only interested in the future," the kid had said.

Markel had shrugged first his left then his right shoulder while he thought, What the hell, you can't win 'em all. Maybe someday soon he'd find reason to drop by the great state of Minnesota with a little more time for the development of special projects, of which a certain English teacher would be absolutely numero uno. And now, with them safely out the front gate, it was back to the telephonic salt mine with a call to New York.

"Marty? . . . Hymie Markel here. I promised I would call you first and let you know what happened in there. . . . Really nothing. It went off very smoothly . . . a few photos for the kid's scrapbook, if he has a scrapbook. I must say, Marty, you do not send us the ordinary souvenir hunter. True to my word, there was no press person within a thousand feet either before the interview or after. The boss was a bit distracted, naturally, with this new Federal Reserve crisis and all, but he did go out of his way to be wonderful to the kid . . . smiling all the time and asking about his school and how high did he get in the Boy Scouts, and stuff like that." Markel was disappointed at the strangely cold tone of his listener's ensuing questions.

Marty should be more grateful. He should know how much trouble and rearranging it had taken to set this thing up.

"Yes, he did give the President the envelope. . . . No, he didn't open it. Just as we were going out the door, the boss handed it to me and asked me to send it over to the National Science Foundation, and that I did. . . . Huh? . . . All right, so it did say 'for the President's eyes only.' . . . Marty, listen to me a minute, will you, and no sense getting so up tight about a little thing like that. You know as well as I do the boss hasn't time to read one thousandth of the material that comes his way. That's what he has a staff for. And while we're at it, I wish you would level with me and tell me why this kid is so important to so many different sorts of people. Why am I apparently the last to know?"

Markel frowned and tipped dangerously far back in his chair as he listened to what he considered a rather unflattering reference to his intelligence. "Come on now, Marty. You know very well we can't have a kid in there alone with the President. . . . Look, I like kids, but I must be frank and say I'm not too sure this one is entirely all there. . . ."

After a moment Markel realized he was talking to a dead telephone, and once more he employed his habitual shrug to placate the sundry evil demons of this day. Two minutes later his secretary said she had Leo Marcusi on the line.

"Leo? . . . I promised I would report back to you first thing. Well, the kid just left a few minutes ago. I don't know what you were worrying about, and/or your informant. Maybe you were beating him at pinochle and he wanted to distract you, but anyway, they had a nice chat, mostly about the kid himself. . . . What the hell else do you talk to a teen-ager about? He goes back to Minnesota sometime this afternoon. So much for that. Meanwhile, unless you have some new tale out of the Arabian Nights, I'll get on to some of the fifty other calls on my desk. I know only one thing, and that is I wish to Almighty God the telephone had never been invented."

Markel advised two reporters, one TV commentator, and one Washington columnist that indeed the President had talked with a young man who did not want any publicity, much less photos taken of him with the President. If they wanted to make some kind of mysterious hay out of that, they were welcome to it. And no, he was not the President's illegitimate son. Jesus, had things gotten to a point where the President of this great country could not even interview a fine young man without the media thinking he was up to something?

Finally, as part of an automatic reaction to a distressing morning, he placed another call, this time to Rudy Distancia. "I must say I admire your taste. Do they grow many more teachers like that in Minnesota? Send your friend Kellogg when you need more funding for the school system . . . or any other system. But next time tell her to leave her class at home."

He heard Distancia's continuing chuckle and found it strangely annoying. What an oaf.

"The boy was very well behaved and seems to relate very well to older people, but I am inclined to agree he may not have a full deck. You wouldn't believe I had to *persuade* him into the Oval Office, and he didn't look very happy when he left. . . . Nope. Never said a word about the end of the world. Of course when the boss really gets turned on, it's sometimes difficult to get a word in edgewise."

When Markel hung up with his usual *"Ciao,"* he lit a

cigarette and blew smoke toward the rose garden. Why had he bothered to withhold part of the interview from Distancia? Actually the kid did say the fate of the world was in the envelope he handed the boss, and he had also mentioned something about how if all the people got together right away the world might be saved, but if the boss had a dollar for every time he had heard that song he would be richer than he already was. By this time he couldn't even hear the tune, must less the individual notes. If you spent much time in the Oval Office, you knew when the old man's attention was about to capsize by the faraway look he aimed at the flag standard which stood on his right.

Sucking on his cigarette, Markel strolled to his outer office. He needed a break before he started another round of calls. He paused by his secretary's desk and smiled. "Did you send that envelope over to the people at the Science Center?"

"Yes, I did. It should be there by now."

"Good. That should give them their laugh for the day."

* * *

It was proving to be such a dismal forenoon that the upper two thirds of the Washington Monument was lost in the clouds. Rain and mist obscured the surrounding buildings as they walked slowly across the little park between the White House and the Hay-Adams Hotel. Alice thought it was like coming out of a movie, the difference being that the film broke before the end. Whatever it was that had gone so very wrong in the President's office would come out eventually, but after a long walk Mike was still not talking. He would break his brooding silence in due time, Alice told herself, and she tried very hard not to appear as sorry for his obvious disappointment as she really felt.

She wondered how much differently things might have gone if Marty had been along. Marty had apologized profusely for his inability to greet them on their arrival in Washington the night before. A long-standing engagement to speak at the Explorers' Club in New York could not be canceled without arousing suspicion.

"But I'll be in Washington the next morning and I'll arrive just in time to escort you to the White House." It seemed Marty could do anything except manage the weather. At eight o'clock, when he had intended to depart from New York, LaGuardia and Kennedy airports were closed with zero-zero flight conditions. They were forecast to remain the same until evening. Damn. The whole east coast was in a meteorological mess.

As they waited for the traffic light across from the hotel, she looked up at Mike and thought, Well, maybe it is getting a little late for me to have a son, but if by proxy—the stepmother bit—if it ever happens, then I hope he looks and acts like Mike, who has not lost his dignity one second throughout this whole morning.

As they crossed the street she ventured, "It's still pretty early, but if you're hungry we might have lunch."

"I think we'd better telephone Mr. Martinson first."

Mike said nothing more until they were in her room and she handed the phone to him. It had been reassuring to hear Marty's voice on the other end.

"I struck out, Mr. Martinson," Mike said. "The President wasn't listening, and there wasn't much I could say to get his interest with three other people there."

"Three? I understood Mr. Markel was the only other person present."

"No. There were two photographers, and I didn't know

who they were. That's the whole point. If the wrong people find out what I know before phase two can be started, they could blow the whole thing. I'm very worried, sir. On the radio this morning I heard a report by NOAA saying that the amount of sunlight in the United States has decreased by one point three percent during the last five years. That's old stuff, based on old figures compiled by someone back when I was a little kid. My figures indicate the decrease is on the order of at least two percent and getting worse every day. The top is still spinning, but the tilt is more every hour. If we wait too long, it could be twilight all the time in this hemisphere." Mike's voice cracked slightly when he added, "We've got to do something."

"When I look out this office window at what I can see of Manhattan, it appears to be already too late," Marty said. "I'm sure sorry I couldn't have been with you at least as moral support, but I'm afraid now all we can do is regroup and attack from another angle."

"Mr. Markel said the chances of getting another appointment with the President were not very hopeful. He was a nice man, but . . ."

"I can handle Mr. Markel. It's the President who worries me. Do you feel you must be absolutely alone with him? Could I be present?"

Mike hesitated. "Not even you. Unless you could arrange even better personal protection than the President has."

"I'll work on that."

"I asked the President himself if we couldn't be alone even for a few minutes, and he just smiled and said okay, this summer he might be campaigning in Minnesota and I could take him for a ride in my Pontiac. Well, if he waits until next summer there isn't going to be any campaign or Pontiac or much of anything else, except for a few strong people hanging onto trees until they start uprooting. I don't want to start a worldwide panic, Mr. Martinson, but the situation is really desperate. Very soon some strange things are going to happen. Do you believe me?"

"You bet."

"Then you'd better do whatever you can . . . fast."

* * *

Because of the deteriorating Washington weather the flights to Chicago and St. Paul had been transferred to Dulles Airport, a tedious forty-minute bus ride from the Hay-Adams Hotel. And because of the heavy flight operations confined to a single airport there was considerable delay and confusion for those passengers who would normally have boarded their domestic flights at the National Airport, near the center of the city. The ticketing lines were long and the agents weary. Very few flights were getting away within an hour of their scheduled time.

Mike Piper stood beside Alice Kellogg for ten minutes in the slow-moving line and offered to take her place in checking the baggage and ticket presentation. "Why don't you go sit down for awhile, Miss Kellogg? I can handle this."

"Really, Mike. I'm not as decrepit as you think. Not varicose yet, kind sir. Why don't you go have a look around? It's a beautiful airport. I'll meet you over there by the bookstand."

Mike patted the briefcase he held and told her he would be responsible for it. He hoped he had not hurt Miss Kellogg's feelings. Wow. She was not really decrepit, like she suggested, and he hoped she didn't think he thought that way about her even if she was old and naturally needed some looking after. She might not be as old as his mother, but it was all the same anyway.

Mike's briefcase contained his toilet kit, a top and string, and a pocket knife. Just before leaving St. Paul he had added several sharp pencils, a note pad, his calculator, a book by Carl Sagan on the solar system which he found rather elementary, his yet to be revised composition on Shakespeare for English VII, and a manila envelope containing the same set of figures and projections he had given the President. Just in case the President's envelope should be lost, he thought. The original calculations advancing his spinning-top theory were already proving out, and even if lost, they were easy enough to reconstruct, given a few full days of hard concentration. The "solution" to the whole trouble was another bag of beans, he reflected—much more complex.

Keeping the briefcase firmly under his arm, Mike strolled in wonder beneath the tremendous and graceful concrete forms which arced high above his head and formed the stalwart beauty of the building. Here, he decided, was flight in all its beauty and utility. Neat.

When he came to a refreshment stand he decided an ice-cream cone might ease his feeling that he had somehow failed the two people in the world who had faith in him. Doggone it, Miss Kellogg and Mr. Martinson were super persons, and he had them all steamed up and they had gone to all kinds of trouble and expense, and now it looked like nothing would come of it. How was it going to be returning home to Susie and telling her you really were with the President that long and had come away without accomplishing anything at all?

He stood at the refreshment stand, licking thoughtfully at a double chocolate-strawberry mix which had cost eighty cents, for criminee sake! He found some relief from his darker thoughts by regarding the magnificence of his surroundings. Wait until he could tell Susie about this pile of concrete which some neat architect had made into a space-age masterpiece. It was super-super-inspiring. It was saying right out loud (for criminee sake), *Do* something extraspecial before I only weigh about four thousand pounds and fly off into space. It's up to you, Mike Piper. You are *it*. Now perform.

* * *

At the same time Mike Piper was coming to a decision, the Lieutenant Governor of Minnesota took a deep breath of the last fresh air he expected to breathe for at least twenty minutes and entered the Governor's office. There he found his precautionary inhalation had been unnecessary since Preston Granger apparently was not in the mood for his usual incense burning at the close of his official day. Instead, Distancia noted with considerable relief, he was not even sitting in the lotus position, nor were his eyes glazed. Perhaps a man might get through to him this afternoon, Distancia thought, while making a silent vow to search the gubernatorial office next time his honor set forth on one of his expeditions. If he was not on grass or hash or *something*, then Rudy Distancia did not know humanity.

"*You* sent for me, Preston?" he smiled, wondering what could possibly be on the fathead's mind.

"Yes. Several days ago I asked you to set up an appointment with a young man who seemed to have some interesting theories. What happened? Everyone you have sent through that door lately has been either a conniver or a frightful bore. I'm not sure I should trust anyone over seventeen or eighteen."

Distancia allowed himself an easy laugh, and why not? It so happened the information his political superior desired had not escaped his fingertips despite the buffing of the comely manicurist who had tended his digits only half an hour previously. "Oh yes, the boy. Just as I expected, that turned out to be a terrible fiasco. Very embarrassing for everyone concerned, and I'm sure glad you didn't get mixed up in it because the kid is obviously demented."

"I don't understand why it was so difficult for him to see me when he apparently had no trouble getting an appointment with the President."

Good question, Distancia thought, and I wonder too.

Without quite kicking imaginary pebbles across the yak skin rug beneath his feet, Distancia assumed his most humble demeanor. "Well, boss, could be the President of the United States doesn't enjoy quite the same quality of protection as a few of our state governors. Maybe that's why he's always getting himself in so much trouble, if you see what I mean."

Granger glumly cupped his chin in his hands, and it was almost with relief that his lieutenant watched the familiar far-off look return to his eyes.

"Well, sometimes I really would like to see more interesting people," Granger mumbled, and Distancia, recognizing his cue, turned to leave.

As he opened the door Distancia heard his name called. "Rudy? Have you read *Searching for Bear Claws on the Upper Khyber*, by Posolosky?"

"No. I can't say I have."

"You should. It's bound to be a best seller."

"I'll bet. Thanks. I'll order a copy."

* * *

When Alice Kellogg came out of the ladies' room, she paused at the airport gift shop hoping to find some little doodad for Mrs. Piper. A guest remembrance for her hospitality at dinner. Good manners, dear, just as Mother taught you. Something not too pretentious, something to bring a smile, perhaps, and a nice thought about Michael's English teacher.

After ten minutes she despaired of the tasteless collection of ding-dangs and claptrap available and settled for a "thank you" card.

She paid for the card and walked to the bookstand. There she waited for Mike and reassured herself they still had twenty minutes before the last announced departure time—which would probably be changed again. She started to survey the book titles and was regretting the blooming garden of bosoms when she thought she saw Mike in the distance. She started to wave, then realized it was another young man. Hurry, Mike, she thought, time is wasting.

* * *

The gloomy afternoon had become an evening twilight, and the President of the United States checked his watch for a possible malfunction. He spun around in his chair and stared through the window at the south lawn. Winter, yes, and it had been a severe one, but why did it seem to be getting darker at such an extraordinarily early hour? He was about to ask his secretary if anyone in the White House had a current almanac so he could ascertain exactly what time sunset occurred when, as if he had actually summoned her, she appeared at the door. A health food addict and an exponent of balanced posture, she minced across the Great Seal of the United States, which adorned the carpet between the door and his desk. She squared herself as if about to make a momentous announcement, but her voice was deliberately subdued.

"Mr. President, I know you won't approve of my shifting the Portuguese Ambassador over to five instead of four, but Dr. Weismuller and his assistant at the Science Center, Dr. Pomeroy, are in my office. They insist they must confer with you immediately. They seem distraught, and they're certainly not making any of their usual cracker-barrel jokes. Could you please see them, sir, if only for long enough to get them off my back?"

"Sure. Send them in. Maybe one of them can tell me why it seems to be getting dark so early in the day."

"I've noticed that too, sir. And by the way, did you feel anything strange this afternoon . . . about half an hour ago?"

"Come to think of it, I did enjoy some agreeable vibrations from a Republican senator."

"The big chandelier in the entrance hall fell down. It didn't hurt anyone, thank heavens, but it made a mess, and now we won't have it lit up for the reception tonight. Someone said it must have been an earthquake because they saw it swinging in a circle."

"We don't have earthquakes in D.C. I'm sure there is a law against them. Probably the ghost of McKinley is wandering around upstairs, or didn't we pay the light bill? Send the boys in."

When Dr. Weismuller entered, the President favored him with his famous oblique smile. He dropped it when he recognized the large manila envelope carried by Dr. Pomeroy as being the same one given to him by the boy he had seen much earlier in the day.

* * *

Hymie Markel prided himself on his computerlike reactions in emergencies. He allowed no wasted thought or motion when the pressure was "right off the gauge," as he was fond of describing a particularly dicey situation.

When things became confused or dangerous, it was Hymie Markel who charged to the rescue, his mind clicking off escape routes, twists, immediate foes, necessary friends, needed data, those to be blamed and those to be credited if only in heaven.

Now Markel emerged shaken from the Oval Office. Never before had he been part of such august company, and for the moment at least a key factor in their plans. In addition to the President, who seemed more worried than Markel had ever seen him, there were the two eminent professors on his scientific advisory staff, Drs. Weismuller and Pomeroy. At their sides, handing them reams of data when asked, were four young assistants who looked too bright for their own good, in Markel's opinion. Additionally present, almost as decorations upon a cake that certainly needed no further frosting, were the Secretary of State, the Defense Secretary, and the Assistant to the President for National Security Affairs. There were also two members of the Cabinet who looked solemn and confused, but for once seemed inclined to keep their own counsel.

And for what was all this brass assembled so suddenly? A tidy question needing a tidy answer. The boss had not offered to make Markel privy to their deliberations, but he had fired off several questions before giving direct orders. How had the arrangements been made for young Mike Piper to visit the White House? What was his record as a juvenile? His school record? Who were his friends, his parents, their friends; who had accompanied him to Washington, and, most important, how long would it take Markel to return him to the Oval Office?

The President explained that Mike Piper's presence was required at once and there were no limits to the resources Markel might use to achieve his return. If necessary an Air

Force jet would be dispatched to wherever the boy happened to be. A Marine helicopter would be standing by to bring him directly to the south lawn. "Off you go," the boss had said without a trace of his oblique smile. "I'll be expecting to hear from you in thirty minutes that he is on his way."

Fine. No problem, Markel decided as he half ran to his office. Of course he would have preferred to know what all the flap was about and why the kid was so important to it, but for now his job was to turn Mike and (happy days) his escort around and get them headed back in the right direction. "Absolutely double-A priority," the boss had said. "Just get him here fast."

With the help of his secretary and a girl recruited from the Executive Offices in the West Wing, Markel kept three and sometimes four telephone lines in almost continuous operation. The Hay-Adams Hotel advised that Miss Kellogg and Mr. Piper had checked out at 2 P.M. The doorman thought he remembered them getting into an airport bus. Call Northwest Airlines. How many flights to St. Paul? The 3 P.M. flights had been transferred to Dulles, along with so many other flights. Passenger list? Yes, a Kellogg and a Piper aboard. Make an AIRINC call to the flight. Northwest operations order same to return Washington immediately. No air traffic delay guaranteed. Call Washington area Air Traffic Control. Make sure same preferential landing approach treatment as for Air Force One.

Leo Marcusi. Tell me all you know about the kid, and that's an order if you ever expect to see the inside of the White House again. And never mind why. I don't know myself.

Call Marty Martinson, who started this whole caper.

Marty not in office. Flying to Washington. What flight? No one knew. What the hell kind of executives did we have in the country these days, and especially the media bosses, whose whereabouts should be known at all times?

Yes. Ma Bell's information has a Benjamin Piper at 2000 Maple Avenue in St. Paul. Get someone on the horn there and build up some background material. What school did he go to, et cetera.

What time did Northwest estimate the flight would be back at Dulles? Could they make it into Washington National and save time, to hell with the noise limitations? The weather out the window was looking better even though it was practically dark. *What the hell do you mean the Captain advises there is no Piper or Kellogg on the flight?* Nonsense!

Check the ticket counter at Dulles. The damn ticket agent gone home for the day. Where does he live? Get his number. Through the yelling of some kids and a television set in the background the agent insists a Piper and a Kellogg are on the flight. He remembers checking them in. All right. Make another AIRINC contact with the Captain. Tell him to tell the cabin attendants to recheck their passengers. Goddamnit, Piper and Kellogg *have* to be on board unless they were carrying parachutes.

Click-click. Call the Piper home in St. Paul. No answer. Check with phone company: line is not out of order. Where the hell is everybody?

Click-click. Get through to Rudy Distancia. What kind of a family does the kid come from? Is there possibly anything between the kid and La Kellogg? Get your dirty old mind on the facts and get right back to me. Like yesterday.

Confirmed with the Marines. Chopper all booked and standing by. No sweat.

Northwest. Okay, you tell me how two people can board one of your flights and then disappear. . . . You want me to tell that to the President of the United States? You guys want a few charters next campaign? Well, get your flying circus in shape then and phone me the flight is on its way back to D.C. with a full passenger count.

* * *

At noon San Francisco time Leo Marcusi tried to contact F. Leslie Nash without success. Miss Perkins informed him that her employer was out to lunch and could not be disturbed under any circumstances short of war. Marcusi, who had his own jungle telegraph system extending from the Arabian oil fields to Alaska's north slope, translated this information according to a previously established pattern. The code said Nash would not be occupying his usual table at Jack's, so there was little use in calling there. He would be al-frescoing it in Sausalito with his current delight, one Naomi Ching, winner of San Francisco's Miss Chinatown contest some six years ago and a dedicated swinger.

Miss Perkins suggested Marcusi call back at three, which he did from the Press Club, since six o'clock Washington time was one hour past his drinking time and there was no wisdom in postponing same simply for the transmission of good news. Hence he had developed a slight lisp when he eventually captured F. Leslie Nash on the other end of the line and informed him, ". . . rest easy. There is absolutely nothing to concern yourself about. The boy did see the President, but he was thoroughly discredited long before he got to the Oval Office. I am told the appointment lasted about fifteen minutes, after which the President had enough. The boy is now on his way back to St. Paul, where he belongs. Anything else I can do for you? Just ask. That's what Leo Marcusi is here for. Johnny on the spot."

* * *

Twenty-seven minutes after the start of his marathon search Hymie Markel was beginning to perspire heavily. At the twenty-eight-minute mark the girl who had come in from the Executive Offices to assist said she had the boy's mother waiting on line six.

Markel punched the wrong button, swore softly, then punched number six. Mothers! With the way things are going she will probably turn out to be a Jewish mother. At this time in my life, yet.

Why isn't Madame Piper at the airport meeting her son? What kind of parental neglect do we have in America these days? And Mr. Piper is not at home yet? Where does he work? They are closed for the day? Very well, Mrs. Piper. When they do arrive have them call me *immediately.* The President wants your son right back here and toot suite. Of course you can come with him if you wish. . . .

Hey, Hymie, slow down. Get one of the girls to send out for something—anything. Okay, make it chow mein. Even it feeds the brain. This has all the marks of being a long session. Tell President's secretary advise boss right on to everything full steam and damn the torpedoes, but all not in line yet. Boy-lost situation. No, for Christ's sake, don't tell him that. Just that there will be a slight delay.

A Miss Kellogg on the line? Who the hell is—PUT HER ON! A winner right at the finish line.

"You're still at Dulles? What's the matter? Where's your young friend?"

Hymie listened intently. His mouth fell open for a moment, then he began the teeth-grinding ceremony he em-

ployed to ease the most extreme emergencies. "Stay right
where you are, Miss Kellogg. Don't move. A state patrol-
man will be along in a few minutes to pick you up and
bring you directly here."

Where is boy—boy—boy? . . . Vanished? What does
she mean—how does he *dare* vanish?

Click-click. Get through to Virginia State Patrol. Quick.
Pick up good-looking woman at phone booth opposite
Northwest ticket counter. Full speed here.

Dulles police. Get every available man on a search of
the airport and get back to me. Scour the joint if it takes
all night. Give me any reports of suspicious persons or incidents which might relate. Now.

FBI. Run a check on any stolen cars in the Dulles area.
Any incidents might relate? Get a hundred or more agents
on this right now and check every bush between here and
Dulles. And try cooperating with the state and local police
for a change. This is a double-A priority, a double-bubble-
gum project, and yes, of course, overtime is authorized.
Just get the kid and bring him here and upgrade your
whole outfit in the eyes of this administration. . . . I
don't *know* what the hell it's all about, and if I did it is
unlikely I'd tell you. Now get cracking.

The CIA? Nuts to them for now. What could they have
to do with a sixteen-year-old kid from St. Paul? Put them
on standby.

Jesus. Suppose the kid has been in an accident? . . .
What? Run over by an airplane? . . . Kidnapped? For what
reason? . . . Marty Martinson, what have you done to me?
Come to think of it, better have a few men from Security
pick Marty up whenever he arrives at National. Bring here
and eat individual out.

Markel sighed. He pressed the intercom button which
connected him directly to the President's secretary. He

tried to keep his voice from cracking or betraying any of his sense of foreboding.

"The President is receiving guests for the reception? Would you be kind enough to tell him that I'm running into some snags? I would like very much to see him as soon as it's convenient. . . . I'll be right here."

* * *

The first call Alice Kellogg made to St. Paul provided her with even more frustration than she already knew. After a long ringing there had been no response from the Piper residence. She called the power company hoping to alert Mike's father. How did you tell a mother or a father their son had disappeared and sound casual about it? When she finally got through to Ben Piper's office, she was advised he had left for the day. Likewise the flight from Dulles to St. Paul, which should, if God were in His heaven, be transporting an English teacher and her student. How could he just evaporate? Help! She dropped her last quarters into the phone, calling Marty Martinson. His secretary explained Mr. Martinson had left the office and was trying to get a plane to Washington. If this was Miss Kellogg calling, would she please stay where she was until he arrived or if she changed locations please call back?

Alice hung up and sat with her head in her hands as she reviewed the events which had brought her near despair. Where had she really last seen Mike? At the counter . . . and they were to meet at the bookstand. Then she had thought she saw him through the crowd, but it had not been Mike. Must need glasses. Or had she hoped so much to see him she had created a mirage?

Soon afterward she had discovered the note fastened to a book in the stand—eye level, in plain sight. Her name.

She had recognized Mike's semi-runic writing almost instantly. Bright he might be, but would the boy ever learn to write?

> Dear Miss Kellogg—
> I am in an awful big hurry or I would have said good-bye. Here is the sitchuachun. (Sp?) I am going away but will be back in a few days, so dont worry. I must fix this matter. Have a good trip back home and remember I think you are neat. No time to explain. Good-bye, Miss Kellogg.

The note was signed "Brain 2000," a title she knew he disliked. And he had drawn a little smiling face beneath it.

There it all was—something your mother would call a pretty pickle.

The call to that Mr. Markel in the White House proved that Mike had not tried to go back there. It was nice of Mr. Markel to sound so concerned, especially since he seemed almost to disapprove of the whole interview. Mike, dear boy, how could you do this to me? Please for the love of God, show your smiling face, even if we missed the flight. I need you, your parents need you . . . the whole world needs you.

She read the note again, her hands trembling so violently she could hear the paper rattling. No doubt about its being genuine. But had Mike written it under force? It did not appear to be strained, despite the message. Then why . . . where the hell . . . ? Oh, Mike.

Alice glanced at her watch. Almost a full hour had passed since she first started looking for him. Now while she was brooding, five more minutes had become history, the world was coming to an end that much faster, and she still had to find the man she loved and needed. How comforting it would be to say, "Marty! It's Alice. Something terrible has happened. Mike has disappeared. No, I don't think he was forced to write the note. It doesn't read that way to me, and I'd recognize his lousy penmanship anywhere."

Then Marty would take care of everything.

Come along now, she thought. Just sitting here and waiting for other people to rush to the rescue was bad for the liver. Do something, *anything* to avoid just having a good cry.

She returned to the bookstand and asked the female gnome who seemed to be in charge if she had seen a tall, rusty-haired young man in the vicinity. The gnome wanted to know how young was young, and Alice told her about sixteen.

"I could have missed him unless he was a flipper. They come here and flip through every magazine on the rack that has pictures in it, which proves they can't read. *Playboy, Penthouse, Oui,* all them sex-maniac rags which they never buy one of. Older men do it too. Once in a while I catch them right in the middle of an ogle and I yell at them, 'Hey, man, you got your jollies yet?' Then they get that look like kids caught with their hands in the candy jar and they sort of ease themselves out . . . still without buying anything. There's always a new bunch to take their place. Now to me this behavior indicates the American male—"

Whatever the gnome wanted to indicate, Alice lacked desire to share.

She was obliged to apologize several times as in her haste she jostled people on the way to the front entrance.

Outside in the gloom she stood tapping her foot uncertainly and thought, Please hurry up with your help, Mr. Markel. Now is when a girl really needs a friend.

What was she going to say when she finally did find Mike's mother on the other end of a telephone line? "Hello there, Mrs. Piper, how is everything back in St. Paul? . . . How's the weather? . . . It's rotten here, and even the White House looked a little shabby in such poor light. Haven't seen the sun since we left. . . . Well, it seems we missed our flight back. . . . How is Mike? . . . Well . . . that's why I'm calling. . . ." Wow.

Maybe Ben Piper would answer, but would that make the difficult any easier? "Well, folks, it's like this. You entrusted me with your precious son and I lost him. Don't ask me how I could lose a six-foot, freckled, reddish-haired kid, but I did. Just plain don't know what happened to him except that he is certainly not available, and according to his own words, he won't be available for at least a few days. I'm awfully sorry, folks, and hope you'll just go about your business as if nothing out of the way has happened and you'll both wait like good parents for him to come home, if, as, and when he decides to get around to it. That is, of course, if he is free to come home when he so desires. That is, if he hasn't fallen down an elevator shaft, or is being held by some terrorist gang who know about his theory and are torturing him right now to get the solution before they execute him. . . ."

THE EIGHTH DAY

Despite the extreme January cold Professor Ho-Po of Peking University decided to lunch with his Advanced Botany students, who were gathered on the lawn of the Sciences Building. They dined on elderly squid while all the time smiling and smiling and smiling like good revolutionaries of the People's Republic. They continued smiling while they indulged in the ancient and honored custom of grasshopper watching. In the old decadent times this custom provided some very exciting challenges to gamblers, a once-upon-a-time instinct of many Asians which is now labeled reactionary and is therefore forbidden.

Professor Ho-Po, however, did remember how the game was played (I'll wager the grasshopper I have chosen will jump farther than yours), and he described it to his eager and ever-smiling students. Lest they wind up hauling night soil in penitence for counterrevolutionary thoughts, he warned them to keep right on smiling even when they were losing.

Later, when he had stuffed his padded jump suit with his winnings, he confessed that even he could not explain what grasshoppers were doing jumping around Peking in January, thus proving himself a true comrade without pretensions of knowledge beyond his capabilities.

Warning his class once again to keep smiling, he beckoned to Lee Pee, the prettiest comrade in the university and, stuffing a wad of expensive and very reactionary rhinoceros horn between teeth and gum, invited his student to some distant bushes, where he suggested a particular species of grasshopper might dwell. There, isolated and inspired by the long-known powers of rhinoceros horn, he attempted to teach Lee Pee some of the more interesting aspects of the revolutionary movement.

Still maintaining her smile, Lee Pee was receptive, since it was Mao himself who declared it was dutiful to take all a comrade teacher could offer you.

Professor Ho-Po was soon disappointed, for the rhinoceros horn proved ineffective against an onslaught of scientific puzzlement. What indeed were grasshoppers doing in Peking at this time of year? Mao had always castigated people who were inclined to exaggeration, yet what had Ho-Po so recently beheld with his own eyes? How could he avoid being denounced as a prevaricator and therefore an enemy of the people if he told anyone what he had just seen? Even when the land was rife with imperialistic, opportunistic liars, he had never heard anyone claim a grasshopper had jumped more than three meters high.

* * *

The Pan American Boeing 747 climbed through the heavy overcast for ten minutes before it emerged into a tinted evening made all the more magnificent by the twinkling of the first stars. In the first-class section Dudley Winslow toyed with the dinner the stewardess had set before him and allowed his thoughts to float as easily from subject to subject as thistledown blown on the wind. Frequently in a state of near trance, Winslow had never been able to discipline his thoughts, which was one of many reasons his long service in the United States Foreign Service had been anything but spectacular. While at first glance he did offer an impression of great strength and dignity, his superiors at State knew better, and in a classic display of good-old-boymanship always devised tailor-made assignments for him—thereby keeping him comfortably on the payroll and still not risking any irreparable harm he might do to the foreign policy of the United States. Thus his present assignment as Deputy Administrator at the embassy in Moscow, toward which metropolis he was presently airborne.

Dudley Winslow was accompanied by his wife, Phoebe, who had once sighed over him as the handsomest of men but now chided him about his marsupial pouch and the dewlaps of flesh draped beneath his chin. The daughter of a Kansas entrepreneur who had made his fortune in pork bellies, she had appropriated the window seat just as her husband knew she would, and was now attacking her meal with her customary devotion. Sometimes she reminded him of a piranha, those voracious fish he had seen during a stint in the upper Amazon. "My dear," he had said gently, "control yourself. Just because we're going back to Moscow, you are not going to starve to death." In a quick transposition back to his days as a yachtsman he added that she was settling down below her Plimsoll marks.

"You sail your ship and I'll sail mine," she managed between mouthfuls.

Returning from Stateside leave to their Moscow post

with the Winslows were their two children, Heather and Geoffrey. Both had devoured their meal with nearly the same enthusiasm as their mother and, having finished, disappeared into the upper lounge. They had been seated behind the elder Winslows, and long before actually boarding the aircraft at Dulles they had done their utmost to ignore their parents' existence. Well traveled teen-agers did not need to be told they were now over Greenland, where a glance at the display of aurora might deserve their momentary attention, or that they would not arrive in Moscow until late morning. In their own considered opinion, there was almost nothing about the world they did not know.

When Dudley Winslow at last finished the éclair he had chosen for dessert (his wife took two), he washed it down with the last of his wine and pulled a copy of *Foreign Affairs* from the seat pouch ahead of him. He began to read at his usual assimilation rate of thirty words per minute, gracing that feat with his customary 30 percent comprehension factor. Few people knew that at Harvard, Winslow was known as "Hipsie" from his habit of moving his hips as he read. The total mental effort involved in reading the story of a colleague who was an expert on the Balkans became such that after ten minutes he was very grateful when a stewardess kneeled in the aisle beside him and smiled her professional smile. She was a dainty, quite pretty little thing, he decided, and as he removed his half-eye glasses he wished his Phoebe were as devoid of lard.

"What a nice family you have, Mr. Winslow," she began.

Winslow gave her the smile he intended to use when the State Department and a President agreed he should be Ambassador to somewhere. "Oh yes, quite," he responded.

"Speaking for the whole crew, we are happy to have you all traveling with us."

"Ah yes. Thank you. We regret leaving Washington, of course, but then duty calls. One must carry the flag, that sort of thing, you know, Miss ——?" He tried to make out her name tag, but vanity forbade the use of glasses when conversing with younger people.

"Just call me Trixie," she said. Her smile faded as she looked back down the aisle. "Is your son all right?"

Winslow twisted around to look at the seats behind him and saw they were vacant.

"I presume so. Perhaps he is up in the lounge with his sister."

"Heather? What a lovely girl. I've been just a little concerned . . . if there is anything we can do to help him have a nicer flight. He seems to . . . er . . . spend a great deal of time in the little boys' room."

"Really? How odd. Well, I'm not entirely surprised. One can't indulge oneself in junk food all day long without sooner or later paying some sort of penalty, can one? My whole family cannot rid themselves of the notion that certain items, mostly bad for the digestion, are unavailable in Moscow. I assure you it is quite the contrary."

"Then you're not worried."

"Not in the slightest. He's young and strong." Again Trixie was bathed in his special ambassadorial smile.

"And very handsome for his age," she responded. "Wait a few years and that rusty hair will drive women mad."

"Ah yes, quite," Winslow said, wondering what on earth Geoffrey had done to his hair, which was as blond as his own at the same age. Indeed, he thought vaguely, you were never quite sure what the young were up to these days. One should not be surprised at anything.

* * *

Mike Piper was nervous, but he was "gathered," as he liked to think of his situation. Here he was aboard a Moscow-bound airplane, and thus far all had gone as planned. Neat. Now he knew the problem would be to remain super-alert, to divert when necessary, and to seize upon every opportunity. Like a general in battle, he must use cover and deception to overcome superior forces, and for final victory even retreat if necessary.

He reviewed his campaign lest he repeat any mistakes. His sure protection was Mr. Winslow, whom he had observed at Dulles stuffing a sheaf of diplomatic passports back into his briefcase. The briefcase also contained books and travel folders on the U.S.S.R. Wow, that had been a race against time, trying to find Miss Kellogg and then having to run for the boarding gate before they closed it. There was the chance, and it had to be taken right now. Stick with Mr. Winslow, but not so much that you become a nuisance. Continue to act as if you are part of the family. Don't argue with success. Passing security had been no problem at all; anyone could walk through to the boarding gate if your X ray revealed no metal and you acted just like you knew where you were going. It was really neat the way Mr. Winslow didn't seem to mind if you kept close to him and boarded the airplane just sort of *between* Heather and Geoffrey. A very cool do. Mr. Winslow carried all the tickets and smiled all the time, and the stewardess seemed to know his name. He was sure a real VIP, and she just waved everybody around Mr. Winslow toward the first-class section. There could have been a nasty glitch if the cabin attendants in that section had asked to see seat assignments, but you were ready for that with phase one of the master plan. All you had to do was slip into the nearest lavatory and sit down.

Warning himself that a successful stowaway must think fast and constantly, Mike had been careful not to lock the door of the lavatory lest a cabin attendant become curious about an "Occupied" light before takeoff. He waited half an hour after the takeoff, until he felt the Boeing was leveling off at altitude. He gave himself an additional five minutes and finally emerged. No one had paid the slightest attention to him as he strode forward boldly to the first-class section.

That indifference he now recognized had been due to factors beyond his control. The cabin attendants were furiously busy about the galley, taking drink orders and generally settling their passengers. Mike heard an announcement from the flight deck that the passengers might like to watch the aurora borealis display out of the left-side windows. He saw the resulting diversion of attention as an opportunity and immediately approached Geoffrey Winslow, who was sitting beside his sister. They had exchanged smiles and a few words en route to the airplane, and Geoffrey had proved a friendly type.

"Hey, would you like to go upstairs in the lounge with me for a look around? I'll bet we would see the aurora better up there."

To Mike's satisfaction, both Geoffrey and his sister rose quickly to the bait. He smiled at their parents, who were sitting just ahead of the first-class section.

Because the upper lounge was the refuge of dedicated smokers and the cocktail hour was still in full swing, it had been difficult to see much of anything, but Mike sensed the interest of Geoffrey and his sister was not really in the borealis, but in a joining with their own kind. They agreed adults were fine in small doses, but were usually too fixed in their ways. Everything had to be done just the same every time.

During the next half hour of rapid-fire exchange Mike had found the answers to many questions he needed to know, and when a stewardess stopped by to ask if they would like some refreshment he had gained enough confidence to ask for an orange juice. Real casual. Cool. Geoffrey, whom he now addressed as Geoff, and Heather agreed they would like the same beverage, and they told Mike how much they yearned for orange juice in Moscow. Mike said he had no idea there might be a shortage of orange juice in Moscow because this was his first trip to Russia. He was to meet his parents there. They were presently in Turkey, where his father was doing advisory work on a new power plant. Wow, he thought while he was explaining how he had been "sort of looked after" by a Miss Kellogg during his parents' absence, he was becoming a practiced liar. But watch it, he reminded himself. Overconfidence is how crooks get caught. From now on try to make anyone you meet talk about themselves. Then they will not be inclined to draw too many lies from you.

As their acquaintance warmed, so did their speed of conversation accelerate. Mike soon learned that Dudley Winslow held an extremely important position, and probably kept the U.S. and Russia from declaring war on each other. He also learned much of Geoff and Heather's trials living in foreign lands, and their longing for Americans of their own age. They were not enthusiastic about returning to Moscow.

"You're lucky you'll only be there a few days. After Intourist is through showing you only the good, come see us for a look at real life."

Finally they all began to yawn, and after a discussion of time zones, which allowed Mike to demonstrate his understanding of minutes of arc and the celestial equator, they agreed it was time to catch some sleep.

As they descended the stairs, Mike excused himself. He was starving, but he knew there was unnecessary risk in expecting a meal. Thus far no one had asked to see a ticket, thanks to his constant proximity to the Winslows, but if there had been a meal count when the food was loaded at Dulles then why was there an extra mouth aboard? The cabin attendants might start making inquiries, and good-bye super spy Mike Piper.

As Geoffrey and Heather turned toward the front of the first-class section, Mike turned aft toward his favorite refuge. On the way as he passed a loaded food tray, he managed to relieve it of one banana without being seen. He stuffed it quickly in his pocket and walked easily to the lavatory. Cool, man, cool. Easy now . . . just cool.

This time he locked the door. Later, when the Pan American Boeing was sliding between the arctic stars, Trixie, who was solicitous of all mankind, discovered Mike Piper in the galley. He had opened a drawer and was devouring one of the sweet rolls which would be served with breakfast.

"Aha!" Trixie smiled. "Caught you."

A chunk of half-chewed sweet roll came to a halt beside Mike's prominent Adam's apple. "I . . ."

"If you're that hungry, Geoffrey, I'll fix you something."

"Geoffrey? Who me? No, I'm not a bit hungry." Mike was shocked at his lack of poise. How many times had he told himself that if he could not handle surprise he would never get through this thing? He tried without success to swallow.

"You look so pale," Trixie said. "I told your father you might be ill. He said not to worry."

"Oh? No . . . no. I always look this way. Maybe I'm allergic to the northern lights." He tried to smile.

"Don't you want to get some sleep? We'll be serving breakfast in about two hours. Then it will be London before you know it."

"Do we have to land in London?"

"Yes. For fuel. But you Moscow passengers can stay right on board if you want."

"I'd like that. Maybe I could sleep right through everything . . . if I could find a nice quiet place without too many people moving up and down the aisle."

"Come with me." Trixie beckoned. "Tonight you're in luck."

Mike followed her forward to the darkened first-class section. She led him past Dudley Winslow and his wife and Geoffrey and Heather. All were asleep.

She stopped at the foremost two seats on the left, removed the separating armrest, and took down a pillow.

"There," she whispered. "You can even stretch out. These seats weren't booked, and no one will bother you up here. I'll tell your parents where you are if they wake up first."

"Don't, please. I'd like to surprise them." Looking down at the white pillow in the dim light, Mike found it suddenly irresistible. He sank to the seat on his knee, stretched as much of his length as he could, and lowered his head to the pillow. "Thanks," he said softly.

Trixie took a blanket from the overhead rack and tucked it around him.

"Gee," Mike mumbled, "you're nice."

"So are you and all your family. What's the name of your brother?"

"Mike."

"You don't look much alike."

"Well . . . he's adopted."

"I understand. Sweet dreams, Geoffrey."

Mike was only half aware she had left him. It had been a long hard day, and here, feeling as if he were lying in a bed of lies, he just wanted to think about Susie and the other good things in life. Presidents and gravity and tectonic plates and the Supreme Soviet and all the other complications of his spinning-top theory were like the well-known "Roche limit." If a moon would stay intact, then it must keep a minimum distance from its parent planet. Such was the law of the universe, and the same applied, he decided, to his present situation.

For a few minutes the vision of Susie executing a double loop and then a butterfly on the Greenland ice cap flickered across his drowsiness. Then even Susie vanished.

*　*　*

At 4:21 A.M. Hymie Markel slurped down the dregs of his twelfth cup of coffee and stared at the chopped liver sandwich he had ordered from the White House kitchen. He had just fielded his umpteenth call from the President, and not one of the brass, he thought, was sleeping. The Secretary of Defense was up, and so was the Secretary of State. He had seen both men sitting disconsolately on one of the settees in the hallway of the West Wing. They were watching one of the maintenance staff wax the parquet floors, and he knew they were speculating on what could have happened to one youngster from Minnesota and what was going to be done about it.

At midnight the search of Dulles and every other airport in the vicinity of Washington had been abandoned. Needles in haystacks, and who, pray, had lost the needle? Truman may have said the buck stopped in the Oval Office, but in the case of this damn kid it stopped eight inches from a chopped liver sandwich.

At least some things had been accomplished, although just how they might help in the search for Mike Piper was still unclear. The teacher, Alice Kellogg, was back safely in the Hay-Adams, in a suite at White House expense. Presumably she was sleeping. How could such a good-looking dish of some apparent competence lose the kid in the first place? She had endured a one-hour questioning by half the Cabinet and the President himself, and had shed only a few tears in the process, but her answers really led to nowhere except zero.

So, if the kid had departed voluntarily, then where the hell did he go? Miss Kellogg could not even guess. Then there was his girl friend, Susie. Who else but Hymie Markel ever had to dig up a sign language expert at ten o'clock at night in Minnesota, then wake up a sixteen-year-old girl who could not hear and had never talked with her mouth and ask her via the interpreter at least a hundred questions? All via long distance with three other phones jangling and people going in and out like war had been declared. Or had it? Hymie thought he had never seen so many generals, colonels, and admirals since the Inauguration.

One private theory had been somehow satisfying, even though nothing much had come of it. At one o'clock in the morning he had called Leo Marcusi at his home.

"I'm just going on a hunch you might have something to do with this, and if so you'd better come clean with me right this minute or I'll leak enough stories about you to make Nixon look like a hero. Where is the kid?"

"How the hell should I know?"

"Because I think the kid has something on the oil companies they are not going to like at all, and it strikes me as most peculiar that you would have known about his arrival here in the first place, and even more peculiar that all of a sudden, when no one was minding the store, the kid just up and disappears. Doesn't that strike *you* as peculiar?"

Hymie was not altogether surprised at Marcusi's reaction. "I am going to sue you, the President, and the Congress of the United States. I don't mind the invasion of my privacy and your flagrant disregard of my constitutional rights, but it is carrying things too far when some silly ass calls from the most revered house in this country at one o'clock in the morning and wakes me out of a sound sleep with a lot of preposterous questions."

"I ask only one question. Where is the kid?"

"I don't *know* where the kid is and I don't care. It strikes me you're making a lot of fuss about nothing."

"That is a matter of opinion. The fate of this nation may depend on finding that kid. May I suggest you would be doing your country a disservice if you don't tell me everything you know about his whereabouts?"

"What have you been drinking? Or smoking?"

"I am deadly serious, Leo. I'm still in my office and expect to be until I find the kid."

"Clue me, maestro. Why is it that during the last few days so many people with a lot of influence are so interested in this particular kid? Is he the Second Coming or something? If so, I want to get my house in order."

"You might want to do that anyway. Especially if we don't find him soon," Hymie finished with what he hoped was the proper ominous tone in his voice. "Sweet dreams. You know my number if you have a change in your cast-iron heart. *Ciao*."

But Leo Marcusi had abandoned all hope of sleep. There were now too many tracks to be covered. What the hell was going on? This whole matter had been so nicely diverted, and now it had surfaced again. It was long after midnight Central time when he reached Rudy Distancia in St. Paul.

"Greetings," Marcusi said. "I'm calling to inquire just exactly what the hell you think you are doing to me?"

Distancia grunted. "What are you doing to *me* calling at this hour? I'm in bed with a book."

"That's a switch. What's her name?"

"*Searching for Bear Claws on the Upper Khyber*, by a guy named Posolosky."

"Is he a Democrat or a party ex-er?"

"You should buy one. It's a real thriller."

Hymie heard Distanica yawn.

"What I want to know, Rudy, is this: Why didn't you tell me the Piper kid really had something important to say? Why did you advise me his meeting with the President would be just one of those things? What was the purpose of the deception? In other words, what do you know that I do not know and should?"

"Am I to understand the President took that nutty kid seriously?"

"Not at first, no."

"You don't really believe that crap about the end of the world."

"I do. The President does. And so do the eminent scientists who are gathered here in mass woe."

"Well, I'll be damned."

"You will be more than that if we can't find the solution. Unfortunately, the solution has disappeared and I am the patsy."

"I don't follow you."

"Hitherto, Rudy, you have always been the model of discreetness. Be advised that if one word of this gets out to the media there will be an international panic such as this world has never known. Do not breathe a word of what I am about to tell you. You would not be told if I did not entertain some faint hope you might offer a clue which we might fit with another clue and foster some new ideas. The kid has disappeared, and apparently of his own volition. Where do you think he might go?"

"Where is the teacher? She would know."

"Negative." Hymie then related all that had happened, and by the time he had finished his queasy voice seemed to be coming from another person. A voice in the wilderness, he thought, the last plea for rescue by one of those who stood center stage during the apocalypse.

His eyes closed several times while he waited for Distancia's response. He asked once if Rudy was still on the other end of the line and heard Distancia say he was thinking. Finally Distancia came through in measured words. "I can't believe anybody that age is going to wander around by himself very long. The Piper boy is part of a happy family, so I doubt if he has anything against home. Sooner or later he's bound to head for the familiar, so I'll arrange for the state police to throw a cordon around the neighborhood and pick him up the instant he shows."

"You don't understand the importance of secrecy in this. How are you going to explain why he's so important he rates ten or fifteen plainly marked cars plus all the trooper trappings? Some news guy would get on to it sure as my ulcer is blossoming."

"Easy. I'll say the kid has been kidnapped, and when the troopers make a rescue that falls right into their hands they'll all be heroes. We'll give them a medal, or some such, and no one needs to know anything more. Okay?"

"Okay," Hymie said reluctantly. "Not too bad. Sometimes, Rudy, I think we might be able to use you around here. *Ciao*."

* * *

At 7 A.M. Pacific time the telephone at the bedside of F. Leslie Nash tinkled circumspectly, as if hesitant to awaken the great man. The telephone, like everything else in the Nash household, was engineered to operate at a prudent level; never let there be commotion of any sort, never let voices be raised, or bells jangled. The kitchen, where preparations had already begun to please Nash's highly selective palate, was soundproofed, and newly hired servants were admonished to wear soft shoes despite the fact that they would be moving across heavy-pile carpeting when performing their duties.

Nash disliked noise of any kind, yet he did not trouble himself to answer the telephone until he had risen from his bed, smoothed the night's wrinkles from his magenta pajamas, and slipped into a somber bathrobe. When at last he picked up the phone he addressed the mouthpiece with a single word of greeting—"Yes?"

"Leo Marcusi here, sir. I hope I'm not calling too early."

"The early bird catches the worm."

Nash was pleased to hear Marcusi chuckle. How aptly and quickly he had chosen his retort.

"Right, sir. As always, you succeed in hitting the nail on the head. I trust you slept well?"

"Reasonably."

"Well, sir, my report to you yesterday that the whole matter of the Piper boy had been taken care of and could be forgotten was premature. A complication has raised its ugly head, and I'm not sure just how far you want me to carry the ball in this rather peculiar game."

"Come to the point, if you please."

"You remember our recent conversations about the boy I referred to as John of Arc?"

"I do."

"The boy has disappeared. What troubles me is that in the present atmosphere of distrust of any petroleum-related enterprise we may be accused of having had something to do with it."

"Why in heaven's name should that occur? I fail to see the connection."

"Some early morning research with a friend of mine at the National Science Foundation revealed some interesting facts. It seems the President took the lad much more seriously than was first reported to me, and a part of the overall scheme seems to be the immediate closing down of all oil wells in certain areas. I know it's vague, sir, but that's all my friend dared to tell me."

"Preposterous. But then anything becomes possible with a Democrat President. I don't understand why this ridiculous idea would even be considered."

"My friend did allow it all had something to do with the possible end of the world. I know, I *know*, sir, it is utter insanity, but there it is. Another contact of mine tells me a massive search for the boy is now in progress. The Army, Navy, Marines, the FBI, the CIA, the whole kit and caboodle are looking for the kid, but so far no luck. What do you want me to do?"

Nash hesitated. There was not an oil-producing area in the world where at least one member of the Petroleum Council was not operating. The closing down of any region even temporarily and for whatever idiotic reason could be disastrously expensive. For a moment he wondered if Marcusi's well-known fondness for the bottle might have finally brought about brain damage. He caught himself. Whistling in the dark, he thought. Bad news did not evaporate on command. Suddenly the superbly lubricated machinery of his self-preservation instinct took over. This was not just a different variety of the crises he faced every day. Extraordinary measures were now in order.

"Find the boy, Leo. Call me immediately you have done so and bring him west in one of our jets. I am not pleased with these developments."

"But, F.L., if all our national agencies can't find him, how am I supposed to—"

"That's your problem. Your job depends on it. Use force if necessary."

* * *

Alice ordered tea and toast, and said her appetite had failed her this morning. Sitting opposite her in the wood-paneled dining room of the Hay-Adams Hotel, Marty Martinson reached for her hand. "Will it distress you if I order a big breakfast?" he asked. "Trouble makes me hungry and food cheers me."

Alice turned to the hovering waiter. "Cancel the tea and toast, please. Bring me a double order of pancakes with sausage strewn alongside."

The waiter smiled and Alice tried to reciprocate, but she thought her lips might crack in the attempt. How now, Mrs. Gloom, how much of your pathos is self-pity and how much concern for Mike? He is all right, somewhere . . . he must be all right. "I feel like a character out of Dostoevski," she said, "I know it's no fun to watch this melancholy face, but it's the only one I could find when I reunpacked this morning."

"What I see suits me so well I'd like the same view more often."

"I hope the day will never come when you regret that illusion." She reached for his hand. "Marty, thanks for the nice words. But the only thing I can think of right now is one very disillusioned kid."

"It's been a long time since I was his age, but if I remember rightly discouragement, like everything else, is very temporary. Teen-agers bounce right back. I'd be willing to bet Mike hasn't quit. I have to believe that sometime today he'll surface. The way things are now organized, there isn't much he can do in this country without someone hearing about it."

"Meanwhile we all go spinning off into space."

"I hope we don't go too far out before you and I have a chance to get better acquainted. Don't misunderstand me, that wasn't just a pass. If the timing weren't so bad, it would have been a proposal."

Alice tried to pretend that her involuntary smile was meant solely for the waiter who placed the pancakes before her. By the time he had departed, she managed to recapture her calm or, she thought, what just might pass for calm in the face of great turmoil. She also thought her smile was properly enigmatic—well, almost.

"Did I tell you about my career as a girl scout?"

"Yes, you did. That first night."

"There is your out. Repeating myself. Imagine how soon you would tire of the same old chatter seven mornings a week."

* * *

Dudley Winslow went to the window of his seventh-floor apartment in the embassy and stared down at the Kalinin Prospect. The wide six-lane street was covered with snow, and the perpetual gloom of wintertime Moscow made the evening all the more sinister. He sipped slowly at his scotch and water, aware that it was his fourth since arriving from the airport, and while he hesitated to label himself intoxicated, he wished he could. What had he, Dudley Winslow, done to deserve extra and most peculiar problems—as if jet lag and family behavior were not enough?

Heather and Geoffrey had gone to their rooms, and presumably to bed, thank God, thereby avoiding the spectacle of their mother's first reunion with the only products of the entire Soviet Union she approved—Mysinchiska vodka combined with precious Ukrainian chocolates. She was now stretched out on their bed, fully clothed and snoring vehemently. "I hear you loud and clear!" Winslow shouted at the ceiling. She reminded him of a beached hippo he had once seen taking a sunbath on the banks of the Congo, and now he could not decide whether it was preferable to leave her be and try to think through the racket or attempt to rouse her and face a crying jag, which almost inevitably followed her occasional overindulgence. For there was more than one side to Phoebe, he remembered. Beneath the blubber lived a frightened little girl who only wanted to please.

He also remembered there was a pressing need to think. Of course he could go hide in his office on the eighth floor and try to gather his thoughts there, but then the Ambassador might be in his office, and after the welcomes-back there would certainly be something gone wrong in the nine-story building which the Ambassador would consider needed immediate attention.

What to do? Winslow pulled nervously at his heavy eyebrows, a signal to all who knew him well that he was attempting thought. How best to handle this most trying situation without embarrassment, or possibly, very serious trouble? Never before had there been a time when his career was so endangered, and if it was now, then the surface evidence had appeared in a most unexpected form—a youngster by the name Piper. Or was he a youngster?

Before she collapsed into incoherence, Phoebe had suggested the Soviets had discovered some kind of youth preservation serum and Michael Piper was probably a highly trained thirty-year-old spy who would report everything that happened in the American Embassy to the KGB.

On the other hand, could he be a plant by the CIA, testing the good old Winslow reliability with a view to coming promotion? A test of Winslow resourcefulness under stress? Perhaps there would be a downgrading to some hardship post worse than Moscow if he failed to perform just right. Djibouti? Patagonia? Baluchistan? Dear God!

Winslow took a long pull at his scotch and tried to recall precisely how he had entered upon his present dilemma. Yes, he did remember the youngster hovering about; in fact, had exchanged a few words with him while the flight was en route. Yet certainly nothing had been said which could be in any way interpreted as even a slight relaxation in the normal diplomatic code of manners. Somehow the boy had made friends with Geoffrey and Heather—also quite normal, come to think of it. And so everything had gone along in the same fashion throughout the flight. Had the presence of young Piper been a carefully arranged camouflage? If not, then how did the lad get on the aircraft in the first place? Haw! And in first class, no less. A fishy circumstance, indeed.

Next, the arrival at Moscow with the usual cool but polite greetings from the Soviet petty functionaries. It had been nice of Gologorsky, who was rather his opposite number in the Kremlin, to send an aide with a bouquet of flowers for Phoebe. There were occasions when the Russians could be amazingly kind and thoughtful. There was never any problem through customs and immigration at any time, but Gologorsky's aide smoothed things even further and there had scarcely been a pause in their walking to the embassy limousine.

Once in the car, after smiles and handshakes all around with the various bureaucrats—yes, that had been the first time he had really noticed the omnipresence of the Piper lad. There he was, sharing one of the jump seats with Geoffrey, smiling and waving just as if he were one of the family. It had been then that you thought it necessary to make some inquiry.

"And who are you, young man?" he had asked. A most reasonable inquiry, succinctly stated—hardly words to give offense to anyone. The answer had been somewhat of a shock and at first incredible. Quite.

"I am here," quoth young Piper, "to see the Soviet heads of state."

Now Winslow recalled it had taken a moment to make sure he had heard rightly and had not lost his wits in jet lag.

"And where are your parents? Didn't they come to meet you?"

"No. They're in St. Paul."

"Ah?" Winslow knew his voice had sounded as if he were gargling, and at that moment he remembered longing for some Lavoris.

"That's in Minnesota," young Piper had informed him.

"Ah? Is it now?"

"I would appreciate it very much, sir, if you would help me see the head commissars immediately."

What kind of a game was this, Winslow wondered, confronting a man who had just completed a very long flight from Washington, a man who was a whole twelve hours off timewise and already constipated? What sort of scheme was afoot? Very obviously this rather nice-looking young man was not acting alone, but then who was his true master?

Phoebe had not helped the situation by wearing her now-I've-seen-everything smile. After a moment Winslow had decided a challenge was in order. "Who sent you to Moscow, young man?" had been his carefully formed question.

"Our President. He is not well informed nor well advised. His attitude left me no alternative."

Winslow recalled he had maintained a sort of mesmerized silence after that declaration. What did one say? What *could* one say to a young American boy who was obviously demented or was on something? Hashish, and so young? A classic example of the breakdown in young America's moral fiber. Shocking. But then what in heaven's name was he doing on the airplane? Worse, perhaps Phoebe, whose maternal instincts were strictly confined to her own brood, was correct in her premise that Piper was not an American at all.

Winslow studied the amount of liquid left in his glass and considered increasing it. He rose, went to the window, and looked down upon the two gates where autos entered the embassy, passed through the inner courtyard, and exited. Nothing seemed out of the ordinary. The usual Russian policeman stood black against the snow and occasionally stepped into the cubicle, where, Winslow supposed, he warmed his feet. There was a formal guardhouse at the exit gate. The usual two bundles of uniforms were stamping on the snow.

He watched a woman walk out of the exit gate and recognized her as one of the maids who performed the general clean-up tasks about the embassy. Nearly all of them, he knew, worked for the KGB and fed a constant stream of useless information to their insatiable superiors.

How soon would this new development pique their interest? An unaccompanied youth presently sleeping in one of the staff rooms on the fifth floor wouldn't attract much attention until it was discovered he was not a genuine Winslow. Then what? Fortunately, a secretary was away on her vacation in Spain or Piper would have had to be put up with the Marine guards, which would never do, or right in the Winslow apartment—for, as usual, there was not an available hotel bed in Moscow. And, good grief, one couldn't just turn the lad loose.

He reviewed the choice of answers that must come with the morning. There were approximately one hundred and twenty-five people in the embassy, all of whom knew each other and had at least some idea what their compatriots were up to. How was he to explain Piper's presence, particularly if the boy maintained that poppycock about the President and his need to speak with the Soviets? And then what about Washington?

Winslow gulped at the last inch of whisky in the glass and agonized over the beginnings of an obligatory cable. "Have acquired a youngster en route who says he must meet with the Supreme Soviet . . ."

Even some of the looser types back at State would hardly believe such nonsense, much less as having been originated by a trusted representative of the department.

He started to compose an alternate message. "Have acquired a boy about sixteen of fair complexion . . ."?

Good God, no! Someone might even suggest he, Dudley Slade Winslow III, had joined the gay liberation movement.

How about, "Runaway youth with obvious mental deficiency now in my custody. Claims American citizenship and intimacy with the President . . ."? Worse! Far worse! He just claimed he had *met* the President, nothing more intimate.

Just the facts, Winslow. If Piper were some kind of a test, be it of the Winslow integrity, perception, or resourcefulness, then surrendering to the obvious—that is, believing exactly what he had been told and relaying same —would bring on him suspicion of naïveté. And everyone in State knew where that put one.

Winslow left the window and walked slowly toward the bedroom. He thought he resembled a sailor in a fog, surrounded by hazards on every hand, knowing there was only one correct course. This moment in history seemed appropriately scored with warning signals transmitted by the slumbering horn on his bed.

He sat on the bed, loosened his tie, and finished his scotch. He stared at Phoebe's ample rump rising and descending with her mighty inhalations and quivering sometimes as if the flesh below her rumpled skirt were deflecting the spikes of little harpoons. As he removed his shoes and lowered himself gingerly beside his wife, Winslow tried to the utmost of his capability to understand why, in spite of his strict conforming to whatever rules and regulations governed his daily life, the world had always seemed so hostile. Perhaps when she sobered, Phoebe might solve his present dilemma. Perhaps she would show him the best way to procrastinate until the whole thing went away.

While the earth continued its gradually increasing rate of rotation and brought the end of eternity perilously near, Dudley Winslow remained in a semicoma for eight precious hours.

THE NINTH DAY

Michael Piper slept a troubled sleep. He dreamed of a great uniting of the earth's people in a common effort. He saw the result of such pooled energy floating upon an ocean of oil, and in the depths were electric eels marching past with opalescent signs . . . Share . . . Understand . . . Forget . . . Die . . . Live.

While Mike Piper was dreaming, an earth fall reburied the tomb of Tutankhamen at 6 A.M. Cairo time. The calamity was not discovered until shortly after 8, at which time a huge crack was perceived in the pyramid of Cheops.

Almost simultaneously the bells in the Vatican began to ring, and their joyous clanging continued long enough for the Pope to rouse from his slumbers and witness the miracle. All of the hierarchy and many of the Vatican underlings knew there were no bell ringers on duty at such an hour, but they were soon content with their master's somewhat apprehensive explanation. "God is summoning us," the Pope intoned. "He is saying repent, the time is almost come."

By 9 A.M. Rome time there were long lines at the confession boxes.

Unfortunately, no one correlated a similar clamor set up in Paris by the bells of Notre Dame. A thorough search by the Parisian authorities, including specialists from the riot squad, failed to discover a handy Quasimodo.

In the time-honored way of official Washington rumors began bubbling to the surface with ever compounding frequency. Repetition served the conveyers well, and by 10 A.M. the following suppositions had simmered long enough to be identified as scoops by the local newsmongers.

1. The President was holding a secret meeting with the Joint Chiefs of Staff and Cabinet at Camp David, where plans for making Cuba a fifty-first state were being programmed.

2. The meeting was a screen to direct attention away from the President's illegitimate son, who had been living with Castro in Cuba (unconfirmed whether adopted or not) and would shortly arrive in Washington.

3. The illegitimate son had already been booked on the "Today"; "Tonight"; "This Afternoon"; "Good Morning," and "Swing Shift" shows, where he would offer undeniable proof of his parentage. His name was Michael Piper (pronounced "Peepair"), and he was the spitting image of the President.

4. Peepair was a nice kid, according to unidentified White House informants, and did not want to make trouble for his true father. He just wanted help with his schoolwork, which he was bringing with him. The President had called upon two scientists from the National Academy to counsel Peepair on his homework problems.

They had already discovered the Cuban school system was far more advanced than the American.

5. Peepair was staying at the Madison Hotel, the Hay-Adams, the Hilton, the Sheraton. The Russian Embassy official who handled such Cuban affairs as there were in Washington seemed confused when queried, but volunteered that if Peepair really was close to Castro (and never mind his relationship to the President) he would certainly be staying at the best of the best.

6. One energetic reporter whose girl friend did substitute clerical work, including some Xerox machine copying at the White House, filed a story about a bright student from Minnesota named Piper who had presented the President with a scientific ultimatum which had in turn so disturbed White House advisers that an immediate conference was called at Camp David. The girl friend was not privy to the nature of the ultimatum except that she thought it had something to do with the earth leaving its traditional orbit and all hell breaking loose as a consequence. The reporter was told by his city editor that he was working for a newspaper, not a science fiction magazine, and to get on to something with more human interest.

By noon Washington time the wide network which the exhausted Hymie Markel had established across the nation was sizzling with vital communications. No less than one hundred and forty-two white male youths in the mid-teen bracket, all of whom were tall and rusty-haired, had been discovered in various environments. None of this assembly answered to the name of Michael Piper. Hymie Markel decided the real Mike was hiding behind a pseudonym. Unfortunately, not one of the youth crop displayed more than an elementary acquaintance with mathematics. On testing, eighteen declared the sum of three and seven to be eleven.

Yet, through some misunderstanding in Markel's original "Confidential Priority Release," one hundred and two of the youths were now standing by for a summons to the White House while six were actually en route, accompanied by their eager parents. "With visions of sugarplums," Markel sighed unhappily. And a pretty penny it was going to cost the taxpayers getting all of them back where they came from.

After he had showered, shaved, and taken a Benzedrine, Hymie Markel was advised of a new and much more serious development. Drs. Pomeroy and Weismuller of the National Academy of Sciences, working ceaselessly with the astronomers at the Kitt Peak Observatory in Arizona, were now positive something was going very much awry in celestial systems hitherto dependable. With the employment of the gigantic Mayall 4-meter telescope a new meteor classified in the sixth magnitude was observed approaching the earth at an ever accelerating pace. No one could explain how the object appeared so suddenly, or where it came from.

Even worse, the Kitt Peak staff became confused when they attempted what should have been a perfectly normal prediction pattern. Cooperating with their colleagues at the Cerro Tololo Observatory in the Chilean Andes and feeding their combined data through computers at Tucson and Washington, they were unable to determine whether the meteor was approaching Earth or Earth was approaching the meteor. Whatever the truth, scientists of the sister observatories and the "Aura" member institutions comprising thirteen universities began viewing the heavens with alarm. They named the meteor "Caligula I," after the Roman emperor who was bent on destruction but could never make up his mind just when or where to commence.

While the "Aura" group were determining that "Caligula I" was composed of 92 percent iron, 7 percent nickel, with 1 percent of undeterminable substances, they also found the closing speed with earth to be approximately thirty-three thousand miles per hour, which Drs. Weismuller and Pomeroy discovered matched very closely with the orbital escape speed specified in the paper delivered to the President by one Michael Piper of 2000 Maple Avenue in St. Paul, Minnesota. The discovery made both men highly nervous and irritable because they could not share what the White House had described with their associates. Weismuller, normally the most placid of men, lost both his glasses and his pipe and became semiblind for the entire day. Moody in his frustration, he finally took his despair to a massage parlor.

Dr. Pomeroy, noted for his learned addresses on religious follies since the first century and a long-time atheist, went to the Tucson library, ostensibly for some research. He inquired of the first librarian he spied where he might find a copy of the Holy Bible.

In Moscow, Michael Piper opened his pale blue eyes with a sense of still wandering among his dreams. He lay quite still while he examined his unfamiliar surroundings. The room was small, and obviously the rightful proprietor was female since he could see a line of dresses hanging in an alcove and three pairs of booties in the corner. He saw that it was snowing outside, the big-flaked, gently falling variety that reminded him of Minnesota. What would his mother be doing now? And Dad? It had been snowing in St. Paul in just the same way when he had accidentally overheard a parental conversation which had puzzled and disturbed him.

Looking out at the window, his mother had said, "I sure would like to go to Florida this winter or someplace where there's more sun than snow. . . ."

And his father had replied, "Doggone it, so would I, Nancy. But unless a miracle happens, we just can't afford it. We have that whack of an insurance premium to pay, *and* the taxes, *and* the payment on 2000 Maple, *and* the various contraptions which are apparently necessary to alter our children's teeth so they will have a socially acceptable smile. That doesn't leave much in the travel fund or any other fund."

Was that the way it was with everyone when they grew up? Did it work out you couldn't do pretty much what you wanted as soon as you got married or were just out of school? It should be the opposite. As soon as a guy finished with biology and English and all that stuff, he ought to be able to do about anything he pleased.

Mike pulled the blanket up just under his chin and stared at the ceiling. He envisioned Susie against its whiteness. She would be practicing at the rink now. . . . No, if it was day here in Moscow then it would be night in St. Paul and Susie would be home. It was tough being away from home so long . . . well, maybe not so long since it had been only four days and nights, not counting the time difference. If the Russians would just listen to reason, they could do the job just as well as the Americans because they had the power to make other nations do what they said ought to be done.

Mike reached beneath the pillow and found his thin briefcase was still where he had put it. He sat up, rubbed at his head for a moment, and then opened the briefcase. Then he sat quite still, yawning occasionally over the figures which he had studied so many times. And once again he assured himself all of his calculations jelled. There were no mistakes and there was no logical argument that he could see which in any way could refute the figures. Weight was weight, mass was mass, and force was measurable. No question. On the twenty-first of February, eleven days from now, there would be no reversing the situation. No matter what anyone did to stop the departure from orbit, no matter how much weight was transferred from area A to area F or area L, the difference would be ineffective. He must see the Supreme Soviet today.

* * *

Dudley Winslow hesitated outside the door. He was dressed for the day, Harvard tie precisely knotted, his gray business suit pressed and immaculate. The sense of unbreakable order stopped at his collar, since from that point upward Dudley Winslow was in near chaos. Everything was fuzzy this morning, and there was so much thinking to be done about the boy or man or whatever he was who was behind this door.

Miss Gengarelly, the girl who worked in Special Projects, would not mind the boy using her apartment . . . hopefully. She was a genial young thing, and it was anyone's guess why the Russians had troubled to place one of their omnipresent "bugs" in her room since she was not privy to any secret material.

Just perhaps, the bug might prove a friend in disguise to the United States of America and incidentally to Dudley Winslow, that country's most obedient servant. If the boy was a Russian plant and attempted to communicate through the bug with his masters, then Winslow had already displayed the foresight to have the bug bugged. Whatever conversations or signals passed to and fro would be recorded upstairs on the ninth floor, where only the authorized counterintelligence spooks were allowed. It might even be amusing to confront Gologorsky someday with irrefutable proof the Soviets were amateurs when it came to the likes of Dudley Winslow.

On the other hand, if young Piper had been planted by the CIA, then thanks to Winslow, who had been on his toes as usual, the mere fact he had so generously provided for the boy and obviously had nothing whatsoever to hide offered proof that Dudley Winslow was indeed a very straight arrow.

Winslow tapped three times on the door, gently, in the manner of a long-trained and thoughtful host who regrets disturbing a guest. When the door flew open and Michael stood smiling, he was momentarily taken aback.

"Well, well," Winslow managed. "Well . . . well."

"Good morning, sir."

"Yes. Of course. It's snowing a bit."

"Makes me homesick for Minnesota."

Clever boy, Winslow thought. Establishing the authenticity of his residence again. "Would you care for some breakfast?"

"I'm starved. Yes, please."

"We'll just slip down to the snack bar then. It's not much in the way of food, but not poisonous either." Winslow was pleased with his description—a touch of the practical along with a touch of humor. Not something to create outright laughter of course, but then that was not the drill.

As they walked down the hall to the elevator, Winslow said, "My wife is still sleeping. . . . Jet lag really does her in. Otherwise we would have been pleased to give you breakfast in our apartment."

"I don't want to be any trouble except for seeing the Supreme Soviet. I hope you can arrange it this morning."

Cheeky boy, Winslow decided. Of course all he had to do was pick up the phone and Brezhnev would grant the lad an immediate audience. Ho-ho, no trouble at all. On the other hand, supposing he did call Gologorsky, and after his usual jinking left, right, and backward he might say that one of the hierarchy *would* see the boy? Wouldn't that be proof there was a great deal more here than anyone would suspect?

The snack bar was overhot and steamy. As he watched Mike attack a mountain of toast, Winslow caught himself just before suggesting that perhaps later in the day Mike might like to join Heather and Geoffrey, who had said something about going ice-skating. Did you invite a spy, never mind for whom, to play with your children?

"Do you like ice-skating, Mike?"

"My girl friend, Susie, is in the expert class. When she fell down, I knew my spinning-top theory had become real life."

"I fear I don't quite understand."

"Well, Mr. Winslow, I guess I have to tell you sooner or later, especially since you've got to help me get inside the Kremlin and talk to the big shots." Mike lowered his head for a moment, took a deep breath, and raised his eyes to meet Winslow's heavy horned-rimmed glasses. "Well . . . I have to tell you, sir, that I'm not quite what I seem to be."

"Ah?" Making his familiar gargling sound, Winslow found his coffee suddenly tasted like Lavoris.

"My parents are not going to meet me in Moscow. If they knew where I was they might even believe some of the things Dr. Patcheck said about me."

"Would they now?" Winslow closed his eyes momentarily. This was *indeed* a test, an ax revealed without warning, and he would be judged on his ability to get out from under it without losing his head. "And who might Dr. Patcheck be?"

"My psychiatrist."

"Ah?" The thing to do, Winslow warned himself, was

to play along with this little ceremony and see where it ended. "And where," he asked with elaborate casualness, "might your parents be?"

"In St. Paul. Worrying about me, I guess. . . ."

Winslow marveled at the boy's easy smile as he added, "Sometimes they call me Brain Two thousand, but I don't like it much."

Winslow reminded himself consistency was the foundation of all spy covers. He had not read John le Carré for nothing.

"May I ask again what on earth you are doing in Moscow?"

"That's exactly it, Mr. Winslow. I am here because of Earth."

Winslow took out a clean white handkerchief and blotted delicately at his brow. Good heavens, why did they keep it so damnably hot in here? Or was this flushing of the face due to the new and quite uncomfortable realization that this fresh-faced American youth might reveal himself as a terrorist?

Winslow noticed a Marine having breakfast at a table in the corner and was pleasantly reassured. After all, this was sacred ground, a little piece of American real estate, where bombs and that sort of thing would be unthinkable.

Thinking unthinkables, Winslow only half listened while his breakfast guest gave him a simple outline of his spinning-top theory and the approaching point of no return for Earth as indicated by his calculations. "The only thing is, Mr. Winslow, I have told you only half the story. You now know what is going to happen, just like the President and very few other people know. But no one knows how to fix it . . . except me."

"And that's all in your head?" My God, Winslow thought. I'm asking him a question as if I really believed him! On the other hand, that's very good, because I'm "playing along," as the saying goes.

"No. I couldn't possibly carry it all in my head. But my figures are in this briefcase, and that's the part I did not turn over to the President. If the wrong people got hold of this information, they could use it to blackmail the entire world. If you were some sort of rebel leader or a terrorist who wanted his pals out of jail, you could say to everyone, 'If you want to keep on living, do exactly as I say.' Just imagine yourself in that position, Mr. Winslow."

"I'm trying."

"There are a lot of people in this world who wouldn't mind if Earth did leave orbit. They want to change things so badly they just don't care how it comes about. That's why I have to be so careful." Winslow was horrified to see Mike caress his briefcase. Did it contain one of those paperlike bombs?

"I guess you could say I have created sort of a . . . What's his name?"

"Frankenstein's monster?"

"Yeah. That's it. Do you think I could borrow one of those briefcases like you people carry when you're transporting secret papers? You know, with a chain and padlock that goes around your wrist. I'd sure feel better."

"I'll see what I can do. Perhaps the courier people will have a spare."

Thoughts ambled through Winslow's mind at a higher speed than their usual tortoise pace. Obviously the boy must be humored, but how far dared he go without informing the Ambassador? If he sought assistance, or even advice, then would that action not count against him in the self-reliance category? The Ambassador might say, "Look here, Dudley, how could you be so unaware that an ingratiating presence is the mark of a true professional?

You should have realized your young man might easily have held you and your entire family as hostage."

Suddenly Winslow's speculations took a new and terrifying turn. Could this young man really be a tall, gangling young girl? These days . . . ah, these days anything could be.

THE TENTH DAY

Two Grumann Gulfstream jets were employed to bring the mighty together on North Haven Island, off the coast of Maine. Despite the low fog which persisted at Rockport the aircraft landed within a few hours and their very important passengers were transported by fast private launch to the island itself.

Millbank owned the house, and used it as a convenient retreat from the noise and pressures of Manhattan. It was a large property yet managed to be very New England, complete with slanting floors and walls out of plumb. Millbank was the first to arrive. Soon afterward came F. Leslie Nash and Lee Brubaker from California, and then Cyril Henshaw from Dubai, Peter Leonidopolis from Athens, and Prince Abu Amryni from Abadan. Jack Eldred eschewed the offer of a third Gulfstream to pick him up in Houston. He preferred flying in his own Lear jet, which flew higher and was more sportive, thereby proving Eldred was a true Texan who believed that he who polishes his own flashiness is seen farthest.

All of this assembly gathered at the urgent behest of F. Leslie Nash, who had framed his mandate succinctly: "How would you like to be out of business in ten days?" From the tone of his voice, even when relayed by satellite, his not so merry band knew he was not mouthing trivialities.

They gathered first in the living room and automatically, as if driven by tribal rite, seated themselves according to their invisible but known rank. Nash occupied the most antique rocking chair (sat in by Benjamin Franklin, according to Jerry Millbank) and Prince Abu Amryni, who represented most of the Arab producers, seated himself in a chintz-covered armchair near the roaring fire. He had brought his own manservant, who plied his master at regular intervals with cups of steaming tea. The others were obliged to make do with the services of Millbank's prized butler, who had lost a part of his tongue in a long-ago accident and was therefore incapable of repeating anything he heard, and Hulda, the household manager. Since her older sister had been the notorious "Beast of Belsen," Hulda knew the value of a closed mouth.

Millbank, still resentful at being hauled off his yacht just when he was beginning to enjoy the Scottish winter, made his welcoming speech. "You're damn lucky it's not solid ice from here to the mainland." Nodding at the gray twilight beyond the mullioned windows, he grunted, "Nobody in his right mind comes here in the winter, so we don't have to worry about security. The only place that's more isolated is the moon."

"Good," F. Leslie conceded. "I hate to think what sort of rumors would be created if some knowledgeable reporter even suspected we were all in the same place. It is of the utmost importance that we conclude our business tonight and disperse in the morning. Whatever our decisions, we must appear to act quite independently and not be accused of collusion." He favored Prince Abu with a faint smile. "Perhaps you have heard of an old saying in English? 'Birds of a feather flock together'?"

Abu returned a half smile, adding one millimeter more to his lip span. "In Arabic we say, 'What one buzzard does not know, the other will.'"

A polite chuckle mixed with the crackling of the fire and dribbled around the room.

Nash nodded his head at Leo Marcusi, who, in keeping with his status, was squatting on a colonial footstool which he had placed next to a spinning wheel. He was too near the fireplace and already thought of himself as a spitted turkey in need of basting, but if one side of his body would be too hot while the other would be too cold, then such minor discomforts had been the burden of courtiers since ancient times. Considering what he had to offer the aristocracy now waiting upon him, he also knew that ancient custom would have caused his head to be removed for bringing such bad tidings, unless he could offer a sweet banana by way of atonement. Well, he had the fruit, and he would withhold it until he was asked to mount the gallows. He took momentary comfort in observing that the Englishman, Cyril Henshaw, was seated on a stiff-backed armless chair so far from the fire that he must be cold all over.

"Leo, would you be good enough to commence?" Nash asked without so much as a glance in his direction. He was studying the low-beamed ceiling as if seeking some wisdom there. "I assume all of you have read the memorandum I prepared for you to digest en route here. Haste made it necessary to skip the usual niceties, and coding sometimes transforms good English into clumsy phrases, but you should have the general gist of the matter. In a word, we are in a hell of a bind."

There was a general mumbling of agreement while Leo Marcusi opened his dispatch case with a loud snap and placed a sheaf of papers on his knee. "Gentlemen," he began, "while I personally believe this information is entirely genuine, may I suggest you remember that paying for information sometimes results in the listener being told what he wants to hear—"

"The wish is father to the thought," Nash cut in quickly.

"Exactly," Leo Marcusi said with a slight bow of his head. "I am extremely reluctant to reveal the sources of my information except by position identities. Names are not recorded in my files. If you so insist, they are in my head, which, as Samson might have said to Delilah, is always at your disposal."

A few rumbles of approval fluttered around the room, but soon subsided. Everyone present knew how many billions in world currency were involved, and in such a shadow too much levity was in bad taste.

"First, here is Colonel Blank, who told me in strictest confidence that the current meeting at Camp David, which includes the President and his highest advisers, has nothing to do with any warlike gesture, plans, or threats by any nation whatsoever. Colonel Blank is in the Pentagon and is one of the several aides to Joint Chiefs of Staff. I am not at all sure the Colonel's so-called confidential opinion was not a deliberate leak."

Marcusi slipped the top paper to the bottom of his pile and read from another. "Next we have Miss Blank Blank, a relief operator at the White House switchboard. She is now a middle-aged lady. In our younger days we crushed a lot of the grape together and a few other things. Fortunately for this research, our now quite platonic friendship has endured. She told me that the day before yesterday, which would be the eighth of February, an estimated forty calls originated in the Oval Office, all to geologists and geophysicists. Other calls were made to the University of Edinburgh and the Sorbonne. Since Miss Blank speaks fluent French, she listened in on the Paris call and heard a presidential request for assistance in contacting some authority in Libya who would not be overly resentful of a tremendous American effort to do something to save the world. Miss Blank did not understand what the tremendous something would be or even why, but she did recall it required the cooperation of those who controlled the Libyan oil fields. Our conversation took place in her Washington apartment at ten-thirty A.M. yesterday."

"My brothers in Libya," Prince Abu intoned, "are lost. They will only do what the Russians tell them to do."

"Precisely, Your Highness." After allowing a moment of silence to grace the Prince's profundity Marcusi resumed. "Last night at a place called Bimbos, eleven to eleven-thirty Washington time, I met with Chief Petty Officer Blank Blank, who works in the coding room at Naval Operations. He was loose of lip when I first sat down with him, and much more so after a second bottle of champagne and the dancer of his choice was guaranteed to be his for the balance of the evening at no expense to himself. He told me, in strictest confidence of course, that a signal he had sent yesterday afternoon at approximately two P.M. Washington time went to the Commander of our Sixth Fleet, ordering same to proceed immediately to the Persian Gulf, occupying the major ports with such vessels as necessary, closing them to all tanker traffic, and to hold his combined forces in further readiness for occupation of *all* Middle East oil fields."

"My God, what will the Russians think?" Brubaker groaned. "Much more important, what will they do?"

"Ordinarily that might be easily predictable," Marcusi said evenly, "but when I challenged my friend Hymie Markel, the White House Special Projects officer, he said the President was preparing a special statement to be transmitted to the Russians before the Sixth Fleet weighed anchor. There would be no problem, he said, since the Russians were reasonable when approached in a reasonable fashion. In this case Russian troops were to be invited to guard all our intercontinental missile sites while theirs could be armed, aimed, and held at our temples until the crisis was solved. When I refused to identify the source of my information, Markel said he would have me arrested and shot as a traitor and a spy. I suggested he would need a double-barreled shotgun, one for each count, and left town."

"Do you think you are being followed?" Nash asked with a new trace of anxiety in his voice.

"Probably. But for many years I have employed a double, a very good little theater actor who unfortunately for him bears a remarkable resemblance to me. He is a taxidermist by profession, a business that is very much in decline, and I have used him several times in the past to make appearances at official functions I knew would be boring. This time I paid my man handsomely and sent him off to the Bahamas with a blonde. Meanwhile I slipped out the back fire escape to my office and took a devious route here. My image has enough pocket money to maintain both himself and the blonde for as long as will be necessary— which might be a very short time for all of us if what the kid says is on target."

Nash allowed his lips to part two centimeters while he asked evenly, "And where is the kid?"

Marcusi took his time. To all who serve, he thought, there comes their day, and this is mine. The banana, the great big gorgeous banana, was protruding from the basket and only Leo Marcusi knew how to bring it forth for the delight of the court. Let those who were inclined to judge him untrustworthy or even inept now stand aside and marvel.

"It pays, gentlemen, for one to know one's way around Washington. One of the last chores I did before Hymie Markel threatened to have me executed was to drop by the State Department. As we all know, China is sitting on a seventy-billion-barrel reserve while producing a mere two million barrels. George Trinton of the Getty company believes he can remedy the situation if he goes there, has a look around, and makes a few friends. The trouble is he wants to take his whole family and there was a hang-up somewhere between the Chinese and our State Department at issuing so many visas, so he asked me—"

"I do not see what this has to do with the whereabouts of the kid," Nash said crisply.

Marcusi recognized the high percentage of acid in his boss's voice and hoped Nash would develop an ulcer before he gave him so much as a nibble of his banana.

"I am coming to that, sir. While expediting the journey for Trinton's family, I chanced upon my old friend Weed— Thomas-the-Weed, as we used to call him at Harvard. Weed, so called because of his overall resemblance to a stalk of marsh grass, works in the Operations room, which receives intelligence in various forms from our embassies and consulates throughout the world. He asked me to go have a cup of coffee with him, which I was reluctant to do since I knew Hymie Markel might have me picked up as a spite thing and I was short of time. Guess what I found out."

"Hurry up, Leo," Millbank growled. "We are also getting short on time and I'd like to start some serious drinking."

Marcusi volleyed a smile at his interrupter. No matter how rich and powerful they might be, he could at last face them down. "The kid," he said so softly they must strain to hear, "is in Moscow."

Only the crackling fire broke the long silence until Jack Eldred said, "Well, I'll be goddamned."

"How do you know?" Nash asked thoughtfully.

"Thomas-the-Weed was in my class at Harvard. We both knew a Dudley Winslow, who, it seems, was instrumental in helping Tom get his job in the State Department. Yesterday Winslow sent a Telex to Tom asking him to conduct a personal check on a sixteen-year-old named Michael Piper, who was presently in his care at the embassy. He indicated the kid might be deranged and he didn't know what to do about him. On the other hand, he thought our CIA might be involved and he wanted to steer clear of the whole thing. He also asked the Weed to explore any hope there might be of his being considered for a more important post."

Prince Abu spoke sonorously. "What position does Mr. Winslow hold at your Moscow embassy?"

"He is the Deputy Administrator—a minor functionary."

"Why should he be involved with the boy?"

"That I don't know. Nor did Thomas-the-Weed. The point is we now know more than the President of the United States and all the various agencies he has looking for the kid."

Nash said there were several things he did not understand at all. Did the Russians know they had a prize so handy? Why had the boy gone to Moscow? Who paid his fare to Moscow since the Piper family could hardly be labeled as affluent? "There is a fly in this soup somewhere," Nash said, twitching his nose like a bloodhound. "What I want to know is: Is the kid a decoy of some kind, and if so, for what? It is inconceivable that a mere teen-ager could have created such a fuss all on his own."

Nash's questions and comments triggered a general discussion. It continued throughout the dinner, which opened with Burgundian snails sautéed in llama butter and concluded with iced pineapple à la Chantilly.

With the port, which Millbank identified as being drawn from a barrel which had served aboard the *Victory* at Trafalgar and had possibly been the very same container in which the heroic Nelson's corpse was shipped home, the discussion took a more organized turn. Obviously young Piper could no longer be allowed to run around loose while expounding his ridiculous spinning-top theory and, worse, being believed. With the kind of people in Washington these days one never knew what to expect. Why, Jesus Christ Almighty, if those ignoramuses shut down one ordinary-sized oil field for twenty-four hours just because of some youthful ecological freak, the cost to the U.S.A. would be on the order of a hundred million—not to mention a nose dive of the stock in whatever petroleum company was involved. And how about the world? Supposing this thing spread like a disease. A return to the Stone Age—no company could call its soul its own.

The obvious solution was to stop the boy before further damage could be done. Henshaw, who had spent some hairy years with England's famous M-5 espionage outfit and hence was quite familiar with derring-do assignments, was appointed chief of what they chose to call "Operation Zap."

Millbank said, "In spite of the fact they are a bunch of goddamned Communists, the Russians may still be classified as human beings. Therefore they are susceptible to money. I should imagine several million Swiss francs deposited with the Banc du Suisse in some official's name would stimulate that person to cooperate with us. We want the boy delivered, preferably intact."

"Where do we want him delivered?" Brubaker wanted to know. "It would be damned difficult stashing him in the United States with every agent in the government on the lookout for him. If he should be found, we would be open to some nasty charges. I gather the boy himself would not be susceptible to monetary reward, so transporting him against his will could mean, in this country at least, kidnapping."

Prince Abu, who in deference to his religion was drinking Perrier water instead of the priceless port, agreed. "Yes, what will we do with the boy after we have him? Mr. Marcusi has suggested he is a masculine Joan of Arc, but I hardly think we can burn him at the stake."

Peter Leonidopolis, who had offered virtually nothing since his arrival except laments for his tanker fleet, which would soon be at the mercy of the American Navy, said, "How can I survive such unfair restrictions?" He moaned repeatedly.

Chiding him, Brubaker said, "Aw, come on now, Peter. Just as scrap your ships are worth about twenty million. I have trouble visualizing you on welfare."

Yet it was Leonidopolis who brought some measure of honesty to the discussion. Licking the delicious savory from the tips of his manicured fingers, he said, "To me it is very simple. The boy has already won the first battle. If we kill him now we will make him a martyr, and that would be very dangerous for us since people will believe anything martyrs say, whether true or untrue. Therefore the boy must have an accident which seems of his own making. Can you arrange that, Mr. Henshaw?"

"Yes . . . reluctantly."

"I don't like to discuss such possibilities," Millbank said testily. "Why not hide him on my boat in Scotland? In the wintertime the area is almost deserted. I'll have the boat riding at anchor, put heavy guard aboard, and give the kid a mechano set to pass the time. In another six months this whole flap will blow over."

Leo Marcusi, who had just lit one of his host's Havanas and was having some trouble getting his lips around its batlike circumference, ventured, "Let us not forget that according to the boy, in six months we will all go phhtttttttttt!"

The shocked silence which greeted a remark he had thought might lighten the brooding atmosphere convinced him he had taken far too much pleasure in the port.

"You don't really believe he knows what he's raving about," said F. Leslie Nash. "Here we are, only trying to make an honest dollar, and this child is out to change the nature of the world. I believe our approach should be direct and, alas, quite merciless. This is a time for brass knuckles, not kid gloves."

He cleared his throat ominously to assure himself of attention. "We are aware of a series of facts which are still unknown to the world's leaders, including our President. Not for ourselves, you understand, but for the salvation of good order and continuing progress in the world it becomes our duty to suppress *all* revolutionaries who would seriously damage international economies. Doesn't it strike you as quite remarkable that a high school boy has caused

234

all this commotion by himself? Time may reveal he has been chosen simply as a symbol of innocence—a young Mr. Clean protesting against the depredations of the evil oil moguls. It seems to me that we have all read this scenario before. While I cannot now suggest exactly *who* may be behind the boy, it is certainly logical to assume there is some powerful organization . . ."

"Are you suggesting the Sierra Club?" Millbank inquired. During his labial pronouncement of the word *Sierra* bits of rare Stilton port spewed from his chops.

"No. Whoever it is must be more resourceful and certainly less vulnerable to our own campaigns. I want it thoroughly understood that I abhor violence, but it may prove we have little choice. We must remove the boy to a place under our control." Nash hesitated, pawed through the vast accumulation of clichés in his brain, and found the exact word he wanted. "He should be *sequestered*. Out of sight, out of mind."

"Precisely," Leo Marcusi echoed, and soon all were in agreement that Henshaw should proceed to his business with vigor. Meanwhile Millbank would return to his yacht, now lying at Inverness, and make such security preparations as he thought necessary.

"As for the rest of us," Nash recommended, "until we hear the boy is sequestered we will simply play things by ear."

* * *

Nicolai Gologorsky's office faced upon the inner courtyard of the Kremlin and the bell tower of Ivan the Great. After he had replaced his desk telephone in its receptacle, Gologorsky lit his third cigarette of the day and inhaled deeply. Ordinarily he would have consumed at least thirty cigarettes by this hour, but he was trying to quit smoking.

He took what satisfaction he could from an obvious improvement in his cough rate and the absence of yellow stain from his fingers. Now he allowed himself only ten cigarettes a day, a quota designed to meet the number of crises and puzzlements he estimated would face him.

The telephone had offered a curious riddle, one which, in his opinion, coincided all too conveniently with the KGB report laid upon his desk by his secretary, Yelena Kondratieva, less than an hour ago. Fortunately, it had been a dull morning and he had read the report only for lack of anything better to do. (In Gologorsky's most secret opinion the KGB was a hangover from the old Stalinist days: bureaucratic fools who adored the scent of paper and contributed absolutely nothing to the true Soviet needs.) Still, it was wise at least to appear to take them seriously, lest they become resentful. Born troublemakers, Gologorsky thought, people to be observed like drowsy snakes, but not roused lest they uncoil and bite.

His morning KGB report contained one item which he now reviewed with more interest. A young American male was presently housed in the American Embassy, having arrived the day before yesterday. At first it was assumed he was part of diplomat Winslow's family (nephew, perhaps?); now it seemed there was no blood relation. The KGB listed optional opinion: "1. Since the young male was obviously too young for any normal diplomatic duties and apparently was not a tourist, he could be an expert of some sort imported to solve various technical problems within the embassy. Possibly an electronics expert? Cryptogram and decoding expert? Photographic? A computer repair expert? 2. The maid, agent Tatiana Morodova, who cleaned the room he presently occupied (Miss Gengarelly's), found several papers covered with numerical calculations. Same were copied and attached herewith for inspection. The figures gave no indication of financial, chemical, or computer usefulness. 3. No record of young male same description passing through either customs or immigration at same time diplomat Winslow. (Note: Winslow known to be slow-thinking and quite stupid. But is that reputation simply a cover for a very clever American spy? Suggest subtle challenge to American Ambassador at next meeting.) Custom and immigration forms still being searched. 4. Is Winslow a homosexual? Did he import the boy for his own pleasures? If so, there are several attractive opportunities to exploit the situation to Soviet benefit. 5. Are Americans naïve enough to think we will accept young male at face value? Either he is a spy or an expert. Ergo, a constant watch is being kept on him and any deviation from the norm will be reported immediately."

Gologorsky folded the plastic cover over the report and, turning to the window, watched the snowflakes descending past the five-domed Archangel Cathedral. Something smelled overly ripe here. Why should that stuffed capitalistic shirt telephone him so airily and, as if it were something arranged for every passing tourist, request an appointment with one of the Presidium or even Leonid Brezhnev himself? Quickly. This afternoon if at all possible. And who did he want the appointment for? His own President? One of the more powerful senators? Jane Fonda? No, the young male whose presence had been brought to his attention less than an hour ago. Who was playing games here?

Gologorsky bared his teeth, then inserted his cigarette between them and maneuvered it slowly up and down. Who, indeed?

He turned back to the window and regarded the large lithograph of Karl Marx which adorned the opposite wall. Suddenly Gologorsky felt sorry for himself because he was certain he could see into the future and he dreaded it. Because of that damned smug-looking German there was communism, which had not worked out the way Marx or anyone else had planned. Now, two generations later, Nicolai Gologorsky, formerly of Tashkent and lately a mover in the highest Soviet circles, wearer of the Order of Lenin, not to mention the Red Star, was about to be tested again. The boy in the American Embassy was most certainly a KGB plant—else how could he have entered Russia in the first place?

And why was he here? How was it Nicolai Gologorsky had been the first advised of his presence? Testing, testing . . . someone was testing him for a higher post? Perhaps even a ministry or the Supreme Soviet? Or a long spell in Siberia if he mishandled the situation?

Very well. As everyone in the Kremlin knew, the only reason the world was not Russia's slave was the overall inertia of the Russians themselves. Through wars and revolutions they had learned to endure perpetual hardship and accept the delays of bureaucracies without complaint. It was the Russian way. There was no boldness of decision because everyone feared the consequences if a mistake was made. Therefore the safest routing for any enterprise was to make no decision at all. File and forget. But now, not Nicolai Gologorsky. Let the KGB bastards of the First, Second, and Third divisions twist and squirm in their haunt on Dzerzhinsky Square as they witnessed true boldness. They would observe a man unafraid of decisions, a man to whom Mother Russia was the reason for existing, a man without thought of his personal career.

Gologorsky strode to the telephone and picked it up gingerly. He asked to be put through at once to Dudley Winslow at the American Embassy, and while he waited he smiled happily and blew smoke rings at the distant snowflakes.

"Winslow old boy," he began in his flawless English, "I'm right back to you. In view of our long and fruitful relationship I have set aside other matters and will see your young friend at eleven this morning. Could you give me some hint as to the nature of his business . . . that is, in case I need advisers present?"

He listened to Winslow's carelessly intoned words and marveled at his ability to say so much without saying anything at all. Could Winslow himself be KGB? No, that was ridiculous . . . but then wasn't the whole thing typical of the Americans? They were born to intrigue and never to be trusted. "I'll send a car. Would you like to come with him?"

When Winslow declined, Gologorsky knew he had acted wisely. The American had deliberately avoided a direct answer, saying he did not *think* he could make it. Of course not. He was too stupid to recognize the fine hand of the KGB, or even his own CIA.

Winslow had not been in Moscow a week before Gologorsky knew more about his quite undistinguished career than he knew himself. "He belongs in one of our bureaucracies." Gologorsky smiled wryly. "He is not bold."

Gologorsky stopped smiling when Yelena Kondratieva entered without knocking. He saw she was nearly breathless, and he took ten seconds of his precious time to admire the rise and fall of her alluring breasts.

"Commissar Gologorsky!" she said in awe. "I bring incredible news!"

"Nothing is incredible, Comrade Kondratieva," he responded in his best paternal style, "only improbable." This sort of wisdom had won him many a romp with the opposite sex, and Kondratieva, who he knew very well had been placed in his office by the KGB, was next on his list of conquests. Once they had been tamed beneath his powerful torso, the devotion of women comrades was, he had found, more reliable.

"You look troubled, *ma chiska*," he said, reaching out to give her ear the most delicate of tweaks. "We have enough melancholy Russians without you."

"Lenin has rolled over in his tomb! He is lying on his stomach!"

Gologorsky took three long and fast strides to the window. By pressing his face hard against the glass he could look down and along the wall of the Kremlin toward Red Square. While he could not quite see the Lenin mausoleum itself, he observed that a great crowd had gathered in the vicinity.

"Comrade Kondratieva, are you *sure?*" he asked, and heard a new anxiety in his voice.

"Yes. I was taught he would be there until the end of the world." She began to sob, and as if to comfort her Gologorsky took her in his arms.

"Perhaps it is coming," he said huskily. "All the more reason to enjoy ourselves while we can."

* * *

Michael Piper found he was sick of lies. They breed like rabbits, he thought. You tell one and you have to tell another to cover that one, and pretty soon you compound those two and have four, and there you are.

He paced Miss Gengarelly's room, pausing occasionally to do knee bends and an occasional series of push-ups—anything to pass time while he was waiting for Mr. Winslow and to distract his thoughts from St. Paul, Minnesota, where he was willing to bet fifty million bucks it was also snowing. But the drifts could be five hundred feet deep and still not bury a guy's guilty feelings, he decided. Too many times now he had pictured what must have happened when his mother read the note he had left for Miss Kellogg. She must have cried, and it was not very nice to visualize your mother crying. And Dad would frown and his jaw would work like it always did when he was mad, and he would not understand at all. For that matter, who would? Even Miss Kellogg might not speak to him again. She would say he had been thoughtless and should have told everyone what he was doing. But how could he have told about it and still do it? Just imagine saying, "Hey, Dad, the President wouldn't listen to me so I'm going over and talk to the Russians." Just imagine. Would he say, "Well, son, now that's the neatest idea I ever heard in the whole world, and here is your air ticket; drop us a line when you have a chance"? Oh sure!

Well, anyway, he had written three cards, although probably they would not reach St. Paul until sometime next week.

Dear Mom and Dad—
    I am fine, and do not worry. Home soon. Please feed my goldfish.

Love,
Mike

PS Say hello to Sandy. Tell her she can use my hi-fi until I get back, but only if she uses her own records.

Dear Susie—
    I am here in Moscow on business. It is an interesting city, but I have not seen too much of it yet. I hope all is well with you and you are not

falling down again. Remember what I told you about spinning tops? I have so much to tell you I could spend the rest of my life doing it.

Love,
Mike

PS And maybe I will.

Dear Miss Kellogg—

I don't have your exact address, so I am mailing this to the school. I was very sorry to leave you so quick, but time was short. Anyway, my geography is improving. It is snowing here, and I guess it makes me sort of homesick. Never mind. I hope to see you soon and promise to make up any English I miss. First I have to do this thing. Sorry no more space on this card. Only can say you are neat.

Your Friend,
Mike

That sort of took care of St. Paul, all right, but the local scene was getting heavier by the minute. The Winslows were nice people, and going to their apartment for dinner last night had been very much okay until Heather and Geoffrey started asking about where are your parents and weren't they supposed to arrive by now? That took more lies.

Funny thing how Mr. Winslow and his wife didn't ask any questions. None at all. They just talked about the weather and stuff, and about the last time they were in London, and they didn't seem to think it was unusual that here was Mike Piper sitting right at their table in Moscow. They didn't ask any questions at all. Not one. And only an

242

hour ago Mr. Winslow had come by to say everything was
fixed with the Russians and to be ready at eleven o'clock.
It seemed too easy, but then Mr. Winslow must be very
important.

Okay, Mike. You are ready. The figures are all in the
briefcase and reworked for the last time. Just be sure you
hold back on the solution until you know they understand
we are all on the same planet.

* * *

The commotion in Moscow's Red Square was soon
brought under control, and several Heroes of the U.S.S.R.
were summoned to put Lenin's body back in its proper position. Twenty-seven bureaus managed to involve themselves in this solemn business, but members of the Academy of Sciences were not invited. This was a mistake,
because the scientists took on a pique which lasted for
days and were unavailable when they should have been at
the ready.

Thanks to Soviet censorship of the event, the half revolution made by Lenin's body remained unknown to the
rest of the world and no one troubled to calculate the centrifugal forces which had activated the corpse of a man
who had been inert for so long. Hence what happened in
Belgravia, Texas, U.S.A., drew almost as much attention.
There a high school freshman heaved a twelve-pound shot
one hundred and eleven yards, three inches. The freshman
was a puny boy weighing only eighty pounds stark-naked.
When he tried to repeat his feat, the best he could do was
five yards. The local paper was informed of the incident,
but applied a peculiarly American form of censorship and
refused to print the story, much less put it on the press
wire. The editor knew a Texas joke when he heard one.

Almost simultaneously with these peculiar events scientists at the Lawrence Berkeley Laboratories were troubled by new data which had been accumulated by NASA's flying Lockheed U-2. From previous information they had determined the earth was transiting through the universe on a heading which would take it farther from the constellation of Aquarius and toward Leo. The speed was calculated as being on the order of a million miles per hour. Now they discovered the apparent speed had increased to approximately 1.2 million miles per hour. Two astrophysicists who had been summoned to join the President of the United States at Camp David now warned him outright that if the acceleration persisted a snowballing effect was inevitable. Earth's envelope would start collecting a lot of spacial debris which would accumulate until somewhere in the atmosphere an imbalance would be created. This would aggravate the present acceptable wobble and eventually lead to a departure from orbit.

"That corresponds with what the kid told me," the President said as a uniformed aide handed him a note from the Secretary of State. The note explained that the Secretary was delayed in Washington by a delegation of Letts. They said their traditional reindeer hunt was ruined because the animals were all running north and south instead of west to east and it was all America's fault. They would forget their reindeer hunt and go home content if the U.S. would float a loan on the order of one million dollars—very small change compared to what the U.S. had granted the seventy environmentalists who were making a study of reindeer movements in Lapland and their effect upon the tundra.

Yet reindeer and Letts held the President's attention for only a moment. He had some very sticky questions to ask those dignitaries who were assembled around him. And his questions were woefully monotonous. To General Shellcase, Chairman of the Joint Chiefs of Staff, he said, "Now that you've had time to make a proper search, why can't you produce the boy?"

"Mr. President, I regret to inform you that so far—"

The General was not permitted to finish his regrets. Knowing his answer from the distress in the General's red, white, and blue eyes, the President turned to the Director of the CIA.

"And you, Kermit. Surely you must have at least a lead on the boy?"

"I regret—"

When the same prelude was repeated by the Director of the FBI, the President wondered aloud what the world was coming to and immediately corrected himself by stating he knew very well what the world was coming to unless someone in his administration found the boy. He was still berating his advisers when the Secretary of State arrived by helicopter and joined the group, who sought what comfort they could find before the roaring fire. Mincing ever so slightly in his moment of triumph, he announced, "We have found the boy and have him in custody."

The President was so exuberant he seized his Secretary of State by his rather prominent ears, shook his head until his hair flew, then hugged him passionately. "God bless you, Marvin Kaplan," he shouted. "Why didn't you bring him with you?"

Secretary Kaplan clasped his hands before him, bowed his head to emphasize his humble role in such a momentous discovery, and said it was really nothing. Skipping lightly over the facts, he explained how he had inspired a member of his brilliant staff, one Thomas Weed, to employ the inadequate facilities of State, and by applying logic to an obtuse situation he had come up with the obvious answer. The boy must be in Moscow. (There was no point, Kaplan mused, in detailing why Thomas-the-Weed was so fucking stupid and unaware that he had kept his knowledge of the boy's whereabouts to himself for the last two days. Nor was there cause at this great moment to contemplate the farthest limbo to which Weed and his colleague Winslow would soon be assigned.)

The President managed to decode the Secretary's statement and, harking back to his days as an insurance salesman, exclaimed, "Hooray for our side! By God, I knew *someone* in this administration would save the day." Turning to General Shellcase, he said, "Get out your fastest flying machine. Send it to pick up the boy and bring him here immediately. There is no time to waste. I want the boy here within twelve hours."

"But, Mr. President, since our recent concession to the Russians that they are only defending their frontiers they have become almost belligerent. It takes three days for them to even look at our request to land a military aircraft anywhere in Europe. It takes five to ten days for a permit to go higher than two thousand feet. They have very itchy fingers, and you certainly don't want the boy shot down."

"Are you afraid of the Russians?"

"Yessir."

"Good point. So am I. But I've been looking for a reason to try that red telephone ever since I've been in office. Maybe I should call Brezhnev."

"I wouldn't, sir. If the Russians get the idea we want the boy badly enough to send an aircraft just for him, then they'll get more suspicious than they already are and not let him out of the country."

The President fixed his attention on his Secretary of State.

"Marvin, suppose I tell the Russians what is really happening. Suppose I explain we have eleven days left before it's too late to stop this whole thing. What would they do?"

"Stall. They would wait for you to play the rest of the American trick."

"We have to know what the boy knows. Maybe this is a CIA job."

The President took a fistful of after-dinner mints from a cut-glass dish and tossed them into his mouth one by one. His aim was so accurate mint never touched lip.

During this demonstration of oral and manual dexterity he directed Marvin Kaplan to call Moscow and find out exactly where the boy was at this moment. If possible he should be taken up to the code room in the embassy, where he could send his overall solution to the problem by satellite communication.

In three minutes the Secretary of State had Dudley Winslow on the phone. Announcing himself, he heard nothing but a gargling sound on the other end and inquired if they were still connected. One minute later the Secretary's face turned gray and his head seemed to sink into his shoulders. He turned to the President.

"The boy," he said as if he hated the sound of his own voice, "is in the Kremlin."

* * *

Dr. Pomeroy of the National Science Foundation moved sheepishly through the bookstacks of the Tucson library. When he finally located a copy of the Bible he made certain he was unobserved, then took it down and tiptoed to a dark corner at the end of the stack. There he seated himself on a hard wood chair, and after concealing the Bible within the folds of a much larger volume (Hogarth's *Pen and Ink Illustrations*), he sought through pages he had not examined since boyhood. Somewhere in his youth he knew certain phrases had been recorded on his brain, but his parents had forced his devotion to the Holy Scripture, with the consequence that he became an atheist.

Ever since his arrival in Tucson and his subsequent dialogues with various colleagues at the Kitt Peak National Observatory, their mutual discoveries in the heavens haunted him. Somewhere he knew it was all written down, and he found it annoying that the memory cells in his brain seemed so barren. Now, in the library, when he was almost in slumber over the sonorous phrases of St. Luke, he found what he had been looking for.

> And there shall be signs in the sun, and in
> the moon, and in the stars; and upon the earth
> distress of nations, with perplexity; the
> sea and the waves roaring . . .

Later he turned to II Peter and read:

> But the day of the Lord will come as a thief
> in the night; in which the heavens shall pass
> away with a great noise, and the elements
> shall melt with fervent heat, the earth also
> and the works that are therein shall be
> burned up.

"Holy mackerel!" Dr. Pomeroy whispered in harmony with the tome he held. "Is someone trying to tell us something?"

* * *

At London's Heathrow Aerodrome, in the crowded terminal building, Cyril Henshaw met with Robin Montague of Barclay's Bank. Both men were tall and gaunt. Both wore Aquascutums, bristle mustaches, tobacco-stained teeth, and crush-type tweed hats. Both were thin of lip and straggly of hair, considering their otherwise sartorial perfection. They greeted each other as if it were not two o'clock in the morning.

"Hello, Cyril. Good flight?"

"Decent enough. You look well."

"Surviving."

"How's Daphne?"

"Smashing, as always."

"Give her my fondest."

"Right."

"And Lady Montague?"

"Dreadful, really. Mother is experiencing considerable flatulence."

"Pity."

"But then there is inflation everywhere."

"Ho! Right. Have you got the loot?"

Montague patted the briefcase he held. "Equivalent of two million quid in rubles."

"That should do."

"I should think."

"The passport?"

"Right." Montague handed him a British diplomatic passport. "Bit of a do getting that. The FO made a frightful flap about it. Whimpered yours was not Foreign Office business."

"Fuck the FO."

"Right. All bloody bores."

Montague handed Henshaw the briefcase. "I don't suppose you'd care to count it here . . . with so many clods about."

"No. Barclay's is still Barclay's, I assume."

"Right."

"Cheers, then."

"Right. Cheers. Good flight."

The two men parted, both tall, both Aquascutumed and tweed-hatted; both touched at their mustaches as they became lost in the crowd.

* * *

In St. Paul, Minnesota, Susie York completed the final lacing of her skates and glided toward the center of the Palace Rink for her afternoon practice. She was greeted by the handful of other figure skaters who knew her, and she smiled in return. Now suddenly more than ever she longed for hearing and power of speech, for with Mike still not returned she could communicate only with her parents, who unfortunately were not very adept at signing in Ameslan, or with her teachers in the special school. It was not at all like talking with Mike.

She made three turns of the rink at an easy pace, gliding over the fresh ice, loosening her muscles, concentrating on what she must practice this afternoon, trying to think about something besides Mike. She would work on her double axles, of course, and her final stems because that was the weak part of her routine. And she wanted nothing but perfection because she remembered what Mike had signed to her just before he went away: "No one in this whole world is as beautiful as you are. You are like the moon in a clear sky. Everything else is dimmed."

Well, it was not to worry so much about Mike. He was delayed for reasons he would tell her about. There was nothing Mike could not do except get good marks in Spanish (and English), which was sort of surprising since he got to be so fluent in Ameslan so quickly.

Susie was completing her third circuit and about to pick up speed for a cut to the center and the double loop, which opened her routine, when she passed a familiar face watching from the rail. She cut to a quick stop and returned to Alice Kellogg. She was smiling, and Susie saw her lips form the words "Hello, Susie."

Susie gave her a little salute, placed the palm of her hand over her right breast, then raised two fingers to her eye. "Hello! I'm happy to see you!" She thought it was pretty wonderful and extremely neat that Miss Kellogg would be here right at the rink. Then suddenly she caught her breath. Had she heard something about Mike? Something bad?

Alice Kellogg had taken out a note pad, and as Susie watched she wrote quickly, "Mrs. Piper had a call from Washington. Mike is okay."

Then Susie wrote, "When will he be home?" And Alice wrote, "Don't know. Soon, I hope."

Suddenly they both knew there were no written words to express their feelings. Their eyes met as Susie made two fists and crossed them over her breast as if embracing something very precious. She smiled when she saw Alice Kellogg's lips form the words, "I understand. We both love him."

* * *

Also in St. Paul, Nancy Piper, who had managed to remain dry-eyed throughout a five-day vigil, now had the greatest difficulty in seeing. I must go to an oculist, she thought. No matter what she tried to do, her vision had refused to cooperate ever since that man (what was his name? Markum? Markel?) had called from the White House. He had said Mike was perfectly all right although he was not at liberty to say exactly where he was. He would be home very soon and not to worry about a thing, and the President himself had sent his regrets for any inconvenience Michael's absence may have caused. How about that? The *President* of the United States sending his regrets to the Piper household! At least it was not his condolences.

The trouble was when she tried to telephone Uncle Victor and Aunt Moselle about Mike being all right her eyes filled up with salt water and she simply could not read the numbers on the dial. The same thing happened when she tried to call Ben at the office, so he was almost an hour late getting the news. But he came home early, as he had ever since Mike disappeared, and this time when he came into the house he took one look and said, "Aw, come on now, Nancy, it isn't going to help matters if you get the blubbers."

That remark really turned on the floodgates, and when he reached to take her in his arms the whole dam burst. Then when she told Ben his son was safe—*well* . . . If you ever heard a man sob inside when your head was pressed hard against his chest, you would appreciate how much Ben himself had been holding back.

When told the same news, Miss Smarty-Pants Sandy brought things nearly back to normal. "Aw, I knew he'd come back. I just busted his hi-fi."

* * *

Almost simultaneously Peter Leonidopolis was having a leisurely breakfast at his villa near Vouliagmene. He sat beneath an acacia tree spitting the seeds of a delicious Israeli orange at the pristine beach far below the terrace. He had been fretting about his tankers until he noticed the impressive trajectories he was able to achieve with the seeds. Truly there must be something very special about these Israeli oranges, he decided. For cause and effect he experimented with another, lofting seeds into the sparkling atmosphere until they actually disappeared. "Order a case of those oranges," he commanded his butler. "If they can do that for expectoration, who knows what they will do for my other departments?"

The slight giddiness Leonidopolis experienced during his seed-spitting interval might have given his thoughts a different turn if he knew that in nearby Athens the floor of the Parthenon increased in arc more than five degrees. The majestic monument took on a bosomy look, and for the safety of the fifty American and five thousand West German tourists was closed for the balance of the day.

* * *

While Leonidopolis continued to indulge himself in morning seed-spitting, night had come to St. Paul. Marty Martinson took Alice Kellogg to dinner at Le Bistro. He had been badgering Hymie Markel at the White House for any news of Mike ever since the boy's disappearance and had finally received the same enigmatic report offered the Piper family. Somehow even such a crumb of good news triggered his resolve. He had boarded the next airplane for St. Paul, and four hours later, after the Alsatian maître d' had changed the wine he wanted to a wine he did not want and passed the order to the Croatian waiter, Marty raised his glass to his guest and asked her to marry him. Her direct response endeared her to him more than ever. She asked if they had to finish dinner first.

* * *

In Texas, U.S.A., Jack Eldred was giving a party on the lower twenty thousand acres of his ranch. The guests were a mere fifteen hundred, and to fend off their possible boredom until the barbecuing of fifty steers was completed, Eldred had hired the Goodyear blimp *Columbia* to take selected friends for an aerial tour of his establishment.

All went well until late afternoon, when Captain Nicolari discovered he could not persuade his bulbous airship to return to earth. One of the most experienced lighter-than-airmen in the world, he tried every trick of his trade to bring about a successful return to the mooring mast. Since the cocktail hour had already begun and four really good old boys were aloft without nourishment, Eldred recognized the situation as critical. Summoning the troop of Texas Rangers assigned as security to the party, he ordered them to hand their irons and shoot the blimp down. Twenty minutes later the good old boys rejoined their host in drinking a toast to the great limp sausage, which had slowly descended on Eldred's front lawn. "What the hell," Eldred said expansively. "I'll buy Goodyear a new one in the morning."

Thereafter all joined in a hymn to Texas ingenuity, and they sang with such fervor no one except Captain Nicolari troubled to speculate on why the *Columbia* had behaved so badly.

* * *

In West Los Angeles, Lee Brubaker was playing with his electric train. It was an elaborate system which wound through the wooded acres of the Brubaker estate. Wearing his engineer's cap, it was Brubaker's pleasure to take his grandchildren and their friends for rides over the system, and he was careful to indoctrinate them with the fact that the oil cars bore the replica logo of his family-held company. "B.B. Oil is best in the West," he taught his young guests between whistle hoots.

On this afternoon, when various other peculiar events were happening in Texas, Greece, Scotland, and Russia, the B.B. Railroad suddenly went berserk. Fortunately, no children were present when Brubaker's favorite locomotive, the *Grand Turk*, accelerated very suddenly and, gathering speed in spite of frantic braking, hit an open switch and catapulted its engineer into the swimming pool. There Brubaker eventually surfaced, to find his butler waiting with a telephone. "It's Mr. Leslie Nash, sir. He said it was urgent."

Still gasping for air and bewildered, Brubaker took the telephone. His temper was not improved when the frigid voice of Miss Perkins informed him Mr. Nash was on another line and please hold.

"Lee, how are you?"

"I've just been in a terrible train wreck."

"Are you in the hospital?"

"No. I'm in the swimming pool."

"Then you must be all right."

"I'm very disappointed. Our safety record is ruined. I can't understand—"

"Never mind. Have you heard anything from Henshaw?"

"Yes. He went into Russia early this morning their time."

"Why was I not informed?"

"I don't like to bother you with details."

"For want of a nail a kingdom was lost. Well, here's a detail for you. According to my friend Distancia in St. Paul, who is the only person we know who has actually heard the Piper boy's theories, straight from the horse's mouth, so to speak, closing down Venezuelan production is not part of his program."

"Does the kid own some Venezuelan stock?"

"I gather the latitude and longitude are wrong to help in rebalancing. Do you realize what that might mean?"

"Even richer Venezuelans."

"Through the Department of Energy we're closing in on

a more than billion-dollar contract to increase our strategic petroleum reserve . . . up to ten months' supply in this country alone. Can you imagine what might happen if this juvenile says don't put it there . . . move it over here?"

"You sound like somebody besides a few nuts believes in spinning tops."

"Lee, listen carefully. I've just finished talking with Leo Marcusi, who has it straight from the White House that our dear President *does* believe in the boy, and so do many of his scientific advisers. They are all meeting at this very moment. This is not funny, Lee."

Brubaker climbed out of the pool, dragging the telephone wire behind him, and walked a few paces along the edge. He needed time to think, and the squooshing sound of his water-soaked shoes seemed appropriate to his general perplexity. When he viewed the obviously irreparable wreckage of the *Grand Turk* in the distance, he fought back tears and resolved to give it a formal burial with some appropriate dirge like "I've been working on the railroad . . ."

The voice of F. Leslie Nash hailing from the neglected telephone brought him back to reality. Sighing, he lifted the telephone and said very softly, "Leslie . . . do you suppose the kid knows what he is talking about?"

THE TWELFTH DAY

The limousine bearing Michael Piper in regal splendor passed through the twin traffic lights of the Kremlin's Spassky Gate. Two uniformed soldiers wearing automatic rifles across their backs waved the car through. It proceeded at high speed and without the slightest regard for occasional pedestrians as it passed the Kremlin Theater and then turned right along the Administration Building. Mike barely had time to appreciate the Czar's cannon in front of the Church of the Twelve Apostles before the car swerved left and came to an abrupt stop at the Council of Ministers Building.

Mike decided this was all absolutely neat and he would have liked to continue, but the door was pulled open and a lady who he thought was about Miss Kellogg's age called his name.

"Mr. Piper? Yelena Kondratieva here. Come with me."

There was certainly no welcome in her voice, Mike decided. She seemed to be just a machine announcing words, and as cold as the surrounding atmosphere. Her only protection against the snow was a thin tan shirt with a red star over the pocket.

As he stepped down to the snow Mike found he towered a full head above his escort. He smiled and said, "How did you know my name? I've never been here before."

She seemed not to hear him. Instead she said one word, "Come." Then she strode rapidly toward a small door facing on the street. Clutching his briefcase, Mike hastened after her. In contrast to Comrade Kondratieva, Nicolai Gologorsky exuded a not inconsiderable charm. He asked Mike if he would like a cigarette, and when told he did not smoke Gologorsky apologized and begged the boy's forgiveness for being addicted. "Terrible habit," he chuckled. "Perfectly dreadful way to ruin one's health. You are such a fine-looking young man, and so tall. It would be a pity if you ever took it up."

Mike said he really did not believe in the theory that tobacco stunted growth, but had no interest in smoking since there were more important things to do.

"For example, visiting Russia?" Gologorsky said helpfully. "Please do not believe the propaganda you may read about us. Of course we are not perfect, but it is hardly fair to class us as barbarians. Certainly the young people of America know that many of the world's greatest thinkers, authors, artists, and scientists have been Russian-born. We are seekers after truth. We prefer to help the helpless of this world and stand firm against all aggressors, no matter of what flag."

Gologorsky smiled very quickly and warmly, and Mike thought it was much neater to be with Mr. Gologorsky than with Mr. Winslow, who mostly complained about his own physical ailments or his family problems. This was big thinking . . . the kind Mike preferred.

Mike became aware that Gologorsky was scrutinizing him very carefully when he said, "I have two sons . . . about your age . . ." Gologorsky elevated one of his heavy eyebrows quizzically. "That is, I suppose you are all about the same age?"

"Sixteen," Mike said flatly.

"Ah yes. Well, they are a bit older, but then you seem very mature for sixteen. My boys plan to stay in the Army. What are your ambitions after you grow—that is, have you planned a career?"

"Sort of. I might like to be an astrophysicist, or an accountant. I'm not sure which."

Gologorsky reached into the top drawer of his desk and turned on his tape recorder with an ease resulting from long and frequent practice. He combined the necessary movement with the business of lighting a cigarette. Exhaling smoke and fanning at it as it drifted in Mike's direction he asked carefully, "What brings you to Russia, Michael?"

"You just turned on your tape recorder, didn't you, Mr. Gologorsky?"

Momentarily taken aback, Gologorsky eyed Mike with new interest. Perhaps, he thought, it is I who have been reading the wrong propaganda. American youth was supposed to be categorically stupid, decadent, and spoiled. Yet there was something about this boy that denied all such labels. Such alertness was a quality Gologorsky had found sadly lacking in too many Soviet youngsters.

Gologorsky pretended to have a coughing spell while he regrouped his thinking. Was the CIA raising some kind of an elite youth cadre? Shades of Adolf Hitler and his Jungengruppen!

"You didn't answer my question, Michael," he smiled.

"Well, sir, I came to see the President of the Soviets, or I might be able to do with a delegation of your big bosses, unless . . . I mean, unless you are one. But I think there should be more than one because what I have to explain is extremely important to Russia and to the rest of the world."

Gologorsky swallowed several times and bit at his mustache. Come along now, what was this? Was he supposed to be amused? Was the boy just parroting Winslow, who had not enough brains to frame the simplest deceit, let alone the subtle overtones of intrigue which now seemed to be developing?

Once again Gologorsky reviewed the possibility that the boy might be some sort of KGB testing plant. He decided against it. The KGB did not have so much imagination.

He watched in silence as Mike opened his briefcase and laid his calculations on the edge of the desk. "Without going into the complete details, Mr. Gologorsky, I can give you a rough idea of what is happening. I guess you have tops in Russia?"

Mike pulled a wooden top from his briefcase and set it on the papers. "I can demonstrate to you right here how my spinning-top theory works. Basically, that is . . ."

Fascinated, wondering if some enemy had put an exotic type of dream drug in his cigarette, Gologorsky told Mike to proceed as he wished.

Mike took a string and a knife from his briefcase, wound the string around the top, and spun it away on the parquet floor. "Watch how it orbits, Mr. Gologorsky. Just like the earth."

Gologorsky thought, If anyone comes in I will be sent off to a "special regime" camp, and I will be gone a long time.

The top spun down, Mike picked it up, and sliced off a thin piece from one side. "Now watch, Mr. Gologorsky."

He spun the top again. Regarding it dubiously, Gologorsky decided he knew at last why all Americans were crazy. They become mad in the cradle, he thought, and throughout their mortal lives their idiosyncracies multiply. Yet this time, as the top took an eccentric orbit, he found himself listening with increasing interest as the young American explained how the removal of petroleum weight from a concentrated area of the earth must soon have the same effect as the wood chip he had cut from the skin of the top.

"Hmmmmmm," Gologorsky grunted. "Hmmm." Sensing the approach of a genuine puzzlement, he lit a second cigarette from the butt of the first. This was not going to be the best of days. Snorting smoke through his nostrils, Gologorsky asked why Michael had come to him with the problem. Simultaneously he strove to remind himself that this whole performance was preposterous, yet he found himself unable to dismiss the demonstration as some sort of joke. He reviewed the various comrades who might be after his job and resisted a temptation to call his apartment and ask his wife if there had been any uninvited callers . . . say a few of the boys from the KGB?

"I came to Russia because my own President was not interested and something must be done now. Time is so short."

"Your President knows about this?" Lead him on, Gologorsky thought, let him rave until he trips over his own lies.

"Yes. I was invited to the White House, but the President preferred to talk about other things. It was not a satisfactory interview."

"To you."

"Yes. But I think that if you Russians will start the ball rolling he will realize what is happening, and then everyone in the world will pitch in. We will have a worldwide common effort toward one thing, and that will be a pretty neat and wonderful thing, Mr. Gologorsky."

Since when, Gologorsky wondered, did they start reading Marx in the American schools? "All very fine and noble, Michael, but you have not told me what must be done to rescue the situation."

Gologorsky leaned forward and picked up the papers of calculations. He flipped through them casually, not really studying the figures because he suspected old Nicolai was not going to be the butt of this childish joke much longer. Any moment now the notations would disappear, since they must certainly be written in that kind of ink, and his staff would come in laughing. It was like watching clowns at the circus, he thought; the droll fellow carried the loudest explosive.

"Mr. Gologorsky, I am not going to tell you or anyone else what the solution is until I know for sure that we are thinking on the same frequency."

"I do not understand this frequency business. You are a wireless expert?"

"I tinker with it."

"Ah? And that is how you came to know Mr. Winslow?"

"No."

The flatness of the boy's negative impressed Gologorsky more than he liked. Joke or no joke, it now seemed that he must get to the root of all this. If some sort of hoax was in progress, then this young American was the greatest actor ever. There was not a flick of nervousness in his eyes, no hint of the telltale twitching, finger-tapping, and assorted quirks Gologorsky had so long witnessed in the multitude of liars who had stood before him. Whatever it was, this boy was telling the truth and he was unafraid of the consequences. If the Americans, through that dunderhead Winslow, were using the boy in some kind of an attempt at entrapment, then they had moved their pawn too far. They should never have shoved him out on the board without protection.

"Michael," Gologorsky said easily, "I have several very important appointments waiting and I would like time to study your calculations. Would you be good enough to accept my offer of a guide and do a tour of the Kremlin for a few hours? There is much to be seen besides this dull office—the Czar's apartments, the Bell Tower, the Palace of Congresses, et cetera."

"It sounds interesting, but something on my project should be started today."

"Do I understand the solution is not in these papers?"

"I have it right here." Mike tapped his head and smiled. "As soon as I am sure you want to do something, then your government must call mine and say so. When you are both agreed, then in a few hours I can give you both all the figures you'll need to begin solving the problem."

"Both? But I understood your government rejected you."

"My President is not my government entirely. He just didn't listen. They will if you will. But the solution belongs to everyone on earth."

Does it indeed? Gologorsky thought as he pressed the button which would summon Yelena Kondratieva.

* * *

Of the usual million billion meteoroids which strike Earth's envelope every day, only one was of a size to survive the usual cremation and enter the atmosphere as a considerable solid. Moving at approximately forty-five miles per second, it struck Earth's surface in Siberia near the crater of another meteoroid, which had made a spectacle of itself in 1908. Like its predecessor, it dug a vast hole in the snow, started a forest fire, and caused pressure-wave damage over a wide area. Since this was the kind of news the Soviet censors considered harmless to national security, the world, including Nicolai Gologorsky, knew about the event within an hour after its occurrence. Thus as he read Michael Piper's papers he experienced some difficulty in persuading himself the predictions and the big Siberian bang were not related.

Acting more upon his protective instincts than reason, Gologorsky promptly assigned two of his staff to research other recent phenomena. Computers at the Technical Institute almost immediately volunteered more information than he was sure he wanted. There was a long list of floods and droughts, crop failures, widespread fires throughout Europe, severe winters, scorching summers. Nor was the computer at a loss for the causes. Gologorsky noted with growing uneasiness that most of the more dramatic changes and events were attributed to a combination of human endeavors.

At the 120-inch telescope at Lick Observatory in California astronomers were perplexed because their most recent photos of the heavens failed to match those taken at identical celestial hours only six months previously. Checking with their colleagues at Mount Palomar's 200-inch telescope, they found they were equally confused.

Their nagging, almost imperceptible sense of disorientation was evidenced much more strongly in Oregon pronghorns, Missouri beavers, yellow-haired porcupines, Townsend's chipmunk, and most of the western tanagers.

A similar distrust of the current American natural environment was observed in the reticence of lousewort to expand, biscuit root and common lomatium to bloom, and the inclination of show phlox to fade.

Mike Piper, accompanied by Yelena Kondratieva, who had warmed somewhat as she explained the iniquities of Czarist Russia, was unaware of such manifestations. Lost in history as depicted in the Kremlin's gloomy Hall of Arms, he hardly noticed when later Yelena Kondratieva escorted him across the central complex of the Kremlin and into the Arsenal Building.

* * *

When Dudley Winslow had completed his conversation with the Secretary of State, he replaced the telephone as if it were made of hot iron. Remembering long-ago days when he was U. S. Consul in Bogotá, he wished fervently they would return. For then an overseas conversation was usually so distorted that half of what was said was lost and the other half open to various interpretations, according to the electronic whims of the atmosphere. Now, with satellite communication and near perfect transmission of the human voice, there was little cause to misinterpret phrase or word, and what his *very* superior had said left no room whatsoever for doubt. Good heavens! Why had Tom Weed failed to warn him the Piper boy was so valuable? How, Winslow lamented, could this thing happen to me?

The Secretary of State—indeed, the President himself—wanted Michael Piper back immediately. But three hours had passed and he was still in the Kremlin. Since the boy did not drink vodka, it was hardly possible they had got him drunk and sent him somewhere to sleep it off, but then what *was* he doing? There was a further question. Presumably the Ambassador, who lived in nearby Spasso

House, was still unaware a certain youth had been his quasi guest for two days. Now if the Secretary of State knew about him, certainly the Ambassador must be told, and he would jolly well want to know why he had not been better informed in the first place.

Surveying his woe, Winslow found it difficult to respond to Phoebe's prattling at lunchtime. Their usual exchanges about the weather and her complaints about the laundry facilities as offered by the embassy became even more stilted when she inquired of Michael Piper's whereabouts. She claimed her mother's sensitivity told her Mike must be very hungry. Her husband patted his napkin at his bristle mustache and suggested he was probably having lunch in the Kremlin.

"In the Kremlin? Eating that indigestible Russian food? What is he doing over there, may I ask?"

"You may ask, but I cannot tell you."

"Why not? I want to know what that poor boy is doing over there with those monsters."

"They are not all monsters. He is with our friend Gologorsky."

"Who I would not trust as far as I can throw St. Basil's." Phoebe Winslow munched thoughtfully on the sausage a junior foreign officer had brought her from Germany. Eyeing her husband carefully, she said, "Something is bugging you. What is it?"

"Nothing. Perhaps I have the pip."

"You also have the responsibility for Mike. I told the Ambassador about him this morning—"

"You told the Ambassador?" Winslow was horrified.

"Yes. We passed in the hall, and he stopped to ask about our trip. I simply said of course he knew we had picked up a guest . . . such a nice boy, and all that."

A silence ensued. Finally Winslow said almost inaudibly, "How was he supposed to know we had acquired a guest?"

"I assumed you told him."

"For various reasons I didn't quite get around to it."

"Oh, me . . . you are in trouble."

Little does she realize how much trouble, Winslow thought. How could he explain Mike's appearance on the scene, not to mention his lack of passport, money, ticket, or anything else? Now he had to be dispatched immediately back to Washington. There was a four o'clock Pan Am flight out of Moscow, but how was he going to get all the paper work done, acquire an exit visa from the Russians, and explain everything to the Ambassador if Mike was going to spend all afternoon in the Kremlin?

He excused himself and, leaving his lunch almost untouched, went to his office. There he placed a call to Nicolai Gologorsky. According to a person named Kondratieva, who identified herself as a member of Gologorsky's staff, her superior had been called away very suddenly. He was en route to Minsk and would not return for several days.

STILL ON
THE TWELFTH DAY...

Cyril Henshaw left his small clothing bag in his hotel room and took the briefcase with him. He paused only briefly to search the hotel room for the bugs (electronic and other varieties) he was certain were standard Moscow accommodations. Leaving the hotel, he trudged through the snow and entered GUM's department store. He bought a pair of gloves, a karakul cap, and walked to the British Embassy. There his business was brief. In half an hour he had the names of the principal officers in the American Embassy and the names of several Soviet authorities in the Kremlin who might have business to conduct with foreigners. He recognized one name, Nicolai Gologorsky, and decided luck was with him on this snow-swept afternoon. In Henshaw's time with M-5, Gologorsky had been known as a relative anglophile in a den of porcupines, and once when Gologorsky had visited London they had even talked on the telephone. The Russian had needed good tickets for a performance of *My Fair Lady* and M-5, through the efforts of agent Cyril Henshaw, had been happy to supply the very best, along with a lovely escort. Gologorsky had proclaimed it the greatest show he had ever seen, and afterward celebrated the occasion with vast amounts of scotch whisky. It was reported that for weeks afterward Gologorsky practiced his cockney accent. Unfortunately, he was much too clever, drunk or sober, for anyone, his lovely M-5 escort included, to elicit any interesting information.

Henshaw had a word with the current M-5 agent, Peter Strathcona, a chap he had assigned to Moscow when he was still with the organization. "I should have thought you'd have worn out your welcome by now."

"I have," Peter Strathcona agreed as they shared a pot of tea in his office. "But I'm only a front and they know it. The real work is done by others. I just give them practice in surveillance when I move from A to B, and I fancy they have actually become rather fond of me."

Later Strathcona called Gologorsky's office and made an appointment for six o'clock.

"That will give you two hours to knock about, and you'd best walk it from here. Taxies are a frightful bore to find at this hour." He paused, and his natural curiosity took over. "I don't suppose you'd care to tell me what you're up to. Confidentially, of course."

"Not yet. But there is another chap I must see. Dudley Winslow, with the Americans. Know him?"

"Rather. What on earth . . . ? Well, never mind. I'll ring up the Americans and see if he's in town."

"I can tell you now. He is."

* * *

Secretary of State Kaplan had departed Camp David and returned to his office, where, through the Operations

Center, he could keep in more direct contact with international events.

The Secretary had spoken twice with the American Ambassador to Russia, trying to impress upon him the urgency of the situation without explaining why the immediate return of young Michael Piper was so necessary. The liaison was awkward because both nuance and inflection were difficult in code and the Russians bugged everything. Additionally there was a risk of starting a worldwide panic if the whole story were told. As a result Secretary Kaplan was reduced to such verbal pirouetting as "The boy's mother is not feeling well and would like him home immediately," and on another conversation, "The auto accident in which the boy was involved has resulted in a heavy liability suit. For the sake of his family's future he must return at once. . . ."

Let the Russians spend the next few days trying to decode *those* remarks, Kaplan mused. He was confident that by the time they completely unraveled the dialogue the boy would be safe in the White House.

Yet things were not going well at all if a true assessment were made. Calls had been made to Moscow every thirty minutes since three o'clock their time, and now at six the boy had not emerged from the Kremlin. Why? After listening to Winslow's less than convincing reassurances Kaplan reminded himself he was trying to communicate with an extraordinarily dull fellow.

When informed of the delay the President had wanted to get on the red telephone right away (that damn thing had a frightening fascination for him), and had insisted he would personally get to the bottom of things. It had been almost necessary to use force to restrain him since he seemed incapable of understanding that if the Soviets thought the boy was important enough for the President of the United States to be concerned, they would be all the more reluctant to release him.

There was still time. Maybe the kid just decided to take a walk around Red Square and became lost. Did he speak Russian? No, but that wood-brained Winslow had commented that during one of his rap sessions with the kid, young Piper had mentioned something about speaking Ameslan, the sign language of the deaf. Unusual, but so what? Kids learned all kinds of things these days. Kaplan recalled that his chauffeur's son was a glassblower of such reputation at age fifteen that his creations had already been shown at the Hirschhorn gallery.

At eight o'clock Moscow time Secretary Kaplan received a short call from his Ambassador to the Soviets. Almost immediately after the call was concluded, Kaplan initiated another call to the President. His words were measured and his voice held deliberately low key. In a time of extraordinary crisis he would show himself as a rock and thereby avoid the ever present political risk of being shunted out of the picture. "We have nothing official from the Russians as yet, sir, but I must inform you the situation is grave. Michael Piper has not been returned to the embassy. The Soviet contact who was originally in charge of the matter has left the city, and presumably the boy is incarcerated."

"What does that mean in real language?"

"A blind cat has met a dead mouse. We can only wait and see what the Russians are willing to tell us."

"We can't wait. The whole world is in trouble."

"May I remind you that is a condition the Soviets prefer?"

"I'm going to use the red telephone."

"Please do not. I beg you, sir. They will cheer if you do and gloat over their prize. Other means must be found."

"Then find them. I'll give you twelve hours."

"Make it twenty-four. The alternates are few and complicated."

"All right. But whatever you do, don't risk the boy's life."

Or my career, Kaplan thought. Obviously the President believed a rescue of Michael Piper was mandatory, but without at least some risk the task would be impossible.

Kaplan sat back in his heavy black leather chair and removed his glasses. The action rendered him nearly blind, but he preferred to isolate his usually overproductive brain from the visual distractions of his office. Now able to ignore the complex reports from all over the world which littered his desk, he concentrated on the thorniest problem he had ever encountered.

How did one extract one young American from the most carefully guarded fortress in the world, which was situated far inside the most assiduously guarded frontier in the world—and in twenty-four hours?

Marvin Kaplan sat immovable for a long time. Then, as if rousing from a deep hibernation, he dialed a number on his private telephone. "Mamma? This is your wonder boy, Marvin. How goes it with the noodle soup?"

Secretary Kaplan's mother expressed her surprise in the heavy accent which was so dear to him. Why, she demanded, was he all of a sudden interested in noodle soup?

"Didn't you always tell me to sit up and eat my noodle soup because it would make me a smart fella?"

"I did. But look at you. Who else has flags all over his office and can call Uncle Haggai in Tel Aviv anytime he wants?"

"Mamma, once you told me that after your fortieth anniversary Papa stopped listening to you. But there still had to be some communication between you. How did you manage to get his attention?"

"Well, sometimes I would put my foot out and trip him

and catch him before he hurt himself, or sometimes maybe I would make pantomime like a fancy actress until he couldn't stand it anymore and he would have to ask what is this all about, Ruth? He would say, 'Stop making like a damn fool and tell me what it is you want, Ruth.' And then I would say, 'Well, I would like to play bridge tomorrow night with the Dubchecks,' or, 'There is going to be a Bar Mitzvah at the Grossmans,' or did he want a chicken sandwich—"

Kaplan smiled and said with all his eloquence, "Mamma! I love you!"

"What's this, boy? Fancy words will get you everywhere. You need money? You spend your allowance already?"

"No, Mamma. But I did need you. Thank you for remaining alive."

After half listening for several minutes while his mother detailed a long list of ailments, symptoms, cures, and comparisons with the inferior physical state of her contemporaries, Kaplan was satisfied she was in excellent health. He bid her good night with a resounding kiss and a promise to visit her on the coming weekend.

After he had hung up Kaplan began a slow circling of his office while he thought about noodle soup. He remained deep in thought, but a strange light had come to his eyes, as if the glasses still neglected on his desk were no longer necessary for true vision.

*   *   *

Mike Piper did not become uneasy until the light failed. The Russian woman had left him in this room with instructions to make himself comfortable—it might be a while, she had told him, before Comrade Gologorsky would be able to see him. Meanwhile she left him with an illustrated brochure on the Kremlin, which was, unfortunately, in French. Hoping to ease his hunger, which had reached a crisis stage, he sought distraction in trying to understand the French text of the brochure. The attempt was a failure, for hunger had taken almost complete charge of his mental concentration. People sure didn't eat very well in Russia, or very often—it wasn't like Minnesota, that was for sure. And they sure didn't spend too much energy for heat.

Experimenting, he found he could blow out his breath and see vapor, which he thought was not exactly the way such a nice room should be climatized. It was a large room; you could hold a ball in it if you wanted, and it even had chairs around the walls for the people to sit in between dances, like in the old movies. At one end there was a large table supporting a samovar, several glasses, and plates, but the whole assembly had an unused look. No sign of food. There were four high windows that must not have been opened for a hundred years. Beyond the table in a corner he had discovered a toilet and washbasin.

Checking his watch for what he thought must be the umpteenth time, Mike became increasingly unhappy. Cripes, but Mr. Gologorsky must be a slow reader. Of course it did get dark early in Moscow at this time of year, but it had been black outside the windows for more than an hour. And a guy could not eat snow.

Food! Cripes, he thought, it was all right missing lunch, but it must be near dinnertime, and even with the jet lag and all a guy's belly was still important. Right now in St. Paul they were probably having breakfast, say orange juice and cereal with at least one banana sliced on top, and about six hunks of toast with butter and jam and eggs and sausage if it was Tuesday or Thursday, which was when Mom usually did such things. And of course, a glass or two of milk and maybe a sweet roll to top everything off. Then a guy was ready for the day.

It was the nagging thought of food which compelled him to try the big double doors through which he had entered the room. Maybe there was someone outside who could take a message to Mr. Gologorsky saying it was all right if he wanted to take a few more hours to study the figures, but holy mackerel, how about sending out for a few hamburgers? With fries, please, and easy on the mustard. Can you hear my belly rumbling, Mr. Gologorsky? But before we eat, please call Mr. Winslow, who must be wondering what has happened.

He decided if there was no one outside the doors he would just keep on going. He was certain he could find his way to Gologorsky's office. The Arsenal Building faced on a sort of open place, and all he had to do was cross it and keep a big flagpole on his right and in another two hundred feet or so he would come to Mr. Gologorsky's building. After that it was through the little entrance door, then up some stairs, and a couple of doors down the hall was Mr. Gologorsky, or at least some people. Did everyone go home at dark around here?

It was too quiet. Maybe the snow muffled everything outside, but there wasn't any noise inside either—nothing except the squeaking of the floors when he moved. Cripes, he thought, I'm cold, hungry, and homesick all at the same time. This is very heavy.

His heels made a hard, flat sound as he marched to the doors. He pushed down on the door handle and found it immovable. He shook it and pulled at it, gently at first and then more forcefully. Nothing moved.

Cripes, he thought. This is no good.

* * *

Not far from the Kremlin, in the American Embassy, Dudley Winslow and the Ambassador stood looking down at a small park across the Kremlin Prospect. They watched a host of formless bundles playing hockey beneath the streetlights. They watched the traffic moving silently along the snow-covered street.

The two men had said little for the past hour. They moved to and from the window, staring at the entrance arch to the embassy, both convinced that the next time they looked down they must surely see one of the unmistakable Soviet limousines turn into the archway and disappear. It would be delivering young Michael Piper, who had so suddenly become the focus of their entire attentions.

They looked frequently at the array of clocks along the wall of the ninth-floor communications room and noted that it was already 8 P.M. Moscow time, and, even more unhappily, 8 A.M. Washington time.

"Of course I could call Mikoyan . . . or even the party Chairman," the Ambassador said tentatively. "Then they would at least be obliged to go through the motions—"

"Secretary Kaplan was very strong on that, sir. He suggested that any undue concern on our part would alert the Soviets to the boy's value."

"It appears they might already be aware of that. How about trying to find him in Minsk?"

"I doubt if he's ever left Moscow. It's the old stall."

Dudley Winslow kept his peace. Now resigned to his fate, he knew that whatever happened to young Piper or was about to happen would be automatically debited against his already sagging account in the foreign service. He was sorry about everything he could think of, and wondered if subsequent events might even pose a threat to his pension. Living somewhere in enforced retirement on Phoebe's pork-belly inheritance, he decided, was more than any human being should be forced to endure.

Winslow was almost grateful when the phone rang, the

one he knew connected the Ambassador directly with the Secretary of State in Washington. He saw the Ambassador move quickly to the phone, listen intently, as he would only to Kaplan himself, then make some brief notations on a pad. When he returned to Winslow he was shaking his head and frowning. "I am not at all sure," the Ambassador said, "that our friend Kaplan realizes the situation. It is the same old story of trying to run things from afar."

"I'm frightfully sorry about all this—" Winslow lamented.

"You may become more so. Kaplan is now convinced the boy is being held a prisoner, and directs us to find out precisely where he is being held. The location is extremely important. He wants to know in what building if it is in the Kremlin, the exact room, all of the details of that room, including a floor plan, and exactly where guards are posted. This information must be in his hands within a maximum of twelve hours."

Winslow paled. This was it, the impossible he knew was coming. He offered in what he thought was a masterful understatement: "Obtaining that information is going to be somewhat difficult . . ."

"It's your bag, Dudley. Sorry about that. Guess what he calls the project."

"I wouldn't have the faintest—"

"Operation Noodle Soup."

* * *

Nicolai Gologorsky was amused, although he could not explain even to himself exactly why. Here before him was Henshaw, one of those self-appointed English aristocrats whose forefathers established an empire that had stretched from sun to sun. Who had he come to but Nicolai Gologorsky, son of a peasant whose forefathers had been peasants since Russian history began. Voilà, as the French said, like throwing a switch, the power change is accomplished.

Gologorsky was convinced there was little cause for him to struggle through the accumulation of figures the American boy had left in his charge. The lad was not a CIA device, or even some fancy of the KGB. He was genuine worth, else why would this Britisher Henshaw open his briefcase and reveal a fortune in rubles, dollars, and Swiss francs? All would be Nicolai Gologorsky's, plus a guarantee of more for life if he would simply turn the boy over to Henshaw and arrange an immediate exit from the U.S.S.R. It was even amusing that Henshaw had not troubled to specify the route of departure.

Most of all Gologorsky delighted in Henshaw's lack of appreciation of the Soviet system. As a former agent of M-5 he should know that accepting any sort of bribe in Russia was extremely risky. If the bargain was discovered, there was no place to hide. One was loyal to the Presidium, for in them rested all real power, and to displease them even slightly was to ask for catastrophe.

And yet? Looking at the man who sat at the opposite end of a small tea table (which in the Russian fashion Gologorsky used to deformalize his more important conferences), it would appear that at least British aplomb seemed unruffled. Gologorsky envied him for his casualness, which suggested that releasing the boy to Henshaw's custody was a matter of little consequence. Only a few millions' worth? Nonsense. If he was worth that much to Henshaw's employers, then he was worth a billion or more. Question: That amount cached in another country or six more stars added to the Order of the Red Star for Comrade Nicolai Gologorsky if the boy was turned over to the Supreme Soviet? A sweet if difficult choice.

"Why don't you tell me who you really work for?" Gologorsky asked while displaying his most persuasive smile. "Only a government has that much money to spread around."

"Several governments," Henshaw replied as if an agreement had already been reached. "The boy is really quite balmy of course, but history tells us deranged youths, whether male or female, have a way of capturing the public's imagination and creating all kinds of trouble. If this should happen in the case of young Piper, my clients might find it very embarrassing as well as inconvenient."

"You mean expensive."

"Precisely. For that reason I have been instructed to request a certain amount of aid within the Kremlin. I came to you first because of our past association, which admittedly was rather slight. If you decline the offer, and I assure you there is more where it came from, then someone else will doubtless accept. This is only a token payment which may help in adjusting your attitude. Before the actual delivery of the boy you may specify a considerably larger amount, and I believe I can arrange it for you."

Gologorsky made a sucking noise as he drained his tea glass and rose from the table. To all men, he thought, there comes a moment of supreme rectification. Measure for measure, indeed. How many years had he envied the English in their glorious confidence, their ability to suggest they had the situation under control even though the very Houses of Parliament were crumbling? Now, to employ one of their very own phrases, which of course was originally a Russian folk saying, the shoe was on the other foot. Henshaw's boldness was a result of that British overconfidence. He had walked into the game without troubling to castle his king, without regard to the skill or wisdom of his opponent, who was about to enjoy the delights of checkmate. Obviously Henshaw was not aware the boy was already in the Kremlin or that the alarming report on the desk was originated by him. Nor could Henshaw know that his arrival was proof enough that the calculations and the boy's spinning-top theory were priceless.

"Fi-fie-fo-fum," Gologorsky recited soundlessly, "I smell the blood of a Englishmun. . . ."

Employing his most ceremonious gestures, Gologorsky lit a cigarette. He rocked back and forth from toe to heel as he imagined several ways he might humiliate Cyril Henshaw. It was like being invited to choose one enticing young woman from among a whole cadre of females who had been liberated to work in a musk factory.

"When do you expect this so very valuable young man will pay us a call?" he inquired. He found it necessary to hide behind a screen of cigarette smoke lest the coming moment of triumph appear in his eyes.

"Sometime within the next few days. He is already in the American Embassy. Frankly, we don't know whom he might contact here. That would be part of your job to find out, and then, if possible, divert him directly to you. If you can arrange it, we would like to keep him from even entering the Kremlin."

"But why don't you just pick him up at the American Embassy? Surely they will cooperate with their English friends."

"The people I represent do not have an altogether harmonious relationship with the present American administration. And they abhor the use of violence . . . particularly in this matter."

"Ah? And what is their business?" Gologorsky asked with a show of innocence.

"That you will find out in due course. I can only assure you money is no problem, as evidenced by the contents of this briefcase. Just let me know when the boy is in your hands and so will be the money."

For a moment Gologorsky thought to dismiss the Englishman with the sneering contempt he deserved. M-5 should be ashamed to let such a graduate loose in the real world.

Gologorsky marched resolutely to his desk and halted. He raised his right hand as if calling for the attention of a symphonic orchestra, extended his little finger, and with the most precise and delicate of gestures punched at the call button for Comrade Kondratieva. She entered immediately.

"We would like to see our young guest."

Kondratieva glanced at Henshaw as a mongoose might regard a handy snake. Her eyes moved to Gologorsky without mellowing. "Follow me," she said in English.

As they walked toward the Nicholas Tower, Henshaw said it was the first time he had ever been in the Kremlin and he wished he had more time to look around. "It must be very old and suffering from a bit of disrepair, if you don't mind my saying so." He nodded at a considerable crack which extended down the face of the Arsenal Building on their left.

Both Gologorsky and Kondratieva stared at the crack, then glanced at each other. "Humph!" Gologorsky snorted. "It must be new because I've never noticed it before. But it is nothing. By morning it will be repaired."

"We keep the old buildings only to remind the Soviet people of the Czars' oppression," Kondratieva recited icily. She led them into the Arsenal Building and preceded them down a long corridor on the second floor.

Kondratieva halted before a pair of sturdy doors at the end of the corridor. "He is here," she said, gesturing at the doors.

Gologorsky smiled at Henshaw, then glanced at his briefcase. "I know that an English gentleman always keeps his word. Right, Mr. Henshaw? You said, when the boy was in our hands?"

"Right."

Gologorsky reached for the briefcase. He hefted it and smiled again. Then he turned the handle on the door and pushed. The heavy door remained fixed. Gologorsky tried a second time without success, then turned a quizzical eye upon Kondratieva. "Push," she said in Russian. "It's not locked."

Still clutching the briefcase, Gologorsky pushed until his face turned crimson. The door remained immobile. Angered, he placed the briefcase on the floor, took three steps backward, and charged the door. His grunt of pain mixed with the shriek of forced wood, and the door opened approximately four inches. Just inside stood a startled Mike Piper. "Hello," he said uneasily.

Grimacing with pain as he rubbed his shoulder, Gologorsky announced he had probably broken his clavicle. Then, recovering himself, he managed to smile at Mike. "My deepest apologies. There is no logical explanation for this embarrassment. The building must be—how do you say?—out of kilter. The door was never locked. You are free to go anywhere."

Both Gologorsky and Mike tried to move the door without success. Henshaw applied his weight, but a four-inch aperture was apparently the maximum.

Finally Gologorsky stood back, panting. "I will send carpenters immediately. Do not fear."

"I'm not scared, Mr. Gologorsky, but maybe I better get back to the embassy. I'm sure hungry."

"Ah, but, my dear young friend, you cannot leave without sampling our native fare! You are our honored guest, and a true Russian meal is on the way. The Kremlin chef is a Tartar, and they are very emotional. He would be inconsolable if his work were for nothing. Please allow us a few minutes to remedy this unfortunate situation."

Gologorsky turned to pick up the briefcase and was dismayed to see Kondratieva holding it. He shrugged his shoulders, winced, and asked himself why he should have such a sense of foreboding. Yet Comrade Kondratieva rarely smiled, and she was smiling now. Something like the painting in the Louvre, he remembered—the "Mona Lisa."

As they retraced their way down the corridor, Gologorsky pulled Henshaw to his side.

"You saw the boy?"

Henshaw nodded.

"I have decided the risk is too great and the reward is too little."

Their eyes met for an instant, and their understanding was absolute. Henshaw reached into his coat pocket and pulled out the fat envelope he had reserved for himself. "Perhaps this fifty million more will convince you the boy will be better off in our hands and on his way out of the country by tomorrow morning?"

Gologorsky thought it was his turn to smile.

Later when he had promised Henshaw all would be in readiness by nine in the morning and had bade him the fondest of farewells at the Spassky Gate, he walked back to his office with Kondratieva at his side.

He reached for the briefcase, but she moved it just out of his reach. "What is this?" he asked.

"Comrade Gologorsky," she said as she stuck out her tongue to catch a few snowflakes, "surely you would not forget the promise you made poor little Yelena? The trip to the Black Sea for the sun we were going to make . . . last summer, when you were going to take me to the

Caucasus just to drink the wine? When the season was right you said it was impossible. Not only would your wife object, but also you could not afford the cost, you said. And you gave me only the very long face so I would be sorry for you. And now? . . . Ah!" She caught several more snowflakes on her extended tongue. "Would you rather take me someplace far, far away where there is sun and pretty clothes . . . or would you rather have me give this briefcase to the KGB?"

* * *

Secretary of State Kaplan was a football fan, and although he was a small and portly man he sometimes dreamed of himself as a superb broken-field runner. Now, sensing a contest which might become the political Rose Bowl, he broke loose from his normal cautious game plan and rushed for the goal. The President had ordered, "Just get the job done. The sky is the limit."

Okay. The skies would be the limit, and the first yardage gain would be against the Air Force. Spurring his secretaries into a flurry of activity, he was soon talking into two telephones at the same time, shifting from one listener to the other with hardly a stuttered word.

Not even General Shellcase escaped his lash. Thus he arranged for six supersonic aircraft to proceed at once to St. Paul, Minnesota; there to stand by for certain passengers. Once they were aboard, the aircraft would take off immediately with highest priority clearance for landings at Andrews Air Force Base, where four Marine helicopters would be waiting to hoist the passengers to Camp David.

General Shellcase complained the operation was too expensive. Recent budget cuts mandated a 52.4 percent reduction in all military expenses. Even generals must now drive their own cars.

Kaplan reminded him of his more recent mandate. "So we don't use all six aircraft? I want no delays. If one of your flying machines breaks down or the pilot gets a bellyache, I want a standby right at hand. This may not be war in your eyes, but it is in ours."

For two hours Kaplan continued his weaving, dodging, spin-offs, and breakaways until at last he was content. He had cut through battalions of bureaucracy which ordinarily would have delayed progress for at least a week, and even the elusive Alice Kellogg, now Martinson, had been tracked down in a resort hotel near Bemidji, Minnesota, where she and the groom were dog-teaming. Odd, Kaplan took time to think, how some people chose to spend their honeymoon. He also thought that now all was in readiness for his final play . . . unless, God forbid, the most important of his chosen teammates turned out to be recalcitrant. To cover that possibility he placed new calls to London, Paris, and West Berlin.

Finally he called Moscow, bowing his head in simulation of prayer as he did so, for here, perhaps in the hands of the most bumbling of his fellow players, lay the key to the entire game. "What have you found out?" he asked Dudley Winslow.

Much to his surprise, Winslow's voice exuded confidence. He sounded like a different man, authoritative and forthright.

"Well, sir, I have a Mr. Henshaw here in my office, and he has seen the boy. Although the Russians pretend otherwise, Mike Piper apparently is confined to the Kremlin. He is in a second-floor room of the Arsenal Building—"

"Ah? He has a window then?" Kaplan remembered the building from his several visits to the Kremlin.

"Yes. It faces north and overlooks the Historical Museum, just off Red Square." There followed a moment's pause while Winslow apparently conferred with Henshaw. "Mr. Henshaw says that he is not sure which window it is along the second floor, but it is between the Nicholas Gate and the Arsenal Tower if you are viewing the building from the street."

"Can someone on the street be seen from the window, and vice versa?"

Again a pause. "Mr. Henshaw says yes, certainly, providing the viewer has reasonable eyesight."

"Who is this Mr. Henshaw and why is he being so helpful? Did he come to you or did you go to him, and what is a Russian doing with a name like Henshaw?"

Despite the geographical distance involved there were some very faint odors emanating from the hearing end of Kaplan's telephone which he decided were not all delectable. Was this the joker? There was certainly no time to do a proper investigation of anyone.

Another conference, this time of such duration Kaplan began to fume. Then, just before he was about to demand that Henshaw himself come on the line, Winslow said, "He says he is a defector of sorts, although he will not tell me what from. He is an Englishman, formerly of M-5, and says that when he saw the boy's eyes and got to thinking about what he really represented he became convinced a true world crisis was at hand and something must be done about it immediately. He decided that if the Russians alone possessed the boy's information the situation would become unilateral, and his only desire now as an intelligent human being is to assist in any way he can. Both nations must know the solution or—"

"Pray, Mr. Winslow," Kaplan ordered in his best Benjamin Franklin manner, "do not, if you please, take precious time to review a situation of which I am most keenly aware."

Apparently there was a snag in Moscow, for the ensuing pause was again almost longer than Kaplan's strained patience could endure. When Winslow returned to the phone he sounded more like his old self: vague, bewildered, and in imminent danger of fumbling the ball. "Mr. Henshaw fears the displeasure of his employers. It seems he is shy two million dollars on their account. Frankly, sir, I do not understand how the Russians took it away from him, but if we will reimburse . . ."

No matter what the crisis, Kaplan thought, Britannia rules the banks. Let not a farthing slip through their fingers lest the tradition of Morgan, Drake, and Elizabeth I be betrayed. If extortion was his intent, then so be it. Henshaw, however unreliable he might be, was the only game in town. "Very well, Winslow. Tell Mr. Henshaw to report to our embassy in Bonn, where certain individuals will request his assistance. Meanwhile we'll run a check on him, and if he cooperates and his sentiments seem genuine, then money will be no problem."

Immediately after concluding his Moscow exchange Kaplan threw himself into such a continuous chain of telephoning that even his staff commented on his adroitness in tracking down and persuading the right people to comply with his immediate wishes. When he had finished at last and removed his heavy glasses, he rubbed at the bridge of his nose and thought that he had reduced the number of unknown factors to nearly zero. There was now some hope for the world, and if both the architect and the engineer of his grand plan were given their rightful due, then the future of one Marvin Kaplan was limitless.

He pulled at his earlobes as if shifting mental gears,

then dialed his private telephone. "Mamma? I have been up all night and I need a few hours' rest away from everyone and everything. Kick the cats off the couch because your wonder boy is going to be using it."

What Kaplan did not know as he left his office was how the tides of the earth, which normally fluctuated two to four inches, were now sashaying between eight and twelve inches, and in certain areas, such as the Malay Peninsula, were expanding even more. If the process continued, it seemed inevitable that record heights and depths of several feet would be reached within a matter of days. Drs. Claudia Sungaipenuh and Lirik Ombalata, who observed the phenomena, were so appalled at their discovery they decided to keep it secret. Scientists who made outlandish claims ran the risk of being laughed at, and like other true scientists, the one reaction they could not bear was ridicule.

* * *

When the options had been typed, Hymie Markel personally inserted them in the green leather folder with the gold embossed Presidential Seal on top. Then he straightened his tie and marched toward the Oval Office, where the President had retreated for a few days' respite from the pressures at Camp David.

Markel was admitted almost immediately. After receiving the usual perfunctory greeting (Markel was acutely aware that, as the staff originator of Michael Piper's visit to the White House, he was the handiest to blame for everything that had happened since) he placed the folder before the President and stood back to await developments. At least, he thought, the options had been framed as succinctly as possible.

The President opened the folder and, as always, ran the tip of his left forefinger down the list of options.

1. Now that contact with Piper has been established we should—

   a. Appoint Sec. Kaplan as Ambassador Extraordinary to the world.
   b. Mount a CIA task force effort to rescue young Piper.
   c. Threaten war if Piper is not returned immediately.
   d. Demand summit meeting with Soviets (threaten end of world). Castro as mediator?
   e. As result of d. persuade Soviets to cooperate in mass effort. U.S. to supply all funds. Soviets to supply labor from their "adjustment" camps.
   f. Leak suitable information through American press that boy is a plant and theory is a hoax designed to divert Soviets from U.S. territorial ambitions. Russians will easily persuade themselves this is fact.

Desiring to clear himself, Markel reminded the President that the first option originated in the State Department. Other options framed by more departments—Agriculture, Indian Affairs, Internal Revenue, and Interior—would be soon forthcoming. No one, it seemed, wanted to be left out now that the scent of crisis was in the Washington air. Whether they understood the problem was not a problem.

After a long moment the President opened the center drawer of his desk, fumbled around inside, and found a packet of digestive pills. He popped two in his mouth, masticated carefully, and belched. Then he placed his left forefinger on d. for the summit meeting. "I will not go for the Castro idea," he said. "We need enemies if they are not too powerful, and Cuba is ideal. Suppose we do start getting chummy with the Russians. Then what will we do for a threat? What would we do with our generals and admirals?"

* * *

Rudy Distancia reminded himself that while the element of surprise had tremendous value it was also shot through with hidden perils, any one of which could backfire and defeat the original plan. Thus he was prepared for a rebuff when he telephoned the White House and told Hymie Markel that he was right across the street in the Hay-Adams Hotel.

"What brings you here?" Markel inquired with a coldness Distancia recognized as "Put the caller on hold until he states his case, then sic him on someone else."

"A matter of grave importance," Distancia said with due solemnity. "I have certain information on the Piper kid and his self-appointed chaperone which I feel it is my duty as a citizen of this country to divulge."

"All right. Divulge. This is not really the White House; it's the madhouse these days, and I'm awfully busy."

"The nature of this information is such that it must be delivered directly to the President." Distancia paused, then added, ". . . with all due respect to your integrity, Hymie."

"I'll clue you right now . . . *impossible!* The boss is going out of his gourd trying to cope with the problems of a nation of people who insist on playing with their toys even when the house is on fire. And anyway, the whole Piper affair is now in the capable hands of our friend Kaplan, who, as he is so fond of saying, is running with the ball. You can catch him at State, and the number is 567-3000. His number-one secretary is Dolores Vinetta."

Well done, Distancia thought as he floated sonorously through the customary verbal minuet in which both parties agreed to meet for a drink if, as, and when they both happened to find so much as an hour when they were not in immediate demand by individuals who would be lost without them.

"Step one completed as advertised," Distancia announced to the furniture in his elaborate suite. This quick journey to Washington had been at the not so subtle urging of F. Leslie Nash, who had suggested the discreet distribution of new information on the Michael Piper-Miss Kellogg duo. He had explained that it was of such a confidential nature he dared not expose it through his normal Washington contact—Leo Marcusi. Coming from that gentleman, the information could only be suspect as part of some insidious Petroleum Council invention. Now how different it would be coming from the lips of someone of Distancia's objective stature! The hinted rewards if Distancia could find time to spend a day in Washington talking to the right people were staggering. Ho-ho! Who needed a lousy little Lieutenant Governor's job when a kingdom was available? Asked when he could leave St. Paul, Distancia had announced that he already had his coat on.

Once more relying on surprise, Distancia eschewed the telephone and went in person to the State Department. He took the elevator to Kaplan's office but did not ask initially for the great man. Instead he inquired for Dolores Vinetta, who, as he had hoped, proved to be of Italian descent. After an exchange of pleasantries, a modest, almost throwaway description of his position in the government of Minnesota, and a jocular suggestion that perhaps in the time of the Medicis the Distancias and the Vinettas might have been of the same blood, he launched his first guided missile. Just checking the trajectory, he thought. Miss Vinetta must by now be aware he was not in Washington just as a tourist, but as the bearer of information of such nature only the Secretary himself should hear it.

"But he is not here. He is at his mother's . . . resting."

"When will he . . . ?"

Distancia knew then the true beauty of surprise, for he had devoted less than ten minutes in groundwork preparation which, if all went well, should net him an interview sometime this very day. Yet even as Miss Vinetta was checking through her appointment book pretending to find a slot where one great man could chat with another, Secretary Kaplan himself marched into the office. He glanced at Miss Vinetta and removed his hat and coat as he continued his determined passage toward his office door.

"Mr. Secretary, this is Mr. Rudy Distancia, the Lieutenant Governor of Minnesota."

Kaplan halted reluctantly, smiled the smile he employed for high and low and especially for cameras, and stated that he was ashamed to admit he had never been in Minnesota. Distancia responded with a promise of a torchlight parade if the Secretary would find time to visit the hinterlands, and as Kaplan resumed his march he moved quickly to his side. "The Piper matter," he whispered. "I have something of the utmost importance."

Distancia was pleased with the immediate results, which he compared to striking a mule between the ears with a two-by-four. He saw Kaplan come to an abrupt halt while the eyes behind the thick glasses surveyed him up and down.

"Have you, indeed?"

Kaplan told Miss Vinetta he was not to be disturbed and, waggling a finger at Distancia, beckoned him to follow. As they entered his spacious office, Distancia wondered how many days he would have waited if he had sought an appointment through normal channels.

Distancia spent four minutes and ten seconds establishing his familiarity with Michael Piper and his spinning-top theory. He chose his words carefully, employing the truth only to ring the bell of authenticity at twenty-second intervals. He was pleased to note that Kaplan was a listener, in this case such a fervent example he turned his head from side to side as if to be sure both ears were picking up the flow of wanted intelligence.

"The fact is, Mr. Secretary, I've been deeply concerned about this matter since the boy was first granted an interview with the President, and if you care to pick up the phone and call Governor Granger I am sure he will confirm my original fears. But I was not then aware of his Soviet connections. . . ."

Distancia let his voice trail off lest it disturb the silence he knew would follow. Let Kaplan make noise now, he thought.

He was satisfied when Kaplan cleared a nonexistent obstruction from his throat and after a moment asked exactly what Mr. Distancia meant by such a statement. Piper with Soviet connections? Unlikely.

"Unlikely? Then how, sir, do you suppose the boy ever got to Moscow?"

Distancia was delighted with the sound of a second Kaplan throat clearing. Now, he thought, an astronaut would safely say, "We have ignition."

"You assume he is there?" Kaplan asked cautiously.

"Where else? His guru is Alice Kellogg, who operates under the cover of an English teacher. Perhaps from your special vantage you have seen some very clever Russian ploys in their American intelligence network. But for country boys like me choosing the Kellogg woman has a touch of genius. Have you met her?"

"No."

"You should. Never in a million years would you suspect she would be even slightly interested in the products and research fields of Minneapolis-Honeywell, which is only one of the many manufacturers in my bailiwick who produce things of vital interest to the Russians. We may be in the boondocks, Mr. Secretary, but that, of course, is the safest place for agents of Miss Kellogg's caliber to operate."

"Have you any proof of this quite serious accusation?"

"Plenty. We are building the case now, but we must move slowly to avoid frightening such a wary bird."

The Petroleum Council was just playing for time, Distancia remembered. If the whole Piper thing failed to blow away in a week or so, then Nash would spend a few million to create a crisis somewhere in the world—a confrontation serious enough to engage the full attention of both Kaplan and the President. If that distraction was not sufficient to make them forget about actual proof of Alice Kellogg's status, at least he was now seeing that seeds of discredit and distrust were firmly planted.

"Certainly you cannot believe this whole thing originated in the boy, Mr. Secretary. It was conceived by the Kellogg woman's superiors, who must have recognized that if she alone presented such a theory she would be signed by some publisher to do a book on it or sent off to the jolly farm. But to have her working through a normal sixteen-year-old all-American boy? That, Mr. Secretary, if you don't mind my saying so, strikes me as pure genius. The Soviets are counting on our becoming scared, even panicking, because they are sure we believe the boy. I would venture to predict the next thing on their agenda will be a

demand of some sort, then more and more as they use the
boy as an ultimate threat. They might even demand a total
surrender of our defenses before they will reveal the boy's
so-called solution. Surely you can see it, sir? This is the
greatest bluff of all time."

There followed a silence which Kaplan maintained long
enough to complete the business of cleaning his already
spotless glasses. Finally he said, "How long do you propose
to be in Washington?"

"As long as you desire." By God, Rudy Distancia knew
when a fire had been kindled, and F. Leslie Nash would
okay an expense account the likes of which had never been
seen even in San Francisco.

"Don't call us, we'll call you," Kaplan said as he ushered
Distancia to the door.

                        * * *

At three forty-seven Moscow time a man and a woman
left the Pekin Hotel and began walking the mile and a half
along Gorky Street to the Kremlin. The man wore cowboy
boots.

They had considered taking the Metro to Red Square,
hoping to be less conspicuous in the late afternoon subway
crowds, but changed their minds when they considered the
possibility of a subway delay. Kaplan had impressed upon
them that timing was all important to their mission. If
they missed communicating with the boy today, he might
be transferred and contact lost forever. Yet they must not
appear too long or more than twice in the vicinity of the
Kremlin lest an inconvenient encounter or some unforeseen incident lead to their exposure. It was an extremely chancy exercise, threatened with such outside factors as just happening to be on the wrong subway car
standing next to an overly curious Soviet citizen. "A paste

and cardboard affair assembled by a confused computer," the man had categorized it.

Yet, with a masterful display of his ingenuity, Kaplan had managed to circumvent the strict Soviet practice of requiring over two weeks to obtain entry visas for any visitors. He discovered that a pair of American country music performers were scheduled for a single concert in Moscow as part of the cultural exchange program. Within hours Kaplan had caused the cast of the tour to be altered. The passports and visas of the singers were picked up, photographs substituted, and a man and a woman of his personal choice sent on their way fully documented.

It was Kaplan himself who declared Napoleon Bonaparte was not just beating his gums when he said imagination rules the world.

Unfortunately, Kaplan's carefully orchestrated research via the personnel computers of the CIA, the State Department, and the Armed Services, provided the name of only one man who was fluent in both Russian and Ameslan. He turned out to be an Army corporal with his Master's in linguistics who had joined the service because he was a devout misanthropist with a history of unhappy love affairs. He was promised he would be assigned to Japan, there to continue his studies. As a consequence he was sent to Stuttgart, Germany, where to pass his time until discharge he had taken up Ameslan and worked with the local handicapped. It had taken some very heavy persuasion on the part of his commanding officer to sell him on a trip to Moscow. When he discovered his partner was to be a woman, he panicked and could not be brought to heel until threatened with charges of mutiny.

The man viewed the venture with even less enthusiasm when he was told his partner could not speak a word of Russian. It seemed she had been a clerk in the embassy at

Madrid, where she had mainly distinguished herself by being mad for matadors and on one occasion had created no little comment by appearing as Lady Godiva at a bullfighting gala. But she could sign in Ameslan, thanks to a sister who had been deaf since birth.

The combination, such as it was, found itself joined (unofficially) in holy matrimony to match a detail of their passports and sent off honeymooning in Russia almost before they realized what had happened. They *were* told that if they could bring off their mission successfully a grateful government would grant their every wish. Having heard such talk before, the man was dubious, but when his commanding officer said he would be damned if he would let him have a blindfold when he faced the firing squad the man finally consented, like a good soldier.

All the woman wanted was a shady-side season ticket to Madrid's bull ring, a reward Kaplan himself took pleasure in arranging.

Now the man and the woman walked at a steady pace toward Red Square and the Kremlin. They intended to arrive during the twilight before Moscow's early winter darkness. If all went as planned, they should be on their way back to the Pekin Hotel by nightfall, complete with a set of figures which they had been warned would doubtless be meaningless to them. Later, when time permitted, they were to transfer the figures to the spacing below the bars of country music sheets which had been provided during their briefing in Stuttgart. If asked, they were to explain that the numbers were fingering clues for deaf guitar players.

It was snowing hard as they walked along Gorky Street, signing occasionally to establish precedent in case they were being observed, and linking arms in accordance with their status of newly marrieds.

Pausing for traffic at Pushkin Square, he signed, "If the snow falls on your notebook, won't it smear the numbers?"

And she signed, "No, I'll use a pencil. What are you, a male chauvinist pig or something? You think just because I'm female I can't do anything right?"

"What have I ever done to deserve you? Just remember to keep your trap shut if anyone says anything. Let me do the talking."

"You better be nice to me or I'll make that marriage stick. And I have a nasty lawyer who could even beat the Army."

"Considering how the Army looks to me, that should be easy. Now give me a kiss on the cheek. There's a man across the street walking right along with us, and I don't like his looks."

As she complied, he tried not to cringe. When the man across the street looked away, she quickly wiped her pursed lips and signed with a gesture he could only interpret as an incomplete karate chop.

THE FIFTEENTH DAY

Mike Piper supposed that under the circumstances he had
nothing to be unhappy about. The Russians, especially
Mr. Gologorsky, could not have been nicer. They were still
having trouble getting the door to swing easily (something
about the building settling on its ancient foundations),
but they had fed him well and had even brought in a TV
set and the latest copies of the Paris *Herald Tribune*.
There was for sure quite some difference in the way they
listened and studied his calculations in comparison with
what had happened in the White House. Mr. Gologorsky
had said they were honored to have him as a guest, and
they sure were acting like they meant it. Wow, had there
been a lot of people dropping by the big room. One was a
very big wheel who was introduced as the Chairman, but
he could not speak English, so an interpreter had to
translate everything. Talking through an interpreter was

sure unhandy. How could a guy know the interpreter was saying things the way you said things and meant the same things?

The food was fairly good, though awfully heavy. Were the Russians afraid a guy might get lonely? It seemed like every meal brought along someone with it—usually a person between sixteen and eighteen who spoke very good English. On the two girls who came together for yesterday's lunch the accent sounded real neat. It was sort of interesting to wonder what Susie would sound like with an accent—if she could speak out loud.

The thing was, this room was beginning to bug a guy. Cripes. How long could you stay in the same room no matter how many people came to see you? If there was one single inch of this room a guy did not know, then cripes, someone should kindly show him exactly where it was. Mr. Gologorsky said he had phoned the American Embassy and found out that Mr. Winslow had been called out of town for several days. But he had left a message saying if it was all right with the Russians maybe Mike could stay in the Kremlin until he got back. And Mr. Gologorsky had laughed and said of course he was welcome. Which was fine, only the view was getting kind of monotonous.

Of course the sticking-door thing was kind of a weirdo, but then what were the guards doing outside? Making sure the door would still swing? Mr. Gologorsky explained that there were just as many kooks in Russia as anywhere else and some of them didn't like Americans because of the bad propaganda of Voice of America, so just as a precaution the guards were there. He had said, "Mike, you can go out anytime you feel like it. Take a nice walk through the Kremlin, go see the Czar's apartments and the Palace of Congresses. Do anything you want, and just remember those men who are following you are your friends. They are along to protect you against any possible harm. We don't want anything to interfere with our big meeting, and I'm working on that right now."

Well, how could you beat that? Wasn't that what you came to Moscow for?

Still, this was something like being a prisoner because just about everybody knew how prisoners knew every inch of their cells. Some cell! There were two big chandeliers hanging from the ceiling and some sort of sculptured frieze, or whatever it's called, running all around the place where the ceiling and walls join. And cripes, those doors alone should be in a museum, which of course was how a person could describe this place—like to Susie when you saw her. She would get a charge out of the big windows with glass that was so wavy it must have been made a hundred years ago.

Mike tried to calculate how many times he had circled the room since his arrival, just walking, getting exercise, and passing the time. Pacing, he discovered dust on the second windowsill from the east end of the room and wondered how he could have missed it before. He was more surprised to find a considerable crack in the wall just between the second and third windows. How could he have missed something that was nearly half an inch wide and wriggled from the floor right up to the ceiling? Maybe the old Arsenal Building was falling down. He would ask Mr. Gologorsky what he thought because cripes, that crack sure was not visible before.

He paused to look out the center window while he thought about the date and the approaching climax of events if the Russians failed to do something soon. But he was not going to give them the solution until they could *prove* they were sharing their efforts with the Americans. It would take the combined support of all nations anyway if things were going to be set back in order before it was too late. No, sir. No mutual agreement, no solution.

He had returned to calculating how many miles he had walked around the room when his attention was attracted to a man and a woman who were on the sidewalk beyond the Kremlin wall. They were standing between two barren trees, and he thought that if it were summertime he would not have been able to see them through the leaves.

Mike was about to return to his walk-mileage calculations when he caught his breath in excitement. Cripes! The way their hands were moving they had to be conversing in Ameslan. He watched them a moment. Absolutely, positively, no question about it!

Then for an instant the man turned and looked directly at him. He signed, "If you see me, place your hands flat against the window."

Hardly believing his eyes, Mike complied and saw the man sign, "Are you alone?"

Mike signed with the affirmative gesture. He made a fist. "Yes."

A third pedestrian appeared between the trees and trudged through the snow, then another. The Ameslan pair hesitated long enough for the traffic to clear, then crossed the street and disappeared beyond a towered building which Mike had been told was the Historical Museum. During their passage he noticed the man and woman ignored him and appeared to be interested only in each other. They were signing, but from his window position he observed them only in profile and at a down angle which he estimated at thirty degrees. He could not follow their gestures, but they seemed to be quarreling.

Once the two were alone again, the man turned to look up at him while the woman watched up and down the street. His hands flying, the man signed, "If we are interrupted, keep watching for us whenever you are alone. We are your friends. Susie sends you her love and is waiting for you. Mother and Father well and know you are here. Your 'early iron' is fine, but needs washing. Your English teacher married a newspaperman and is now with Susie in Washington. Now do you believe we are your friends?"

Mike made another fist, but it was suddenly very hard to see the man's hands at such a distance. Cripes, what was going on? He was crying like some little kid. He wiped away the tears, sniffled hard, and signed, "Why are you here?"

"It is very dangerous. We can only be here a few minutes at a time. The President believes you now. He will do anything you say to save the earth. He needs the solution. Have you told the Russians?"

Mike shook his head vigorously. Then he signed, "If the President agrees, I will leave for Washington and tell him the solution."

"You cannot. Don't you know you are a prisoner?"

Mike again shook his head vigorously.

"You are. You will certainly not be released until you give the Russians the solution. Can you give it to me now?"

"It is too long and complicated. I have to write it down. So would you."

"Okay. Please have it ready. We'll be back before dark."

"Wait. What is the name of my little sister?"

The man gestured the letters S-A-N-D-Y. Then he signed, "She says she is sorry she broke your stereo set."

"What is the name of our school principal?"

After a moment's hesitation the man signed, B-U-N-K-E-R.

"Good. I'll be waiting for you. Bring something to write with."

There was no further signing. The man and the woman

simply locked arms like lovers and moved away. Mike saw them momentarily, bent against the wind. Then the Historical Museum obstructed his view and he could not spot them again.

He turned reluctantly from the window and went to the large table the Russians had provided as a desk. He regretted he had not requested an electronic calculator, but perhaps it was better this way. The fundamentals were all in his mind, but the actual numbers were going to take a long time to come by using nothing more than paper and pencil. Yet it must be done, and now.

He began to concentrate, his pencil moving slowly at first. Brain Two Thousand, he thought, where are you when I need you?

He began his calculations as he had originally, with the weight of the new island of Heimaey, south of Iceland. It was only a recent pucker in the earth's mantle and there were more in the Aleutians, but the creation of Heimaey was the touchstone for his basic computations. The summit, he recalled, was a hundred and eighty-five meters high, and fifteen million cubic meters of lava were emitted. Now for the equations. . . .

Despite the frigid temperature of the room Michael Piper found he was perspiring.

* * *

Nicolai Gologorsky had his orders, and he was a good socialist. He was also acutely aware of his own mortality, and had decided that indeed, the reward as presented by the Englishman was not sufficient for the risk. Why be hounded throughout the world for the rest of what the KGB would vow must be a very short life when he could prove his devotion to the Soviet and still keep the money? Later, say in a few years when all interest in the matter had dissolved, he could take a brief "vacation" in any one of the satellite countries, more of which were being added to the Soviet roster every year. Once in a looser society it would be *desvedanya* to the whole socialist mishmash and on to better things. Yelena Kondratieva might prove a stumbling block unless he kept the promises coming, but words were the most economical form of protection, and perhaps in the interim she might be run over by a handy tank. One should not fret about such matters, he decided —at least not yet, when the preservation of his own neck required his complete attention. Instead of awards of at least a few more red stars, revealing the presence of the American youth in the Kremlin had brought him suspicion and some hard questioning by his superiors. Gologorsky had been reminded very testily that the Soviet Union was in the midst of a fifty-billion-dollar program to develop gas and oil reserves in Siberia. What, the Chairman had wanted to know, would the American boy's spinning-top theory do to that massive effort if the Presidium decided something must actually be done to alleviate the situation? Those several Russian scientists who joined the meeting (after a thorough investigation of their political records proved they were correct thinkers) had astounded the chief party members by declaring that indeed the oil had been pressing on the earth's mantle for eons and any great release of its weight could result in a "pop-up" effect somewhere in the crust. Could it happen even in the Workers' Paradise? Yes, it could, the scientists affirmed.

Beneath the very feet of the Presidium members? Again the possibility was confirmed.

Gologorsky's orders were cut before the meeting had terminated. By whatever means necessary he was to drain the youngster of all the information he might have, including the solution. Here, the Chairman surmised, to the unanimous agreement of his comrades, was an opportunity to throttle the capitalistic, imperialistic, chauvinistic, aggressive nations and once and for all bring glory and the power of the people to the world.

* * *

Phoebe Winslow regarded her husband over a crystal bowl of the caviar she had bought on her last journey to the Caspian. It was teatime, and usually the contemplation of any sort of food caused her to mellow and sometimes even become civil to the distinguished-looking human being who had shared most of her adult life. Yet this glum afternoon, with the apparently perpetual Russian snow glissading past the windows, she found little to approve in her partner.

Gobbling at the caviar so voraciously she dropped twenty-three eggs on the floor, she said, "You really are a pain in the ass, Dudley. All these years in the foreign service and you're still an errand boy. While you are admiring yourself in the mirror, does that ever get to you? Does it ever occur to you that a hair out of place or a necktie that doesn't match your eyes is not going to change the fate of nations? Do you ever ask yourself *why* a man of your age . . . a graduate of Harvard, a man of good family, with the exception of your embezzling uncle . . . did you ever ask yourself during your self-admiration sessions why some men are ambassadors while you are just the guy who holds the door open for them?"

Dudley Winslow kept his peace and only half heard what she had said a hundred times before. The addition of a generous dollop of scotch to his tea, he had found, usually erased his ever gnawing sense of inferiority. He tried to smile at his wife as she ladled another mouthful of caviar

into her maw. He cautioned himself to remember menopause.

"I'll tell you what, Dudley. You are fifty-three years old,
and there is still one thing you can win. That is a contest
for which I will contribute both the seed money and the
grand prize. Just to make sure I get my money back, probably with a dividend, I'm going to enter you. You'll be
wearing my colors in this contest to see who is The Most
Boring Man in the World. You'll lead the field from the
opening gun. All you really care about is jogging. Jog-jog-
jog every morning of your life just to keep your figure.
Someday, I keep hoping, you'll stop running and grow
up."

Phoebe allowed a moment's pause while she ladled an
inch pile of caviar on an inch of toast. "Why don't you say
something, Dudley, like 'Isn't the snow pretty this afternoon?' Something exciting like that."

"Sticks and stones may break my bones, but words will
never—"

"There you go! What a wit. Sometimes I get so lonely
just looking at you I wonder if you are really there. I look
in your eyes and all I see is the color blue. Sometimes I
think I can look right through your head and see furniture
on the other side of the room. Then I tell myself no, that's
a crazy idea. Surely there must be something in there.
Bone? Gristle? But just like my daddy said . . . 'Keep him
on the mantelpiece for decoration. Don't, whatever you
do, ask him to think.' He also warned me never to trust a
gentleman."

"I doubt if your father knew any."

"Say there, Buster, you are in great form this afternoon!
Just get that worried look off your face and no one will
know you."

"I'm worried about the boy. He is such a pleasant young

man. Henshaw said he sent me his best regards. I was rather touched. I wish there were something I could do."

"Are you sure he isn't a Russian spy?"

"Absolutely. Kaplan himself is so concerned about his rescue that he is taking personal charge of the project."

"And how does he propose to accomplish that?"

"I haven't the faintest . . ."

Phoebe licked at the deposits of eggs on her fingers. "I don't know why I bothered to ask."

* * *

Mike was waiting at the window for them. All of his calculations were complete and written on a small piece of notepaper, small enough to crumple and stuff in his pants pocket if he heard anyone at the door. Yet when he saw the man and the woman stop and sign to each other something about the man being a chauvinist pig and the woman a crabby liberated shrew, he had certain misgivings. Who were these people, really? How did they know he understood Ameslan? And how did they know so many things about his personal life?

When the man turned to look up at him, he saw the woman take a note pad from the folds of her coat. She continued to survey the opposite street and the square.

Mike signed, "Before you start copying, tell me, who rents my teeth braces?"

The man hesitated, shrugged his shoulders, then signed, "Sorry. We weren't briefed on that."

Mike was disappointed. Maybe he had asked too much, since very few people knew about the deal with Kevin McCoy. Briefed? Maybe he should try another angle. He signed, "What did I leave Miss Kellogg at the airport?" The answer, he decided, would be available only to someone who knew or had talked with her.

"A note. You left it at the bookstand."

Greatly relieved, Mike smiled and signed, "Okay. Here it comes."

For the next ten minutes, as the light faded and the visibility through the falling snow decreased, Mike signed a long series of numbers, coordinates of latitude and longitude together with quotas of ships in gross tonnage. The man stopped him several times when he had apparently missed a numeral or when the woman fell behind in copying. The relay was broken off twice as pedestrians passed. Mike knew a nervous moment when a male pedestrian stopped and seemed to take too much interest in the couple, but finally the man shooed the stranger away with a laugh and, somewhat to Mike's amazement, seized the woman in a bear hug and held her in a long kiss. As soon as the intruder had disappeared, the man released her and signed that they were ready to copy again.

Mike sent, "This is only the temporary solution to hold things until the permanent solution can be arranged. Okay, here goes—ten ships totaling eight hundred thousand tons to latitude sixteen degrees, ten minutes north, and fifty-seven degrees, twenty-five minutes east . . ."

He was just starting on the final row of his figures when he heard the door open behind him. As he crumpled the paper in his hand he turned to see Nicolai Gologorsky.

*   *   *

As the fifteenth day of Michael Piper's original garage revelation faded into the Russian snows, various events were taking place elsewhere. A new delegation of scientists, selected and inspired by F. Leslie Nash, was advised of a potentially troublesome "spinning-top" theory which Drs. Pomeroy and Weismuller now claimed as their own. Through the efforts of Leo Marcusi the scientists were invited to meet with the President of the United States. Michael Piper was never mentioned as the new arrivals puffed on their pipes and mouthed significant-sounding pooh-poohs at the very idea of the earth going out of orbit.

They did not directly disdain the various phenomena which had supposedly been observed. "Just as there are rashes of flying saucer observations," one distinguished professor from MIT sneered, "it is now common for people to witness earthly fantasies."

Dr. Esteban Keim of Stanford pointed out that during the forties there occurred such a warming of arctic air masses that ice flows decreased vastly and such warm climate birds as the Baltimore oriole, scarlet grosbeak, and wood warbler made tourist flights to Greenland. Meanwhile the regular resident arctic specie fled even farther north. So what was new? Dr. Keim wanted to know.

Winsome Courtney, one of the most honored women ever to graduate from Mills College, pointed out that her plotting of the solar wind cyclonic systems rose and fell according to weekly patterns which matched periods of bad weather across the United States. Any changes corresponded to like differences in solar wind intensity and variations in the earth's magnetic field. "Mr. President," she said crisply, "we are moving into years of increased sunspot action. By the mid nineteen-eighties I foresee the occurrence of even more natural phenomena. From the purely scientific standpoint I must endorse the view of my colleagues who believe the so-called spinning-top theory as created by the removal of oil weight from the planet is utter nonsense."

As the President was thanking the delegation and expressing his particular gratitude to Dr. Winsome Courtney for her reassuring words, Hymie Markel entered the Oval

Office unannounced. He went directly to the President and placed a typed note before him.

FROM: U. S. Consul. Tangier
CLASS: Urgent
Rock of Gibraltar just broke in half. Native apes departed on own initiative prior to upheaval. Unexplained why. Human residents now being evacuated.

Hymie Markel had scribbled two lines across the bottom of the note.

Just had a call from Prudential Life Ins. Chairman of Board wanting to know if rumor true. Very concerned about corporate image.

The President reached into his center desk drawer and found four digestive pills. Clasping them in his fist for later use, he instructed Hymie Markel to give the scientists a tour of the White House. He went directly to Camp David, where he hoped to find some comfort in the company of Marty Martinson and his bride, Alice, and perhaps hear some explanation of this Gibraltar thing from Drs. Weismuller and Pomeroy.

Although news of the Gibraltar episode (9 on the Richter scale) had reached him promptly, it was not until cocktail time that the President was informed that the eastern rim of the Pacific tectonic plate had moved eleven feet to the north, a transformation which had previously been predicted as requiring at least a century. The movement of the plate, with its edge marked by the San Andreas Fault, had been ominously quiet, and the effects were still unobserved by the general public. After his second martini Dr. Pomeroy suggested that if the present rate continued or even increased Los Angeles would sneak up and capture San Francisco within the expected lifetime of the average inhabitants. Such an eventuality, the President commented after his third martini, could cause very grave problems for both Democrats and Republicans.

Cocktail time at Camp David corresponded with six in the morning Moscow time. There a phenomenon occurred which was unlikely to be reported abroad. Known to geologists as "the intrusion of magma," a current of warm rock just under the lithosphere ascended and met the cold winter material beneath the Kremlin. As had occurred for eons, the warm currents divided into two streams. Solid rock was pulled in two directions, forming two tectonic plates, and as they separated a crack developed. All of this occurred very slowly and with relatively little audible commotion. Michael Piper was rudely awakened by a noise he later compared to his dog crunching a bone, then his bed slid the full length of the floor and was stopped abruptly by the opposite wall. Opening his eyes, he saw that it was still dark outside, and it was a moment before he realized the crack he had noticed the day before was now a yard wide and beyond it he could plainly see one of the illuminated spires of the Historical Museum. He heard bells clanging at the far end of Red Square and wondered sleepily if the Russians were launching some kind of a celebration. Then the sound of the bells ceased abruptly, and shivering with the cold, he rose and made his way barefooted across the slanting floor. Examining the separation of the wall, he saw it was like a mountain crevasse, and he thought immediately that if he spread his arms and legs and was extremely careful about how he moved he stood a fair chance of descending within about fifteen feet of the ground. Then, if he had the nerve, he could jump the rest of the distance just as he had that long-ago night when he had vaulted off Susie's porch. Once again the snow should cushion his landing. Beyond was freedom. As he started to dress he marveled at his easy acceptance of the obvious fact that the wall had not separated simply for Mike Piper's convenience. There had been some kind of an earthquake—a rather sneaky shifting of the earth's crust which resulted in a single tremor. No perceptible aftershock, which should indicate a minor shifting of the local tectonic plates. All quite natural and in line with his predictions. A human being, he decided, could get used to anything as long as the gravitational force remained reasonably constant. But when that began to change everywhere in the world—wow!

As he pulled on his pants Mike heard the sound of boots pounding in the hallway and men shouting in Russian. There followed a heavy thumping as someone threw his weight against the door. Mike could find only one shoe in the darkness, but he hesitated to turn on the light. If anyone outside was looking up at the crevasse in the wall, that person would see him silhouetted and his whole plan would fail. Cripes, where was that damn shoe?

He scrambled around near his bed, sweeping his arm across the polished floor, listening with apprehension to the increasing commotion in the hallway. Bless the door! Whatever happened must have thrown it even farther out of plumb.

Just as he discovered the missing shoe, he gasped. The door had given way enough to allow a paper-thin sheet of light to slip through. He could hear the grunts of the guards, then more voices shouting. Cripes! The door could not hold forever . . . like maybe only one more minute . . . so *beat* it, right now!

He paused at the desk, swept the papers covered with his calculations into a thin pile, and stuffed them inside his shirt. Then, in a half crouch, he started an awkward slide across the slanting floor. With his street shoes on he found traction poor and fell down. Recovering, he glanced back to see the shaft of light from beyond the door had widened.

When at last he reached the wall he breathed deeply of the fresh cold air and eased himself into the crevasse. Then he whispered to himself, "Easy does it now," and, moving only one foot and one hand at a time, began a careful descent. The old masonary crumbled often beneath his feet, and for one terrifying moment he literally hung by his fingertips. But he swung his feet until he found what felt like a reasonably secure projection and, pressing his body as hard as he could against the inner wall, half slid until he was in contact with both sides again.

Hey, he thought, I'm a human fly.

He had struggled downward some thirty feet when he heard the distant splintering of wood and knew the door had at last given way. There was no time left for caution. He glanced reluctantly at the distance still to go and told himself it was now or never. He took a nervous breath and leaped toward what he prayed was a deep drift of snow.

* * *

Nicolai Gologorsky was dreaming of sugarplum fairies and spinning tops when his telephone rang. "*Moi chizok*," his plump wife said, "it is for you. *That* woman," she added acidly.

Gologorsky padded to the telephone in such fear he did not notice the cold of the morning. Even with his special perks as a commissar and party member the heat in his apartment was limited, and for an ordinary call he would have delayed long enough to put on socks and his soft house boots. But it was just becoming light outside and he knew no one called at such an hour except KGB, who were all insomniacs. Still, it was better if they called than if they were knocking at the door.

He was even more unnerved to discover his wife was right and indeed she had recognized the voice of Yelena Kondratieva. By what special sorcery did wives know all the things they should not know? Now, in a tone which instantly ruined his day, Yelena Kondratieva told him that an American invasion team, sponsored of course by the imperialistic, capitalistic tool of the aggressors, had somehow managed to blow a hole in the Kremlin and kidnap the American youth. She urged immediate action in view of Gologorsky's scheduled appointment with the boy and the President of the Supreme Soviet that very morning. "And the money," she added. "Let us not forget, my dear comrade, there must be more available. But we need the boy's body to collect."

Trying his best to forget the whole folly, Gologorsky half stumbled to the window which overlooked Pushkin Square. He yearned to step out on the balcony and inhale some early morning air, thereby perhaps relieving his fast-growing premonition that at the very beginning he should have turned the matter of the American youth over to someone less vulnerable. But the shoddy workmanship in the construction of his luxury apartment discouraged balcony visitations. Far too many had fallen off the side of the building even without the burden of extra weight. It was like the elevator of the building, he brooded, which according to his estimate worked less than 50 percent of the time. And it was like his last interview with young Michael, which upon reflection had been even less than 50 percent productive.

He had been mystified at the apparent change in the boy himself. Michael had seemed highly nervous when Gologorsky first entered the room. Previously he had always seemed easy; they had in a way become friends, and planned to play a few games of chess as soon as Gologorsky could find time. Had he not provided paper, pencils, an atlas, and a book of weights and measures in English, just as the boy had asked? Perhaps he should have approached him with chessboard and box in hand, sat down for an hour, and probed Michael further while his concentration was on the game. *Da*, he might have made a mistake in his initial approach. The fierce look, the growling threats and hints of physical persuasion, had only seemed to make the boy more stubborn about revealing his solution. And without the spinning-top solution who was Nicolai Gologorsky but a relatively minor government functionary with two million dollars in hand and no place to hide? A "schmuck," as the few Jews left in the U.S.S.R. would say. Thank you for your efforts, Comrade Gologorsky, and *desvedanya*.

Young Mike had said, "I'm sorry you are angry, Mr. Gologorsky, but I'm just not going to write down the solution until I know for sure my own government has it and I have some proof you are going to work together. That's the way it has to be."

Now Gologorsky could easily remember how the boy looked standing in the big room, so alone in the early evening twilight—a young man he would have been very proud to claim as a son. What gave him that confidence he was right? How could an absolutely helpless juvenile stand there, eyes shining, and say *nyet* to the only official he knew personally in the Soviet Government? *Guts* was the American word, Gologorsky recalled.

Now, he thought regretfully, he must turn the hounds loose on the boy. How sad. No matter how resourceful the Americans who had retrieved him from the Kremlin might be, their chances of escaping alive beyond the borders of the Soviet Union were virtually nil. Yet somehow he must prevent an accidental shooting of the boy.

Gologorsky sighed unhappily as he placed his first call to the KGB.

* * *

Nicolai Gologorsky was not the only early riser on this chill Moscow morning. A representative of another government, Dudley Winslow III, had been up since long before dawn, pacing the rooms of his apartment in such mental anguish as he had never known. Could what Phoebe had said be true? Was he really just a stuffed shirt, the world's champion bore? What could he do to refute such an accusation—not that he cared all that much about what Phoebe thought, but what about the opinion of his peers and, even more important, of himself? Had the house of Winslow come to such a pass that one of its blood was merely tolerated? Excepting Uncle Byron, who had embarrassed the family with his overlight fingers at the Bank of Boston, there had not been a blot on the family escutcheon since the pilgrim Nathanial Winslow tried (unsuccessfully) to seduce Hiawatha.

Writhing beneath such complex thinking, Winslow decided it would be useless to go back to bed and listen to the 1812 *Overture* as rendered through Phoebe's respiratory apparatus. He would go up to the communications room on the top floor of the embassy and see what cables had come from Washington, which should at least provide something different to think about.

He dressed with deliberate carelessness, as if determined to show the world Dudley Winslow III was, after all, a regular fellow. He encountered some difficulty in creating an imperfect knot in his tie, but finally managed to his satisfaction. For a wild moment he considered wearing a blue cashmere sweater instead of a jacket, but changed his mind. After all, one did not throw aside one's pride after fifty years of indoctrination.

He was just leaving the apartment when the annunciator box at the side of the door buzzed. Winslow was confused. Callers at this hour of the morning?

He pressed the annunciator lever and made the only response his surprise would allow. "Yes?"

Winslow recognized the gravel voice of one of the Marine guards. "Sergeant Tonney here, sir. I was just finishing my rounds when the gate police brought me a youngster who says he knows you. He doesn't have a passport or papers of no kind whatsoever, and I don't know what to do with him because he claims to be an American."

Winslow caught his breath. "Is his name Michael Piper?"

"That it is, sir."

"Send him to me immediately."

While he waited Winslow tried desperately to gather and concentrate his thoughts. Although he did not smoke he took a cigarette from the coffee table and puffed at it nervously. Mike back in the embassy at this hour? Was this in answer to his secret prayers—a moment of truth? Certainly the Soviets were not going to give Mike the key to the Kremlin, and if he had just escaped the Russians must even now be in hot pursuit. Logic, old boy. Use your noodle, as Secretary Kaplan was so fond of saying. The first place the Soviets would look would be the embassy itself.

Visualizing the embassy besieged, in defiance of international law, Winslow tried very hard to specify his duty.

He opened the entrance door and waited impatiently until he saw Mike emerging from the elevator. He was smiling, there was still snow in his hair and on his shoulders, and he was shivering with cold. "Hi, Mr. Winslow. I'm sorry to wake you up, but it's sure neat to see you again."

Five minutes later, after he had listened to Mike, Dudley Winslow III saw his duty clearly. There was no time for protocol, and certainly no time to rouse the Ambassador in Spasso House. Mike was not a refugee Cardinal Mindzenty, with world opinion to protect him. If the Russians really wanted him they would find some way to remove him from the premises regardless of diplomatic protests. And now, quite to his own surprise, Winslow discovered he had a plan.

He took his son Geoff's heavy parka, gloves, and boots from a closet and told Mike to squeeze into them somehow. Then, excusing himself, he went directly to the top floor of the embassy and entered the only room in the building considered electronically bug-proof against the Russians. It was a room within a room, a large Plexiglas box where important staff meetings were held or highly classified and single side-band telephone calls were made. Winslow hoped its security was as tight as it was supposed to be, since the dangers inherent in his scheme were almost overwhelming.

There were two telephones side by side on the small conference table. One was red, which he knew was connected directly with the White House or wherever the President might be. The other telephone was black, and Winslow had never seen anyone use it. Yet he knew very well what it was for, and he also knew that less than four or five people, including the Ambassador, had ever used it. He turned on the air-conditioning system, which was deliberately designed to frustrate electronic listening devices. Then he picked up the black telephone. He heard a humming ring, and instantly a male voice came on the line with one word, "Colorado."

Winslow took a deep breath and said simply, "Winslow. Status one. I have an applecart. North side. Sixteen hundred Zulu."

"Stand by."

There was a moment's pause, then the male voice enunciated distinctly, "Square D . . . twenty-five . . . thirty-one . . . Melrose. Dally it. You copy?"

"Right. Thank you very much."

Winslow heard a click in the receiver and hung up. He put the data in his coat pocket and left the Plexiglas room. Moments later he passed a Marine guard and entered a much larger room on the floor below. He marched through a double row of locked file cabinets and in the center of the room stopped before a concrete pedestal. A small propane-fueled furnace stood nearby.

The pedestal held two safes, and both alarms, he noted with satisfaction, were armed. Ignoring the larger safe, he deactivated the alarm on the smaller safe by dialing the combination he had memorized for Saturdays. Jolly good that this *was* Saturday, he thought as he twisted the opening numbers on the safe, for that fact had been the first trigger to his plan. Every Saturday it was his duty to meet the *Red Arrow*, the train which came down from Helsinki and carried not only the U.S. diplomatic couriers and their important pouches, but also new employees for the embassy, mail from home for U.S. residents, and usually half a truckload of free world amenities which the diplomatic community thought necessary to their contentment. It was Winslow's duty to see that all went smoothly, prevent any possible confrontation with the Russians, and frustrate (as had once happened) a hijacking of the goods truck by its Russian drivers.

The train always arrived at six in the morning, and Winslow though the timing was, for once, most convenient. Unfortunately, on this morning he might be less than meticulous about his duties. The main thing was to behave for the benefit of the Russian police at the embassy's street exit exactly as he had always behaved on Saturday mornings.

He opened the small safe door and took out a green loose-leaf notebook. He flipped quickly through the index tags to the M section and found "Melrose." There he found "Square D" interpreted as "Open field. Pasture—1500 meters. High fir trees east end approx. 20 meters high."

He found the two numbers he had copied, "twenty-five" and "thirty-one" were interpreted as 56 degrees, 30 minutes, 27 seconds north, and 38 degrees, 20 minutes, 13 seconds east. The words "Dally it" translated as "5 to 10 minutes either side of specified hour. Be ahead of time and wait."

Winslow turned to the back of the book and pulled out a colored map of Moscow and environs, including the surrounding countryside to a distance of forty kilometers. The Russians had long ago set a limitation on travel without proper passes at thirty kilometers from the center of Moscow, but there were ways to go farther if the regular routes could be abandoned. A pair of dividers were taped to the leather binding of the data book, and now he removed them and measured the coordinates of latitude and longitude on the map. He made an X where they intersected at a point thirty-eight kilometers to the northeast of the Leningrad Highway. "Beautiful," he sighed. It was comforting to know someone had done his homework right. He checked his watch, closed the safe quickly, rearmed the alarm system, and half ran to the exit.

Soon afterward, at ten minutes until six, an embassy Ford, driven by a still yawning Marine, left the arched exit from the courtyard and sent up a spray of snow as it swerved left toward the planetarium. In the back seat was a single figure, wearing an astrakhan hat and heavily bundled in a fur coat. The figure waved lazily at the Soviet gate police.

The car proceeded at high speed to Gorky Street and continued past the Pekin Hotel. It pulled into the parking area of Belorussian Station, and the bundled figure left the car for ten minutes. Returning, the same person climbed into the back, and the car sped away toward the Leningrad Prospect. Now the dawn revealed a second bundled figure in the back, and moments later the entire car disappeared behind a lonely rooster tail of snow.

All of the car's eccentric maneuvers were executed according to the crisp orders of Dudley Winslow. The Marine driver said, "I sure hope you know where you're going, sir, because I'm plumb lost. This sure ain't the way back to the embassy."

"Exactly," Winslow replied with confidence. "Let us hope the Russians will also become confused." He turned to smile at Mike Piper, who now sat erect beside him. "I hope you weren't too uncomfortable on the floor. That parka is not a bad fit."

Mike asked, "Do you think they'll follow us?"

"I am sure they'll try. I must tell you we are gambling on time and Soviet bureaucracy. First, news of your escape must be transmitted to the proper authority, who will close all the normal exits from Moscow. Then someone will interrogate the gate guards at the embassy and find you had indeed been there. That should require at least half an hour, hopefully more. When I fail to return from Belorussian Station, they will start piecing things together, which will take some time. Perhaps another hour or two in our favor. Before that time has elapsed, we should be with my friend Sasha."

"Who is Sasha?"

Winslow chuckled. "A man I met because we both like birch trees."

Mike decided there was something about Mr. Winslow that made him quite different from the rather sad man he had known before. He seemed to be enjoying himself. His eyes sparkled and he spoke with assurance. Mike thought he sort of reminded him of the athletic coach back at Central High. He also thought this new Mr. Winslow was pretty neat.

Mike watched the weak sun, a golden ball bouncing along the tops of the birch forest which stood on both sides of the road. They passed a group of peasants riding in two horse-drawn sleds. They were heavily dressed against the cold, and their breaths made clouds of vapor around their fur caps.

"Does your friend live around here?"

"Not far now. Another ten miles or so. When there isn't snow on the ground, I like to jog in the early morning. I drive out to this area and jog through the forest trails . . . four or five miles, depending on my disposition. One morning I met a Russian who also likes to jog, and after several weeks we became good friends, I suppose because we both appreciate the birches and jogging. Sasha is a blacksmith who lives alone just beyond the next village. He is a very strong man with one weakness . . . the Russians call it *spekulatsiya*."

"What's that?"

Winslow pointed to the heavy box in the seat beside the Marine driver. "*Spekulatsiya* is black-marketing. That box is full of American cigarettes. Sasha doesn't smoke himself, but he has a lot of customers who do. And, what's more, he has something we need very badly. I am hoping we can make a trade."

* * *

Nicolai Gologorsky stood morosely between Colonel Boris Krasnayov of the Soviet Army (Hero of the Soviet Union etc.), and Comrade Yuri Lomonosov, Deputy Chief of the KGB. They stood in the snow and stared at the great crack in the side of the Arsenal Building as if they were unwilling witnesses to something obscene.

Colonel Krasnayov brushed at the icicles which his exhalations had formed on his mustache and said, "Obviously a Commando effort. Special Forces technique straight through. Cleverly disguised to make it look like some sort of natural earthquake. They must be using some new kind of blasting material. Not a trace of smoke or fire. But how did so many men get past the frontier?"

"Perhaps they came as tourists," Gologorsky offered nervously. "There have been increasing numbers lately." He did not like the continued silence which seemed to have wrapped itself around Comrade Lomonosov—a man not noted for his tolerance of anything which displeased him.

Colonel Krasnayov said, "We shall have some very interesting information when the bandits are caught. I can hardly wait to chide their military attaché. What foolishness! There is no possible way for them to cross the frontiers. All points were notified over an hour ago."

"What about the U. S. Embassy?" Gologorsky asked because he longed to make a sound of some sort. Deputy Chief Lomonosov's continued silence was ominous.

"We've cordoned it off. No one can leave or depart. Locked up," Krasnayov said tersely.

"Ah? Very good. The Soviet Army is far ahead of me." Shifting quickly to the side of the least menacing of his companions, he added, "How very perceptive of you, Colonel. Of course if this was some kind of a Commando effort, they would not all be sitting inside the embassy."

"We must remember the Americans are never logical." Yuri Lomonosov finally employed his vocal chords. In a high thin voice, as chilling as the early morning, he turned his black astrakhan hat to face Gologorsky and asked, "Why did you choose to confine the boy to the one place in the Kremlin where the outer wall would not be further protection? I await your answer with the same interest that the President of the Presidium will await my report."

"It simply seemed the most logical and convenient place. And . . . I thought the boy might be more comfortable there and be more willing to cooperate—" Gologorsky was sweating despite the cold.

"Is it not conceivable, Comrade Gologorsky, that you might have become the tool of the Americans? Is it possible that the Englishman, Mr. Henshaw, provided you with tempting funds which might in fact have been a guarantee the boy would be placed in a location where, with relatively little effort, he could be freed? Do you prefer to confess now or later?"

"How can you even think I—"

"Is it not as apparent to you, Comrade, that someone *inside* the Kremlin must have been cooperative in this matter . . . someone in authority? How else would an American team of any kind know so exactly where the boy was located? If the boy was worth so much effort as we see here, then he is valued by our American friends at more than a few million rubles. Dare I conjecture that you might have some future travel plans . . . say to a country beyond the frontiers of our beloved motherland?"

Gologorsky tried to stifle the panic he felt rising like yeast in his throat. He was being called a traitor, the oldest technique in the Soviet Union. By offering a scapegoat who would at the very least spend the balance of his days in Siberia, Comrade Lomonosov relieved himself and the KGB of any involvement in a national error. Conversely, Lomonosov might even become a hero in uncovering the guilty party.

"I should say offhand," Yuri Lomonosov whined, "that your travel plans might be altered."

* * *

The Soviet-flot T-144 airliner landed at Copenhagen three hours later than scheduled. Before departure from Moscow's Sheremetyevo Airport there had been a long and unexplained delay while the authorities queried every foreign passenger and checked the past history of every Russian. Baggage was not searched, since whatever the authorities were looking for apparently was of such size it could not be concealed, and a rumor circulated among the passengers that the search was for certain individuals.

All passengers were eventually released to board the aircraft. Among them was a honeymoon pair whose devotion to each other had achieved such intensity even the officials were inclined to smile. Later, when they were safely in the air and could not be heard even by their nearest seat companions, they whispered various sweet nothings and endearments to perpetuate their visual image.

The woman said, "Listen . . . this thing is going too far. You're getting me all excited."

"The word is *aroused*. I find this not entirely unpleasant. You have a nice smell about you."

"It's essence of Pekin Hotel, a very special fragrance. Do you really hate me?"

"Now that I'm not so scared I look at you differently. What are you going to do after we deliver the notes?"

"Stop that. Keep your hands out of mischief. I'm going to the bullfights. Stop it, I say!"

"How do you know I'm not the wild bull of the pampas?"

The woman pushed him away—gently. "What are you going to do, Toro?"

"The Army says they will make me a sergeant. On that kind of salary and perks we could have a nice relationship."

"You mean get married?"

"No. I believe in long courtships."

"Forget it. They don't have bullfights in Germany."

"I'll get transferred to Spain. The Army said I could have anything I wanted after our mission was completed."

"Okay. It's a deal. Now stop that . . . well, not altogether . . . we have to keep up appearances."

* * *

At the air base in northeastern England, Major Charles Fuller was pleased to hear his name called on the paging system at the Officers' Club. Better yet, he was advised to report immediately to the squadron commander's office, and since it was just past mail time he was sure the summons meant but one thing—the arrival of his official confirmation as lieutenant colonel.

"Greetings, Chuck," his commander said, grinning. "Glad they found you before you got away for the weekend."

"I'm going down to London unless—" He winked, knowing his commander would understand his impatience. The commander himself had said promotion was overdue. "I hope they're not out of silver leaves in the PX."

"There will be a pair waiting for you when you get back."

"Of course if I've finally got it made I don't have to go to London. I can celebrate right here. You're invited."

"I accept if you're buying the drinks. And I'll donate the silver leaves."

"That's just great. I sure appreciate it. Boy, are we going to have a Saturday night bash!" Major Fuller smacked a fist into his palm to display his enthusiasm.

"We may get a late start because first you have to make a little journey." The squadron commander handed him a sheet of paper covered with computerized numbers. Fuller studied them a moment and frowned.

"Wait a minute. You can't do this to me. Why am I always the boy to get these special missions? This could be dangerous, and I should be about out of luck."

"You do such a good job I can't bear to try anyone else."

"Now listen, Tom Sawyer . . . !"

"This caper is super important. Not only will you get shiny new silver leaves on your shoulders, but I'll put your name in for another DFC also."

"I already got three. I don't want any more medals and I don't want to wind up in Siberia, or worse. I puncture very easily, and both my parents were hemophiliacs. I am no longer interested in this kind of hinky-do. I want a staff job."

The commander smiled easily and stared at the ceiling. "Your country gives you a ten-million-dollar flying machine, the only one in the world that can fly hands off fifty feet above the ground and take you to a pinpoint anywhere within range while all you've got to do is sit there and watch the scenery go by, and you're unhappy? I never heard of such ingratitude."

328

"When that scenery is going by at five hundred knots while I'm looking up at telephone poles, barns, birds, and God knows what else, I don't see much that doesn't raise my pucker factor."

"Then don't eat too many prunes. Your coordinates and rendezvous time are all on that sheet. This is a very big one, so don't goof it. Good-bye, old friend. I'll have a drink waiting for you at the club."

* * *

The blue embassy Ford continued its race along the Leningrad Highway, passed over a bridge spanning a frozen river, then plunged once more into a heavily wooded area. Moments later the Ford skidded around a blind turn and almost immediately came to a skidding stop.

The Marine driver turned his attention to the back seat. His eyes were appealing as he said, "Sir?"

"Well . . . well," Winslow said for lack of a more definite response. Obviously a further exchange was unnecessary, for a barrier obstructed the road and four Russian soldiers stood in front of it. Winslow noted that in spite of their being bundled to the eyes against the cold they held their short assault guns at the ready.

One of the soldiers approached the car and peered inside. He seemed to be displeased and said "Nyet!" several times.

Winslow rose to the occasion by opening the box at his feet and removing a carton of cigarettes. Handing them to the soldier, he smiled warmly and explained his little party had not intended to go beyond the barrier. If the good comrade soldier would be so understanding, he would permit Dudley Winslow of the American Embassy and his companion to step out of the car and breathe of the crisp ozone. In such a way they could begin their admittedly peculiar American ritual, which the good soldier comrade would understand was performed every morning regardless of the weather. "Come on, Mike," Winslow said in English. "This is the place I usually start." Then in a less hearty tone he added, "Do exactly as I do."

Once out of the car, Winslow took off his heavy coat and tossed it carelessly onto the back seat. Mike duplicated his actions. As the Russians watched in puzzlement, Winslow rose on his toes, extended his arms, and took a deep breath. He exhaled a great cloud of vapor into the cold morning air. He repeated the exercise several times, and Mike tried to imitate his smile of satisfaction.

Finally Winslow pounded his chest vigorously, and when he had finished he said to the Russian, "Now we come to the best part of the morning. We jog ten kilometers back toward Moscow."

Winslow wished the Marine would not look so unbelieving when he told him to turn the Ford around and follow them. "Stay well behind. We don't want to breathe your filthy exhaust fumes."

As if he turned his back on poised submachine guns every morning, Dudley Winslow III started an easy jog along the way they had come. Stretching his long legs, Mike was soon jogging at his side.

"A bit awkward, that," Winslow said, emitting large puffs of vapor. "Something I hadn't counted on. As a lifetime bureaucrat I failed to credit my opposite numbers with such speedy reaction."

"What can we do now, Mr. Winslow?"

"Keep jogging to stay warm. You do have a good stride and you'll need it. About a mile from here we should be hidden by the trees. We'll wait for the car, retrieve our coats, then double back through the woods. If the snow is

not too deep, it should take us only about an hour on foot
to my friend's place, and we have time to spare."

"Super," Mike said. "I can't wait to tell Susie about this
morning."

"Of course we could get ourselves shot. You should
know that."

"You seem to know what you're doing, Mr. Winslow. I
have a lot of confidence in you."

Winslow blew out a cloud of vapor and said, "Thanks,
Mike. I haven't heard that very often . . . if ever."

* * *

At Copenhagen's Kastrup Airport, Marty Martinson
waited outside the Danish customs for the man and the
woman. During his Washington briefing he had been assured he would have no trouble recognizing the pair. "Just
look for some rather open displays of affection."

It had been Secretary Kaplan's idea to use Marty rather
than anyone in the Copenhagen Embassy, and his concern
for security had been endorsed by the President. "The
Russians know every member of our foreign service in the
Baltic nations," Kaplan insisted. "I want the man and the
woman's cover to be complete and not see them get
knocked off or lose the data ball just at the goal line. They
must deliver to an unknown . . . an unknown we can trust
implicitly."

At Camp David the President had pointed his decision
finger at Marty and said, "You are elected." Then, smiling
at the former Alice Kellogg, he expressed his regret at
separating the newly marrieds so soon after their ceremony.

All very well, Marty thought as he fingered his stubble
of beard. Yet both Kaplan and the President had ignored
the human factor. It had been a unique experience to have
the British Concorde delay its departure until he had been

thoroughly briefed, and equally impressive on arrival in London to be whisked away almost immediately to a nearby military field where a supersonic fighter capable of even greater speed than the Concorde awaited him. The elapsed time from Washington to Copenhagen had been merely four hours and thirty minutes, including ground transport. The trouble was now in the Martinson body, which insisted it was only 2 A.M. and past a bridegroom's bedtime. Bedtime? How could any husband explain to the President of the United States that he had just married the most energetic woman he had ever known? Alice Kellogg had put her full heart into her bridal role. Her enthusiasm for post-nuptial affection had left him staggering, and in his rare moments of rest he had mentally written the first chapter of a book to be entitled, *The Short, Happy Life of Marty Martinson.*

Marty looked at the scud above the red and white Danish flags whipping in the wind and wondered how he could manage to stay awake through the return journey. "I know it may seem incredible to you," Kaplan had warned, "but so are the Soviets incredible. They can hijack you on our very doorstep, and if they have even the slightest suspicion you might be involved I'll guarantee they will. Therefore you must not fall asleep either mentally or physically . . . not even for a moment. Stay constantly alert. Bear in mind the fate of this entire planet may lie in those few bits of paper you will bring back with you."

Marty Martinson's pulse rate increased alarmingly when he saw a pair of cowboy boots approaching. The man in them fitted the description he had been given, and there was a woman with him.

Marty let them stand a moment, their eyes searching the crowds of Europeans making for taxis and buses. He wanted to be sure they were not being followed, and he saw how easily an elaborate plan could trip over a detail. What would have happened to these two if for some reason he had not been standing where he was? Suppose there had been some unforeseeable accident—a car collision while en route between airports, a mechanical malfunction of an airplane, a bellyache—any of which might have prevented his being where he was. According to his briefing, the woman and her escort had been told only what they needed to know to accomplish their task. Lest they be apprehended, they knew nothing more. Was there some sort of a double for protection then? Another couple? For that matter, was there someone serving as a double for himself who would suddenly step right up and accost the pair with the proper key phrase if Marty Martinson fell asleep standing up? It was now obvious he also had been told only what he needed to know.

Marty raised his hand at the man and said, smiling, "Did you bring the country music?"

The man hesitated, searched Marty's eyes, and sighed with relief. "Yessir. Ah got the best goddamn tunes y'all ever heard. Right here."

The man opened his dispatch case and handed Marty several sheets of music. "Ah jes know it's gonna be a hit," the man said.

"Let's hope you're right."

Marty turned away and, walking rapidly, soon melted into the crowd.

* * *

The snow was deep through the woods, but the surface was frozen hard and only occasionally did they break through the crust. A pallid sun dappled the whiteness with weak highlights where the birches stood sparse, and cast an eerie glow over the hillocks along the horizon.

Mike was impressed by the heavy silence as they moved toward a darker portion of the forest. When the birches gave way to a thick stand of pine, the only audible sound was their breathing and an occasional squeaking beneath their boots as their weight compressed the cold snow more solidly. They took turns carrying the box of cigarettes which they had taken from the car along with their coats. Winslow was carrying the box now, and the more Mike watched his broad back moving tirelessly ahead the more he liked the man. Cripes, he had seemed so stiff and unapproachable before; now he was a different person. But then most adults were weirdos, and a guy could never be sure how they were going to behave.

During the next half hour Winslow paused several times and glanced at the fragment of red sun visible through the trees. Once he whispered that he was having trouble orienting himself because the snow cover made everything look different from what he remembered.

At last they came to a frozen stream and heard a bell tolling in the distance. Nodding vigorously, Winslow said that he now knew exactly where they were. His friend Sasha's house would be just at the head of the stream.

They continued along the twisting bank, slipping occasionally on the snow-covered ice. The stream turned sharply, and beyond a low peninsula they saw two log structures—a cottage and a barn. Smoke curled upward from the chimney of the cottage, and Mike saw a man in a peaked cap gathering an armful of wood from a pile of birch logs. Winslow set the box of cigarettes down in the snow and whispered, "That is Sasha. We'll wait until he goes inside and save him embarrassing explanations if any of the villagers happen to have dropped in on him."

They sat down in the snow and waited until the man entered the cabin and they saw the volume of smoke from the chimney increase. Then, after cautioning Mike to remain concealed until signaled to follow with the box, Winslow made a wide curve around the peninsula. Finally Mike saw him move across the clearing to the side window of the cottage. After a moment he beckoned. Mike hoisted the box to his shoulder and struck out for the clearing.

* * *

Opposite the Children's World store in Moscow's Dzerzhinsky Square, Yuri Lomonosov presided over the feverish activity within the KGB Building. Lomonosov and his assistants were busily sifting through the numerous reports which had come from the outside world, but the local situation demanded their major attention.

Ten suspicious-looking individuals had been seen on the road to Vnukovo Airport. Eight males and two females. Arrested. Five individuals who appeared to be (or were pretending to be) eating their noon meal one half a kilometer from the ZIL auto factory had just been questioned —and arrested. All male. A mixed bag of skaters had been arrested on the Moscow River near the Krutitsky Monastery. At least on first questioning none of those detained seemed to be of American origin or speak English. One of Lomonosov's aides pointed out that after a few hours of severe treatment they might loosen up. His suggestion was rejected as unnecessary since a new and startling (if true) report had just come in.

Vasily Kozlov and Peter Arbatov, two of the policemen who had been on duty at the gates of the U. S. Embassy the previous night, had been awakened from their day sleep for questioning. They claimed that sometime before dawn an American boy fitting the description of Michael Piper had presented himself to them and asked to be admitted. Since it was common for Russian dissidents and other misguided Soviet citizens to try for asylum in the embassy by claiming they were really Americans and needed help, the policemen had at first refused the boy entrance. They had also considered administering the customary beating, which usually discouraged further visits by such twisted individuals, but at the last minute decided they would check with an American Marine who was passing across the inner courtyard. The Marine questioned the boy a moment, made a telephone call, and took the boy within. Apparently he was, indeed, an American.

Lomonosov was perplexed. If the boy had actually presented himself at the embassy, then where were the commandos who had released him? Launching an investigation within an investigation, he demanded to know precisely when the last drop of vodka had caressed the policemen's lips. Any sober person would find it hard to believe that a sixteen-year-old boy simply walked out of the Kremlin, crossed Red Square, and walked all the way to the American Embassy so early on an extremely cold morning. Were the policemen inside keeping warm? Had they been asleep, or drunk and asleep and imagining things?

Lomonosov was further puzzled by a series of reports originating with the Soviet maids who served the U. S. Embassy—good KGB agents all. Observing as they cleaned and polished, they insisted the boy was not presently in the embassy unless he was confined to the top floor, where they were never admitted. Furthermore, electronic bugging of that area (admittedly incomplete) showed no indication of the boy's presence.

He was chewing on the lower fringes of his mustache when an assistant laid a two-line report before him. A peasant (unidentified), on his way to early market, had observed a dark blue Ford stop on the Leningrad Highway.

Two men had joined the vehicle and removed coats and a large package from same. They had then disappeared into the forest.

Lomonosov had been about to dismiss the report as inconsequential when he changed his mind. A blue Ford? Only the American Embassy used such cars. Was it still there? And what could it be doing on the Leningrad Highway at that early hour?

Suddenly Lomonosov thought he might see a twinkle of light in the frustrating confusion about him. It was noon, and he must take his midday meal lest his ulcer protest—yogurt and bean curd were the best for his affliction. But while he was compromising with his peptic, others would be working in the finest KGB tradition.

Lomonosov's high voice squeaked out orders in rapid succession. "Find the peasant. Want more details. Check time of sunup against story and advise me." Could he really see, or was he just seeing things? Vodka, he thought angrily, was the curse of the entire U.S.S.R. "Call the Army. Send troops to suspect area. Check for footprints in snow. Follow same, if any. Order two helicopters patrol same area. Survey anything unusual. Report immediately. Check further at U. S. Embassy. Furnish names and rank of any missing officials and/or their families. Same for clerks, typist, etc. Bring on immediate completion of engineers' report on damage to Kremlin. Accomplish items one through twelve by time I return from lunch. And while you're at it, arrest Comrade Gologorsky."

* * *

At 1400 Zulu (Greenwich) time Major Chuck Fuller walked through the drizzle which seemed to anoint the North of England air base perpetually. He wore a heavy flying suit and a white helmet with his squadron insignia painted on the sides. His name, scratched from wear and somewhat faded by the upper elements, was on the front of the helmet in bold letters—FULLER, C. D., MAJOR. His crew chief, in a moment of ill-timed humor, had crossed out the MAJOR with a crayon and substituted LT. COL.

Fuller approached his F-111 swept-wing aircraft impressed, as he had been since first sight, with its bulk. It stood in its dark camouflage like a forbidding monster against the bleak sky. He barely glanced at the 111's exterior. Hell, the wings were still there. He had counted them himself—two. The crew chief would have seen to the innumerable mechanical details, and the electronic boys hopefully would have their crazy world in some sort of order. Captain Hal Fenner, as the regular navigational officer of this most exotic aircraft, would have occupied the right seat if this were an ordinary mission. Now he had already been in the cockpit for an hour, setting up the computers for a flight he would never make. His seat was needed for a passenger.

The information Fenner was feeding into the elaborate inertial navigation and terrain-following equipment on the right side of the cockpit had been hard and expensively won. It represented numerically the combined computations and information gathered from countless satellite flights over the Soviet Union and adjoining countries, plus an enormous input of local knowledge obtained either accidentally or by trained agents operating in the desired areas. Long ago choices had been made of possible landing sites on the European continent which were not genuine airports until, on certain maps, the areas around most cities under Soviet domination resembled a checkerboard. Thanks to the superb capabilities of the F-111 aircraft, Fuller could fly with bulletlike precision to any of the designated areas, land, and take off his heavy machine in less than two thousand feet if necessary. Where it was advisable to avoid surface radar, the flight could be performed at nearly ground level, night or day, rain or shine. The 111's terrain-following equipment was designed to automatically avoid towers, bridge projections, and even high-tension wires.

As long as everything worked, Fuller thought glumly.

He climbed the long ladder to the cockpit and tried to smile at his good friend Fenner. "How we doing?"

"Fine. You're practically in the suburbs of Moscow."

"I don't want to go to Moscow. I want to go back to Houston and smell magnolia blossoms until my sinuses say quit."

"I know what you mean. What is it this time? They didn't give me a clue beyond the route out and back."

"I like the back part. It's another guy has to be sprung. God knows why. I'm getting sick and tired of this cloak-and-dagger stuff."

"I've set you up to go all the way from launch point at fifty and one hundred feet. Four hundred and eighty knots. On the way back you're set to go high and super-sonic. Once you're over Finland at forty-five thousand you can hit the afterburners all the way home because you'll have plenty of fuel. How's the weather at the target?"

"Good if you're an Eskimo."

"Got your snowshoes?"

"Yup." Fuller fastened the strap on his white helmet and flipped through the pages of the small leatherbound book which comprised the F-111's pre-takeoff checklist. Fenner hoisted himself over the edge of the cockpit and lowered himself on the ladder until just his head and shoulders were visible.

He smiled mischievously as he employed a phrase professional aviators never used. "Happy landing."

"Go fuck yourself." Fuller did not bother to turn his head.

* * *

For the first two hours they were in the cabin, Mike decided Sasha Sokolnicki was absolutely the most far-out individual he had ever known. If Miss Kellogg would let him write a theme about this Russian, maybe he could balance the last disaster, when he had tried to write about the rebirth of the Pontiac.

Sasha Sokolnicki was a huge man with a great red nose sprouting from beneath a pair of tiny furtive eyes. A heavy black beard obscured the rest of his face and surrounded his mouth like moss hanging at the entrance to a cave. A seldom locked cave, Mike thought, for Sasha talked unceasingly, roaring and bellowing for emphasis and pounding his massive chest with enthusiasm for whatever long story he was relating in Russian. Mike soon learned the meaning of Sasha's favorite word, "*Nichevo!*" for which Winslow said the rough English equivalent was "What the hell!" or "Who cares?"

Winslow also reported that a part of Sasha's interminable speeches concerned his admiration for Winslow and for Mike, who "looked like the young man he had once been before he chose vodka over women." Sasha had long ago found he could not handle both, he explained, so he had made a choice. He enjoyed jogging only because he believed it increased his capacity for his favorite liquid. Cost was his curse, Sasha roared. An old troika, or horse-drawn sled, used as a tourist curiosity and in winter festivals, brought him a small income from Intourist—barely enough to cover feed for three horses and an insufficient supply of the local brew.

Ever since their arrival Sasha had laced his tea with a

generous splash from a stone jug, and had offered a sample of the same to his guests. Winslow declined for both Mike and himself, saying there was much to do within the next hours. He also cautioned repeatedly that it was imperative they arrive at the appointed place somewhat before the appointed hour, using Sasha's troika, if they might.

Sasha said *"Nichevo"* innumerable times, and told Winslow to stop worrying. Bad for the liver, he declared, rolling his miniature eyes.

As noon passed and the weak sun slid down into the birches, Mike learned why they had come to Sasha. First and most importantly he despised the Soviet system and his favorite epithet for the party Chairman was *Kakoy duray!*—what a fool! As a consequence of his opinions he had spent ten years in a Siberian "adjustment camp" which had only succeeded in confirming his scorn. After Winslow explained the help he needed would involve an indeterminate amount of physical danger and certainly imprisonment if Sasha were caught, the bearded Russian's response had been brief. *"Nichevo!"*

With his great boots planted firmly on the box of cigarettes which he announced would bring him a fortune, Sasha agreed there would be no complication whatever in providing his horses and precious troika for transport over the snows. It might even bring him a sort of vengeance on his oppressors. He also claimed to know well the area Winslow described—indeed, the exact field where Winslow had made an X with his pencil.

Yet Mike knew that Mr. Winslow was becoming increasingly concerned. According to his plan, they were scheduled to leave the cabin at two-thirty. If Sasha's estimate of his horses' speed was correct, then the troika should arrive near the field with approximately half an hour to spare. But at one o'clock, without his ever having stepped outside to harness his horses or make other preparations, Sasha's speech began to slur. Suddenly, as if struck between his tiny eyes, he rolled off his stool, hit the floor with a resounding thump, and slept.

Winslow kneeled beside him and propped up his head. After listening to his heavy breathing a moment he slapped him gently, without result. The great inert mass of Sasha Sokolnicki remained sprawled in total relaxation, a hint of a smile barely detectable behind his mossy mouth. "Anyway, I'm sure he's not dead," Winslow said in relief. "I saw a pump on the side of the cabin. It was wrapped in straw, and there was a bucket beside it. Get some water, and we'll wake up our friend."

Mike opened the door and closed it immediately. He swallowed hard, and when he spoke he hardly recognized his voice. "Mr. Winslow . . . there are several Russian soldiers on the other side of the stream. It looks like they are coming this way. . . ."

* * *

Major Charles Fuller left the dank void of northeast England and climbed through a solid overcast with the wings of his 111 still partly extended. He pursed his lips to whistle silently within his plastic helmet, and between tuneless cadenzas wished with all his heart the balance of the mission could be as relaxed as the launching. All he had to do presently was pay reasonable attention to the crisp diction of the female English controller who was vectoring him around possible collision with other aircraft, then wait for dismissal. That would occur once he had reached forty thousand feet. From then on he would be a priority target on English radarscopes, but he would not be called. Such little traffic as there might be at flight level four zero would be vectored to avoid him. Thus to anyone interested he would simply appear as a westbound aircraft, possibly a military ferry returning to the opposite side of the Atlantic. How far he should continue westbound was determined by the range of Soviet radar. Once off their screens, he would be very much on his own. Then would begin the dicey part.

Fuller broke out into brilliant sunlight at thirty thousand feet. He lowered his helmet glare shield to protect his eyes and rechecked all the F-111's navigational components to be sure they were fully operational. Then he turned away from the sun.

Fuller set his engines at maximum economy cruise and continued floating in the upper solitude for thirty minutes. Two hundred nautical miles west of Ireland he muttered softly to himself, "Well, here goes nothing." He switched off his transponder and throttled the engines to minimum thrust. Then he rolled the 111 over on its back and started a dive toward the vast layer of cloud which hung momentarily below his head.

Fuller spoke once into his microphone. "The thief is on the way."

He did not receive a response, nor did he expect one.

* * *

"I hate to do this," Winslow said. "It's totally unlike me. It is the sort of thing one did as a college undergraduate."

Mike's announcement of the approaching soldiers had spurred Winslow to immediate and desperate action. He searched quickly through the simple cabin for anything containing water, then did his utmost to shake Sasha back to consciousness. But the man's bulk was too much, and he remained blissfully dormant. "We simply must wake him up. If the soldiers come, he is our only chance."

It was then that Winslow spied the matches on the wooden box which served Sasha as a cotside table. He took two and inserted them in Sasha's boots where the soles joined the tops. Then he lit the matches and moved quickly to the small window.

"We used to call that a hotfoot," he said, dividing his attention between the slumbering Sasha and the soldiers who were now crossing the stream.

When the first match burned to the boot seam, Sasha grunted ominously and jerked up his leg. The other match brought more satisfying results. Sasha let out a roar and leaped to his feet. He swung his arms wildly, seeking an antagonist. Winslow got behind him immediately and propelled him toward the window. Sasha blinked at the sight of the approaching soldiers, said *"Nichevo"* several times, and whirled around the room in search of his vodka jug. Winslow got to it first and, backing warily toward the little iron stove, said he would smash the jug in a thousand pieces if Sasha failed to get rid of the soldiers.

Sasha stood immobile while he seemed to be mustering his wits. Gradually his menacing scowl turned to a smile and he broke into raucous laughter. He wiped at his little eyes and nodded, then muttered a few words in Russian and turned for the door.

When he had left, Winslow interpreted his passing comment for Mike. "The gist of what he said is that the soldiers probably saw our tracks in the snow. He's going to tell them we were here, but went off along the rocks of the stream so our tracks wouldn't show."

They moved to each side of the window, but remained far enough back to avoid any possibility of being seen. They watched Sasha stagger ponderously as he approached the soldiers. He conversed with them a moment, then raised a huge hand and pointed toward the stream, back over their heads.

"I guess thataway is back where they came from," Mike whispered.

"Amen," Winslow said, wondering that he also found it necessary to whisper when there was no possibility of being overheard.

* * *

Sliding over the foam-streaked waves at only one hundred feet, Major Charles Fuller noted that all except one thing was going according to plan. Funny, he thought as he chewed methodically on two sticks of Doublemint gum, only not so funny for him, how all the brains including his own had forgotten that a 111 or any other aircraft flying over the sea north of the British Isles in winter was almost certain to encounter a full gale. At very low altitude a fine salt spray would be carried high enough to cloud the cockpit glass. And there was no way other than landing to clear it.

Here, eastbound for the Shetland Islands, the partial opaqueness of the forward windows was only annoying, a tolerable annoyance Fuller concluded, since the less a lonely man could see of the gray and forbidding landscape the better for his spirit. Navigation was no problem since the autopilot coupled with the inertial navigation computer was flying the aircraft and the same would hold right through to destination. Once arrived however, Fuller knew he would be entirely dependent on his own visual resources for a landing which must be followed almost immediately by a get-the-hell-out-of-there takeoff.

Fuller tried to convince himself that he was employed in his present job and would soon sport two silver leaves on his shoulders because his superiors had somehow convinced themselves that he had never been the worrying kind. Really? At least if he was going to get in the bad habit of worrying he shouldn't start quite yet. He should save his concern for the last hour of this caper, so aptly code-named "Thief."

Fuller thought he saw the Shetlands faint along the horizon, but between the salt spray on the windows and the several rain squalls intervening he could not be sure the dark shapes were not imagined. He was satisfied when he noted the autopilot was turning the 111 smoothly from northeast around to an almost due east heading. It should be clear sailing now until the coast of Norway, which was reported to be shrouded in heavy cloud. That approach, Fuller knew, would be enough to drive a pessimist to straight terror. For he would simply have to sit with his arms folded while the terrain-following system sensed the obstruction in the sea ahead and told the autopilot to climb, turn, and otherwise maneuver to keep man and machine from becoming instantly one with the mighty rocks of Norway.

*　*　*

At eleven minutes past three Moscow time a Soviet army helicopter flown by Lieutenant Serge Spenskayov hovered ten kilometers east of the Leningrad Highway near the village of Nevel. Spenskayov, an energetic youth who liked action of any sort, was now bored almost beyond his toleration, for all day he had been squinting down at the empty snowscape, and he was certain he knew every centimeter in his assigned area.

When Spenskayov had first arrived on the scene he had noted foot tracks which left the highway and wriggled off toward the east. But those tracks had suddenly disappeared into thick forest, and in spite of the absence of tree leaves he had been unable to follow them to their destination. He had radioed that report to his unit commander, and soon afterward it looked as though half the Soviet Army arrived in a long line of vehicles; so many that to Spenskayov's disgust, they soon obliterated the very signs which might have led them to any quarry. Ever since, the forest had been full of soldiers, trudging around in the snow and making so many tracks that Spenskayov thought the scene from aloft was hilarious—a sublime example of foot soldier thinking. It was his understanding they were supposed to be looking for no more than twenty desperate men, not several divisions of an invading army. Thereafter Spenskayov lost interest in the proceedings below and passed the time simply by staring into space.

At fifteen minutes past three Spenskayov saw the sun approach the distant horizon and realized he had at the most another hour and a half of patrolling before it would be too dark to see much of anything. Although it promised to be a clear night, he knew there would be a long twilight. Even now the milky sky was beginning to merge with the snow horizon and the contours of the terrain below were melting into the vast mauve-colored flatland.

Suddenly Lieutenant Spenskayov saw something moving across the snow he had not seen in a long time. Boredom evaporated instantly as he descended for a closer inspection. It was a rare sight these days, a genuine troika with all three horses charging through the snow in magnificent style. How Russian, he thought, how pleasantly in the great tradition. The sight filled Spenskayov with nostalgia for his native town of Kirov, where there were still two troika clubs for those interested and contests were held twice each winter. The winners were chosen on authenticity of harness and personal apparel and their driving skill. As a teen-ager Spenskayov had always envied the members of the club and had thought of joining one in

Moscow, but the Army was unreasonably demanding of a young officer's time.

Thus enchanted, he fancied he could hear the bells tinkling on the troika's harness above the sound of his engine. Spenskayov brought his helicopter down until it was only a few feet above the snow. Yet he was careful to remain at some distance because, he thought, If I were driving such a fine threesome, I should not be at all pleased if some bumbling idiot came along in his chopper and stampeded the horses.

Matching his speed against the troika, Spenskayov found it was moving across the open country at twenty kilometers per hour, a fine pace considering the depth of the snow. He longed to land and stop the troika, tell the occupants how very fine they looked, and perhaps suggest they apply for a permit to visit the contests in Kirov which would be held this very month. Then he saw something which changed his mind. As he watched, the driver and his two passengers waved gaily at him, and he saw they were laughing. How could he ruin such merriment by intruding with his silly and unbearably noisy flying machine?

Spenskayov held his position and watched in fascination as the troika headed toward a nearby stand of timber. As it bore down on the trees, he could not detect the slightest decrease in speed. Were they all drunk? If they managed to miss the first line of trees they must certainly smash against the second or third. Yet the driver continued straight on, and even cracked his whip to urge the horses on.

Then suddenly the forest swallowed the troika and Spenskayov wondered if he had been dreaming. Only the parallel tracks in the snow remained.

Regretfully he pulled up to a hundred meters, seeking

one final sight of the troika. But in the forest below the late afternoon light had almost become the indigo of true night and little could be seen but the trees. Spenskayov smiled. If the lucky occupants of the troika were still alive after their wild dash through the trees, then it must be because they were indeed very drunk. Such truly good times were difficult to come by in the Army. For the first time in his career Spenskayov wondered what it would be like to live the life of a civilian. Certainly it would not be necessary to spend an entire afternoon fluttering over the snows with only a lone troika to relieve the monotony. And certainly it did not make sense to report that the only thing he had seen were preservers of a great Russian mode of transportation who knew how to enjoy themselves.

* * *

Mike sensed that things were not going as they had hoped. His initial delight in the troika's apparent high speed over the snow and his amusement at Sasha's wild yelps as he urged his horses onward turned to disappointment for obviously Sasha was not the most unerring of guides. Worse, the countryside seemed to be swarming with soldiers, and within the first hour they had twice barely escaped a meeting with Russian patrols.

Mike had seen the graphic sketch Winslow showed for Sasha's enlightenment. There was a square with the coordinates of latitude and longitude specifying their intended destination, and Winslow had made an X at the approximate location of Sasha's cabin. All of which, in spite of the Russian's vodka-soaked brain, appeared to be comprehensible to him. He knew exactly that field Winslow desired, he claimed. It was located between a large collective farm and an area of very small truck farms. It was isolated, he said, and there should be no one in the vicinity so late in the day. Winslow insisted he would know if they were at the correct field when they arrived. Mike wondered how he could be so sure without any sort of navigation equipment.

Thanks to Sasha's fumbling with the harness, their departure was twenty minutes behind schedule, but the clinking bells and the swirling snow were so invigorating Mike found the only reminder that this was not a very special pleasure journey was the filthy and stinking horse blanket Sasha had thrown across their legs.

They had been en route for almost two hours, and Mike longed for a compass, because he had been watching the declining sun and knew they had more than half completed a huge circle. Long ago, it seemed, they had left the more heavily wooded country and were now without concealment of any kind.

Leaving an open field, they turned onto a narrow road, and almost immediately Mike saw trouble was unavoidable. Ahead, coming toward them at high speed, was a Russian army half-track festooned with soldiers. There was no room for normal passing, and as Sasha brought his horses to a halt it became obvious a confrontation was inevitable.

The half-track stopped, and an officer who appeared to be nearly the same age as Mike approached the troika. He carried a short assault gun and looked cold.

For what seemed like a long time the snorting of the horses, the clink of harness, and the rumble of the half-track's engine mixed in forbidding harmony. Mike thought his own heartbeat added to the noise, and for an instant he wondered what he would do when he was returned to Mr. Gologorsky and if the commissar would carry out some of his threats. Then, to his astonishment, he heard Winslow laugh and follow his merriment with what sounded like a war whoop. He hauled the jug of vodka from under the horse blanket and tipped it to his lips. He swallowed long and enthusiastically, then handed the jug to Mike.

"Pretend," he whispered as he wiped at his mouth.

Mike hoisted the jug and pretended to swallow. The liquid burned his tongue, and he did his best to yell. Sasha then reached back with his long arms and jerked the jug from Mike's hands. He let out a yell before he brought the jug to his lips. He swallowed hard, and Mike knew he was not pretending. Laughing and spewing vodka droplets into the chill air, he handed the jug down to the officer. Their eyes met in understanding as Sasha began a long tirade in Russian.

As if he were having trouble with his equilibrium, Mike leaned toward Winslow and whispered, "What is he saying?"

"Sasha is telling him we are on our way to a wedding celebration down the road and he ought to be ashamed for obstructing traffic. You are the groom and I am your father, and Sasha says he must deliver us there before we get too drunk. He asks the officer if he is such a monster he would break the bride's heart."

Mike saw the officer stare at him curiously through the gloom and he deliberately crossed his eyes.

Out of the side of his mouth Winslow said, "Now he is asking Sasha if we have seen a group of foreigners—about twenty, he thinks—and they would probably be armed."

Sasha passed down the jug to the officer again, and the vapor from their breaths mingled as the officer became more at ease. When at last he turned back to the half-track he directed the driver to pull off to the side and waved Sasha onward.

As the troika passed the half-track, Mike was relieved to see the soldiers smiling and waving at him. He joined Winslow and Sasha in yelling back.

*　*　*

Major Fuller felt some four g's in the seat of his flight suit as his 111 left the gray sea and plunged into the low overcast. As the aircraft climbed rapidly, he knew the mountains of Norway were hidden in the murk below and the terrain-following equipment was responding to their stony presence. So far, he thought, I continue the human experience.

It would be twenty minutes to the backbone of Norway near Ustaoset, then the autopilot would start the 111 in a descent and follow the lower terrain all across Sweden. The real ground hugging would start when he left the Swedish eastern shores and slipped into Finnish territory. He would have things to look at then for sure—frozen lakes and hillocks, miles of forests, all viewed from the altitude of a flying chicken.

And I am both chicken and the chicken, Fuller thought. If I don't get a steel enema from below, big brother will sure be watching me from on high.

Fuller was not overly concerned about the Russian ground-based radar. At fifty to one hundred feet and a speed of four hundred and eighty knots his appearance on any local screen would be so brief he would probably be mistaken for a malfunction of the equipment, and there was very little chance of radar targeting any hardware that would catch up with him. But the Russian satellites in space would be recording every inch of his journey, and if they could get things organized fast enough, then there could well be a gross strain on the pucker factor. "An unpleasantness," as the helmet-and-goggle aviators used to say. He would have one trump card to play just before landing, known as "the joker." The rest of the game was an open gamble.

As he reviewed his dismal luck at poker recently, Fuller wondered what was a decent, God-fearing American boy doing out here all alone in Norwegian limbo when he should be watching the game at the Cotton Bowl?

* * *

Soon after they had left the road Sasha found concealment in a small stand of trees, and he brought the troika to a stop. Steam rose in great clouds from the sweating chargers as he turned to look at Winslow and Mike. He sighed, wiped the mucus from the end of his fiery nose, and told Winslow that he had unhappy tidings.

"What's the trouble now? We must keep going or we're going to be late. And that just can't be."

Sasha pointed at an open field beyond the trees and said it must be the field they were looking for. Winslow regarded it suspiciously. He took off a glove, reached into the pocket of his coat, and brought out a small black metal box. Holding it between his fingertips, he pointed it at the distant field and said immediately, "He's lying, Mike. Or he's stalling for some reason. I'm not sure which."

"How do you know?"

"If that were the correct field, one of our agents would have planted a device in it last year, or even the year before. They are located strategically all over the Soviet Union. They transmit a signal which will illuminate a red light on the back of this box. It's called a verifier. If we fail to receive a light, then we do not have the correct field."

"But couldn't the Russians discover the frequency and destroy it?"

"The odds are one in several million. The device is buried deep underground. It is no bigger than your fist, and it selects erratically from over four hundred frequencies. Any one of them will light this light. Now I am going to tell Sasha he is either a rascal and a liar, whom I shall later expose to the KGB, or he has just made a dumb mistake he must rectify immediately."

As Winslow harangued him in Russian, Sasha's face fell into dolorous folds. He seemed about to cry. He gulped and swept his hand across the surrounding trees, and he told Winslow he had thought the field he desired was where they had now stopped, but it was obviously not the right place. "The field I remembered must have moved," he added apologetically.

"Are you trying to tell me you are lost?"

"*Nyet!* Only my memory is confused. We will find it eventually if it takes all night."

"We can't wait for eventually. We have exactly thirty-eight minutes to find that field or there is no need to bother."

Sasha pulled off a mitten with his teeth and muttered something unintelligible. When Winslow asked him to try talking without a mitten in his mouth, he removed it and pointed at the horse blanket. "You have my medicine under there," he said unhappily. "Perhaps a small dosage will clear my memory."

* * *

Colonel Vasily Kutuzov had one year to go before his retirement from the Soviet Army, and on this late afternoon he thought that he had never in his entire career known such a series of confusing orders—which of course should be expected since they originated with civilians, in this case the KGB.

Early on this very morning he had been ordered to deploy his men and equipment over a wide area and apprehend at least twenty obviously determined commandos. The order also stated they had a boy with them who must not under any circumstances be harmed. A neat trick, Kutuzov thought, if only someone would show him how such a miracle could be accomplished. Were such combatwise troops supposed to just throw their arms around their pursuers as, Kutuzov mused pleasantly, he had witnessed amid the ruins of Berlin during that long-ago war when Russian and American troops joined hands?

While his English was then most elementary, and was not much better now, he tried to remember the American soldiers' phrase which so aptly described a military situation which was not going too well—for example, the present search for twenty ghosts.

How had they managed to vanish so completely? If an airlift was out of the question, then did not the stupid bureaucrats in the KGB assign his effort to the wrong area? Only a few hours ago a counterorder had come through—continue to look for the twenty commandos and also for a blue Ford car from the American Embassy. Now he had just received a report the blue Ford was back in the embassy compound, and so was the driver. This was work for Soviet soldiers? Chasing Fords?

Colonel Kutuzov shook his head unhappily and wondered why, with apparently every damn stupid or drunken bureaucrat in the Soviet Union authorized to order the military around like toy soldiers, those who did the work were obliged to remain sober.

Suddenly Colonel Kutuzov smiled. For he remembered the American military phrase for just this sort of situation.

"FUBAR!" was the word—fouled up beyond all recognition.

Ah yes.

* * *

At zero minus five Major Fuller brought the power on the big General Electric engines back to 45 percent, and the F-111 slowed to two hundred and sixty knots. A few minutes back, which had seemed like hours, Fuller had seen the sun drop below the horizon as if it had been shot down. His own speed and easterly course had accelerated the coming of night, and on the return flight he might even raise the sun again. It would be a phenomenon, he brooded, which would be like returning to another life. ". . . having heroically disposed of this one," he muttered into his oxygen mask.

He had left the northern wilderness behind; the emptiness of Finland and of Russia to the east of the Leningrad area had been relatively easy on the nerves, but now there were occasional roads and villages, and Fuller likened himself again to a rabbit pursued. Hopefully there was no one on the ground who might witness his swift passage long enough to question the absence of any red star markings on the F-111. At fifty feet, according to his personal calculations, even a trained person would have at the most two seconds in fading light to evaluate his big bird, and would certainly have every reason to believe it was a Soviet aircraft. Additionally, "the joker" would supposedly divert the attention of local radar. Just before landing he would fire the "joker" missile, which would continue for thirty seconds on the same course as the 111, then make an abrupt turn and fly off at ninety degrees to the left. The missile was a harmless but extremely complicated electronic device designed to emanate a radar echo identical to a flying 111. It had a full duration of twenty minutes, more than long enough for Fuller to complete his landing, make a pickup, and take off.

Yet his intestines gave him needless reminder of a watchful eye he could not escape regardless of altitude. There would still be the worry of a Russian satellite orbiting at one to two hundred miles above the earth. If positioned just right it would pick up both "the joker" and the genuine 111, but since the data would be transmitted numerically it would be impossible to tell the difference.

There was the gamble. How long would it take the Soviet interceptor command to analyze the information, separate the real from the decoy, and do something nasty about it? Fuller knew it depended on many factors, including the disposition of the watch officer on duty. Would he be inclined to procrastinate and call an alert on one target or go for an all-out scramble, or both? Fuller knew his own troops took from five to fifteen minutes between first alarm and getting into the air—again depending on whether one human being thought a real threat was involved. He hoped with all his heart there was some unknown flaw in the Russian chain of command which might take them a shade longer.

At zero minus three minutes Fuller watched the digital characters flashing on his inertial navigation system and saw he still had twenty-three nautical miles to the target. Once more he took a moment to study the small booklet of photos on his knee board. They depicted a large open field with a forest to the east. There were several eye-level views, a remarkably clear enlargement of a satellite photo taken from five hundred miles, and a graphic diagram illustrating the perimeter hazards. Fuller decided it would be a piece of cake for landing if its geographic location were not in the heart of the Soviet defense ring.

At zero minus two minutes he slowed to two hundred knots and extended the 111's wings to full landing configuration. Trying to ignore the film of salt spray which still clouded his windows, he left the aircraft on autopilot and began looking anxiously ahead for visual sight of his target. He supposed, unhappily, that if the Soviets were not already in the air there must certainly be a considerable flap at the nearest interceptor base.

He waited until he dimly saw the field two miles directly ahead, then planted a kiss on the flashing numerals of the inertial navigation system. With the same finger he reached for the firing switch of "the joker."

* * *

They sat waiting in the troika on the very edge of the darkening forest. Vapor from the three horses' heavy breathing hung all about them, remaining fixed like clouds about their heads and flanks. Sasha emitted his own cloud of vapor, spiked, Mike realized, with a strong odor of vodka. He also realized that Sasha had sobered somewhat and was becoming increasingly nervous.

The Russian twisted in his seat and pointed his huge bear-paw mitten at the open field beyond. Winslow aimed his verifier at it and smiled at the bright red light he observed.

Sasha complained of the near presence of the soldiers. He whined at the risk they were taking and insisted they would never get back to the safety of his cabin unless his energies were restored with a long pull at the vodka jug. He said they dare not wait much longer.

"*Nyet*," Winslow answered. "Another few minutes will only improve the taste. If you are shot meanwhile, you won't miss the vodka."

He turned to Mike and said, "Give my regards to the

U.S.A. I must say it has been quite an experience knowing you."

"I thought you were going with me."

"You won't need me anymore. And I can't just walk away from my job until the Russians declare me PNG, which they will certainly do."

"They won't shoot you, I hope."

"PNG means persona non grata . . . in other words, not welcome."

A silence fell between them. The occasional squeak of cold leather as the horses moved in their harness sounded abnormally loud in the hushed forest. Then in the distance they heard the faint whine of jet engines. The sound increased rapidly.

Winslow said softly, "I guess this is it. We won't want to keep him waiting. The routine is, you run as fast as you can to wherever he stops. He will not shut down the engines, so avoid the tail. Run to the right side, up near the nose. The pilot will have a ladder out for you. Get up that ladder as fast as you can climb. The pilot will close the hatch and take off immediately. Got it?"

"Got it." They climbed out of the troika and left the woods together. Mike turned around once and waved at Sasha, then followed Winslow into the open field.

The big aircraft was suddenly upon them. It made a half circle of the field in a near vertical bank, then straightened for final approach. The engines throttled down to a relative whisper, the F-111's dark bulk dropped below the background of dark trees, and it sent up a spray of snow as the wheels touched.

Mike said, "I can't tell you how much . . . there is no way I can thank you, Mr. Winslow."

Winslow tried to smile. "I can't explain what you've done for me. Far more than you'll ever know."

They took off their mittens and clasped hands. Winslow said, "I suppose it will be quite cold in Minnesota."

"Yes. Please say good-bye to Mrs. Winslow for me."

"That I'll do. She'll be sorry to have missed you."

Winslow reached out deliberately and grabbed Mike by the shoulders. He turned him toward the F-111 and shoved him toward it. "Now . . . beat it, son!" And Mike ran, stumbling through the snow.

Winslow trudged back toward the wood, his head bent as if he were having trouble retracing their footprints. He did not look back. In the distance he could hear trucks whining—probably a Russian patrol closing in.

THE SIXTEENTH DAY

At Goddard Space Flight Center in Maryland the techni-
cians fell into one heated argument after another. Nimbus
6, the U.S. meteorological satellite which had been passing
faithfully over the North Pole every one hundred and eight
minutes, was now crossing every ninety-six minutes and
dropping one minute and twenty seconds from that time
every day. There were those who insisted the satellite was
out of whack, and those who believed the rumors of the
earth's rapidly increasing rotation might be true.

The President of the United States was having his own
rotation problems, chiefly in the figure eights he was cutting as he paced the Oval Office. The pattern became
more erratic as he reviewed various phenomena which had
come to his attention. He recognized that some had been
included among the more shocking reports simply to
relieve his own tension. In Berkeley, California, home of

the self-liberated, four hundred university students had joined with their professors in building a spaceship, for which state funding was available. They proposed to load it with selected humans and animals of both sexes, and a certain Timothy Leary had been appointed commander by the Governor. He immediately bought a splendid uniform with gold braid epaulets and a cocked hat with large rosette. When Leary appeared on the "Today" show and asked for applicants as his deputy commander, he was barely off camera before he received a long-distance call from one Rudy Distancia in Minnesota who claimed he had just the man for the job.

This touching scene, replayed on the "Tonight," "Tomorrow," and the "Day After Tomorrow" shows, told the President that the public was at last aware something was not as it should be.

There were other manifestations that certain forces were definitely out of alignment. A ship flying the Leonidopolis flag had foundered off Malta after striking a reef that had not troubled any mariner for two thousand years. While the Lutine bell at Lloyd's was still ringing in London, Alice Mills, who owned one the finest stables in Virginia, reported that one of her expensive steeplechase mounts had sailed easily over her highest paddock fence and was never seen again. Locals were asked to be on the lookout for a flying mare.

Far more serious was the recent opinion of the cluster of scientists now encamped in what little hotel space remained in Washington. They theorized that the heating of the inner earth by the radioactive elements of uranium, thorium, and potassium seemed to be compounding itself as gravitational force weakened the planet in certain areas. Thus the same source of heat energy which had created the original pool of molten iron in the center of the earth was thought to be liquefying the encompassing rock. This process was creating an uneven sloshing effect in the molten iron core, which in turn greatly accelerated the planet's customary wobble.

The learned scientists now proclaimed the eccentric wobble would soon propel the planet earth out of normal orbit, which was something the President already knew because, he thought ruefully, a sixteen-year-old boy had told him so. The difference was that the boy had predicted exactly when the departure from orbit would become irreversible, a mere eight days from the present. And, unlike the scientists who had to the last man applied for grants to study the situation, the boy had asked for nothing except something about people working together in a common cause.

As his home planet seemed about to hurl itself into infinity, the President of the United States did his utmost to curb his impatience. He summoned Hymie Markel to his office at eight o'clock in the morning. "What, may I be so bold as to ask, is the status of our young guest?"

"He is still sleeping."

"Don't you think it would be prudent to wake him up?"

"No, sir. Not yet. I have a hunch we should follow his instructions exactly. He told me that unless he had some sleep, Brain Two Thousand could never deal with the complex logistical problems he foresaw. And he was not smiling when he said it."

"When can we have him on deck? Damnit, I've got the President of the Presidium of the Supreme Soviet landing at Andrews in half an hour. Leslie Nash and his whole gang, along with a representative passel of Arabs, will be here within the next two hours. If we fail to get the numbers of the Petroleum Council on our side we will run into a delay we can't afford. Every minute counts."

"If I may remind you, sir, Mike has had a very tiring experience, not to mention frightening. He wants to sleep nine hours, and twenty-five minutes, according to his calculations. When he wakes up he wants seventeen minutes to brush his teeth and shower, then a breakfast, which he says will last for twenty-six minutes. He wants jelly-roll pancakes, and it's all laid on. The chef phoned his mother for the recipe, and it sounded so good I suggested you might like to try the same for your breakfast."

The President went to his center desk drawer for a digestive pill. "I am not Nero," he grumbled. "I cannot eat while the world collapses around me and while people like F. Leslie Nash insist on doing business as usual. Have you heard what happened half an hour ago in the great state of Minnesota?"

"Sir, I've been very busy making arrangements—"

"The goddamned dome of the Capitol Building popped off like the cork out of a wine bottle, that's what. It simply rose out of sight and has not been seen since."

"That must have been quite spectacular. Have you declared St. Paul a disaster area? They'll sure want federal aid to buy a new dome."

"Guess what Granger, that pristine new-consciousness politician, had to say on the matter."

"I can't. If Rudy Distancia didn't say it for him, it must be in Sanskrit."

Although the President tried to speak evenly, his voice showed the effects of such great strain it became almost a squeak. "Governor Granger of the great state of Minnesota said, and I quote, 'All things live. Therefore all things as well as humans can learn to levitate. Yoga is the only solution to our current problems.' Unquote."

"Perhaps he can consult his guru and find out where the dome will land."

"How am I going to describe an incident like that to the President of the Soviets and not have him think I'm deranged? He'll get right back in his *Kremlin One* and return to Moscow."

The President made another figure eight, but stopped before it was completed. "Did Kaplan get his country music score?"

"Right. It's being transposed onto computer sheets. We should have it all in hand by the time Mike wakes up."

"When are you going to rouse him?"

"I'm not going to, personally. I've made some special homecoming arrangements which I hope will dissipate any lingering resentment he may have about his last visit here. Trust me, sir."

"I will. As far as I can throw the White House—which, unless we do something very quickly, may be quite some distance."

* * *

When Mike Piper awakened he was convinced he had died and gone to heaven. The surroundings of the Lincoln Room were vaguely familiar, but the faces on opposite sides of his bed were out of his past life. The first ghost was Miss Kellogg, who smiled and said, "Good noon, Mike. It is really five minutes past noon, which gives you nine hours and twenty-five minutes."

Then his mother said, "How's my boy?" And his father took his hand and held it a moment without saying anything.

Mike turned his head and saw Susanna York. She smiled and signed, "Welcome home. I've missed you very much."

Mike wiped at his eyes and said that he could no longer believe the things he saw. Cripes, heaven really was neat.

One hour later, when he was ushered into the White House East Room by the President himself, Mike found he had become temporarily inarticulate. As he was introduced to one dignitary after another, he could only grin and nod and shake moist hands and try to remember at least a few of the names. There were several Cabinet members, three generals, and two admirals. There was a Mr. Nash from San Francisco, who did not seem very happy to see him, a pair of professors—Pomeroy and Weis —man? There were two men who identified themselves as being from the National Academy of Sciences, and three Arabs in such beautiful flowing robes Mike cautioned himself not to stare.

At the end of the long room he was introduced to the President of the Supreme Soviet and two of his staff. Mike wanted to ask them about Mr. Gologorsky, but could not find his voice before he was led away to meet a pair of Chinese who expressed great surprise at his youth and height.

Finally the President seated Mike at the center of a long table covered with green felt. There were several pitchers of water placed along the table, and drinking glasses, notepaper, and pencils at each place. When all the visitors were seated, the President made them welcome and gave a brief review of the reason for the meeting. Then he handed Mike a leather folder and whispered, "Here is your country music. Play it with all your heart."

Mike opened the folder and glanced at the figures, which he recognized instantly as the same he had given from the Kremlin window. Trying to bolster his confidence, he began with his familiar spinning-top theory and managed to hold his listeners' attention while he spoke of plate tectonics, earthquakes of the past ten years, Wegener's theory of moving continents, the precession of the earth's axis, and the changes in its magnetic field since the present increase in rate of rotation.

". . . so we are not scientifically a collection of nations with different problems. We are all sitting on the same lawn, and unless we join to keep it green it will dry up and blow away. Things are always changing in our galaxy. Five thousand years ago our north star was the Thuban, and twelve thousand years from now it should be Vega, but cripes—excuse me—it won't be unless we do something to reestablish our balanced orbit."

Mike continued with a long list of consequences if people failed to realize their neighbor's problem was their own. He reminded them that the temperature at the center of the earth is nearly as hot as the surface of the sun, and if even an infinitely small proportion of that energy escaped, the results could be equally disastrous for Russians, Americans, Chinese, or any nationality.

Mike saw several yawns and much staring at the ceiling as he spoke of one world. Yet now he had lost his awe of his audience, and he decided to shake them up a bit. "Eight days from now, to be precise at fourteen hours and twenty-one minutes Greenwich time, our speed of rotation will begin to increase from the present two thousand meters per second to three thousand meters per second, and will continue to increase at approximately one hundred and twenty-five meters per day. The effect will be like a centrifuge spinning at too high a velocity. Even if we do not fly apart, all objects, from salt cellars to locomotives, will be difficult to keep in place unless they are firmly secured to the earth's surface. The Gulf Stream, the Humboldt Current, and the Japan Current will definitely change course and immediately affect the climate of the American and European continents. If you now weigh one hundred and fifty pounds, you will then weigh a mere one hundred, which will make walking an enjoyable experience, but extremely dangerous."

Mike paused, took a sip of water from the glass before him, and said that yes, he had taken into consideration the slowing effect of the tides on speed of rotation.

"But the tides are not nearly powerful enough," he continued. "At the same time our gravitational security is being reduced, the home we share in common will be bound on a new journey. Our present orbital speed of thirty-five kilometers per second will increase to fifty. Even if we manage to avoid colliding with other planets such as the moon, we will certainly experience a drastic change in climate. As you know, we are now ninety-three million miles from the sun. According to my calculations, which admittedly are very rough because I had to squeeze them out of my pocket computer, we could be within seventy million miles of the sun in two hundred and four days. That would give us almost twice the intensity of sunlight now falling on earth and a climate comparable to Venus. There would be very few places on this planet where humans could breath unless you Russians would welcome us all to northern Siberia—"

Suddenly Mike was interrupted by the sound of metal clinking against a glass. Across the table he saw a tall, distinguished-looking man tapping a water pitcher with a thin golden pen. The man rose and identified himself with the assurance of one who took it for granted everyone knew him.

"My name is F. Leslie Nash, and I apologize for this interruption, but I think it absolutely necessary before this young man's astonishing talent for alarmist oratory twists facts any further. While I salute the courteous patience of the intelligent minds in this room who have been listening to such nonsense, I must question the need for further tolerance."

Smiling gently upon the faces around him, Nash reached for his glass and took a sip of water. "Of *course* there have been a few isolated phenomena—or should I say phenomenae? If you will simply check with any good record book you will discover an endless procession of strange happenings which have been occurring since the dawn of recorded history. Why should it be any different today? To blame the extraction of oil for a few odd incidents is preposterous. This is a big earth, and oil weight is insignificant. I have brought with me two world-renowned scientists. They are waiting outside to tell you in technical terms precisely why this so-called spinning-top theory should be classified in the same category as the findings of the Flat Earth Society."

Nash expected a more general expression of amusement than he received. Instead, a stiff silence seemed to have captured all who sat about the green-covered table. They had suddenly become immobile, poised like mannequins waiting to be adjusted. Only their eyes were alive, abnormally wide, and fixed on the surface of the table.

Nash made a slight adjustment of his tie while he tried to remember his next angle of attack as prepared for him by Leo Marcusi and Rudy Distancia. What was it they had suggested? Something about proof the boy had already been under psychiatric care?

Nash wiped the perspiration from his forehead. He was suddenly feeling giddy, and his mouth was strangely dry. As a crutch to regain his composure he reached again for his water glass. He missed it by half an inch. Grinning foolishly, he made a second attempt and missed again. During all his public speaking career he had never known such a sense of embarrassment. Why this disorientation?

He reached for the water pitcher, catching it so clumsily that it capsized and spewed water over the sheik who sat on the opposite side of the table. The sheik showed no reaction, but remained transfixed, his mouth half open in awe. He was staring at the middle of the table.

While he was framing an apology Nash wiped his brow with his fingers, passing them across his closed eyes as if to relieve some hidden pain. On opening his eyes he saw what so enthralled the others. The table had scarcely slanted, yet all the glasses on it, as well as the pitcher, were sliding slowly along the green felt. They moved evenly, like soldiers on parade, keeping their distance from each other and never hesitating. Then one by one, pitcher-glass-pitcher-glass, they reached the end of the table and tumbled to the floor.

Except for the spasmodic crashing of glass, there was not a sound in the room. The silence prevailed even after the last glass had disappeared over the edge of the table. Then, very slowly, thirty pairs of eyes came to life and focused solemnly upon their neighbor's.

F. Leslie Nash sat down, and no one said anything for a very long time.

At last, after it had become obvious someone must reactivate the meeting, the President rose and regarded the walls of the East Room suspiciously. When it appeared that no more surprises were due, he said quietly, "If you all agree, I suggest it is time for Mr. Piper to give us his solution."

Mike opened the leather folder and began reciting the requirements he had drawn up and revised in Moscow. The figures were all based on compensation for weight and immediate mobility. ". . . the weights are so relatively small in comparison with the total mass that we must be very precise about their location. It will be something like achieving perfect balance on a delicate fulcrum. Remember if we place a peanut on our hand and move it just right we can influence the movement of an elephant."

One hour later Mike was still calling off numbers to a battery of secretaries who had been called in to copy and translate. ". . . a total of two hundred tankers, minimum of eight hundred tons each, to be distributed as follows: fifty to the west coast of Ceylon; twenty-five to be very precisely anchored in the Gulf of Venice at thirteen degrees, thirty minutes east, and forty-five degrees, twenty minutes north . . ."

Mike paused while a portrait of President Polk fell off the wall and clattered to the floor. In a surprising display of aplomb the President commented that he had never liked it anyway.

Mike continued as if there had been no interruption. ". . . pumping from Alaska's north slope is most critical, and must be shut down immediately. The same applies to the pumping along almost the same latitude in Siberia. The shutdown need only continue until the ships are in position, and then may resume at a limited rate, which I haven't figured out yet. There must be a fifty percent cut in the North Sea pumping, but Venezuela can continue at its present rate. The future is not altogether dark if we can all get together and produce enough heavy pumps to fill abandoned wells with sea water. Once that is done, my calculations show that equilibrium will be restored except for the influence of Saudi Arabian production. If the oil people will give me the figures, I can calculate how much rock must be moved to that area to maintain a normal rate of rotation and to keep us at least fairly near our present orbit. You better hurry, and I thank you."

Mike sat down to prolonged applause, but it was not

until the following morning that he realized he had become a hero.

Hymie Markel had pleaded with Mike to help him satisfy press interest and also to allay the wildfire rumors throughout the land. Thus, he spent most of the day on television programs which preempted everything except commercials.

Appearing on the ABC Network News, the lugubrious interviewer said he wanted to thank Mike for bringing the peoples of the world together—right after this message from Zippo Polyestcr Carpets. When the commercial was finished, he asked Mike what he intended to do next. "Well, I'll try to pass my midterm English exam and work on radio reception for my girl Susie's braces. She can't hear."

"What would you say to her by radio?"

"Oh, I guess, 'I love you.' It would be a miniature diode rig tuned to the wavelength frequency of her brace wires. . . ."

F. Leslie Nash saw Mike on the television set in his Gulfstream while bound for San Francisco. He paused in mentally reviewing his vast financial portfolio long enough to consider taking up Catholicism. If the Vatican was for sale, maybe that would be a good place to find sanctuary. But first he would have to get somebody to track down that treacherous bungler, Cyril Henshaw.

It would not be easy. Henshaw had taken his reformed conscience and a few hundred thousand leftover Swiss francs (which he deemed were owed him by the Petroleum Council for risks duly taken) to a hideaway in the Greek isles, far from the madding tube and his disgruntled colleagues.

Had it been projected on a six-foot screen before his

very nose, Charles Fuller wouldn't have seen the Mike Piper show too clearly. He was deep in his fifth glass at the air base pub, celebrating his promotion to lieutenant colonel.

Rudy Distancia saw some of Michael's video performances, and in the process found comfort, for he was lonely. Governor Granger had been advised that his Capitol's hurtling dome must eventually land in Katamandu and had left immediately. Now there was no one around to make Distancia feel superior. Only the myna bird, and he, if possible, had even less sense of humor than the Governor.

Nicolai Gologorsky did not see Michael. He was en route to Siberia as a guest of his government, scheduled for "psychological readjustment."

Leo Marcusi saw Michael on the set at the Press Club bar and considered—very briefly—becoming a teetotaler.

Secretary Marvin Kaplan saw Michael on his mother's TV set and said they were honoring the wrong hero.

At the end of the day Hymie Markel decided to bet on a night horse race in Miami. He bet on a three-year-old long shot named Orbit and won two thousand dollars.

Nancy and Ben Piper watched their son on several television shows, and they agreed he seemed to handle himself reasonably well. Holding his wife's hand and getting a bit misty-eyed as he contemplated his son's world prominence, Ben even allowed that it was he who should have seen Dr. Patcheck, not Mike. "It's not just the world he's getting back into balance," said Ben. "It's his old man, too." Nancy wasn't listening; her mind was wholly on her pride and joy.

Daughter Sandy took a different view. "Smarty-Pants," she snickered as her brother's image glowed on the screen. "Brain Two Thousand, indeed. Cripes, this is just too heavy. Why, it's the . . . the . . . very end."